For Gail,

With appreciation for your commitment to our Earth and her life!

All my best wishes for your own great journey towards the tomorrows!

Rio

THE
OGLIN

A Hero's Journey
Across Africa . . .
Towards the Tomorrows

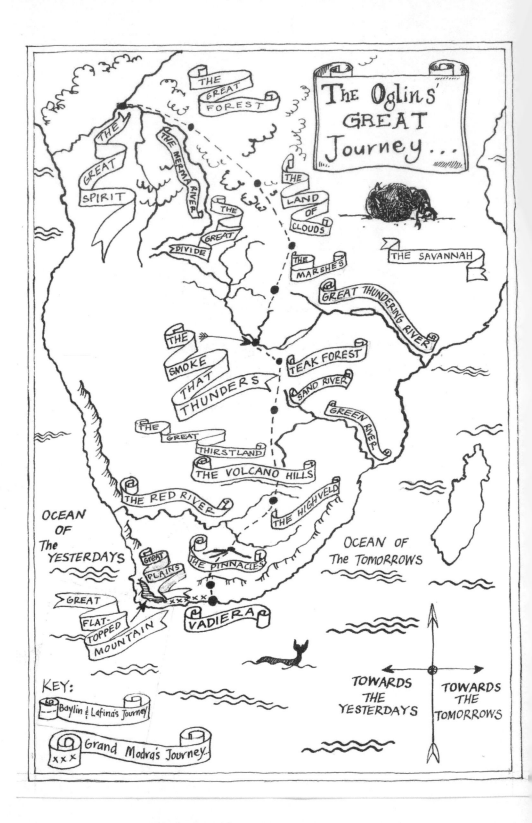

THE
OGLIN

A Hero's Journey Across Africa . . . Towards the Tomorrows

DICK RICHARDSON
With Rio de la Vista

Illustrations by Cathy Feek

MONTE VISTA, COLORADO
VRYBURG, SOUTH AFRICA

First printing 2005

ISBN 0-9759440-3-7   LCCN 2004095085

**ATTENTION CORPORATIONS, UNIVERSITIES, COLLEGES, AND
PROFESSIONAL ORGANIZATIONS:** Quantity discounts are available on
bulk purchases of this book for educational, gift purposes, or as premiums for
increasing magazine subscriptions or renewals. Special books or book excerpts
can also be created to fit specific needs. For information, please contact
Savanna Press, PO Box 777, Monte Vista, CO 81144, USA;
PO Box 1806, Vryburg, 8600, South Africa
Phone 719-850-2255
email: savannapress@rmi.net

To all the pioneers
of Holistic Management
for the trial, error, hardships
and mistakes that cost them dearly,
so that we and the next generation,
the little people,
may find the tomorrows filled
with dreams coming true.

ACKNOWLEDGMENTS

*We wish to thank the following people
for inspiration and inestimable help:*

Allan Savory, Jody Butterfield and Judy Richardson

For story editing, publishing assistance and encouragement:

Ella Erway, Cary Ellis, Gina Lake, Cathy McNeil, Natalie
Atkins, Frank Horley, Sally Ranney, Gregory Hobbs, Krystyna
Jurzykowski and Paul Falconer

For support and encouragement of all sorts:

Sam Law, Deb Lathrop, Tim and Judelon LaSalle

For all the spelling and grammar checks:

Bill Gates (via Microsoft Word!)

*For all of the above and their extraordinary
support and interest in us, our book and
what we believe in:*

Steven Vannoy, Jim, Daniela
and Savanna Howell

TABLE OF CONTENTS

FOREWORD

Every once in a great while, a story emerges that captures the hearts and minds of readers of all ages. Hearts are healed, minds are opened and spirits are lifted. Such stories are a turning point in the lives of the readers. They will never see the world in the same way again—and somehow their sights are forever directed towards a higher purpose.

The Oglin is such a story.

This tale brings the African bush to life in language so real that the taste and smell of the dust and beauty of the land we know surrounds the reader. Told in an authentic "African" voice, the story transmits a deep knowledge of African wildlife, bushcraft and traditional lore, all woven through the adventures of the endearing Oglins. For lovers of wildlife and Africa's splendid beauty and for all who are enchanted by the worlds of magical beings, this story will touch your heart and delight your mind.

While "merely" a story, there is deeper substance here. Embedded in this enthralling tale is the essence of how the Earth can be healed—and it reveals vital keys to living in harmony with the Earth and all her creatures. As a sportsman, I have traveled widely and seen much of the problems that beset the Earth we call home and her people. Poverty and destitution threaten the status quo in many places, including Africa. The loss of biodiversity on a worldwide scale threatens the very fabric of society, as we know it today. The cost to humans and economies from the decline in ecological wealth is immense. In the face of all this, one becomes acutely aware that the kind of knowledge and inspiration presented in this book is sorely needed around the world today.

While *The Oglin* is imminently timely in this era of great challenge, it is also a story for all time. I am proud that such inspiration emerged from a fellow South African and in the spirit of the Oglins' call for worldwide movement towards a better future, it is fitting that it was developed in partnership with an American. As one who loves a wonderful tale and who shares this story's passion for a healthier, happier tomorrow, I heartily endorse the hope that "everyone in the world will read this book!"

Gary Player,
South Africa

CHAPTER 1

HOME LIFE

The land here is peaceful.
It is bathed in golden light which smooths out
The edges of harshness so that everything is right.
Is it any wonder that we love the land the way we do?
We dance to the beat of it and perceive its rhythm as our own.

—Nancy Wood, *Many Winters*

An Elephant

Luka stiffened. Lifting his head in alarm, he let out a low, protective growl. There was a deadly silence. Baylin opened both eyes but did not move another muscle. Total silence, though lasting only seconds, is always a clear danger sign in the bush. Noise is something synonymous with the bush. With all the bugs, bees, birds, there is never a moment's silence, unless there is danger. Imminent danger!

Without further warning, the tree began to move above them, shaking violently, groaning deep within and showering down plump, ripe figs. Baylin shot to his feet. He knew instinctively what it was.

Silence. Baylin and Luka stood dead still. In the utter silence, they made no movement.

1

Then the whole tree began to shake once more, swaying violently, branches creaking. The leaves and figs of the tree showered down upon their heads and all around them onto the ground.

While the turmoil continued, Baylin and Luka backed away from the tree and finally saw the cause of the uproar. It was just as Baylin suspected. What had looked to be a huge grey rock behind the tree, was actually a great, full-grown forest elephant! With his trunk bent backwards over his head and tusks on either side of the tree, the elephant was battering the massive tree with the full weight of his huge body to get at the tasty figs hanging in the upper branches.

At last, Baylin released the breath he had been holding, now that he was sure what it was. A smile stole across his face as he watched the elephant at work. He knew he was lucky to see the secretive giant up so close. Quivering, Luka trusted his master. With Baylin's soft curly-haired hand clasped around his muzzle, Luka relaxed slightly. Slowly, creeping, one furry foot at a time, without making the slightest sound, they backed further away from the tree. Once they were safely away, Baylin and Luka turned onto the well-worn Oglin path leading out of the deep, dense forest.

Baylin had sunk down with a soft sigh of pleasure onto the cushion of moss at the base of the tree, for a rest in the cool shade at the edge of the forest. Luka had settled down beside him, head resting on the soft fur of Baylin's feet. The golden sunlight filtered down through the canopy above them, dappling the ferns and lush forest floor with a dancing light. A slight breeze fluttered the leaves of the tall trees, and the ferns gently waved like giant green fans. The sweet smells of the forest filled Baylin's head as he took a deep breath and let his head fall lazily back onto the pillow of soft moss. How long he had been there before the great elephant disturbed his rest, he wasn't sure.

Baylin shook his head as he made his way towards the edge of the forest, still finding it amazing that a giant elephant could move so silently through even the densest forest. Elephants normally cannot be heard moving unless they are feeding or want to be heard. But, he laughed to himself, they eventually give themselves away by the sounds of their stomachs working, by passing huge wind, or by grumbling noisily in a distinctively elephant way!

Baylin and Luka stopped at the lovely stream that flowed out from the forest. From its crystal clear water, icy cold, running down between grass- and moss-covered banks, with bracken and fern overhanging, they drank. Baylin broke off some bracken heads, the curly new tops of the fern, and crisp stalks of wild asparagus to take along to his Merma for the evening meal, knowing she would dearly appreciate it. He tucked them into the bundle-hide pack that hung over his shoulders and strode out onto the path towards the open savanna and home.

Evening

Walking along, Baylin felt the rush of fear from the surprise encounter with the forest elephant slowly wash out of him. As Luka picked up the scent of home on the wind, his tail started wagging. Strolling out across the lush African savanna, they began to extend their pace. Rising in the distance, the kopjies came into view. These granite outcroppings rising out of the grasslands made a natural shelter for the Oglin clan homes.

Along the slight ridgeline that the path followed, Baylin could see for miles across the savanna to the edge of the deep blue and green forest that surrounded Vadiera. Towards the tomorrows, where the sun awakes each morning, he could just see the edge of the sea, glimmering in the late afternoon sun, deep shining blue with the white lines of the breakers curving along the sandy shoreline and crashing against the rocky cliffs.

In the distance, they could hear the gayla yipping around the heels of the bundles and pala, bringing them in for the evening. The gayla were herding their charges home to their night-time kraal or stockade. Working like stock dogs, the gayla were keeping the bundles and pala close together in a tight bunch, breaking them into a trot now and then and occasionally just yipping with pure excitement.

4

Luka, trotting along in front of Baylin, stopped, stiffened and listened intently to the familiar yips and calls of his siblings and companions playing their vital role in the life of the Oglin Clan. Luka was Baylin's personal gayla. Being close companions, they did everything together, yet at times like these, Luka's instincts called for him to be herding the animals of the Oglins with the other gayla. All day long, they kept the pala and the bundles in tightly packed groups as they grazed, helping to protect them from lurking predators. The gayla herded them out into the veld in the mornings when the Oglins opened their kraals, took them to water and shade in the heat of the day, and then brought them back home again each evening.

Baylin's nostrils filled with the thick scent of acacia blossom, the heavy sweet fragrance wafting on the evening breeze from the little yellow pompom-like flowers that bedecked the thorny trees. The lush dark green grasses of early spring growth rolled in gentle waves across the plain.

Another smell made him stop and look down. The fresh green dung of the herds of bundles and pala lay scattered through the trampled and eaten grasses where they had spent the day grazing. The dung was especially soft from the fresh spring leaves. Baylin crouched down and opened up the dung to see it visibly moving, as if with a life of its own. He watched intently as at least six different types of black, brown and iridescent purple dung beetles, of all different sizes, worked hungrily through the dung.

Some of the beetles were burying their treasure where it lay, pushing the soil up in fluffy mounds. Others just seemed to rush around in it and still others were gathering up balls of dung to roll away. Some of the balls they had formed were already twice the size of the beetles themselves, even though some of the beetles were as big as a small bird! Some of the rolling beetles worked in pairs, always in a terrible hurry, scurrying along, occasionally rolling one another over with the dung ball, as they tumbled it away to bury the balls and lay their eggs in them, deep in the ground.

Further along the path, a covey of francolin flushed out from under Baylin's feet, protesting loudly at the disturbance from their scratching and gathering of a dinner of insects and dung beetles. The sudden rush through the grass, the ear-splitting cackling and the hard, urgent wing beat would be enough to make anyone leap back and send their heart racing!

Then a roar of tiny wings and what looked like a cloud of smoke made its way through the sky above them, moving forward quite quickly, yet seeming to be almost lazily rising and falling in serpentine motion. Baylin stopped to watch and Luka flopped down beside him on his haunches, tongue hanging out. The cloud settled into a small thicket of dense thorn bush and a crescendo of twittering bird sounds rose, almost like the bubbling of boiling water, as the huge flock of queleas came in to roost.

Not far off, Baylin saw the glint of a horn, reflecting the now reddening sunlight. A magnificent kudu bull stood tall and majestic. The kudu's wide, spiralled horns leaned slightly backwards, as he stared down his nose in regal elegance. Nearby, a small herd of females and young kudu stood watching, their tails twitching nervously at the noise and disturbance of the queleas coming in.

To be a young Oglin in Vadiera was a lovely life, Baylin thought to himself as he made his way home. In the midst of the magnificent savanna, his clan's homeland of Vadiera lay surrounded by huge forests on three sides. The forests rose to the mountains in the towards the yesterdays, as the Oglins called the west. The sea in the east, towards the tomorrows, completed the enclosing circle that protected the land of Vadiera. It was a beautiful place. And being an Oglin was a good thing to be.

The Ruck Burrow

After the evening fare, it was time to visit all the animals before the battends could begin. The gayla were happily scoffing their way through the leftovers. Baylin's little badras and sadras were all rushing around in excitement for the battends and

helping to settle the bundles and pala into their kraals for safety. The youngest bundles were separated from their mothers, in a corner of the kraal by a simple scherm of thorn bush, so the Oglins could get a share of the Merma bundle's milk the next morning. As the skies looked heavy with rain, the bundle-rug saddles were also brought inside the burrow for the night. Used for riding the pala, they were made from the beautifully soft hair harvested every season from the bundles.

Battends were characteristic of the evenings in every Oglin family's life. After all the chores were done, these stories were a ritual at the end of each day and were shared by everyone. Evening by evening, all would take turns to tell a battends. In fact, one of the biggest competitions at the gathering of the clans was the telling of battends. The best battends tellers of the different clans would be given an opportunity to show their ability, much to the delight of Oglins from across the land. Some clans had even developed the art of telling battends in pairs or in groups. That made it far more exciting, because they would act out the parts, speaking in different voices and playing the roles of different animals and characters. With such close relationships between Oglins and their animals, as well as the myriad of wild creatures that shared their world, it was natural that many of their battends were about animals.

As the Ruck family finally settled in, all the young Oglins gathered themselves up in a circle around the fire with their Merma, Modra, their Grand Modra and their Grand Merma. The gayla curled up in the corner, their eyes watching the Oglins' every movement as the evening battends began. This night was Grand Modra's turn. As always, he regaled the family with stories of great beauty. Often he spoke of the vast herds of animals on the Great Plains that stretched beyond the forests and ring of mountains surrounding Vadiera, where the Oglins would occasionally venture out on hunting forays.

This night the young Oglins pleaded for a battend about the gathering of the Oglin clans, as already the preparations were well underway for the gathering soon to be held at Vadiera. This would be the first such event for many of the younger Ruck family members and the first gathering in Vadiera for many, many years. So Grand Modra happily granted their requests and told a tale of trekking towards the yesterdays, where the sun abides, to a gathering many, many seasons past, when he was only a young Oglin, about Baylin's age.

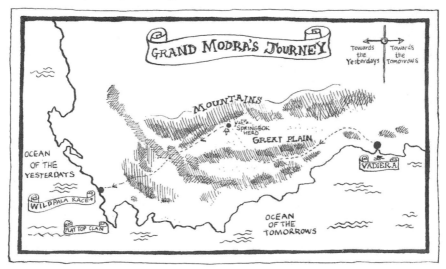

On the way there, he and his companions had made their camp up on a rise of granite boulders, similar to the kopjies in which the Vadiera Oglins lived. There they rested up amongst the boulders for the night. Just below them stood a huge tree on the edge of a little stream of cool, clear water flowing across the vast plains. They were awakened in the middle of the night by sounds of chewing, grunting, the click of heels and ligaments and the occasional snorting of animals. All around them, as far as they could see in the night, the moon was glinting off thousands of horns and from the lyre shape, they could tell they were springbok!

In the cool of morning, in the first pale predawn light, they could see that they were completely surrounded by a vast herd of springbok. As the light gathered strength, so too the vista opened up to their wonder. The light played them slowly, slowly, into the incredible scene. There were literally millions of springbok. As far as they could see across the endless plain, there were springbok, moving ever so slowly. The soft sunlight of dawn washed them in a golden glow, and the early morning stillness enhanced the clarity of their sounds. The front and sides of the herd were slightly spread out grazing or resting, while the middle of the herd was a mass of tightly bunched, ever-moving buck, cheek by jowl.

Grand Modra and his fellow Oglins were forced to stay there in the kopjies for five nights and four days, waiting in wonder for the whole herd to pass by. The Oglins had plenty of time to observe the behaviour of the herd. When the back of the herd eventually arrived, they discovered where the continuous stream of buck coming up the middle of the herd stemmed from. It seemed that in fear of being left behind the animals at the back turned into the stream of moving antelope and headed forward. They walked on until the press around them eased enough so that they could spread out and graze. The discovery of the fresh, unfouled veld out in front of the herd enticed them to put their heads down to grazing. Then as more newcomers arrived at the front, they slowly pushed the others out to the side until they were on the edge of the herd again.

Out on the fringes of the herd, the animals would get enough time for grazing and resting before they would once again discover themselves at the back of the herd. In fear of being left behind, they would dive back into the moving multitude and make their way to the front again. Being isolated at the extremities of the herd meant the best available food, but at a price, because that is where huge packs of carnivores caged their meals. The herd moved in a wide current of living animals flowing like a river, with eddies forming and circling on the sides between banks of hungry predators, before re-entering the main flow and passing on.

In the dusty, trampled aftermath of the herd, Grand Modra and his travelling companions had finally gone on towards the yesterdays and the gathering at the very point of the continent. The clans assembled on the spit of flat land that almost joined the peninsula to the mainland. The Ocean of the Yesterdays was on one side and the Ocean of the Tomorrows was nearby on the other. Towering above them were the beautiful cedar forests and the Great Flat Top Mountain, for which the hosting clan was named. Grand Modra reminisced about how amazing it had been to sit under that mountain, to see the sea on both sides and to watch the swirling clouds that occasionally would shroud the flat summit above.

Grand Modra told his rapt audience that the cloud had a legend of its own. It seemed that when the first Oglins had moved into that area many, many years before, they had come without any bundles accompanying them. However, the Spirit Ancestors had sent a sign to remind them of bundles and their importance in the life of the Oglins. The sign came in the form of a cloud, as soft and as white as a bundle's fleece, pulled down over the mountain. With the mountain's head sticking out on the end, the cloud looked just like a bundle! The Wedrelas, the spiritual leaders, told their clan that the cloud was sent to remind them that it was time for the Oglins to gather bundles together. For they could not survive without the warmth provided by the hair of the bundles, the sweet milk they produced and the many other gifts of their hides, meat, sinew and bones. All of this bounty made the Oglins' way of life more abundant and comfortable. The Great Flat Top Mountain Clan had then sent out a trek party towards the tomorrows again to find and trade for bundles with other Oglin clans.

It was at that particular gathering where Grand Modra had met Grand Merma, and they had come back to Vadiera together. Part of the wealth that she had brought with her was the first of the brown-and-white pala to come to Vadiera. These were now a speciality of the Ruck family, who were highly regarded for their pala breeding and training skills over many generations.

Grand Modra could not help but brag once more about how he had won the untrained pala race at that gathering. On the white beaches across the water from the Great Flat Top Mountain, they held a race in which the young Oglins were each given a pala that had never been ridden before and then had to race them down the beach to the finishing line. He had taken the young pala, the first brown-and-white one he had ever ridden, down into the water to distract him, talking gently to him all the time to calm his nerves, and there he got on his back. Coming up out of the water, he had managed to hold the excited pala back long enough to have the reserve of strength and energy for the final gallop to the winning post. Grand Modra not only won the race, and the pala as a prize at the gathering, he also won the heart of Grand Merma!

As Grand Modra paused to smile lovingly at Grand Merma, Baylin's mind wandered to the upcoming gathering of the clans, soon to be held at Vadiera. He wondered what excitement that would bring! He had never experienced a gathering before. Being a young Oglin, and the gatherings occurring only every fifth summer season, this was the first time he had been old enough to go to one and to have the possibility of competing as well. He had been practising quite intensely with Arto, his own brown-and-white pala stallion. Baylin had an advantage as a rider, as he was a little tall for an Oglin, a bit gangly and not grown to the muscular form of the older mo Oglins yet. He had a special

13

knack for working with the pala, something he had obviously inherited from his Grand Modra and which was strengthened even further in him from his Grand Merma's lineage of famous pala Oglins. He was really looking forward to taking part in the mounted hunting skills competition and had put in a lot of time practising with his team.

Baylin missed the end of the battends that his Grand Modra had been telling, because his mind had been far away. He came back to Earth as his Modra closed the evening proceedings with some serious words about the upcoming gathering. It seemed to be shaping up to be a much more serious event than previous gatherings. Typically, there was much joy and excitement for everybody. This time, though, the Wedrelas, who were the medicine Oglins, had been gathering early in Vadiera from the different clans. Some had arrived many moons early. Something unusual was obviously brewing. The Essedrelas, who were assistants and apprentices to the Wedrelas, were normally much more relaxed and approachable than the Wedrelas. Yet they too had kept themselves very scarce, very quiet and very secretive for some time. There were whispered undertones that there was something major going to happen at this gathering. Baylin hoped very much that this wouldn't get in the way of his efforts.

As the evening drew to an end, the Ruck family all made off to their sleeping rugs. On his way there, Baylin wandered across to give Luka a good night pet and out to the kraal to rub Arto's nose. Climbing into his bundle rugs, he instinctively fingered his pacha, a simple amulet pouch that hangs around every Oglin's neck. It, as always, was made from the skin of the youngest bundle belonging to the family on the day he was born.

Holding his pacha, Baylin thanked Great Spirits for a wonderful day and for allowing him to experience the magnificent elephant in the forest and yet come home without mishap. Evenings were cool in Vadiera and it was nice to snuggle up under the thick rugs of woven bundle hair. The quiet nickering of the pala, occasional swish of a tail, and the stamping of hooves could be heard from the kraal.

Just before closing his eyes, Baylin gazed at the granite walls of the burrow, the grey-brown rock with the black and silver crystals reflecting the flickering light of the fire. He could hear the soft murmur of his Merma and Modra's voices, talking quietly in their rugs. He could feel the little fidgeting of the deep sleeping movements of his little badra lying next to him. With a contented sigh, Baylin fell into a deep and peaceful sleep.

CHAPTER 2
THE GATHERING

When you get into a tight place
and everything goes against you,
till it seems as though you could not hold on a minute longer,
never give up then,
for that is when the tide will turn.

—Harriet Beecher Stowe

Preparation

Slowly and surely, the members of the other clans began to arrive in Vadiera. Every Oglin who possibly could, everyone who was capable of making the journey, came to these clan gatherings. Only the very old, those with very young, those who were too young, and enough youthful Oglins to look after the gayla, bundles and pala remained behind. Baylin had done his duty five summers earlier when his Modra had gone to the home of the Pinnacles Clan to the north of Vadiera. Baylin had stayed at home to help his Merma run the Ruck burrow and look after his younger badras and sadras. Now he and the entire Vadiera Clan were thrilled to be hosting Oglins from across the land. Preparations had been underway for months, and at last the time had arrived!

The visiting clans came in and set up their camps in areas that had been marked out by the Bacor, the council of elders for Vadiera. Each day, Eldrin and Essine, the mo and the mer partners who were the leaders of the Bacor of Vadiera, wandered around, greeting the new arrivals and showing them where to settle in. The little valley near the kopjies was beginning to fill up with the lights of cooking fires at night. The lively evening battends, including singing and a little dancing, were the beginnings of the fun, the feasts and the enjoyment for everyone.

It was an especially festive time for young Oglins, with many young mo and mer Oglins coming in from all around the land. They were busy eyeing each other and watching the hunting skill practice runs of all the clan teams.

Though he felt slightly shy and a bit nervous about meeting so many new Oglins his own age, Baylin always felt quite proud when riding past the others on his rather large pala stallion, with such pretty markings of brown and white. As Baylin was a bit tall for an Oglin, the pair made quite a striking sight. Baylin was especially interested in the young Oglin mers of the different clans, who would watch him with bright golden eyes from under their curly blond and brown hair. When passing by, he would collect Arto and push him into a prance, his neck arched and noble.

The afternoon before the official opening of the gathering, Baylin found himself watching the young mo Oglins holding a practice for the pala-mounted hunting skills competition, the very event in which he and his mates were entered. One team was from the Red River, far to the north and towards the tomorrows from Vadiera. The other team was from the Great Mountains, way off towards the tomorrows. He was wondering if he and his team would have a chance against them. They looked remarkably good, lithe and fit. He also couldn't help wondering what sights they had seen on their trek across to Vadiera, through the outside world. As yet, Baylin himself had never gone far beyond the boundaries of his homeland.

Baylin watched as a young mo from the Red River Clan streaked across the flat ground, with both hands free, his pala running dead level. He expertly swung his spear and thrust it into the stuffed skin of the pig-like dummy used in the hunting competitions. He raised the dummy high above his head and leaned back in his saddle to bring his pala to a sliding halt. It was one of the best practice runs that Baylin had ever seen! His nerves drew a bit tighter as he wondered how his team would fare in the upcoming competition.

The Vadiera team, meanwhile, had a secret practice ground where they could practise the new style and method of hunting that they had developed. None of the other clans had seen anything like it before. It was still a closely guarded secret of the Vadiera Oglins, who were all wondering how their innovations would compare to the time-honoured methods of hunting. Baylin made his way down to the secluded valley to meet his teammates for the competition and to run through their paces together once more before the big day.

Finally, all the clans had arrived and were comfortably camped in the open veld around the central area, where the grass had been grazed nice and short by the bundles and pala in preparation for the gathering. As evening drew near, everyone gathered round for the official welcoming by the Vadiera Bacor. With great ceremony and celebration, the gathering was begun and a night of feasting and battends was underway. Many older Oglins wandered happily through the camp, greeting old friends from previous gatherings and catching up on the news. The Oglin mers and mos that had left their families at previous gatherings, to be joined with a partner of a different clan in a new home, were happily reunited with their families and clan members.

Baylin's own Grand Merma's family members had come from the Great Flat Top Mountain Clan, though none of her sadras and badras had made the long journey, being too old for such a strenuous trek. But some of her younger relatives had come on their stunning brown-and-white pala mares and stallions. They had brought a young brown-and-white stallion especially as a gift for her and the Ruck family in Vadiera. Baylin's heart soared as he imagined all the lovely offspring that the pala would sire and the great joy he would have raising and training them in the years ahead.

It was especially interesting at the gatherings to see how the different clans had developed. Each had its own unique dress and arts, hunting forms, tools and pachas of different design and colours. The shell beadwork, patterns, dye colours, the softness of their leather, the design of their tents and bundle rugs were all distinctly

Oglin, yet they were delightfully varied. The variety made for lively trading at the gatherings and much was learned as each clan shared their innovations and incorporated new ideas into their fine crafts and tool making.

Through all of the excitement, the Wedrelas and Essedrelas were busy scurrying around, talking to the odd Oglin here and there. Many an older Oglin was being taken off and questioned by the Wedrelas. One entire clan was even taken aside for a number of hours to discuss the journey that they had made to Vadiera. There was a hum in the air; something was going on with the Wedrelas. They seemed exceptionally serious and very, very absorbed with the mysterious business. A lot more was going on than was usual for a gathering.

Baylin had a wonderful evening! He spent the time at the battends sessions of his Grand Merma's clan and met all of his cousins for the first time. Wondering what it would be like to go and visit them one day, he tried to imagine the splendid place that they came

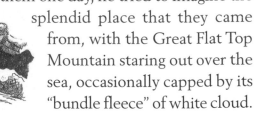

from, with the Great Flat Top Mountain staring out over the sea, occasionally capped by its "bundle fleece" of white cloud.

The Competition

The competitions began the very next morning. They were to go on in heats for a number of days. Baylin and his mates were entered for Vadiera in the pala-mounted hunting skills competition. Soon their secrets would be revealed for all the Oglins to see! They had come up with a new addition to their saddlery. The Vadiera team had contrived straps made from the hide of an animal, which hung down on both sides of their riding bundle blankets, creating "stirrups" that they could put their feet into. This meant they could balance their bodies more easily on the pala. So far, while in public, they had hidden their innovation beneath their blankets and carried on riding in the normal Oglin fashion with their feet hanging free. Only when they were practising in their secret valley, hidden from the other teams, had they let down their leather stirrups and practised riding with them. They believed this modification would give them a huge advantage in the competition, as none of the other clans had anything similar.

Traditionally, the Oglins hunted with a long spear-like lance, held in one or two hands. The Vadiera Oglins had developed a new implement for hunting as well. They had begun using a very short, stabbing assagai, rather than the traditional long lance. Theirs was held only in one hand, although the handle was long enough to hold with two hands if one wanted to. The new hunting tool worked more like a sword than a lance, though it had only a sharp elongated spearhead, not a long sharpened edge like a sword.

In the veld, three riders would approach a bush pig or a warthog at speed, ride it down, stick it with a lance and kill it. In these competitions, an artificial pig was used, made from a stuffed hide and tied to long pieces of rawhide. Mounted Oglins at each end would pull it, so the dummy would move across the ground and change direction at high speed like a real wild bush pig or warthog might do. Normally in the competitions, teams began with their three riders spread out, slightly facing the pig. Then at a shout, the dummy would start to move and the pala would be urged forward at full gallop. The pig could change direction quite drastically at any moment, as the rawhide lines that were attached to it could pull it in a number of directions. At least one member of the team had to stab it right through to make the "kill." It had to be done with three riders, so if the pig broke slightly right, the outside rider on that side would pick it up, or if it broke to the left, the outside rider on that side would pick it up. The task was not something one Oglin could easily do alone. The Pinnacles Clan team was drawn as the first competitor. The riders headed out nervously to line up and have the first run in the tournament. At the shout, the three young Oglins took off with their pala at full tilt. The pig was drawn hard across the grass in front at high speed. The pig broke to the left, and the rider on the outside managed to draw his lance towards it as it raced underneath his pala's feet. The pala actually had to jump to go over the top, or it would have tripped and fallen, and the lance glanced down the side of the dummy pig, only ripping open the edge of it, but not scoring a direct kill.

There was a huge discussion from the group of older mos that came from various clans to be the judges of this competition. It was a skillful rider and a well-schooled pala that managed to get the rip on the side of the pig as the pala leaped over. It was a very, very difficult one. Had they been actually hunting in the bush, they would have had a chance to kill the pig with another try, especially if the wound incapacitated the pig. But the competition allowed for only one stabbing attempt on each run. So, the decision was reached that the team would score only a wound, not a direct kill, for this heat.

The Red River Clan team that Baylin had been watching the previous day was next. They came prancing out onto the field, very, very proud and boastful and obviously very good at what they were doing. They lined themselves up, holding in their eager pala. The next pig was ready. The pig-pulling team signalled that it was ready to go. The pig was pulled, the shout came up, and out they came at pace, leaning well forward as they raced across the field. They had themselves spread so that the two outside riders were slightly ahead of the middle rider, a clever idea especially when hunting live pigs, as this formation actually herded the prey. As the inside rider was just about to reach it, the pig veered to the right, going underneath the back legs of the right-hand pala. That rider had to turn ninety degrees, but he still managed to slam his lance right through the pig as his pala skidded to a halt. He scored a direct hit, a kill!

Baylin had never seen such impressive riding before. Their riding was brilliant and their pala so responsive. He was pretty sure that none of his own teammates would have managed nearly that well. So, the Red River Clan team achieved a full score of a kill. Though there were many more heats to come, Baylin felt the pressure building up. His team's turn was next.

The tension was considerable as Baylin and his mates mounted up and rode out for their first heat. Baylin's whole body tingled and he felt a spreading, numbing heat in his stomach, warm and alive. Even the pala were on edge, moving with extra spring and tension in their strides. Instead of using the tactic of the previous team, placing their two outside pala slightly ahead, the three Vadiera riders chose to position their two outside riders slightly behind the middle one. That way, when the pig broke to one side, the two outside ones could turn on it very quickly without the danger of overrunning it. This was fine when the field was dry, but when it was wet, it could be quite dangerous.

The crowd had swelled as the competition got rolling. There had been whispered rumours from the Vadiera Oglins to the other clans about how good their riders were this year, with superior pala-mounted hunting skills. And they had hinted that there was something unusual that had to be watched, so nearly everyone from the entire camp had gathered around by the time the Vadiera team was set to do their first run.

When Baylin's team lined up, a gasp of surprise arose from the crowd as they realised there was something different about the way the riders were seated on their pala. Baylin and his teammates had drawn down their new leather stirrups. With the riders' feet placed in them, the stirrups would give them extra balance and the ability to reach out further from the bundle-blanket saddle.

Another shock followed seconds later when three old Vadiera mos walked forward and handed the riders their new short stabbing assagais, instead of the long lances that had always been used. Soon, amazement turned to concern. Many of the older Oglins were pointing, shaking their heads and muttering, "This isn't how it is done! This isn't how it is supposed to work!"

However, the Wedrelas and body of official judges had already granted the team permission to use their newly designed equipment. Sworn to secrecy, the Wedrelas, judges and various clan Bacor members had come out to the secret practice area to observe a couple of practice runs firsthand. They had discussed it at length and finally decided that if the changes worked, and worked well, it would be good for the Oglins. If Vadiera could win the competition, it would prove that the innovations could be good for all of them. So, after careful consideration, the stirrups and assagai were allowed in the competition, for all the Oglin clans to see for themselves.

Throughout time, the Oglins had traditionally welcomed new ideas that could benefit them all. Normally, such things were simply made known to everyone, but in this case the Vadiera

Oglins were very proud of their inventions and wanted to test them and, hopefully, win the competition. The improvements were so obviously valuable, the judges had no difficulty reaching consensus.

Still, a hum of dissent began to rise from the crowd. "What about the rules? Has Vadiera forgotten the rules of the competition?" The disgruntled voices began to shout their disagreement. Suddenly a group of mo Oglins, including the coach of the Red River Clan team, ran out onto the field with their hands held high in protest to stop the run before it began.

Baylin's heart sank. If they were now forced to take the stirrups off and change back to their old discarded lances, they would be utterly useless. They were totally unpractised and more than likely, would not even be able to compete in a style they had never really learned. All three of them were young Oglins and they had been schooled as the first team to use the new methods. They had never actually even practised the old way of hunting.

Obviously playing along for the dramatic effect, the head competition judge stepped forward and with his most regal bearing, he raised his hands to still the complaining crowd. Slowly they quieted down.

Arto and the other pala of the team were now really overwrought with excitement. The chase of the competition created shivering anticipation enough on its own, let alone the additional confusion. The disruption and noise finally settled into silence. It was tense for all, waiting on the start line for their first official run in a tournament. The pala were champing, pawing and prancing. Arto had spun completely around twice already, very nearly unseating his rider the first time. Baylin stroked Arto's neck gently and whispered reassurances to his fired up mount, remembering how his Grand Modra had calmed the untrained pala in the waters of the sea so many years ago. Gradually, Arto settled down and Baylin was able to keep him contained for the time being.

The judge's voice finally broke the tense silence, with a well-worded speech in which he explained that the innovations had been approved for the competition. He described how the decision had been made in consultation with all the judges, Wedrelas and Bacor of the various clans. He asked all the individuals who had been consulted to rise and show their support of the decision, which had been made unanimously after the Vadiera team had performed a private demonstration for them. One by one, they all stood and in loud clear voices made it plain that all the clans had been consulted and sworn to secrecy on the matter. Standing proud, their blond and brown curly locks wafted around by a gentle breeze, they confirmed their support.

The head judge had the final word. He asked everyone gathered to please quiet down and assess the new innovations in the Vadiera team's performance on the field rather than prejudge them on the pride that was at stake. So amongst all the murmurs of the crowd, everyone returned to their places.

The Vadiera team circled their pala around at a walk to try to regain their composure and prepare for the run. Concentration and anticipation finally replaced distraught nerves, and the riders lined up once more in a deadly, expectant hush. The shout was given and they sprang forward into a flat gallop. Baylin was the left-hand rider. This was the most difficult position. If the pig broke towards the left, Baylin either had to turn very sharply to get on the correct side for his right arm or he had to lean out to the opposite side, across his body to stab the pig. This was something he had mastered well to win his position on the team. It would have been an ideal position for a left-handed hunter, but they did not happen to have a left-hander among them at the time. Baylin had to hold Arto slightly behind the middle rider, ready to turn at high speed if necessary. Arto was well practised at this, and quite able to stop and turn instantly in response to a shift in seat and the lightest pressure from Baylin's legs. Such a sharp turn would be really dangerous only when it was wet.

The Vadiera riders were racing along at a flat gallop. Just as the pig was in front of the short lance of the middle rider, it veered to the left, rawhide rope and pig almost tripping up the pala in the process. Baylin had to swing Arto instantly around to the left. The pig was moving a lot more quickly than he had anticipated. Already leading on the near side, Arto was able to dig way down and swing in the new direction with the slightest touch from Baylin. Just in time Baylin leaned right out of his riding blanket, to the very end of his reach, his little hairy feet sunk solidly in the leather stirrups. He drove the sword-like lance deep into the back of the pig and left it there. The roar of the crowd confirmed it immediately. He had scored a direct hit. Such a thrust would have killed a wild pig immediately.

The crowd was amazed at the great display of skill and daring they had just witnessed. All could see the advantage the stirrups gave Baylin, allowing him to reach out much further from his pala's back. They could see the difference made by the one-handed short assagai as well. It was much handier than the unwieldy lance. The three Vadiera riders brought their pala to a halt and turned back towards the pig. Baylin drew out yet another assagai from under the covers of the bundle-rug saddle. This was in case he needed to finish the pig off, had it been a real life hunt in the bush. They had decided to do this in their first heat to show the versatility of the weapons in real situations.

With the crowd still roaring and leaping about, Baylin and his team-mates rode back to receive tumultuous congratulations. Hundreds of Oglins swarmed around them to have a closer look at the assagais and a feel of the stirrup leathers. Endless questions were asked of them, with everyone wondering how they worked and how they were attached and so on. Animated discussions were carried on long after the heat.

Once the surprise was over, it was fine for the Vadiera Oglins to let everyone have a close look at their innovations, for now they belonged to all the Oglins. True to tradition, all such new and useful developments were shared among and made common to all Oglins. The Vadiera Oglins already had the advantage in terms of the competition, as no one else would have time to first outfit themselves and then to practise in time for the remaining heats.

However, anticipating the interest and having faith in the new equipment's usefulness, a number of Vadiera Oglins had already been making these items to barter with other Oglin clans. Thanks to their team's impressive first performance with them, the interest was already keen and there was sure to be a lively trade in them over the remaining days of the gathering. Many Vadiera Oglins had made them in hopes of trading with the Great Flat Top Mountain Clan for their coveted brown-and-white pala.

It was quite unsettling for Baylin to be the centre of attention. Although he was feeling shy, he couldn't help but notice the twinkle in the eyes of the young mers looking at him with newfound interest. For the first time in his life, he was the hero of the day. He was feeling pretty proud, even though he was still shaking like a leaf from the pressure and tension in the moments leading up to the start!

The competition was far from over, however. Many more heats were to be run. At the Vadiera team's second heat, the pig also came left. Each time the mounted Oglins pulling the ropes could decide to run it straight, veer it slightly, or turn it all the way around to the left or right. Once again, the judges were testing Baylin's ability to turn in time and use the new stirrups to keep his balance while swinging the assagai around to stab the pig. Baylin had to make very much the same kill that he did in the first heat. His success, twice in a row, helped convince some of the more sceptical Oglins that perhaps his first performance had not been a fluke, and that there was really some benefit to the Vadiera innovations

In their third heat, the pig broke to the right, and the right-hand rider managed to score a kill as well. With ease, he had made a slight turn on his pala and using his stirrups, leaned way out of the bundle-rug saddle and scored a clean kill between the "shoulder blades" without any trouble at all.

By then, the majority of the mos could not deny that these new tools were superior. Though the other teams displayed great skill, the stirrups and assagais made a difficult task a bit easier and increased the chances of success. When harvesting the clan's favourite food depended upon a successful hunt, such an advantage would surely be welcome.

Baylin's life as a quiet and unobtrusive Oglin changed dramatically. His time was now taken up with answering the numerous questions on the use of, fitting of and value of the stirrups. Different ideas were already springing up, now that the creative mind of the all the Oglins was released on the same task. The short stabbing assagai, much like the forerunner of a sword may have looked, was also discussed. Baylin, though he loved the sport dearly, and clearly was relishing being the centre of attraction, really wanted to retreat for a while.

Lafina

Escaping the attentions, Baylin rode out on Argyl, Arto's full brother only a year younger. Stretching out into a trot across the savanna, he was startled by a mer running into his path from the side. She forced Argyl to a wrenching stop with a square stance and a level, golden-eyed gaze. He recognised her immediately as Lafina. She was just a few years his senior and from the Pinnacles Clan. She had an uncanny way of making him uncomfortable. She seemed to stare at him a lot and to always be near him when there was any opportunity. He was sure that he just blushed bright red every time she looked at him.

She was beautiful in a different way. Not beautiful in a fragile and delicate way, like an orchid; no, she certainly was not delicate at all. She was not big and heavy; she was trim, wiry, stringy and hard. In fact she could wrestle most of her mo cousins down in no time, even those of the same size or bigger than her. She could ride a pala like a whirlwind, as well as any of the mos. Yet she was extremely attractive. Her eyes looked through him as if they knew him and what he was thinking. She had an earthy trustiness about her. They had not spoken much but they had caught each other's eyes quite a lot. He felt, in fact, they had both drawn comfort and assurance from that eye contact even across a crowd. It was as if every time he looked for her, she was searching for him. When their eyes met they would lock for a while, until in a flush he would have to look away. He realised suddenly that he really felt good when he was with her, or near her, and was actually gaining a strange sense of strength through their moments of deep eye contact. He would have loved to be around her more, if only he had the pluck to say something.

It didn't seem important now, as she asked if he was going off for a ride on his own. He simply replied, "Yes." He got stuck for words, and didn't really know what else to say.

Again it didn't matter; she was in charge and he was happy with her lead. "I am coming with you," she said. "Move up."

He shifted forward on his rug. Placing a curly blond-haired foot on top of his and a soft-haired hand on his thigh, she lithely swung onto Argyl's back behind Baylin. She put her hands on his thighs, leaned her long, supple body into his, and with a shout kicked Argyl into a gallop up the path towards the forest in the distance.

Baylin and Lafina melted together. She rode and moved like he knew she could. He had seen her enough times by now, performing with the Pinnacles Clan riding-skill team. They raced, did tricks and showed off their general talent. He had also watched her play a brilliant role in the Pinnacles Battends team that was sure to make the finals. She did not bump against him or upset his balance at all. She rode with him and Argyl as if they were all one animal, with one movement, without discomfort and without difficulty. He was intensely aware of her breath in his ear, her hair tickling his face as it blew in the wind, and the feel of her body moulded to his as they slowed to a canter and rode out onto the plain. Out into the veld away from the others, just them, the pala, the veld and the wind.

They rode out to the spot where the elephant had roused him from his afternoon nap, in what seemed a lifetime ago. Baylin and Lafina sat there for hours in the safety of the enveloping arms of the giant tree and talked and talked. He found out all about how she had grown up in the clan of the Pinnacles. She told him all about her clan's home territory, the mountains, and the importance of their dung beetle totem. They held hands to start with and later sat in each other's arms, snuggled up and very content.

They rode back at a walk, not wanting to break the magic spell of the afternoon as the sun left the sky behind them. The light turned the huge storm clouds out to sea a bright oyster-shell pink. Slowly the inky blue colour of a truly heavy African savanna storm rose in the cloud as the pink climbed higher. The stark difference between the beautiful greens and yellows of the veld, with the last light reflected against the dark purple blue of the clouds, was so awe inspiring that they both just fell silent and watched the beauty unfold.

Baylin dreamed that night about the beauty of Lafina. He dreamed about her company, her laughter and, most of all, the feeling of closeness and companionship that they shared. He awoke later in the night in a cold sweat, with bad dreams brought on by a battends one of his cousins had told him about, an incident that had happened on their trek to Vadiera.

His cousin had described walking through the deep forest and hearing a roar of something they had never heard before, and huge trees coming crashing down. One of the mos had been sent to investigate. He was a real bushman. All Oglins were skilled in bushcraft, but this fellow was a legend. He had crept forward, towards the noise. There, from a hidden vantage point, he saw a man, dressed in yellow with an orange thing on his head, holding a smoking, screaming machine in his hands. The roaring machine had teeth that could eat through a tree in seconds. The tree would come crashing down with a shattering noise and a stunned silence would follow. The whole forest was wreathed in a deathly silence.

The Oglins, according to his cousin, were starting to feel pressure from the people "out there." The Wedrelas had questioned their whole clan when they arrived at Vadiera to find out more about their experience. Strange things were now starting to show up in the Oglin homelands, which until now had seemed totally unaffected by people or influences from the outside world. There was a lot of speculation that something different and worrisome was occurring, although no one really knew what it was about, and the Wedrelas would never speak out of turn. Still, it hung a storm cloud over the whole gathering. This was not made any easier by the wild storm that ravaged the camps of the Oglins that night, bringing howling wind, driving rain and the most stunning flashes of lightning and deafening rolls of thunder.

Baylin was deeply disturbed. In his dream, his favourite little sister, Aga, was slowly getting further and further from him. More and more African veld seemed to be coming between them, separating them. They reached for each other. He could hear her calling but he could not make a sound 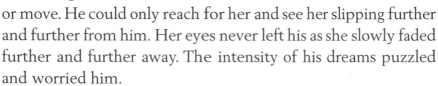 or move. He could only reach for her and see her slipping further and further from him. Her eyes never left his as she slowly faded further and further away. The intensity of his dreams puzzled and worried him.

To make matters worse, the driving rain was causing him even more apprehension about tomorrow. At this rate, the finals of the competition would be played out on a field of mud: wet, slippery and very dangerous.

The Finals

On the fifth and final morning of the competition, only three clans were left in the running for honour in the hunting skills competition. Tension and excitement were at an all-time high. Speculation on the Vadiera team's chances was the topic of the

morning. The rain in the night had been very heavy. All across the wide valley of the encampment, the Oglins had spread their tent hides out in the morning sun to dry on bushes and poles and rawhide ropes. There were hundreds of colourful bundle rugs adorning the flat-topped

thorn trees. Many tents were being repaired following the ravages of the violent storm.

The going was still wet underfoot. The normally dense grass of the playing field had been churned and dug up by the previous days of competition, so the surface was quite slippery. A team of pala had been brought in to drag two thorn bushes back and forth across the pitch to try to flatten it out a bit and fill in some of the bigger divots. This hadn't really worked, as the continuous heavy trampling of five days of competition had compacted the soil somewhat. With no time for the soil life to fluff up the soil in repair, the field itself had not accepted water very well. The surface was slippery and treacherous.

Finally, it was time for the first heat. The first team was from the clan of the Great Mountains, highly skilled riders that everyone had been talking about. The run would be a tough one, but they were ready to try it. It was almost certain that the pig would break left, because they would be testing the outside left rider to see if he had the reactions and the ability to get around and get over to kill the pig on its turn. The question was: Would it turn left and back into them, or would it break straight to the left?

The Great Mountains team got itself lined up. The shout went up, the pig was pulled and they ran out at a flat gallop after the pig, straight down the field. The pig swung to the left. At high speed, the left-hand rider pulled up his pala. It sank down on its haunches and checked with its front feet, bits of sod lifting out from under the front hooves every time they hit down. The young rider was trying to stop and turn his pala, and at the same time straining to get his lance around further to his left, to follow the pig. With one hand on the pala's neck and leaning out as far as possible, he swung his lance down. The point passed just over the top of the pig. With all the force of his stab, the lance dug into the ground, lifting the rider off backwards. With the lancer's weight suddenly gone, the pala flipped suddenly onto its side. Eyes rolling back in fear and struggling to rise, the pala skidded along the ground. Bits of grass, dung and soil flew over its ears before it came to a stop and wobbled to its feet. Out of the settling debris, the dapper lancer arose, shaking himself off.

The dummy pig, of course, got away free without any trouble at all. It was that team's first miss. They may well have scored a hit if it hadn't been for the slick footing that prevented the pala from stopping and turning quickly enough. The crowd cheered loyally, for they knew what a great effort it was and all were relieved that both rider and pala were uninjured by the spectacular fall.

The second team to ride was the Vadiera Oglins. While mounting, they had a quiet chat with the older mo who had been the captain of the team and was now serving as their coach. He said, "That first team was the one everyone thought was really set to win this, if it hadn't been for us doing so well with the short lances. Now that they've pulled the pig left for them, you can almost bet that the pig will break the same for you. So, spread yourselves a little bit more. Extend the distance from the front rider to the back rider a little bit. If you drop back too much, you may well be too slow and miss it entirely. When they change its direction, it will have to be in front of the middle rider, otherwise the middle rider will get it. So, you lot may just manage to score with less danger if you leave enough of a gap. All right, let's do it, my young ones!"

They set up just as he advised. The shout went up. Baylin pulled back a little bit so that Arto's head was just on the hindquarter instead of on the stirrup of the lead pala. The pig flew across the field, with the riders galloping at full speed after it. Leaving it to the very last moment, the pig was almost underneath the leading pala when it was pulled to the left. The middle pala had to actually jump to clear the pig, causing his rider's assagai to just lift clear. The pig's new direction took it practically under Arto's neck. Baylin pulled in, leaned back, and Arto dropped right down onto his haunches, checking on his front feet. From their months of practice, Arto knew exactly what was going on. He understood the movement of the pig and the need to track it, so he was able to follow every movement. He was already checking when he saw the pig change direction. He followed it with his ears, getting down low for the turn. Baylin was able to free himself up completely, not holding on to Arto at all. He leaned out with a completely loose body, to follow the pig around and help Arto through the sharp bend. As the pig began to make ground away from underneath Arto's neck, Baylin was able to lean over onto the near side and arch above the pig, to thrust down with his short assagai and stab into the right hindquarter of the pig. The short lance stayed in the pig as they rode on past.

All three of them were pumped up with pride, standing in their stirrups and thumping each other on the back as most of the crowd were leaping up and down and throwing their hands in the air. While there was no doubt of a score, there ensued a great discussion as to whether that counted as a kill or not. The assagai was in the pig. The pig was punctured in the right hindquarter. "Would it have died? Would it have immobilised the pig? Would it count as a kill?" The crowd roared with excitement, clapping, whistling and shouting its appreciation for the great performance. Everyone knew that no one would have even come close with a longer lance, because they were so unwieldy in comparison. Being able to swing a lance around to get a pig passing behind was almost impossible with a long lance, and the rider would also run a serious risk of stabbing another pala in the process. They knew that nobody could have reached that far out of the saddle without the leather stirrups to balance upon. Neither could someone stop at that speed without letting one's weight slip too far forward, as happened with the rider in the previous heat, with his pala subsequently falling. With the advantage of the stirrups, Baylin was able to lean well back and keep his balance with Arto. It was the combination of the new lance and stirrups that made the kill possible, topped with plenty of skill and courage. There could be no question of that.

At last, the decision was made to withhold judgement until they saw what happened with the third team. Depending upon that, they would either make a difficult decision or hold a rerun.

Baylin's teammates and coach congratulated him warmly. Arto was very shaky afterwards. He had obviously been under immense strain to perform as he had. The uproar and stress were having an effect. In fact, Baylin wondered if they had to do another run, maybe Arto would not be able to do it. It could be that he would have to borrow his Modra's pala. Baylin's own heart was still thumping; he stroked Arto to calm them both down. The whole team was pretty excited about their run but still nervous about what the third team would manage to do.

In a show of good sportsmanship, the Vadiera team wished the mos from the Great Flat Top Clan the best of luck as they rode out onto the field for their final run. They were the team that included Baylin's cousins and Lafina's brother. So the rivalry was even more intense now. The cousins were extremely excited about the shorter lance and the stirrups and looked forward to trying them out. They were, however, sticking to the old methods they had practised with and were going to do their level best to win.

They lined themselves up, using the same strategy the Vadiera Oglins had just used, holding back the two outside pala a little bit further than normal. By then, the excitement was really up and running. Their pala were difficult to control as they were beginning to dance and spin in excitement for the hunt. The shout went up and they took off. The pig was being pulled straight down the middle until sure enough, once again the pig was pulled left. This time, it angled not backwards but forwards and left. The rider on the outside left was able to check his pala in, swing him towards it, and bring his lance around to bear. The speed of the pig was slower than anticipated, and he managed to only score a wound on the left hindquarter as they went roaring past.

The crowd roared for this tremendous effort. The judges huddled together to discuss how things were going to work. There was great but friendly rivalry from the cousins as they rode past with their pala prancing and sweating. Joking with each other, they said, "Look out now! Things are happening! We're going to have a runoff for first place!"

Eventually the head judge came out and announced, "To be fair, we are going to have to award a wound to the Great Flat Top team. Well done to them under such difficult conditions! I am afraid to say, the judges are unanimous, that the Vadiera team will have to be awarded…" The silence roared in Baylin's ears and his heart sank to his fury feet as his racing mind sprang to the shaky, excited Arto beside him. Could he manage another run? The judge continued, "…a kill because the assagai stayed in the pig!"

The rest of the announcement about Vadiera being declared the winners was lost in the thunderous applause that broke loose from the crowd. Vadiera supporters and many others were hugging and yelling their pleasure. The Vadiera mos had won it with a kill in their final run. To all the thundering crowd, it was clear that the stirrups and the assagai were definitely the answer. They were bound to take off, and it would be extremely exciting to see what new developments would stem from them. From that moment, many Vadiera mos had deals and trades that were finally sealed. The supply of short lances and stirrups they had made for the gathering were in great demand.

The Vadiera Oglins were the heroes of the day. By then, everybody knew who Baylin was. In addition to drawing great interest from the young mers, many mos would stop him and his mates for a chat. There were endless questions and animated discussions about their techniques, practices and so on. It was great excitement for all of them. With the glow of their win and the pressure of the competition behind him, Baylin looked forward to a night full of feasting, celebration and Lafina.

Battends

On that evening, the finals of the battends competition were to be held. The three leading battends teams would perform for all the clans. Throughout the gathering, battends sessions had been held each evening. The Vadiera battends team was already out of the running. Each clan had performed one battends before the finalists were chosen. The three leading teams all had something new and unique in their battends. One team in particular used a lot of movement. Up until then, dancing and acrobatic movement had rarely been seen in a battends. Always a lot of singing had been included, but never before as part of the tale was there such beautiful dancing by the presenters. Everyone was all ears and eyes about these developments. All the Oglins were gathered for what was sure to be a display of extraordinary performances.

As the night drew on, the excitement built. The first two battends teams were brilliant, and everyone wondered how they could be topped. The last to perform were the members of the Pinnacles Clan. They enchanted their audience from the beginning. The whole story was narrated while Lafina, two other young mers and one mo acted it out with mime and movement. Their fine singing and dance entranced the crowd, drawing them into the story. Lafina in particular caught everybody's heart.

39

Lafina's soft golden curls and bright lion-coloured eyes shone as she sang her part with a sweet lilting voice. With lithe and supple grace, her dance included difficult acrobatic movements. Her effortless backwards somersaults and flips drew gasps from the crowd.

The whole story was about the importance of the dung beetle in the life and health of the savanna grasslands. With great creativity, they acted out this cycle of life. They showed how the bundles and pala graze and browse the plants and then drop their dung and urine on the ground, where it is immediately fallen upon by hordes of different size and types and colours of dung beetles. In many different ways the various beetles take it underground. Some form the dung into balls, often twice their own size, and roll it away to bury it in the ground and lay their eggs safe beneath the surface. There are so many different kinds of dung beetles, even some that will steal another's dung ball!

The players' backwards somersaults were near perfect imitations of the way dung beetles roll their balls of dung along. Each time the dung beetle would roll over the top of his dung ball, it forced the ball ahead a little bit quicker. The audience laughed with delight at their antics and ability to mimic the industrious insect burying the dung, usually within minutes of it hitting the ground. They skillfully showed how this allowed for the recycling of the nutrients, so that the next season, new life could grow from those old plants. How wonderful a part of the Oglin world they were! As Lafina had shared with Baylin, the revered dung beetles were the totem of the Pinnacles Clan.

The team's battends came to an end with the dung beetles all curled up together after laying their eggs. The little eggs, played by some of the youngest Oglins to make the trek to the gathering, were waiting expectantly to hatch and start the cycle again. With a roar of appreciation from the gathering of Oglins, the battends tellers rose and thanked their audience, bowing in different directions and accepting the praise graciously. Everyone's eyes were on the star of the show. As she made her bows left, right and straight ahead, Lafina's dazzling golden eyes suddenly locked onto Baylin's.

All the battends teams were asked to stand and share in the applause while they awaited the final call of the judges. Baylin's mind was racing. He had a funny feeling in his stomach. It was a burning, tight feeling that was actually disturbing and confusing his thoughts. He suddenly thought of Lafina again, the nightmare, their ride and of other wonderful moments together. Suddenly he knew something was going to happen. Something was going to happen! He felt the cold grip of fear in his throat.

He was so engrossed in his own feeling of dread that he almost missed the announcement. The Pinnacles Clan battends team had won it! There were great whoops of joy from the Pinnacles Clan members and applause from all around. They were truly worthy winners. There was great jubilation and roaring laughter as the winning team was paraded around on the shoulders of their clan mates. There was always great festivity involved with the battends. While Baylin and his teammates had been the centre of attraction earlier on, now the young Pinnacles Clan battends team, and especially Lafina, who had performed the main part in winning the battends, took the limelight. Now she was getting a lot of attention from all, yet twice more her eyes locked onto Baylin's. It was a challenging yet beckoning look, one that made him weak at the knees.

The Choosing

The time had come when the leaders of the Vadiera Bacor, Eldrin and Essine, called for silence. Hushed, all the Oglins drew near to listen to the important news about to be divulged.

"My fellow Oglins," Eldrin began. "First I wish to personally and on behalf of all the Oglins of Vadiera thank all the clans that have come so far to be with us here. Thank you for making the effort to travel the great distances and to go through extreme hardships in making that journey. We have been honoured by your presence here.

"As always, this clan gathering has once again been a time of celebration and fun for all. It has been such a special time for all to gather and be reunited with family that we haven't seen in many moons or seasons. It has been a time to be reunited with those from our own burrows that have moved to other clans for reasons of the heart. It has also been a time to reconnect with friends from other clans, made before at such gatherings as these. And as always, we all enjoy the friendly rivalry between the different clans and were eager to see who would win the various competitions. It has been a wonderful gathering for our clans! Congratulations to all who came and all who participated."

A great roar of applause went up from the gathered Oglins, slapping each other on the back and whooping and whistling their pleasure. Slowly the sound subsided and suddenly, all recognising that a crucial moment had arrived, silence descended upon them.

They could have heard a pin drop as Eldrin continued. "However, as you are all aware, this particular gathering also has a very serious side to it. The time has come for that to now be addressed openly. There have been a lot of rumours and discussions about it already. Our Wedrelas and Essedrelas have spoken with many of you. During this gathering, they have been in consultation with the Great Spirits and are trying to do important things for all the Oglins. Certainly a lot of the clans need something to be done soon."

The Great Wedrela made his way to Eldrin and Essine's side and began to speak. "Each of our clans has a beautiful and healthy homeland surrounding its burrow. We have our territory that we steward and which in turn provides for the life of the Oglins to carry on as normal. Beyond that there is always some sort of boundary, such as the forest that surrounds Vadiera, keeping the clan secure from discovery by people. Some of us have mountains that ring our lands while others have borders of rivers or high cliffs. Beyond these boundaries, we Oglins seldom venture.

"Occasionally we do, though," he continued. "At times we go out to hunt for game to feed our families, or for the traditional hunting expedition that is held for young mos to become adults. We also venture out in large numbers to attend the gathering of the clans like this one. Young Oglins also often go off on treks of their own to distant clans to satisfy a need for discovery. All this is part of what makes us Oglins, Oglins," he said with an attempt to lighten the mood.

"So it is a source of great concern that it is becoming more and more difficult for Oglins to survive when going outside of their home areas and crossing through our boundaries to the outside world. A great many of you had a very difficult time making it to this clan gathering, having to pass through grave danger. Things have changed a lot in the outside world and it is now beginning to affect our everyday lives." The Great Wedrela's words hung in the air like a threatening thundercloud.

"We cannot ignore these changes. Even though we do have our own lands that are safe and healthy, if the outside world isn't healthy and cannot sustain itself, the destruction will eventually reach our clan areas and everything we have and care about will also be at risk, " he warned ominously.

"It seems that more and more and more problems are cropping up out there in the Great World. Even though *our* lands are healthy, it seems that the Earth around us is drying up. Although as much rain still falls as always, its timing is becoming less and less predictable. Unlike here in Vadiera, when it rains in the outer world, the water just doesn't seem to get into the ground anymore. Instead, the water leaves the land, before it has done its job of growing plants, and takes the precious soil with it. The rivers run the colour of the soil and bleed the land of its future.

"All over it seems that people are changing things, and seldom for the better. They are trying to make Earth produce for them what she used to produce normally anyway, without allowing her to work freely and naturally.

"The biggest problem is the disappearance of habitat for all the plants and animals that have shared this land with us ever since our earliest ancestors. The great grasslands are drying up and becoming shrub deserts. More and more beautiful riverine woodland is being washed away out to sea by the floods. The banks of the rivers are becoming straight up and down cut banks, which are very difficult for animals to cross. Against these odds, survival for all life becomes more difficult over time. So, we Wedrelas and Essedrelas have been together discussing this. We have also been in communication with the Great Spirits to ask for direction and to learn what we need to do to fulfil our responsibility to nature, to help reverse these terrible losses and restore the health of the World.

"The Great Spirits have decreed that a critical journey must be made. They have chosen two Oglins to make this journey that will take them far out into the Great World. They must make their way across wide distances, all the way to the Great Forest, where the Great River flows through the land of the Great Spirit. There they must meet with the Great Spirit, who will give them the answers. These will be the keys to our future. They will be the keys that we need to be able to survive as Oglins. They will also be the keys to making the Great World out there able to sustain us and bring us joy and food well into the future. Discovering these keys is to be the mighty task that two chosen young Oglins will be charged with."

The Great Wedrela let the importance of the moment sink in with a long pause. There was a hush over the whole gathering as all the Oglins contemplated the immense challenge that lay ahead for those who would make such a journey.

Then he went on, "It will be dangerous. It will be difficult. But it can be done. There is one old Oglin right here who once made that journey. Three Oglins left and only one returned." There were gasps and murmurs as he continued. "This time the Great Spirit has decreed that only two Oglins go. The Oglin that returned is Grand Modra Spola of the Vadiera Clan. Grand Modra Spola made the Great Journey many, many seasons ago."

Old Spola stood up and moved over beside the Great Wedrela. A huge grin spread across his furrowed face as everybody cheered for him.

"Old Spola will help us," continued the Great Wedrela. "He will help us to train and give the right information to the young Oglins who will make this journey. But the future of all Oglins as a whole lies in the hands of the two that the Great Spirits have helped us choose."

The Great Wedrela paused once again for effect. This time there was silence, deep and apprehensive. "So," he resumed, "we want everyone here to reach for their pacha and feel around in their amulets for one that doesn't belong there. If you find an amulet that is new, raise it high above your head, for you are one of the chosen ones."

Fear washed over Baylin in a prickly rush of heat that travelled quickly through his whole body. His heart was in his mouth and there was roaring in his ears as his mind struggled with questions: "Will I be chosen? What a great adventure, but would I really want to go? I'll be really, really nervous if I'm the one that's chosen. It's such a huge responsibility being given to a young

Oglin." The thoughts crammed into his head as he began to reach for his pacha.

Baylin carefully felt into his pacha, his hands going lovingly around the amulets that he knew so well. Then his fingers went ice cold as they turned around something different, something new, an amulet that did not belong! His heart dropped immediately, right down to his furry feet. What did he feel? He felt fear, then elation. Fear of the huge responsibility of this long and dangerous trip. His heart was racing. Elation followed, because the Great Spirits had faith in him and had chosen him for such a task.

Slowly, Baylin raised the strange amulet up above his head. It was a brilliant, shining stone that caught the glint of the fire as if it had a light of its own. He held it high. The murmurs in the crowd began to grow louder.

Holding it way up above his head, he wondered, "Who is the other Oglin? Who am I going to travel with?" His eyes darted to the right, left, forward, left, right and there he saw, across the crowd, a lithe and supple figure, raising high above her blond head, a dazzling white seashell. Her eyes were also moving around the gathering, trying to pick out the other figure, to see with whom she would be travelling.

Finally, their eyes met, locked on one another. It was Lafina! She was still glowing from her lead role in the battends about the dung beetle. Their deep golden eyes locked.

"So, we'll be travelling together," they both thought. Both of them suddenly felt elated. This was the right thing. It felt good. The Spirits had chosen well.

The Wedrelas blew on their kudu horn trumpets and beat on their drums, and the Great Wedrela called out, "The Spirits have chosen. Baylin of the Vadiera Clan and Lafina of the Pinnacles Clan, you are the Oglins that have been chosen for this task. May the Spirits be with you and hold you in their

hands with the strength of those amulets that you have been given. I will come and fetch you from your clans in the morning.

"Now, my dear Oglins that have gathered together, it is time to rejoice in the health of the land, the beauty of the summer sun and in the rainfall that the Spirits have sent us. Let us celebrate that we have all been able to be here for it. Let us feast and enjoy this occasion together. It is the beginning of a great tomorrow for all Oglins."

For Baylin, the rest of the night was lost in a roar of happenings. Too much, too soon, all at once! Feasting and celebration followed with overwhelming excitement and continuous chatter among all the gathered clans.

CHAPTER 3

THE GREAT WEDRELA

*What we need is
more people who specialize
in the impossible.*

—Theodore Roethke

Down to the Beach

As promised, the Great Wedrela fetched Baylin and Lafina from their respective bundle rugs early in the morning and simply walked with them most of that day. They walked and sat and talked and wandered all over the countryside of Vadiera. They did not really discuss any specifics at all. Besides getting the young Oglins out of the limelight for the day, it was mostly an opportunity for them all to get to know each other.

It was a day to break the ice and an attempt to get the two young Oglins to learn to relax in the presence of the Great Wedrela. Because of his great power and knowledge when he was talking to the crowd, and the fact that he was one of the most powerful members of all the Oglin clans, he seemed intimidating. However, Baylin and Lafina soon learned that he was a gentle old soul, with a lovely sense of humour and a joy to be around. He always had a twinkle in his eye even in the middle of the most serious situations. The Great Wedrela's attitude helped them learn to see the lighter side of things, a lesson that would serve them well later on when they found themselves in the gravest of difficulties.

It was indeed a special day for both Baylin and Lafina. The excitement of the gathering and the implications of the great task they had been chosen for had them both fairly wrought up. The exposure to the Great Wedrela's composed confidence and maturity helped them to begin the process of growing up rather quickly through the whirlwind days that followed.

By the next day most of the clans were leaving Vadiera and Baylin and Lafina's preparation for the Great Journey began in earnest. In the early morning, they met at the Wedrelas' warrens, still a bit nervous and shy about what they were to do. The Great Wedrela had asked them to join him there for their first lesson in the skills and knowledge that they would need for the impending dangerous task that lay ahead of them.

After greeting them warmly, the Great Wedrela announced that they would take a walk down to the cliffs overlooking the sea. It was beautiful weather, as it so often is in Vadiera, and the long walk through the veld to the shore was a lovely way to begin the day. By now the summer was really upon them and the flowers here and there through the veld added brilliant splashes of colour to the deep green of the grasses and soft grey green of the bushes and shrubs.

The cicada beetles, too, were in full cry and their high

pitched incessant squeal stopped for only a moment as they walked past each bush. It always seemed so noisy when the cicadas first started, but within a week or two everyone would be so used to them they wouldn't even notice them anymore. It is funny that everyone always hears them start but no one ever hears them stop. Only once the season turns and temperatures start to drop, one might notice they are no longer there.

The Great Wedrela led them off the well-worn path where it split at the base of the ridge. One path went down to the sandy beach and the other away to the top of the cliffs. They struggled through the thick coastal bush, crouching down to follow tiny little footpaths created by bushbuck, bush pigs and the small duikers that frequented the area. They had to bend low and even crawl on their hands and knees in places to work their way through the thickness and darkness. Webs, spiders and scuttling reptiles were their only companions in the thicket. Very soon they burst out onto yet another well-worn path, which led them round towards the face of the cliff, just above the ocean's seething surface.

Baylin was utterly amazed at the existence of the path. He had spent days upon days exploring the rough terrain around these very cliffs and had never discovered this path. The old Wedrela noticed his surprise and pointed out that only a Wedrela could find it.

"No normal Oglin could ever find it," he said, "just as the people in the Great World will never be able to walk into Vadiera or any other Oglin area. Only an Oglin can find the paths that enter our homelands. People simply cannot find them. This one is just for business with the Great Spirits. Only a Wedrela can find it."

The path was well worn but still narrow and winding. The bush hung overhead in a canopy, turning it into a tunnel. There was a dense, heavy smell of moist, rotting plant material with a slight salty taste to it from the nearness of the sea. As they moved closer to the water, little rays of sunlight began to break through the green shade. The crashing surf sounded all about them and spray swirled in through the tunnel of bush. The water fell from the leaves in little droplets and the sun's rays shining through seemed to become living things, ones that could almost be grabbed and caught, as they shone through the fine swirling spray. Baylin and Lafina felt the need to walk around them to avoid disturbing them. They could feel the magic of the place, and though it was delightful, it sent a shiver up their spines!

The sunlight, glowing green in the canopy above, then disappeared; suddenly it was cold. The smells also changed to a heavy and almost unbreathable odour of wet bat droppings. Baylin recognised the scent immediately and knew they were now in the caves in the coastal cliffs. As quickly as they had entered the bush it disappeared from overhead and they were in the actual cave proper. Wet, cold, water-worn rock closed in around them. They had to get down on their knees again to crawl through a narrow opening in the rocks. They stepped out the other side into a natural hidey-hole lookout point.

Standing in the full sun, they could see the open sky above, yet they were surrounded behind by tall bush, completely shielding them from view. A white sandy floor, edged with low vegetation in front, ended in a shear dropoff to the ocean below. There was either sun or shade to choose to sit in, and the grassy ground cover looked soft and welcoming after their morning trek.

Gazing out, they saw the deep blue ocean in front of them. On both sides stretching away into the distance were the shores of the Bay of Vadiera. To the right was the sparkling white beach, curving around the protected waters of the bay and backed by huge dunes and the bush vegetation behind them. To the left was the steep and rocky cliff face under the onslaught of crashing waves breaking into white water and spray. The opening into the bay was hidden and protected from the Great World by a narrow opening in the cliffs, an opening that no people's eyes could see, nor their ships enter. The deep blue sea swelled through the cleft in enormous rollers. On both sides, the waves crashed into the rock and plumes of spray shot up in a great explosion of water, like a volcano spouting into the sky.

The three Oglins looked down into the sea. Orange and red slabs of rock lay half in the water with creamy-coloured barnacles spread where the showering sea spray kept them glistening and wet. Sitting safely, quite high up they could watch the rollers crash into the rocks below. They could feel the rocks vibrate slightly from the force of the waves. Each initial crash was quickly followed by the spattering hiss of the back spray. Seconds later, deep inside the cliff, they could hear the resounding thump of water being trapped into a high-pressure cave deep inside the rock. The whole cliff face seemed to shudder slightly.

The Whale

Having reached the enchanting spot on the cliffs, Baylin, Lafina and the Great Wedrela sat upon the soft grass, taking in the scene before them. This was the first time Lafina had been so close to the sea. Its power and beauty filled her with wonder.

The Great Wedrela proceeded to tell them about the oceans, how exceedingly big they are, how they meet up with all the different continents of the globe, and how in the end, the oceans are all joined as one.

"Somewhere the waters of this ocean will meet with the next and so on until the last one will once again meet with this one," he told the young Oglins. "There are very few animals that are able to get around the whole world, but there are some that do. The greatest of these is the whale. The whale travels the whole globe, ocean to ocean. While they can and do go all over the place, to anywhere they choose in the oceans, they always come back to this same place, time and time again, to give birth to their young.

"The whale is a very special friend of Oglins," the Great Wedrela explained for Lafina's benefit, "and is the totem of the Vadiera Clan. The whale is the one being that communicates with the rest of the world for us. The whale is our means of being in touch with far-off places and friends, keeping us informed about Oglins and other beings on all the other continents that the whales travel to. They are enormous in size and travel vast distances. They are incredibly clever, and their ability to communicate is extraordinary. All around the world, Wedrelas and a few chosen Oglins can communicate with any and all animals, anytime, including the whales. So as the whales travel, they link up with animals and our kindred Oglins on the ocean shores around the whole wide world. Then the important messages and knowledge can be passed on to other Oglins further inland.

"Baylin," he asked, "surely you must have seen the whales?"

"Oh, yes!" replied Baylin eagerly. "My whole family always comes down here towards the end of winter to see the whales playing. We camp up on the cliff top and spend a night or two so we can watch them and hear their beautiful songs."

"Yes, that's one of the very best things about being a Vadiera Oglin!" said the Great Wedrela. "But tell me, have you ever spoken to a whale?"

Baylin and Lafina both giggled slightly at the very idea. Baylin shook his head saying, "No, I've never spoken to a whale. I've never even thought of speaking to a whale!"

"Then I think it's time you did!" exclaimed the Great Wedrela. "In fact, there's a whale coming in just now. I'm sure that when you listen to her, you will hear and understand what she has to tell us. She's coming in quite quickly! Keep an eye out!"

Baylin and Lafina, wide-eyed, stared intently out across the deep blue sea. Suddenly, much nearer than anticipated, a magnificent, iceberg-sized whale rose straight up into the air until she was almost standing on her mighty tail. Then she breached over onto her back and fell with a tremendous crash, spraying water in every direction, just like a wave against a cliff. As she hit the surface, her enormous weight came to a stop on the mass of water. She rolled over, and they could see her huge flipper up in the air and the changing colours of her massive, yet sleek, form as her body spun.

The sea settled down around her as if she had poured a bucket of oil on it. The water just stopped moving around her and she was the only movement, as she slid, gliding gently forward and down again. First, her head sank under the water and then slowly, her whole body arching over, nose first, she submerged. She just slid, seeming to ooze forward, playing absolute mockery with the power of the sea. The only way they could really tell that she was moving was because she appeared to get thinner and thinner. Suddenly, from out of the water came her massive tail fin, an astonishingly beautiful shape, so sleek and so fine, and yet so powerful. As the tail came out of the water, the last little bit of water ran off it like a smooth waterfall. Then like a great dancer, she raised her tail fin up in the air, slapped it down on the water twice and disappeared beneath the surface.

Seconds later, the water boiled once again and they caught a glimpse of her back appearing. With a blow, a spout of water and mist rising high into the air, she disappeared again. The waters closed over and the sea returned to normal. There was no trace of the magnificent giant.

Baylin and Lafina were smitten and speechless. Never had Baylin seen a whale up so close. And never had Lafina seen anything so immense and impressive as a great whale. The Great Wedrela sat there just smiling, watching the two young Oglins' surprise as they looked into each other's gleaming golden eyes, both lost in wonder at how potent nature and the world really and truly is!

Then the whale surfaced gently, circled round and came to rest, basking in the sun on the swells just below the little group of Oglins. As if Baylin and Lafina were not in enough shock already, she began to speak!

"Hello, Great Wedrela! Hello, young Oglins! How are my friends this fine day?" she asked in a deep, resounding voice.

Both Baylin and Lafina leaped up and stared at her, their jaws literally hanging open in utter astonishment.

Amused at their incredulity, the Great Wedrela asked the obvious, "Can you hear the whale speaking?"

"Yes...we...can! We can hear the whale!" they nodded, glancing at the Great Wedrela and then looking back at the whale expectantly.

"Well, then, answer her."

Tentatively, Baylin spoke, "Oh, Great Whale! Can you hear me?"

"Yes, of course I hear you!" boomed the great grey giant in a friendly tone. "I can hear everything you say!"

Baylin and Lafina both turned to the Great Wedrela asking, "How can this be? How can this happen? We've never been able to understand an animal before, let alone talk to one!"

"The Great Spirit gave this gift to the Wedrelas long ago," answered the Great Wedrela. "And now, the two of you have been given this same gift. You must be able to speak with the animals, for it is from the animals that you must learn on your journey to the Great Forest to see the Great Spirit. The animals can teach you everything we need to know about our world.

"Now, greet our special friend, the whale, and ask her about her life," he instructed them.

So, the two young Oglins turned again to the sea. Searching for what to say in such an extraordinary conversation, Baylin finally blurted out his words to the patiently waiting whale. "Greetings, Great Whale! Please excuse our bad manners," Baylin began. "This is our first time speaking to a whale and we have much to learn. Where do you come from?" he managed to ask.

"Please, dear young Oglins, call me by my name. I am Wallo the Whale," she replied kindly. "I was born right here under these very same cliffs where my mother would come and speak to the Wedrelas, many, many seasons ago now. So every season I come back and I give birth to my own young ones right here, because this is where I come from. This is the place of my birth."

"Where else do you go, oh Great Wallo the Whale?" asked Lafina bravely.

"I'm glad you asked that," the whale answered. "I travel in all directions. I travel south to where the Earth is covered in huge mountains of ice. I travel north to where the waters are warm and the air balmy, where the beaches are soft and sandy and coconut trees stand tall upon the shore. I travel beyond the warmth too, to where the seas are wild and windswept and often even further to where the oceans are themselves covered in a thick blanket of ice. I travel the whole wide world."

"How do you decide where to go, Wallo the Great Whale?" Baylin asked. "What makes you go from here to there?"

"Well, there are many things to bear in mind," she replied. "I consider my ancestors and where they have been. I consider the great knowledge that they have passed on to me. It is knowledge that I have, just as you Oglins have what you are born with. Using this knowledge, and what I know of the weather patterns, the seasons and the availability of food, I make my decisions about where to go."

Baylin and Lafina stood listening in rapt attention. They were so absorbed by what the great whale had to tell them that they gradually lost their shyness about talking with her.

"There is one last thing that makes up my mind," she continued. "After everything else, like all whales, I ask myself a final question before I ultimately decide. That question is: *'Will this upset or divide us from those whose help we need?'* This way, I check that I will still have the support I need in the future.

"We whales have to be very careful nowadays, you know," she went on. "It is very dangerous for us. It is all too easy for an unsuspecting whale to wind up dead at the hands of the people who hunt whales. We hear that it is a horrible death, one that ends with the chopping up of our bodies in the bowels of the hunting ship!"

Lafina gasped in horror at the very thought of it! How could someone kill such a beautiful and wise being as this whale? 'How utterly sad,' she thought, and tears welled up in her eyes.

"Yes, it is beyond comprehension, dear Lafina," the great whale said, seeing how deeply the little Oglin cared for her. "If only the people would ask themselves this question before they go off and do things!" Wallo the Great Whale lamented.

"But there is hope! Many of the people are on our side. All up and down this coast now there are people who come out, spending time and effort to come and watch us play and give birth. They drive around us in their little boats, trying to hear our voices, trying to listen to us. But we don't seem to be able to communicate with them the way we can with you Oglins. We have tried quite seriously, and we will keep trying. I do feel that they care and are doing everything that they can to help us. Obviously, the forces of habit and patterns of past behaviour do not change as easily for people as they can with you Oglins.

"Anyway," she went on, "I'm sure that if people asked themselves this question before they did anything, the hunting of my family and cousins would be stopped to allow us to replace ourselves and keep our population healthy. We whales understand that we are part of the whole and that we must eat and sometimes be eaten in turn! However, not so that our numbers are decimated and that we should disappear entirely. That way, we could be here for many seasons and generations of both people and whales to come.

"This is only one of many challenges in the wide world today," Great Wallo continued. "Everywhere we go, we hear stories of Oglins like you who are facing similar problems. All around the world, every community of life is facing dire threats to its health and its future, just as we are. That is why, my dear young Oglins, your journey to see the Great Spirit is of utmost importance to us all. We must learn to see the whole picture or we all share a common fate.

"Always remember this, dear Oglins," said Wallo the Great Whale, "This question is the message of the whale and the beginning of the keys to the future. You will discover the other keys as you go; they will build upon this one and they will lead us all on a better course towards the future. Take care on your great journey. Go well," she said, giving them the traditional Oglin farewell for a safe journey and timely return.

"Oh thank you, Wallo the Great Whale! We will remember you all the way to the dwelling place of the Great Spirit and beyond," cried Baylin and Lafina.

"Well done, then," said the whale. "Now, young Oglins, it is time that I get on with my own journey. You have a great and important job to do. When you get back, come and spend some time with me here by this cliff, and we'll chat again."

With a slow forward motion, she glided gently beneath the surface until only her tail was visible. She raised it in salute then slapped the water twice and the ripples closed quietly to mark her disappearance.

Baylin and Lafina were so deeply moved by their meeting with Wallo the Great Whale, that they decided to compose a verse, to help them remember her words of wisdom always. They repeated it to themselves until it was burned deep into their memories.

THE OGLIN

Wallo the Whale opened our eyes
to animals as mentors true.
From travels on the sea so wide,
she cautions that the deeds we do
we must with care and wisdom choose,
for we affect all others too.

She taught us thus to always ask
"Will this a new divide give rise?
Or upset those whose help we need?"
For if we use our ears and eyes
our choices then can fortify
the strength of those most vital ties!

CHAPTER 4

A GIFT

Such a gift has been given,
It can never be taken away.

—John Denver, *On the Wings of a Dream*

Old Spola

The days just flew past after the gathering ended. Each morning, Baylin and Lafina met with the Wedrelas in the Wedrelas' work warrens. They had their own section of the kopjies where all the Wedrelas and their assistants and trainees, the Essedrelas, gathered to study and perfect their craft. It was here that the healers practised with potions and lotions. They cooked up their restorative remedies, the recipes for which had been passed down through communication with the spirit world over generations of Oglins. All the Essedrelas' rigorous instruction and training took place here. Lafina and Baylin spent a great deal of time with the Great Wedrela and his leading Wedrelas, learning all that they possibly could to prepare them for the journey ahead.

Lafina was given a sleeping place with Eldrin and Essine and their family who lived near the Wedrelas' burrows. Baylin came in every morning on foot, because there was no fitting place to leave Arto and Luka nearby. Luka joined the other gayla at work, taking out the bundles and the pala to graze each day. Arto was running with the other pala on the veld. In many ways, these were actually rather sad times for Baylin. For the first time in his life, he was no longer free to go out and wander the savanna, the forest and the seashore with his friends as he wished. It occurred to him that this was what growing up was all about. It was simply a huge increase in responsibility coupled with many things that had to be done every day. To think he used to be in such a great hurry to grow up!

Old Spola was given a sleeping place in the Wedrelas' warrens so he could be on hand to share his knowledge with them. Every day he had to be spurred on by the Wedrelas to tell one or two battends of his own great journey so many years ago. Baylin and Lafina had listened very carefully to his accounts and often had to ask him to repeat things or provide more detail so that his memories could become their own. There was no map from Vadiera to the Great Forest. All the knowledge had to be conveyed in a series of battends, all of which were told with the fine wording that the Oglins use in their graceful language.

The words of the Oglin language are extremely descriptive. One word can identify one's exact location or even describe an entire scene. Many of their words have three or four, even five or six syllables to describe an entire scene. One word might describe what one would see coming up over a particular ridge, such as the scene of a great valley with a broad river flowing through it past a lone kopjie nestled into a copse of towering winterthorn trees: *Eêbreëmfuletchalaâna*. Even a specific kind of smell, like that of Matabele ants in the evenings, for example, can be conveyed in a single word. The language is such that if one came to be in the particular situation described, that place would be immediately recognisable.

After many days of intense meetings and constant learning, there came a morning with a very different mood. The Great Wedrela seemed to be exceptionally quiet. Old Spola was particularly difficult that morning, too. In old age, some Oglins become less keen to communicate, a bit grumpy and disinclined to tell any more battends. Old Spola was playing the role well that morning as he said to the Great Wedrela, "I've told all these battends before. Everyone is sick of them and I've heard them so many times as it is. I can't even remember them properly anymore. Who wants to listen to an old mo like me? Surely nobody wants to hear what I've got to say!"

The Wedrelas had to practically kick the reluctant Old Spola into life and remind him that without his knowledge, the two young Oglins would have no idea where to go. They had to keep reminding him how critical the journey was for the Oglins. At trying times like these, the Great Wedrela's sense of humour would shine through and with a twinkle in his eye, he could always cajole the old mo into action.

They would normally seek the sun in the morning and the shade later in the day to keep Old Spola happy. "To keep my bones at the right temperature," he would keep saying. Dear Old Spola's eyes had faded from the usual bright gold of an Oglin's eyes to a sort of dull yellow, a little bit rheumy, and tearful near a fire or on a windy day. His old yellowy eyes shone out from a deeply wrinkled face surrounded by soft grey curls. When Old Spola would get to a particularly emotional bit of his battends, tears would roll happily down his face, as his memories took hold of him. He was a dear old thing who often forgot where he was in a story he was telling, sometimes stopping and questioning whether he was telling them in the right order, backwards, forwards or whether he even had the right story! But the Great Wedrela would prod him along, and the Wedrelas seemed to be happy with what he said. They kept checking questions on these battends with the Great Spirits at night so they could verify Spola's information. Every now and again, the Wedrelas would come out with leading questions to bring out highlights from dear Old Spola's memories.

On that particular morning, however, the Great Wedrela wasn't even at all interested in arguing with Old Spola. The Great Wedrela seemed to have some greater calling and he was a little distant. Sitting in the little patch of sun where they would normally go and talk, they waited for some time. They all just sat quietly, listening to the calls of the birds. The Great Wedrela didn't seem ready to speak. The other Wedrelas were pensive and hesitant, waiting for the Great Wedrela. Baylin and Lafina snuck a look at one another, feeling a bit nervous and concerned.

At last, the Great Wedrela began to speak. "Well, dear ones, the time has come for the two of you to start out on your journey. There's not much more information we can provide for you. We've drawn out all we can from our Old Spola and it's been a battle to get him to talk. So, the dear old thing has basically done his job. We have also done everything the Great Spirit has advised to prepare you for your great journey. There is so much that simply cannot be known. The rest remains to be experienced and discovered by the two of you. Now the time has come for you to leave, and you're as ready as you will ever be."

Baylin took a deep breath and held it. Being so absorbed in the intensity of preparation, he had not actually thought much about this moment. He felt a tingling of anticipation, tinged with a bit of fear. Looking over at Lafina, he saw that she too was taking in the realisation that now their preparations were complete and the time had truly come.

"We'll have a small feast this evening," the Great Wedrela continued, "just the Ruck family and Eldrin and Essine. The other Wedrelas and Essedrelas will also be there and, of course, Old Spola will not be forgotten, if he does not forget himself." He gently rubbed the old mo's grey head. "Baylin and Lafina, this will be your farewell feast and we will send you off on your way in the morning."

He paused for a moment to let his words sink in. Everyone was silent and felt the preciousness of their last day together.

"Today we will cover the final preparations with you," the Great Wedrela started off again. "The Great Spirit has spoken. Baylin will take Arto and Argyl. One of them he will ride and the other will carry a pack. Lafina will take her pala, Lara, to ride."

Lafina sat bolt upright with a look of surprise on her face. The Great Wedrela looked at her from under his bushy, greying eyebrows, with eyes that seemed to be able ferret out anyone's very deepest feelings. Lafina searched his face for a clue.

As if he had found what he was looking for, he smiled, and said, "Yes! I had your family leave her behind. She has been well cared for, of course, but hidden away where I was sure you would not see her. You will be reunited this evening."

Lafina's smile was dazzling. Her glimmering golden eyes shone out of her charming face, contrasting with golden tanned cheeks, surrounded by soft blond curls. The prospect of being reunited with her friend and companion, Lara, pleased her greatly and took the edge off the serious mood of the morning.

As is too often the case, though, good news was followed by bad. "But I'm sorry, Baylin," the Great Wedrela continued, "Luka will have to stay behind. You must travel without him. This is the wish of the Great Spirit. Without the help of a gayla to watch over you and to be your eyes and ears for you, you will have to remain so much more alert and watchful. It will force you to observe much more closely for yourselves so that you won't miss any of the clues you must find.

"The message of the Great Spirit was that you are to travel mounted on your pala for as far as you possibly can. You will need to be even more vigilant, because your feet will not be in direct contact with the soils of the Earth. You will also be able use the pala's sense of danger to keep you shielded, and there is a risk that your own senses won't be as keen as they need to be for this journey. So this is a warning: You will have to work very diligently at being as observant as possible, or the Great Spirit will have to rob you of your companions so you will use your own senses, rather than depend upon theirs. If that should happen, then you'll have to carry on with just those hairy little feet of yours and keep going!"

They all had a little laugh at this, but no one, especially Baylin and Lafina, missed the importance of the Great Wedrela's warning. He was never one to say such things lightly, and the two young Oglins had learned to take in every word he told them. They both had every intention of following his instructions as closely as they possibly could! They knew their own lives and the future of the Oglins depended upon them.

Assured that they had taken in his words, the Great Wedrela spoke again. "You can begin your Great Journey by heading up to the Pinnacles Clan first, so Lafina can bid her clan and family farewell."

Lafina smiled once again at this welcome news as the Great Wedrela continued, "From there you will go on into the north, knowing that you have all the time you need for the journey. There is nowhere on this great continent where you would be frozen in for the winter if you don't make it through in time. There is also nowhere that floods completely, making it impassable for months at a time, except for the great swamps. You have no real need to go there anyway. This great continent is available to you to travel across, as you need.

"However, as you have been learning, there are many risks, from nature, the animals and people. Sleeping sickness, dangerous river crossings and great heat in the deep valleys are just a few of the challenges you may face. There are many predators all across this land. Besides the warnings of Old Spola, the effects of people are likely to create many unforeseen dangers that lie between here and the Great Forest. These will also test you.

"We Oglins are good at working things out as we go along, and that you will do. You have been prepared all your life for living off of the land and its bounty. Your very growing up gave you many of the skills you need."

The Great Wedrela paused to think for a moment before he went on. "Baylin has lived in this abundant savanna and knows the kinds of animal and plant life that live in such areas. Lafina has had a different life experience; she knows of the drier lands and the forms that life takes there. So between the two of you, you have enough diversity of knowledge to help you survive and succeed on this Great Journey. Old Spola has done his best to give you the directions and orientation that you need. While it doesn't seem like much, that is all the specific knowledge we have to offer you. That is all that is known about where to cross the rivers and what to watch for along the way. You have heard all there is to hear from the old mo. Between his snores!" He smiled briefly in his eyes as he teased the old mo once more to lighten the mood.

Then, in a more serious tone, he added, "The Great Spirit will always be guiding you, too…"

He lapsed into silence as the gravity of the situation hung over them.

"Now," he said, drawing in a deep breath and sitting up straight. "There are only two tasks remaining before you depart. First, is to help you to understand the great importance of the white seashell and the stone with a fire of its own. Then we must discuss the creed of the Oglins."

Baylin and Lafina snapped out of their own thoughts, knowing that the Great Wedrela's last instructions must be heard carefully.

"These two amulets must stay in your pachas all the time," he instructed. "They must become part of your daily practice of speaking to the Great Spirit, just like all the other amulets. The Great Spirit gave these amulets to you as a special connection with him. Always remember that they are part of the key to the future of the world. This key lies within you, your journey and the Great Spirit. You must take these gifts to the Great Spirit."

The Great Wedrela's bushy eyebrows stood out over piercing, cold gold eyes as he delivered this most important directive.

"Now, the Great Spirit has warned that you are not going to be taught the keys to the future by him. The keys are not known to only one, but they await your discovery along the way, from the many. Then the Great Spirit will give you the final knowledge that will bring it all together and complete the keys. You have to be very wary and very diligent all along the way. Everything you come across, everything that you do, and everyone that you meet will be part of the learning for those keys."

His eyes caught each of theirs and held them for a moment. Baylin and Lafina glanced at one another. Slight smiles stole across their faces as they realised that they had both unconsciously reached for their pachas as the Great Wedrela had been speaking. In awe of the task that lay ahead of them, they were already needing the support of the spirits and feeling it through their amulets. They each felt a sense of relief and confidence, knowing that they would face the journey together and with all the help that the spirits could provide.

The Great Wedrela continued. "The very last thing you need to know about is the Oglin Creed. It is a new gift that has been given to us by the Great Spirit. It is a gift of guidance that will help us to create and sustain the way of the life that we want. By creating and referring to the creed constantly, it will guide us to the dream of the life we truly want.

"It will give you strength and guide you on this journey, like a star to steer by. Everything you learn along the way and everything you learn from the Great Spirit will be so that we can achieve this creed."

The very idea of such a creed immediately sparked a sense of joy and hope in Baylin's and Lafina's hearts. What a marvellous gift it must be indeed, if it could truly be such a guide to live by for all Oglins!

"While the idea and the guidance are given to us, the creed itself is something we Oglins develop for ourselves and by ourselves," the Great Wedrela explained. "In that way, we are always the ones who dream of and are responsible for creating the life we truly want. It is very simple, and yet one of the keys to its success is that it is created in three steps.

"First, we define how we want to feel most of the time to have a life of meaning. Second, we describe how and what needs to be, for this way of life to become a reality. Third, we portray how things must be: how we must be seen by others, how our living environment must be, how our communities must be and how our land must be, far into the future, in order to sustain this way of life we so value.

"We developed our first creed for the Oglins as a whole with all the Oglin Clan Bacor leaders who were at the gathering and have been referring to it ever since. We have found that it grows on us every day and becomes more and more valuable to us as we internalize the commitment we each have to it. We will share it with you now so you can learn it and carry it in your hearts with you. Later, all Oglins will create their own creeds and gain direction and strength from them."

The old Wedrela was obviously feeling better already. He was lighthearted again. Just thinking of the creed reminded him why this great journey had to happen and the hope for the future that it represented.

The Oglin Creed

The way of life we most value: We want to feel close as families with strong bonds between our clans and friends. We want to feel healthy, loving and at peace with ourselves. We want to feel in close contact with nature and in harmony with the world around us.

What needs to be for this way of life to become a reality: We Oglins need to live with loving, open hearts, sharing our thoughts and feelings honestly while caring for one another. We need to have respect and recognition for one another and all life around us. We must live close to and constantly learn from nature. Everything we do must be good for us, must be good for and enhance nature and must lead to the health of the whole world, for both the near future and the far future. We must create opportunities to grow, to learn, to explore and build upon the beauty and artistry of our way of life.

Far in the future: Others must see us as being kind and fair, as sharers and keepers of great knowledge that serves as guiding principles for Oglins and the world. Our clans must be in harmony with one another and with all the world's living things. We must have the ability to understand one another and to communicate freely.

Our warrens must be comfortable, safe and pleasant places where we and all of our animals can enhance one another's lives.

The land where we Oglins live and all the lands around the clans must be healthy and thriving. The soils must be covered and sheltered by plants so that they teem with an abundance of life and activity. When it rains, the water must go into the soil so that the springs will have life and the rivers will have water that is living and clean. All the plants and animal droppings and all manner of nutrients on the land and in the oceans must be absorbed quickly in order to be useful again for other living organisms. A great profusion and mass of plants must capture the sun's life-giving energy, and support abundance and an ample variety of life forms.

Baylin and Lafina thoroughly discussed and learned the creed with the Great Wedrela. They committed it indelibly to memory. As all Oglins, they were exceptionally good at memorising. It helped lighten all their spirits on the eve of the great unknown. It was clearly what all Oglins wanted and it was clear that without the hope their journey offered, there was no way that they could achieve it.

"This is much more than our vision of the future," explained the Great Wedrela. "It draws upon all that we have come to value from the past. At the same time, it expresses our deepest desires for the present. If we are to provide a future for our younger generations, it is what we must bring into being. It is what we must work for in everything that we do as individual Oglins, as families, as clans and as a whole. Thanks to this gift from the Great Spirit, we now have a star to steer by. This is the first step of this great journey towards the future. Now we must learn how to navigate and make real progress towards it. Everything we do must lead us towards the life and the future we describe in this creed. Your journey to the Great Spirit will enable you to learn how we can achieve this, for it is not enough to know what we Oglins want, we must also know how to achieve it, in harmony with the world around us."

Once again, the Great Wedrela's eyes locked on theirs as he finished his instructions.

The Great Wedrela's words sank deep into the hearts of Baylin and Lafina and took root there. This vision of the present and the future was everything they could dream of as well. Nevertheless, they well knew, from the reports of the other clans and what the Wedrelas had taught them, that the future was at great risk. Again, they felt the weight of the world on their shoulders, knowing that so very much depended upon them and the success of their journey.

The Great Wedrela reminded them that they must remember this creed each night as they fall to sleep. "It will guide you," he said gently, knowing also of the responsibility those young Oglins were taking upon themselves, and that they alone could accomplish the journey.

To help themselves remember the important lessons of the day, Baylin and Lafina composed a beginning to their verse:

A GIFT

This life is oh so sweet and fine,
on this we heartily agree.
Smitten by the vast savanna,
sheltered by the towering tree,
smiling under sunlit sky,
and joyful by the wild blue sea!

Yet all of this is now at risk.
There is no destined guarantee.
To make our future more secure
we must seek our capacity
to serve the self and help the whole
and share responsibility.

We look to the past for wisdom,
and live by our hearts for today.
Together, we do dare to dream
and face the challenge of our day.
We reach for a bounteous future,
where life can prosper in every way.

In each and every heart there dwells
a creed for life to be drawn out.
With care we craft it part by part,
a common goal found and vowed
to live our joy and to protect
what we most fiercely care about!

With this guiding star to steer by
as we traverse along life's way,

we follow it unfailingly
making choices day by day.
And find that in the run of time,
steady on our course we stay.

Finally, the Great Wedrela stood up to break the serious mood. He smiled and said to them, "Now, dear ones, go to your warrens. Baylin, you go and spend time with your Modra, Merma, little badras and sadras. You had better give Luka some special attention, too, while you prepare Arto and Argyl. You will not see the dear little gayla for some time!

"This evening we will gather back here." As he reached across and poked a hairy finger into the old Oglin's ribs, he continued, "We'll try and prod Old Spola into telling us a final battends tonight. In fact, if he doesn't, we might just call on the Great Spirit to take him away to the world of the spirits!"

Old Spola broke into a toothless grin. The dear old thing had not a tooth left in his mouth. He smiled and the tears rolled down his cheeks once again.

A Farewell

That last afternoon flew past in a whirl of activity. So too did the wonderful evening's feast. It was especially arranged so that the little Oglins, like Baylin's badras and sadras, as well as Eldrin and Essine's little ones who had grown so fond of Lafina, could also attend. One thing kaleidoscoped into the next and before they knew it, Spola had finished his battends. It was time for the Great Wedrela to close the evening proceedings.

The Great Wedrela rose and everyone fell quiet. After a moment's silence, he began to speak. "For that great tale and all the others, we wish to thank Old Spola for all he has done. Now these two young Oglins will embark on the greatest challenge and opportunity of their lives as they go out and do as Spola did:

journey to meet the Great Spirit. Whether they will return or not to our shores, we cannot know. Yet it is something we do not have to fear, because wherever they go, even if the Great Spirit calls one or both of them into the world of the spirits, it is for the good of all Oglins. Whatever you do, dear Baylin and Lafina, it is for the good of the Earth. You will always be honoured among Oglins for your bravery and willingness to take this great risk!

"Like all Oglins, when we say goodbye, we are never tearful. We are only tearful when we are reunited. The time we lose while we are apart will make us sad and thus bring tears at our reunion. We will not be sad at your going, as when someone goes there is always hope. Rather when we separate, we will rejoice for the times we have had together, and be thankful for them.

"Now, dear ones, go home to your burrows and rest well. Tomorrow morning before the sun awakes, you will leave. You need to begin the long journey on the path that we have shown you, out across the Great Plains, to the Pinnacles and then beyond into the unknown, towards the place of the Great Spirit.

"May the spirits watch over you and speed you on your journey."

The old Wedrela bowed his head, then turned and left the burrow.

The Ruck family's burrow was very quiet and subdued that night. Baylin slept fitfully, dreaming and waking a lot. Everyone, it seemed, was having a difficult night. Each time he woke, he could hear the others tossing and turning in their rugs, as though there had been an invasion of bed bugs.

Once again, it was Lafina that filled his mind. He remembered how she had suddenly appeared at his side, with her arm around him and her body moulded to his, as he had walked out into the night for a moment of solitude after the excitement of being chosen by the spirits. She had led him away by the hand and they had climbed the Vadiera kopjie. They had sat there holding each other in the moonlight. It had felt so right. They had talked and held each other until the early hours. She had told him how she wished to share the beauty of her Pinnacles homeland with him one day. He told her that if he hadn't been chosen to make the journey, he would certainly have made the trek to the Pinnacles Clan homeland with her and her family. They would have had the chance to spend more time together and get to know each other better anyway. They were very grateful to both be chosen. To think that only one of them might have been chosen was unbearable. Their hopes and growing dreams to be together would have been dashed before they could have evolved.

That last night in his family's burrow, though, he was racked with guilt. He had seen and thought little of his family through the recent activity while he had been growing closer to Lafina and her beauty captivated him. They were spending so much time together. The attraction of his home and family were fading away. He felt like a betrayer, and his dreams were wild with confusion.

The next morning they all rose very early. No one looked rested at all. Sitting around the Ruck burrow, draped in their sleeping furs, the whole family was very quiet and introspective. Baylin was busy doing his final packing for the great trip. He saddled and packed his pala and shut up his packs for the final time. He lovingly ran his hand over his new pack and remembered his homecoming the previous afternoon when he shared the news of his final departure with his family.

His Merma had not said a word when he had broken the news. She had just turned and left, only to return a moment later with her hands behind her back.

She looked up at him and said, "Baylin, I have something special for you. I've made it for your journey." From behind her back, she produced a new carrying bag made of kudu hide. She had lovingly tanned it by hand, using the fat of a warthog. It was beautifully decorated and lovingly painted with different colours from the extracts of different roots and plants, as only an Oglin Merma knew how to do. Only mer Oglins were taught how to do this. No mo Oglins knew the secret workings of the colouring of leather. The bag had a fine patchwork of tiny little bits of seashell sewn into it, making pretty little patterns of flowers, the moon, the sun, the sea and the small kopjie of Vadiera, all to remind him of home.

"The smell of the leather and the fat that's been put into it is a very special smell," she said tenderly. "It will always remind you of home and your family here."

Baylin's Modra then presented him with a special walking stick made out of whalebone and a slender tree branch. He had carved lovingly into the handle all sorts of etchings of home as well, to remind him of Vadiera. They were more signs than actual pictures. In particular, the central theme on it was an image of the stars of the Cross of the South and the Two Sadras pointing the direction to the south.

"That, my young Oglin, is so you will find your way home to Vadiera," said his Modra. "It is my personal request, I've written it here in a language all of my own, to ask the Great Spirit to return you to us."

As Baylin carefully examined the fine carving, he realised that the point of the handle was carved into the head of a pala.

"That, my young Oglin, is to remind you of your other animal friends who await you here and to remind you of the importance of Arto and Argyl in your life."

The beautiful pala's head was windswept and
stretched out as if in a full gallop. Baylin stroked it
lovingly with his furry forefinger.

"Yes," said his Modra, reading his thoughts, "that is so
when you touch it, it will remind you of the whistling of the
wind in your ears when you are riding. You will need to be
cautious and so at times will be moving very slowly. I wish that
the speed, strength and agility of the pala carry you with great
haste, energy and ease across the land to see the Great Spirit
and home again to us, with your purpose fulfilled."

One by one, all his little badras and sadras had come up to
give Baylin little farewell gifts of some type, little "remember-
me-by's" such as seashells and tiny pebble stones. One
of his sadras had given him a farewell gift of a flywhisk
especially braided of hairs from Arto's tail.
Laughing with delight, Baylin had leaped up and
ran across the burrow to see how Arto's tail
had been docked to make the whisk. Arto was
swishing his now much less efficient tail around
and giving Baylin an embarrassed look.

Finally, Baylin's littlest sadra, Aga, the sweetest
one, his favourite one, who spent a lot of time on
his knee and who would sit up in front while he
rode Arto, had come up and given him the pod of a camel thorn
tree. She had also tried to carve something on it, just like her
Modra had done. She had taken a sharp stone and drawn various
scratches and crossings on it. Aga quietly and seriously told Baylin
that the markings were a special map to remind him of the places
that he had taken her. She had made it so that when he came
back, he would remember where they were and could take her
there again. Fondly, they remembered together the visits to the
little pool right in front of their warrens in the kopjie, where
they often used to go and sit together, playing with sticks in the

mud and water and watching the fish, frogs and water bugs. Tears were beginning to well up in Aga's little golden eyes. Baylin held her tight and told her not to worry.

"Oglins don't cry when they say goodbye," he reminded her. "You can cry as much as you like when I get back!"

Bravely, she had held back the tears as she stood there looking up at him. With her hand resting up on Luka's back, Aga had solemnly promised to take very special care of Luka and be sure that he was never lonely while Baylin was gone.

As his mind returned to the present, Baylin ran a hand over the rumps of the now fully prepared pala and walked back into the burrow. His Modra, having helped him load in silence, walked with him and hung his arm over Baylin's shoulders. They strolled through the herd of still- sleeping bundles, calling them each by name, and hearing their gentle breathing and familiar bleats of greeting. They went inside and sat quietly around the hearth.

Then he heard his name being softly called by the Great Wedrela from outside the warren. He hugged each of his family members in turn. Then, hoisting his new carrying bag onto his shoulder and picking up the carved walking stick, he stepped to the door and turned for his final farewell.

"Stay well, dear ones," he said bravely to all his beloved family, in the traditional Oglin words of parting. "May the spirits look after you."

And the family returned all in unison, "Go well, dear Baylin. May the Spirits walk with you and guide you on your return."

Baylin stooped and petted his dear Luka, tugging gently at his ear as he rose. Then he turned and stepped outside to meet the Great Wedrela who was waiting with Lafina and Lara. They walked off wordlessly, leading their pala down the path in the moonlight, away from Vadiera for the last time in many, many moons; or for the two brave travellers, perhaps the last time ever.

A beautiful silver light flooded the landscape. They could see and hear the herds of zebra, kudu, wildebeest and hartebeest that had wandered a bit closer to the kopjie in the night. They knew the herds would soon move further away again at the coming of day, avoiding the busy activity of the gayla ferrying the bundle and pala herds in and out from the warrens to the grazing areas on the savanna.

They rode across the savanna as the first rays of the waking sun washed the coolness out of the sky. By the time they entered the cool of the forest, the heat and humidity of the summer morning was beginning to bring a touch of discomfort to the day. Once they were in among the trees, the path began to climb the escarpment. The trees were immense! Standing tall and straight, they stretched towards the patches of sky that showed through the canopy. They followed an elephant path that led out of the secret land of Vadiera into the forests and lands beyond.

The ground seemed to almost move underfoot, wonderfully soft and moist. They were walking on a sponge of old plant material with an earthy odour that only great forests can exude. It was almost silent in the half-light; birds called now and again, but generally it was a muffled feeling of quiet. It always took a little getting used to after the openness of the savanna. The forest exerted an almost overpowering feeling of oppression, seeming to push them down into the path as they walked along. It made the Oglins feel even smaller than they really were!

Every now and again, there were clearings where a big tree had fallen down and created an opening to the sky. Here the luminous green-dappled sunlight seemed to dance and splash through onto the ferns and young trees. With the abundance of sunlight and warmth created by the incoming rays, a rich profusion of new life grew right out of the trunk of the fallen monarch competing to fill the space.

The pala splashed happily as they forded the streams that they frequently encountered. The water was clear but it had a gingery brown colour from the roots of the plants and the mass of organic matter in the soil. The water looked like light ale being poured, as it occasionally gathered into patches of froth, only to be broken up again into silver bubbles in the little falls and rapids.

The Great Wedrela continued on with them all the way through the forest. At the far edge of the trees, he bade them a final farewell. He reminded them once more to hold on carefully to the two amulets that the Great Spirit had given them and most importantly to keep the Oglin Creed close to their hearts and always in their minds. Together they thanked the Great Spirit and asked for his guidance on their journey. The Great Wedrela briefly hugged them each, and said, "Go well, dear Baylin and Lafina. May the spirits walk with you and guide you on your return."

He then mounted his midnight black pala and rode back into the darkness of the forest, leaving the two young Oglins to go forward on their own.

Lafina and Baylin looked at one another and reaching out, they lightly brushed each other's cheeks. Too overwhelmed by the gravity of what they were beginning, their shyness melted away. They hugged one another with a squeeze of reassurance, strength and companionship. Then, not wanting to let the sadness of leaving take hold, they turned and scrambled up the rough and rocky mountain, leading their pala across the rugged surface. The stones were grey and light blue in colour and covered with lichen. Strewn between were exquisite flowers of every imaginable shade. Brilliant reds, oranges and yellows, set off by lovely blues and purples speckled the greenery of the landscape in a vivid display of colours that only nature can achieve.

Reaching the top, the two Oglins and the three pala stood, catching ragged breaths. Below them spread the vast Great Plains of the dry interior where the rain seldom gave the kiss of its blessings to the parched Earth. In brown and blue hues, the land stretched away, seemingly into forever. Behind them, the dense green mat of the forest filled the valley. In the distance through the haze of moisture, they could see the change in colour where the sky met the sea. Vadiera itself was not visible from beyond the forest.

Not pausing for long, they nimbly slid and scrambled down the far side of the mountain to the plain below. By the time they reached the flats, the sun was high above them and the beauty of the land was dulled by the harshness of the midday heat. Mountains that in the morning light seemed so near appeared to recede into the distance as the heat waves marched their daily dance across the broad expanse.

They mounted their pala in silence. Baylin rode Arto and had Argyl on a loose lead next to him. With Lafina astride Lara, close on his other side, they set off. They were travelling north, towards the Clan of the Pinnacles and Lafina's homeland. Behind each pala a lazy dust cloud rose. Ahead of them stretched the Great Plains, with long vistas, and pale blue skies. Even farther on lay the horizon, shimmering, unsure of itself, and hazy blue in the great distance. A slight breath of wind held the promise of a change in the weather, confirmed by the wispy windswept clouds overhead.

They stepped out briskly and bravely across the shrubby grasslands of the Great Plains, towards whatever awaited them on their Great Journey.

CHAPTER 5

THE GREAT PLAINS AND THE PINNACLES

Brave is simply
those with the clearest vision
of what is before them,
glory and danger alike,
and not withstanding,
go out to meet it.

—Unknown

The Great Plains

The Great Plains of the Karoo are not just a flat expanse all the way. There are mountains to cross, which are occasionally cut through with steep-sided poorts that can serve as shortcuts. Each successive mountain range has a huge effect on local climate, usually cutting off the rainfall on the inland side, while in some cases catching very high rainfall on top, where thick strong grasslands stand up to do battle with the spring winds and winter snows. On the slopes below, thickets of bush offer protection to the birds, animals and ticks alike. On the northern side, where the clouds having tightened their bellies to cross over the mountains and seem to forget to drop their rain, the veld becomes almost pure shrub land. Further from the mountains, it rains enough to sustain the shrubs and grass in places, but it is still harsh and generally very dry.

The most striking thing about the Great Plains is the heat. It rises in shimmering waves off the bare ground in between the shrubs and the grass tufts. The hard soil becomes so hot it is impossible to walk on. It can even burn the feet of an Oglin, which are as tough as old leather and furry around the edges, making their footfalls dead silent. That's a special trait of an Oglin, which means they will never be heard walking in the bush. An Oglin can sneak right up on someone at a full sprint, and they still won't hear him coming. Suddenly, he'll be there, before they know it, just right there alongside. That's the nature of an Oglin. You have probably had more than one sneak up on you and you don't even know it.

To an Oglin, "bush lore" is absolutely innate. That deep knowledge of the bush, the ability to live and thrive in the wild open veld with nothing but a bundle rug to throw over them in the night, is knowledge that is embedded and practically part of them from birth. So Oglins do not have to learn much of anything about life in the bush; they know it already. These inherent skills were what sustained Baylin and Lafina as their journey took them north.

Slowly the veld changed and more grass became evident as the rainfall increased again. They rode out across the endless sea of cream and green vistas towards the blue of the horizon. The tawny grasses contrasted sharply with the green and darkish grey colours of the bushes and shrubs. Here and there under the ridges were darker green thickets of bush and small patches of grassy savanna with widespread, low-growing trees. The waterways, with occasional pools of stagnant green water, were edged with thickets of deep-green trees that smelled sweet and kind. These thickets stood out starkly against the harshness of the endless vista.

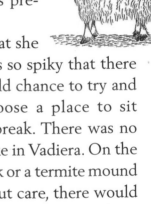

The scents on the air changed all the time. The various herbs and shrubs each released their distinctive fragrance as the passers-by disturbed them. Baylin was reminded of the taste of the game meat that came off the Great Plains, and Lafina of the taste of bundles raised on the shrubs in the veld near her home. The meat of any animal in the Great Plains of the Karoo takes on the special taste of the aromatic shrubs and herbs upon which they graze. The meat is pre-spiced in the most natural of ways!

Lafina pointed out a shrub to Baylin that she called a "bird-can't-sit-bush." The bush was so spiky that there seemed to be no way that even a bird would chance to try and sit on it! Baylin quickly learned to choose a place to sit thoughtfully when it was time to take a break. There was no simply flopping down on the soft grasses like in Vadiera. On the Great Plains, he very carefully selected a rock or a termite mound to perch on. If one were to sit down without care, there would certainly be a painful "remember-me-by" for a while. These bushes don't just prickle; they sting for some time. The pala also soon learned to pick their footsteps very carefully to avoid harm.

As they walked along, Baylin and Lafina thought about the battends which had been practically forced out of Old Spola about the Great Plains. Spola had eventually, under duress, conceded to tell them about the Great Plains. He complained bitterly that no one would believe him because he knew that the Great Plains of the Karoo were so different now.

Most Oglins from Vadiera had been to the Great Plains on hunting expeditions. Even Baylin himself had been before and

Lafina had been there even more recently en route to Vadiera. They all knew it was now quite different than in Old Spola's day. Yet, in the end, the Wedrelas had forced it out of Spola because they wanted him to tell the young travellers how he had seen it all those many seasons ago, not as it looked now. If they could know firsthand how much the Great Plains had changed since Spola's journey long ago, it would give them an idea of what drastic changes to expect further on. The hope was that seeing the difference between then and now, while still early on in their journey, would help the young Oglins. Perhaps they would be able to make some sense of what they found later on when they got into country where neither of them, nor any of their kind, had been since Spola.

In telling about his long-ago quest, Spola described the magnificent rivers that he and his two companions had crossed. He spoke about the beautiful crystal-clear water running in many of the streams and waxed eloquent about the thick matted grass veld, peppered with the herbal, aromatic bushes. He had also told of patches that were almost purely shrub—which now, they realised, was what most of the veld looked like. He certainly didn't mention much about the nasty thorns and very prickly bushes Baylin and Lafina were encountering everywhere!

Spola talked of pods of hippo in the rivers where they had seen none and where they knew that none could survive. There was not enough water in the rivers for hippo and there was no longer enough grass around the rivers for them to graze either.

The stagnant pools of water that remained had stood for far too long by the look of it. They were green and smelled a little stale. Not really hippo water, although the travellers still drank it themselves, for that was all they had. They were certainly very different to the thriving hippo pools of Vadiera, where the streams flushed through all the time with a constant course of fresh clean water, teeming with all kinds of life.

Things were indeed very different now. Spola had never mentioned the strings of wire that crisscrossed the land in straight lines, making it hard to travel freely. He certainly never talked about being able to cross huge stretches without ever having to step on a single plant, just bare ground everywhere.

The banks of the rivers that Baylin and Lafina came to had high and steep cut banks where the ravaged soil stared out over the dry riverbed or over the stagnant green pools. Spola's stories were just outrageous compared to what they were actually seeing. It was no wonder he thought them no longer worth telling. He had described healthy riverbanks, with a tight cover of tall grass and interspersed with reeds, hiding throngs of crocodiles and hippo. Huge leguaans had lived in the occasional thickets on the banks that were teeming with birds of many colours, shapes, sizes and sounds. Spola's battends told of streams flowing into the main rivers, each fed with little bubbling springs and shaded by thick banks of overhanging grasses and shrubs. Sadly, Baylin and Lafina now had to make wide detours around just such riverbeds, to find a route down the vertical dongas, their banks too steep and deep to cross.

In the apron veld, on the edges of the hills, there were ragged scars in the land, deep purple and red in colour, where the dongas opened out into huge deltas of cutting-edge erosion. It was not at all like Spola told of it, with thick grasses and shrubs growing up to the bottom of these ridges. In the flat areas now, there were sections of hard bare soil, crusted over from the rain and siltation. The glare on these barren areas made Baylin and Lafina squint their eyes in pain. Occasionally the bare areas were followed by a little strip of vegetation, grasses and shrubs, beyond which there was another band of actively moving soil, followed by another hard bare pan. The soil was eroding in huge sheets.

Lafina spoke, startling Baylin from his dismay. "Look at this land, and think of our precious creed. The land in our creed is healthy, soft and vibrant. This…this is dry, hard and…dead!" she exclaimed, shrugging her shoulders and shaking her head. "And it is so much worse than what Old Spola saw here. Even though he seems old to us, it was not all that long ago! It has deteriorated to this in less than one Oglin's lifetime! It is not only moving away from how it must be according to our creed; it is doing so at an alarming rate! There must be clues for us to find, as to why this is happening."

Baylin silently nodded his agreement. Looking into his eyes, her own shining with tears of sadness and determination, she went on, "We must find the answers before it is too late."

They fell into silence once more. Deep in thought, they rode the pala at a walk across the barren plain and the dust rose cloyingly around them. Towards the tomorrows, a dust devil swirled its way across the plain. Viciously it tugged and shook, trying to rip the few persistent plants out of the ground, while with invisible fingers it plucked up all the loose soil and twisted it up into the air. Baylin and Lafina stopped and waited to let it pass in a rush in front of them. It whipped at their hair and clothing as it went.

In spite of all the changes since Old Spola had seen it, it was still exceptionally beautiful country. There was a bluish hue interspersed with the green-blue and grey shrubs across the plains. Up against the hills there were contrasting sprays

of brighter green where the elephant food trees grew. The mountains stood over them, like well-mannered gentlemen, stark and looming against the skyline. In the mornings and on cooler south wind days, they appeared so close and tall and the sky above them was burning blue and brilliant. One could imagine the mountains as ancient sentinels, towering over the plain and looking sternly down, giving the feeling that they had seen it all before. The landscape seemed to just stretch on forever around them; the endless vistas seemed to even alter time itself into timelessness.

It was quite extraordinary how the Great Plains created a feeling of silence without end, although of course it was never truly silent. Nothing in Africa is ever silent. There are always bugs, beetles, barking geckos and slithering skinks, bird calls, the movement of air and the rustle of the leaves. No, never really silent, but always awe-inspiring.

The Tortoise

They had been out on the plain for days that felt like weeks already when they spotted in the distance a lonesome dust spiral seemingly rising from the depths of the Earth. Baylin and Lafina welcomed the prospect of a diversion of any kind and eagerly changed direction to have a look. Their curiosity piqued, they encouraged their willing pala forward into a trot and stood tall in their stirrups to try to see better. As they drew closer, they were amazed to discover that the stir was caused by the clambering efforts of a huge tortoise trying to climb the vertical sides of the deeply eroded donga. The poor creature was making no progress whatsoever; he was simply sliding back after each struggling attempt. Judging by the smooth slide marks on all the banks around him it was clear that he would soon exhaust himself if he kept up this fruitless effort. And yet there was no other route of escape!

The tortoise was the size of a large boulder, his shell smooth and gleaming. Of course, there are countless Oglin battends about "Ufudu," the revered Great Tortoise, as there are for all the people of Africa. Oglins have always lived in great awe of the tortoise because of its ability to live for so very, very long.

As the pala both stamped and snorted in distrust, Baylin and Lafina dismounted and approached respectfully on foot to have a closer look at the massive tortoise. Realising that they were there, the tortoise froze in place, his beady eyes watching them carefully. Then, to their utter astonishment, the tortoise casually spoke to them in a gravely old voice, "Greetings, young Oglins! How are you today?"

With their eyes open wide in amazement and a little bit of a cold sweat beading on their brows, Baylin and Lafina remembered.

"Of course! We can talk to animals now!" exclaimed Lafina. "We mustn't forget that animals can talk to us, too!"

Recovering himself and his manners, Baylin managed to respond saying, "We are quite well, thank you, oh Great Tortoise. We were on our way to see the Great Spirit when we came across you. We're actually quite new at this talking to animals and we didn't realise that we would be able to talk to you! Please pardon our surprise," said Baylin.

"Yes, of course, no harm done. Pleased to make your acquaintance indeed," said the tortoise, speaking slowly, as a tortoise is wont to do. "As you might expect, there's not much opportunity for conversation out here. I knew I was supposed to meet you and talk with you today, but then I fell into this blasted donga and landed in a spot of bother, I'd say!" he explained, trying to make light of his serious situation. "You must realise, however, that most animals are not going to stop and talk to you just because you can talk to us. There are a few of us, though, that have especially been asked to meet you along the way and speak with you." Pausing for an instant to eye the Oglins and their pala behind them, the tortoise continued, "By the way, you may call me by my name, Thutha, 'the one who goes with all his belongings.'"

"Oh Great Thutha, perhaps we can be of some assistance," Lafina offered, knowing that they must try to help this grand old creature.

"Yes, indeed, that would be greatly appreciated," nodded Thutha, keeping his fine manner and dignity, even while in such a compromised situation.

"I'll put a riem around you," proposed Baylin. "Then we'll tie it to a pala and pull you out."

The tortoise hesitated a moment, not eager to be tied to one of those flighty beasts. Having tired of battling on his own, however, and being too heavy for the little Oglins to push up the steep bank, he reluctantly agreed.

Baylin quickly set about rigging a harness for the giant tortoise. He carefully lowered it over the edge and asked Thutha to step through the loops. Baylin tugged the reim up tight on the smooth worn shell and tested it with his weight. Baylin then approached Arto, who was almost as sceptical as the tortoise, but trusted his Oglin friend entirely, and attached the other end of the riem to Arto's saddle.

"Back now," Baylin encouraged Arto gently but firmly. As Arto pulled, the slack riem tightened and started to dig into the loose soil on the donga's rim, showering clods of soil down onto the tortoise's hard shell.

"Wait!" cried Lafina. "We need something to run the reim over the edge with or it might break."

Baylin halted Arto and kept him calm while Lafina found a thick branch of a dead shrub. Tugging at it with all her weight, she managed to free it and drag it to the edge of the donga. She shoved it under the taught riem and settled down to hold it in place with her hands and feet. Baylin carefully backed Arto up again and slowly began to raise the tortoise up the side of the vertical slope, which was well over the height of a few full-grown Oglins!

Finally the tortoise's shell appeared at the crest of the bank and with a sudden lurch and skid, Arto pulled the massive body over the edge. The Oglins gasped in relief as Thutha's head shot out in surprise to see where he was. Baylin moved Arto forward to slacken the rope and unwind the grateful tortoise from the harness.

"Oh Thutha, are you alright?" Lafina asked him with grave concern.

"Why, yes," answered the tortoise, slowly as ever. "I do believe I am! That was quite a scare for an old tortoise like me. I haven't the faintest idea how I would ever have got out of there without your help. My thanks to you both, and to your pala there, too!"

"We are very happy we could help you!" exclaimed Lafina. "What luck that we came by in time to get you out of there. I hate to think what would have happened to you otherwise."

"Well, I will be forever grateful," Thutha said with a bow of his head towards the Oglins. The emphasis on "forever" really weighed on the young Oglins, as tortoises live for a very, very long time.

"These dongas are becoming quite a hazard for us tortoises. We can all too easily fall off of these straight cut banks, which do after all sneak up on a tortoise suddenly, you know. We tortoises don't have much of a view from this height. Anyway, where was I?" he wondered out loud. "As you now know, the trouble is we are unable to climb back out of a thing like that

93

once we have fallen in. So many of our Great One's shells lie at the bottom of such 'tortoise traps.'"

Lafina and Baylin marvelled at how such a slow-moving animal as a tortoise could have something happen to them suddenly! Yet they certainly understood how one could never escape from the kind of deep dongas they were seeing as they crossed the Karoo. Lafina had, of course, seen them before, while on her way to the gathering at Vadiera. She had heard battends of previous treks and had learned that the land had not always looked that way. The dongas were a rather recent development. And increasingly, she could see what a serious problem they were for the animals of the Great Plains.

"Well, anyway, all's well now!" continued the tortoise.

"Oh Great Thutha, tortoises live so very long and you are so very large, how old would you be?" asked Baylin politely. Even as the words popped out of his mouth, he realised he had blundered in asking the old tortoise his age. Embarrassed, he drew a circle in the hot soil with a hairy foot.

"I'm not really sure," mused Thutha, with a twinkle in his sad old eye when he noticed the young Oglin's discomfort. "I've been around the sun more than a couple of hundred times I suppose."

Baylin and Lafina's eyes widened in amazement. That was a very long life, especially compared to their few years.

"Oh what have you seen, Great Thutha?" asked Lafina respectfully, as Oglins are especially appreciative of their elders and indeed of any living thing that has seen a great many years.

"I have seen ever so many things in my life," Thutha said, ever so slowly. "And I am sorry to say that many of them are not particularly good. Over time, I have seen the great decline of the land upon which we live. We have seen a frightful breakdown of the community of tortoises that live here mainly due to the arrival of these huge wire fences. You must have seen some by now?" asked Thutha.

"Yes, we've seen the crisscrossed wires stretched across the land. The older Oglins never spoke of those in their battends," replied Baylin. "In fact," he went on, "we have found them very difficult to cross with our pala."

"They haven't been here very long at all," agreed Thutha. "You see, they were built to stop jackals and lynx from getting to the people's goats and sheep. What actually happens, though, is that they stop us tortoises too! We just can't get through most of those fences. We used to be able to wander the great wide world, go here there and wherever we wished. Go there for our food and go here to find mates and such. Not that we did much travelling or move very fast, but we could get around. We are now confined to the same little patch of ground! Which means that as a tortoise, life has become a little bit boring and rather difficult. We can only know the same tortoises we've known before. So now we are almost a little breed of tortoise of our own on this patch, and the next-door patch is becoming another breed of tortoises.

"Another alarming development has been the installation of a new kind of fence with wires that carry a jolting shock. They're a bit like lightning! These are less visible than the old fences," said Thutha sadly. "And they are probably more dangerous for us as tortoises when set up too low, because if one of us steps into them, it sends a huge bolt of lightning into the back of the neck. Of course, we tortoises immediately pull our heads back into our shells when there is anything wrong, and then we sit still for a bit. Slowly but surely, once the stricken tortoise feels brave enough, he puts his head out again, just to collect another bolt of lightning and he pulls his head back in!

This will, of course, go on and on and on until eventually, exhausted, unable to reverse, unable to understand what is happening, the tortoise will die. We find this very, very sad," sighed Thutha.

Baylin and Lafina's heads hung low and tears welled in their eyes at this desperate state of affairs.

"Luckily, in this particular area, we haven't had any of those put in yet," continued Thutha. "But we will have to see how we get along when they do. All in all, things are looking a bit gloomy for us tortoises, really.

"You know, it is all such a sad thing and so unnecessary," sighed Thutha, with a big tear rolling from his ancient eye. "If only people would learn to think a little bit ahead. In fact, all animals should be doing the same. We should learn to think about the future! And whether the things that we do will actually create the kind of world that we want to live in. Each and every one of us should be doing that. Every time we do anything, we should be asking ourselves, *'Will this lead to the future we must have to sustain the life we truly desire?'* Because if we don't do that, we're going to be caught short and discover that we haven't got a future at all!"

After a momentary pause to allow his words to sink in, the tortoise resumed.

"Likewise, the moment anyone makes a decision to do something, then the next stage has to kick in! They must start keeping an eye on it right away. They must watch very carefully to make sure that the desired result actually happens. Whether it is occurring or not, they must make constant adjustments, large or small as the case may be, to make sure they end up with what they want.

"I'm sure that none of these people, or their goats and sheep that wander here and there between the fences, actually want this area to end up with no grasses and no topsoil. Nor do they want the last remaining shrubs to be few and far apart, unable to support a sheep or a goat. Nor, if you asked them, would they want to harm or wipe out us tortoises! But because of the way they are doing things, that is how it will most likely end up. Few of them seem to be checking on the results of what they are doing, let alone trying anything new to change that probability. I think it would be worthwhile for all animals to learn to look ahead and ask themselves those questions. After all, the survival of all life on Earth is what we must concern ourselves with!"

Baylin and Lafina looked at one another knowingly and Baylin said, "That's very interesting, oh Great Thutha. The very last and most important thing that the Wedrelas gave us before we left was a creed for Oglins. Our creed has a section in it which refers to how our land and lives must be in the future."

"Yes," nodded Thutha. "Well, it's that part of the creed that the question, '*Will this lead to the future we must have to sustain the life we truly desire?*' should refer to. Then it is clear that everyone should be checking to ensure that whatever happens actually leads towards their creed. It is not much use if the things we do lead us away from that, is it now?"

"That sounds so very obvious once you think of it," said Lafina thoughtfully. "I expect we will be doing that from now on. In fact, I think we will have to start considering that with everything we do."

"How did you come up with this, oh Great Thutha?" asked Baylin, nodding his agreement with Lafina. "You are so wise. But where did you learn this?"

"Well, of course you know the many folk stories about us tortoises," Thutha replied, "like how we do take a long time to get anything done, but we eventually win in the end. There are great stories about us tortoises racing against the speedy hares. You've heard of the legendary race between Ufudu and Kalula the hare? The tortoise always wins in the end, because the rabbit rushes off and comes back to laugh and then takes a nap in the middle, and eventually the tortoise always gets there first. Because, as a tortoise, we just keep plugging away at things.

"We live such a very long time that we learn to think a long way ahead and see the effects of things that happened a long time ago. Moving slowly all the time has also made us better than most at carefully watching our progress. We have learned to appreciate the little things in life! Thus we make changes early rather than late. We can't afford to go very far out of our way, or we might never get where we are headed!"

Great Thutha slowly lifted his beak up and seemed to give a long and slow wink, which is quite unusual for a tortoise! He looked fondly at the two young Oglins and said ever so slowly, "Well, dear Oglins, I have enjoyed our visit immensely. And thanks to you, I have my life to prove it! But now I have got to wander off and carry on eating. It takes quite a bit of time for a tortoise my size to find enough food nowadays! So, you had better leave me to carry on. And you two still have a lot to learn and a great distance to put under those furry little feet. Off you go, then," he said kindly.

As he moved away, the Great Tortoise Thutha turned his head once more and said, "Young Oglins, don't forget the old folklore that says, 'If you see the tortoise walking around actively in broad daylight, you know there is rain a-coming.' So think carefully about where you lot sleep in this Great Karoo."

Calling after him, Baylin and Lafina thanked the Great Thutha profusely and wished him well. They mounted their trusty pala once more and rode on to the north, across the plain towards the mountains in the distance.

That evening they composed a verse for Thutha's teaching:

Old Thutha lives for centuries,
and with tortoise's common sense,
he looks so very far ahead
to see the future consequence.
He cautions that our deeds may well
have unforeseen significance!

To best proceed we ask ourselves
with each and every step we take,
with plans and dreams and choices made,
with actions and the words we state:
"Will this sustain the life we love,
and a most splendid future make?"

The Storm

The next day was unusually humid for the Karoo. The heat in the deep valleys, combined with the high humidity, was very oppressive. The air itself felt thick and difficult to breathe. Baylin and Lafina were getting up closer to the mountains they had seen ahead of them for the last three days. They still had to climb into the high country and cross over some mountain passes to reach the higher plains, beyond which lay the Pinnacles.

Finally in the late afternoon, the heat became too overwhelming and they decided to rest in the shade of a Karoo

thorn tree. The tree stood high above a cut bank, overlooking a dry riverbed. The Oglins sat and watched towering bright white clouds build up against the mountains, ominous and threatening.

They could hear the growl and thud of the thunder in the distance and see the flickering of the lightning in the clouds. As Thutha had warned them, they had seen a tortoise walking in the daytime and so they knew that there was "rain a-coming." As they rested and watched the billowing of the clouds against the mountain, the wind clawed up the dust with invisible nails and whipped the orange-coloured soil into living devils. Becoming wilder, the dusty devils thrashed through the bush and grass, making them beat themselves against the ground. Perfect circles were scribed in the sand where desperate plants clung with their last remaining roots. They spun and spun again in the swirling wind.

"It looks just like a giant pattern of perfect circles in the sand!" exclaimed Lafina. "If we hadn't seen it happening, we would be very confused about what kind of animal would leave spoor like that!'

As the storm descended upon them in its full fury, Baylin and Lafina sought shelter behind a large rock and huddled together. The pala turned their backs to the wind and stood side by side. The airborne sand flayed at them, stinging as it struck and still making its way into their eyes even though they were tightly shut. Then the cloud showed its dark, purple underbelly as it moved towards them, away from the mountain into the teeth of the wind. Still the sun shone clear on top of the cloud. They could see how the thermals boiled within, just as the sea seethed out from under the rocks below the cliffs of Vadiera. The cloud surged on, climbing ever higher into the clear blue and seemingly gentle sky above it.

Slowly the belly of the cloud closed in overhead, bringing with it the first fat drops. They could still see the mountains, grey and ghostly in the distance. Then the full force of the rain hit them. The first drops were huge and heavy; they dug the loose soil up and tossed it into the air as they hit the ground. Gradually the drops got smaller as the intensity increased. The water was ice cold as it beat down on them. The rain cloud moved further overhead; they were now truly in the grips of the storm.

The two young Oglins sat with their backs to the pounding rain, their leather capes flapping uncontrollably in the wind. They hunched down low, trying to stay as dry as they could, huddled up against the rock. The thunder boomed directly overhead, almost deafening as it crashed about them. A bright flash of green light ending in a blue crack and a smell of burning was followed almost instantly by a deafening clap of thunder. The little Oglins both bolted upright, frightening each other even more. They grinned sheepishly at each other in the murky light. Obviously, the lightning and thunder so close together meant that the storm was right on top of them.

The rain got heavier and heavier. The wind was driving it almost horizontal now, in exactly the opposite direction to before. The wind was now blowing with the storm's movement. The Oglins had to turn away from the mountain for shelter, so they scuttled around and pressed themselves against the other side of their boulder. The pala's hooves splashed in the new puddles as they also turned their backs to the fury of the raging wind. The silver reflection of each flash of lightning revealed the water around them getting deeper and deeper. Each subsequent glimpse exposed wilder waves and rapids, moving faster and faster. Suddenly the water was spinning around their toes. They had to stand upright to keep clear. Just as quickly, it was up around their knees!

The current tugged hard at their legs now as it swirled around. Gripping one another, they began to move through the torrent. It seemed to drag away at their feet, as they tried to move to higher ground. Shouting above the wind, they called to the pala as they struggled towards safety. In dismay, Baylin caught a glimpse of the pala in the next flash of lightning and saw them heading off through the deluge in the opposite direction. He turned to Lafina, pulling her closer to tell her when she suddenly slipped and fell, almost wrenching them apart. They caught each other and he steadied them. She swept 'round past him and suddenly was standing again, teetering in front of him, face to face.

She thrust her face up against his. "We are going the wrong way. That is the main stream I fell into. We turned around, remember?" she shouted with all her might over the noise of the storm.

Nodding in response, he reacted quickly and they struggled to turn through the surging water. Still locked to each other in support, they followed the pala towards higher ground. As quickly as it had got dark, it was beginning to get light again. They could now see the chocolate brown water, wild around them. Above them, the pala were on safe ground already, standing still with their backs to the wind, bundle-rug saddles flapping and their heads held low. Baylin and Lafina scrambled out of the stream as the light returned and the storm passed over them. That's when they noticed the rocks, branches and other debris being swept down the torrent below them. The rocks, clattering against one another made a roaring din only now audible above the thunder.

As quickly as it hit, the storm completely disappeared. The young Oglins shook themselves off vigorously and looked at each other in amazement. They broke into smiles of relief as the hot sunshine broke through, drying them off as quickly as they had got wet. Looking up at the sun, and wondering at the power of it, they both started talking at once. Then stopped. Yes, they were very lucky. For some reason, they had not unloaded the pala or they would have lost all of their supplies. They had also been really foolish to go the wrong way. Well, they had certainly now learned not to sleep or even relax too close to a dry riverbed when there was rain around, as the tortoise had warned!

Steam rose from the soil and rocks that had already been superheated by the sun. The air became hot and humid as evaporation started with a vengeance.

Hearing a great roaring sound from just over a slight rise, they went to investigate. There, right in front of them, was a river where just moments ago there had only been a dry donga! It was now a roaring torrent of chocolate brown water. Huge boulders were tumbling down the river, clattering against one another and smashing up against the banks. Whole sections of the exposed banks were caving away and disappearing down the river in front of them. Large trees were floating past. Right across from them, a thorn tree collapsed into the river, hanging upside down and turning and twisting on its roots. It pulled and pulled like a pala that had been caught for the first time. It was a fight between the raging current and the last roots struggling for a hold in fast-eroding soil. Finally it seemed to give up and

slipped from the bank. It sank as it was pulled under and suddenly surfaced again, thrust almost clear of the water. Again, it stopped dead against the roots. This time the current was too much and the tree tore loose. Quickly and violently, the thorn tree was snatched away by the current and turning as it went, was swept out of sight.

Baylin and Lafina stared at each other in alarm, wondering what would have happened to them if they had been sleeping in the bottom of one of those water courses when the flood came.

"We would have been gone, swept downstream," said Lafina. "It happened so quickly! But in a little while, we'll be able to walk across this riverbed again. It will be dry. I saw it happen on my way to Vadiera. Very soon after the sun comes back out, the rivers and soils dry up very quickly."

"It is incredible! And we are very lucky," agreed Baylin, his voice filled with relief that they were safe and with respect for the power of the flood they had just witnessed.

Baylin and Lafina sat down quietly. In awe, they watched the river as it slowly dropped again. Even though the water they were looking at was deep brown in colour, the sun was shining and accentuated the movement of the waves as the water boiled around, swirled and flowed swiftly past. The dancing reflection of the sun off the water actually hurt their eyes.

They talked about the differences they noticed between this rain and the rain at Vadiera the night before the hunting competition. Although it had in fact rained much more that night, the stream in Vadiera still ran clear in the morning. Certainly the stream had been full, very full, even over its banks in places, but the water in it was still clear. It was not laden with silt nor carrying debris, such as the branches, trees and tumbling rocks that the Karoo flood swept along. One could probably have seen a fish in the stream in Vadiera. Also, that stream's flood had not peaked until the following day. That was some time after the rain; not immediately like the flash flood they had just witnessed. At Vadiera they had seen how some of the dead plant material that made up the sheltering blanket for the soil surface had been shifted around. Yet, most of it was still held in place by all the living plants that cover the soil there. Immediately after the storm in Vadiera, the last water on the surface soaked away into the soil.

Here at the bottom of the mountains in the Great Plains, the water stood in puddles on the surface, directly slaking the sun's thirst as they dried up, rather than soaking into the ground.

The drastic difference between the two storms and their effect on the land shocked Baylin and Lafina.

"Now we understand," said Lafina, "why our creed says: *'When it rains, the water must go into the soil so the springs will have life and the rivers will have water that is living and clean.'* This rain that just fell here is certainly not going to serve this land very well. It is so dry here anyway! How is any of this water going to grow anything here when it has all just left in such a hurry?"

In fact, in the short time before they were able to cross the river and move on towards the Pinnacles once more, some of the higher areas of bare ground were already dry through evaporation and the baking sun. The humidity was unbearably intense in the steam rising off the ground as the glaring sunshine burned the new moisture off. Hardly any water had actually penetrated the soil. Most of it had run off in the flash flood and now the bare soil was drying out quickly. Baylin pointed out the few spots that were still wet and those in particular were in the deep hoofmarks of the kudu that had crossed the plain sometime before the storm. Small puddles remained in the indentations formed by their hooves. Even where their own broad, hairy footprints had sunk into the soil, the moisture had pooled. Where there was some sort of plant matter lying on the ground and in the little hollows where leaf and grass shaded the captured moisture, the soil stayed moist for a bit longer.

The two young Oglins were trying to make some sense of these observations. So much had happened in such a short space of time! They were still feeling the aftershock of the fear of almost being washed away themselves.

To settle herself down as they wandered on, Lafina began to tell Baylin about life in the Pinnacles.

"Our ancient battends tell of storms with the same effects as the one in Vadiera. The battends tell of this both within and outside of the Pinnacles Clan homeland. But now it seems, as we Oglins go outside of our own special territories, we all observe the devastation of the storms like we have seen today," she pondered. "It's actually just a small amount of rain that fell, and yet it causes so much damage as it runs off the land so quickly. In a dry area like ours, if the rain doesn't work for us, that is, if it doesn't go into the ground, it won't grow anything. The rainfall in the Pinnacles is not much greater than out here, and yet our land has solid grass and shrub cover over all of our soils. Grasses, bushes and shrubs produce lots of food for all of our animals and all the wild animals that live there, too! There's plenty for all of us!"

Baylin listened carefully and shared her deep concern and wonder at the decline of the land that they had experienced firsthand.

They spent that night nearby rather than climb into the cooler climate higher up. It gave them an opportunity to dry out their belongings and check that the pala were unharmed. It was a warm and balmy night with no hint of the day's violence to be seen in the beautifully starry sky. The air was crystal clear now that the dust had been washed out of it. The biggest difference between this night and the previous ones they had spent on the Great Plains was the swelling racket of the frogs and the relentless onslaught of the mosquitoes.

From their vantage point, the purple Earth stretched out in front of them endlessly in the semi-dark of the night. Gradually, the bright stars filled the whole sky, with myriad pinpoints of light shining down from above. To the east shone the great constellation of stars known as the Great Wedrela in the Sky, who stands broad-shouldered and proud. His digging stick, the tool the Wedrelas use to dig for the mighty potions used in their trade, hung from his belt, pointing straight to his head where all the knowledge is stored over generations. What's more, a line drawn through the digging stick and the Wedrela's head extended all the way to the horizon identifies north, "the direction from whence we all came," thought Baylin, remembering the ancient saying.

In the southern sky, there was the Great Cross of the South, occasionally present, often not present at all. The cross, along with the twin sadra, off to one side, was used to find south. South is found directly below the point where a long line, drawn through the length of the cross, meets a line drawn straight across through middle of the twins.

Either the Great Wedrela or the Great Cross of the South are in the night sky at any one time. So there is always one way or another of being guided if the sky is clear.

The Cross of the South

The Sadra's

South Horizon

107

Sitting there wondering at the stars, Lafina told Baylin that they would be at the Pinnacles within two days. She could feel her own excitement building at the prospect of seeing her home and family. She sighed happily as she imagined their arrival there soon.

The Pinnacles

It was early morning when the little group of travellers stopped on the point of a ridge with a magnificent view stretching out in front of them. Close at hand, the yellow grass was dotted with green and grey bushes. The ground sloped away quickly towards some low cliffs, beyond which a small flat plain spread out. Surrounded on three sides by hills and open on the fourth, the little valley gave an impression of beginnings; a place where things started and still had hope to continue. This was emphasised by the view of the endless plain stretching beyond the horizon through the open side. In the middle of the hemmed-in plain stood a solitary pinnacle, towering and majestic. It seemed to stand sentinel over all the surrounding land. The rocky pinnacle was round at the base and narrowed upward in perfect symmetry to a sharp-sided nipple, balancing precariously on top.

Behind the sentinel, a flat-topped, vertical wall of cliffs blocked the path in front of Baylin and Lafina. The slant of the early morning sun caused the shadows to be cast long onto the floor of the plain. The new light washed all the cliffs and the nipple in a coating of warm red. The veld on the hills mixed its brown hue with the red of the dawn, and the scene turned the colour of drying blood. It was an eerie sight, yet it was not intimidating, as life in the veld was already active and busy.

Following the recent rains, the clapper larks were happily displaying their flying and minstrel skills. Clapping their wings, they flew upwards, steeper and steeper until they stalled. Then folding up their wings and swooping down, they whistled a sweet, clear, high-pitched, ascending note. Just before striking the earth or running out of breath, they pulled neatly out of the dive and rose again, clapping their own applause.

Below them on the plain, Baylin and Lafina could see a black Korhaan standing on a termite mound, sounding off his cackle for the world to hear. Apparently, something had disturbed him. The bird then fought its way into the air with agitated wing beats and an even more hysterical cackle. The Korhaan, now in view, turned slowly into the wind then dropped its legs down, as if it were wounded, and with a curious overhead wing beat it slowly parachuted to earth. The crescendo of noise did not stop until the bird finished off its display with its proud neck extended, white ear patches stark against the black of its head and neck and its bright red beak open wide.

They peered across the plain to see what had disturbed the bird and soon they spotted it. A busy sheep dog was rounding up a few sheep, dust flying behind them as they flocked together.

Barking occasionally, the dog darted from sheep to sheep, spread out as they were, and raced them into a tight group. Baylin and Lafina watched in amazement. This reminded them so much of their own gayla working the bundles at home. Yet this was the first time they had seen a dog working with sheep or even, for the matter, sheep in a tight group. Up until now they had only seen sheep and goats spread out widely, each grazing on their own. They had not even seen a dog working with them. They watched keenly as the dog lay down with the sheep nervously watching.

A man that they hadn't noticed at first walked to one side and, as if on command, the dog moved and the sheep raced past the man's raised arm in a narrow jumping line. The last sheep shot past and the dog bounded up to the man, barking in excitement to receive a fondle of appreciation. They watched as man and dog headed off along a path and disappeared through some trees.

The Oglins sat quietly while their pala munched away at some sweet grass. They were sure this was part of the Great Spirit's teachings, but they were not yet sure where it fitted in. All they could really come up with was how similar this had seemed to the gayla working with the bundles, yet it was unusual. They had seen sheep before on their travels, but had not come across a dog working with them. They had seen none of the huge herds of game of Old Spola's days, either. Only the sheep and goats, and once or twice cattle too, but always few and well spread out. They stored the experience away in their minds for later reference, realising there would be many pieces to the puzzle and some would probably not fit in until further along their journey.

They rode along the hill a little way further until Lafina pointed out where they were going.

"We line up the Pinnacle with the nipple and that point of the cliffs," she explained. "Behind that we go into the kloof, the secret entrance into the land of the Pinnacles Clan!"

Baylin examined the cliff face but could see no hint of a gap at all as they rode down onto the plain below.

While riding across the flats where the sheep had been, Baylin suddenly called out and leaped hurriedly off Arto. He scrambled around on his haunches, studying the ground. Lafina rode up fast, and Lara skidded to an impressive halt as she stepped down out of her stirrups to see what had excited Baylin.

"Look!" Baylin cried, pointing at the soil surface. "There is concentrated dung here, the soil is all disturbed. The plants are all trampled down and bits of old dead grey bush have been broken off. This is where those sheep were gathered together earlier, and it looks just the same as when our gayla have moved the pala and bundles through. It looks just like the ground where the wild herds in Vadiera have passed! This is the first time since we have left Vadiera that I have seen this."

"Quite right!" agreed Lafina. "Everywhere else that we've seen sheep, they were too spread out, wandering on their own, to have this kind of effect on the soil."

Baylin placed his hairy foot next to the people's track and giggled as he pointed out to Lafina, "Look my foot is only half the size!" Then they both began to laugh as Baylin stretched, battling to keep his balance, to try to match the stride of the shepherd person. An Oglin would have been only as tall as the person's mid-thigh in comparison.

Just then a sizeable dung beetle buzzed in and made a crash landing right in front of them. Lafina was overjoyed to see her clan's totem. It was the first one they had seen since leaving Vadiera.

"It must be from the Pinnacles!" she cried and excitedly leaped back on Lara, spun her around and galloped off towards the cliffs and home, the importance of their recent find seemingly already forgotten.

"Come on, Baylin," she yelled and hooted over her shoulder. "Come to the Pinnacles! It is time!"

Arto and Argyl had difficulty catching up with the flying pair. The packs didn't sit as well as an Oglin can on a pala's back and could come adrift with hard riding. Baylin kept a close eye on Argyl's load as he tried to race after Lafina. Luckily, with no mishap, they caught up just as Lafina and Lara seemed to ride straight into the wall of cliffs in front of them. Blowing hard, the pala were catching their breath again when Lafina disappeared. Baylin pushed on, suddenly worried. Fortunately, he caught a glimpse of Lara's tail swishing, as it seemed to disappear into the rock. Moving forward towards that slightest of clues, he entered the hidden opening in the cliff face. Steep slabs of red and grey rocks rose straight up, surrounding him and stretching up to the patch of sky above. It was very hot in the narrow passageway where no air could move. They walked slowly on, in single file, following the path into the rock in front. Baylin felt like an ant going down a tunnel.

In front of him, what appeared to be an absolutely impenetrable wall suddenly opened up into a further bend in the crevasse that they were riding through. Occasionally he would only be able to see Lara's tail as she disappeared into the seemingly solid rock ahead.

The colours were amazing. The smooth rock streaked with red, blue, yellow and grey lichens. The yellow was so deep it was almost green against the dark and lustrous blue of the sky.

Out of nowhere, he thought of home, his family and his little sister, Aga. He had been having such a wonderful time with Lafina. They were now so easy and relaxed in each other's company and they had so much to discover that other than when he was feeling through his pacha and thanking the spirits, he had forgotten to think of home. Even though he knew they understood the importance of their quest, he felt that his family would be anxiously awaiting his return.

Warm special thoughts of little Aga suddenly vanished when he rounded another bend and the very rock opened up in front to reveal a magnificent vista before him. Lafina was waiting there, visibly proud to survey the view and share it with Baylin for the first time.

A broad flat plain of grassland stretched out before them with flat-topped thorn trees dotted about and a silvery ribbon of a stream running through it. Lovely mountains and cliffs stood in a ring around the plain. In the middle rose another spectacular pinnacle, nearly identical to the one they had seen earlier. Baylin noticed that the grass wasn't just yellow here; it had a greener hue to it.

"It's because the rain we get here actually gets down into the soil," Lafina explained "The rain that falls in the outside world either runs away or evaporates from the bare hard surface of the ground. We don't get more rainfall here; it is just more available to the plants. That is key."

The young Oglins travelled along the well-worn little Oglin path with Lafina in front. She led Baylin off eagerly towards the warrens of her home, situated in a jumble of huge rocks, the remnants of a couple of collapsed pinnacles out in the middle of the open plain. Behind them, the rock face seemed to stretch off into the never-never and the opening they had come through was now invisible to Baylin.

As they neared the burrows at a steady trot, they heard the sound of music in the distance. All the Oglins were gathered together singing and dancing, the activities the Pinnacles Clan was most famous for. They were always greatly appreciated at the gathering of the clans for their exceptional ability to dance and sing. Baylin was enchanted by what he saw and heard.

The travellers rode happily into the midst of the welcoming group. A feast was laid out, and all the Oglins of the clan were there to greet them. The Pinnacles' Wedrelas had seen them coming in a vision when communicating with the spirits, so they were expecting Baylin and Lafina and had prepared a celebration.

The excitement could not have been higher. Having Lafina back amongst them and the arrival of their new hero, Baylin, made the occasion a very special one. After an extraordinary feast of all the clan's specialty foods, the battends told by groups of mos and mers that evening were all about the recent gathering of the clans. They depicted the brilliance of Lafina and the Pinnacles Clan team in winning the battends competition. They also poked fun at and praised the young Vadiera mos, including Baylin, for winning the hunting competition at the gathering. The final morning's run was re-enacted as part of the battends and Baylin could recognise himself being portrayed by one of the young mos. The cheers from the crowd were very real as all the Pinnacles Oglins joined in to be part of the thrilling story.

As the battends finally came to an end, an old Wedrela arose and made a formal request of the young mo from Vadiera. "Honoured guest," he began, bowing to Baylin, who bowed back shyly, "before you continue your journey, it would be in the interest of the Great Spirit for you to spend some time with our mos to teach them how to use the assagais which they have now made. We would greatly appreciate that."

Baylin, feeling very proud, graciously accepted the honour while Lafina glowed with pride for him. It was a very special moment for them as their hearts filled with the warmth of the welcome and home, which is an Oglin's greatest joy.

CHAPTER 6

THE HIGH VELD

Animals are not brethren,
they are not underlings;
they are other nations,
caught with ourselves
in the net of life and time.

—Henry Beston and William Ralph Inge

Farewells

No sooner had they arrived at the Pinnacles, it seemed, than it was time for farewells again. The days had rushed past in a whirlwind of activity. Baylin had an exciting time coaching and showing off his skills while running wild with the young mos of the Pinnacles Clan. He had rarely seen Lafina except for their evening sessions with the Pinnacles' Wedrela, with whom they held long discussions to further prepare them for the next leg of the journey. Baylin had also got to know Lafina's Merma and Modra and some of her sadras and badras when he occasionally joined them for feasts and their family battends.

Baylin had lodged with the leaders of the Pinnacles Bacor and slept exhausted every night. The only ones who had really rested were Arto and Argyl, whose stud potential had quietly been optimised through various pala mares around the Pinnacles burrows. (The Vadiera and Great Flat Top Oglins have still never understood how there came to be brown-and-white pala in the hands of the Pinnacles Clan!) The two visiting pala were well treated and enjoyed their time there immensely, of course. Baylin was far too busy to even know it was happening. The time had flown by and it seemed to be over much too quickly for all of them.

As is the custom with Oglins, there was no crying at their farewells. All the crying occurs at the reunions. Compared to the tearful welcome that Lafina had gotten from her family and dearest friends on their arrival at the Pinnacles, the farewell was a subdued affair.

Once again the decision was made to leave very early in the morning. The Chief Wedrela of the Pinnacles Clan, who had been instrumental in setting the day for their departure or they may well have stayed longer, walked with Lafina and Baylin out of the valley.

It was actually quite a sad moment for Baylin. He had grown rather close to the mos he had been spending time with. He knew he would miss them and the fun they had had. It was all the more difficult, knowing that in leaving the Pinnacles, they were leaving "known territory."

Up until then, Baylin had been able to rely on Lafina's knowledge, as she knew the route and had crossed the country before. This had made things quite a bit easier for both of them. Now, though, they were truly stepping out into the great unknown, and things would certainly be more difficult. Fear and apprehension would now always be a little closer at hand.

As it was when the Great Wedrela at Vadiera had led Baylin and Lafina out, the Pinnacles Wedrela did his best to convey confidence to the two young travellers, with his manner, his eager stride and relaxed conversation. He talked about their journey, the guidance and protection from the Great Spirit, and the significance of their quest to all Oglins. Once again they felt proud to be entrusted with their profound purpose. So, when they finally headed out across the wide open spaces, it was with a light step and eagerness to achieve their mission.

The Red River

Back on the Great Plains once more, Baylin and Lafina pointed north towards the crossing of the Red River. Ahead of them lay the grassy plains of the High Veld. Through this otherwise dry and brown landscape flowed the Red River between a wall of green trees and reeds growing up around red muddy beaches and islands. The green ribbon stood in complete contrast to the dreary brown, parched landscape on either side. After a few days' travel, they rested for a day, swimming and cooling down in the red-orange water, lying in the shade and letting the pala graze for the day.

Standing on the edge of the river, Lafina had said, "Well, Baylin, when you've been through this river, the hair on your feet is going to be ginger-coloured for days. It's interesting because this river is in our battends now all the time. They tell how we can come down here and bathe ourselves in this river and go back and be red Oglins for some time! Yet, the old battends about this river are not the same at all. According to our older Oglins, this river used to be a very different colour. Although it would run a deep orange occasionally, the water was typically only a slightly orange-grey colour. The rocks were still visible below through the water. And the riverbanks themselves were held together by the strong roots of the grasses that covered them. There were pretty tall trees along both sides, not much bigger than they are now, but with grass growing in the shade between them and lots and lots of animals grazing down the sides of the river bank."

Lafina's observation fuelled a deep discussion about the relationship between land and water that remained a theme with them for the rest of their journey. Wistfully they left the river behind them the next day and continued on their way. As they moved further north, there was more and more grass in the veld. The grasslands grew slowly thicker as the rainfall increased.

To start with, they occasionally got a glimpse in the early mornings of the Great Mountains. They lay far off towards the tomorrows, and in winter would sometimes proudly show off their cap of snow. Initially there were occasional mesas and buttes to break up the landscape, but as the travellers progressed, these features became less frequent and the plain more vast and monotonous. On the Great Plains of the Karoo there had always been a hint of a brooding mountain in the distance. Here on the High Veld, the flat plain seemed to stretch on into eternity. There were places where an Oglin could stand and turn in a complete circle and still not even be able to see a single mountain, a single ridge or even a kopjie!

Mesa

Butte

Mostly their travel consisted of endless days of tramping across the grassy plains of the High Veld. Day after day, they rose in the early hours, saddled and packed their pala, and headed north. There were no trees except for those that the people had planted near their homes, standing out like islands from the sea of grass. As there was always a flurry of noisy activity around these dwelling places, the young Oglins avoided them entirely. This meant that they often had no shade to rest under in the afternoons. Every few days they would come across a stream or a river with some trees along the edge of it, stunted in height but massive around the girth. Here the Oglins were able to hole up in the shade and rest in the afternoons while the pala grazed nearby. They knew that they had to pace themselves on this Great Journey and the pala needed to fill their bellies where they could, in case of leaner times ahead.

The two young Oglins got to know one another better and better over these seemingly endless days on the grassy reaches. A biting chill woke them before dawn every morning. On the high plains, the temperatures could drop very low at night, and Baylin and Lafina felt lucky that they were passing through in the warmer season.

Some afternoons brought the traditional summer thundershowers of the High Veld. A deluge of cold lashing rain and hail would drench them from huge blue and dark purple clouds towering above. The sun would often catch the white heads of the cloud above the bruised purple of the storm. This set a contrasting backdrop to the pale yellow and green of the endless grassland spreading out before them, washed in the golden afternoon light.

On some evenings, they were entertained by the spectacular display of the lightning in distant thunderstorms. High overhead there were huge flashes of lateral lightning, starting from a single stroke, then branching out into a candelabra of light. Spreading left and right and off in every direction, they eventually touched up against flickering, pink clouds in the distance.

Each night Lafina and Baylin would take a turn at telling battends about their youth, growing up and where they lived. They shared the history of their clans and talked about what life was like in Vadiera and the Pinnacles. Afterwards they would curl up under their bundle-wool rugs and sleep beneath the vast sky of stars.

The Amazing Maze of Maize

They crossed another river that morning that ran through a pretty valley with lovely wild olive and Karee trees spread out in it. Taking a break from the hot and humid afternoon weather, they swam in the little rocky pools and feasted on the small black olives. The pala had a very good graze and all were feeling rested and refreshed as they made their way up out of the valley.

They reached the crest, and for the first time in days, they had a view from the rocky ridge and onwards across the high plains. Things were distinctly different here. The grass they had become so accustomed to was nowhere to be seen. Instead, they faced an endless sea of dark green that was broken only here and there with straight lines of yellowy looking vegetation. The greenery turned out to be rows upon rows of all the same plant. The broad-leaved plants stood much taller than the tallest Oglin

and were very dark green in colour. It was obvious to the Oglins that this was not likely to be natural! The Oglins were aware of the randomness and variety of nature. Nowhere in nature, in their experience, did only one type of plant live cheek by jowl in rows on bare earth with only an occasional straight break of something else. They were soon to learn that the plant was maize and was planted there by people. Already they knew one thing, that their route lay directly through it!

Spola had not mentioned this, of course. It was obviously not around when he had made his trek. So another new and unexpected challenge had presented itself to the two young travellers. Bravely mustering their courage, they headed down off the ridge and were soon enveloped by the maize. It was even more deadly hot and humid inside the endless rows. The soil underfoot was crusted and bare, yet the pala sank into it with every step. Each hoof fall crunched and sank in as the soil crust broke, making progress both difficult and unsettling, much like walking on crusty snow. After a short distance, the two Oglins had dismounted and walked on themselves, leading their pala to make it easier on them. They had also found that lower down the drier leaves of the tall plants were more brittle and easier to push aside.

There was not a breath of air, and the heat and humidity soon became oppressive. An unfamiliar smell scratched their eyes and caught at the back of their throats. It was going to be a long hard pull.

They had crossed many breaks during the day but one would not turn up when it grew dark and came time to rest. Therefore, they had slept the night in the rows. Their bodies itched all over. The pala, also quite uncomfortable, stamped all night from the irritating fine hair that dusted off the plants and the tiny little cuts that the leaves made as they pushed them aside. Worst of all was the harassment and bites inflicted by the clouds of mosquitoes that lived in the maize. They were all utterly exhausted from their efforts.

The Duiker

The following day, having struggled through the endless maize all morning, they stopped for a rest in a broader alleyway. Here at last the young Oglins were able to come out into the open and see the sun properly. They took the opportunity to check that they were heading in the right direction. It was difficult to tell under the high canopy of the whispering maize plants.

A little duiker that had also holed up on the edge of the amazing maze of maize bolted upright when it saw them. The duiker, a delicate and tawny-coloured little antelope, quivered as she looked wide-eyed in alarm at the Oglins. She didn't spook and disappear in a flash as a duiker often does; rather she stood watching them with her soft brown eyes. Baylin and Lafina likewise looked in wonder at the duiker. Tentatively, Baylin decided to try once more to speak to an animal, to see whether it would work. He was still not completely sure of himself.

"Oh dear duiker, please do not fear us," he began. "We are the Oglins making the journey to see the Great Spirits."

"Oh, of course!" answered the little duiker in a lilting and lovely voice, causing Baylin and Lafina to start in surprise once more. They were just not used to being able to talk with animals yet! With a sound of relief in her voice, she said, "Now I see, you are the Oglins who can speak with the animals. We've been told that you were coming. Please, call me by my name. I am Dainty the Duiker."

"Greetings to you, Dainty," Baylin answered. "I am Baylin of Vadiera and this is Lafina of the Pinnacles. We are very pleased to make your acquaintance, though we certainly wish it were under better circumstances. We have come such a long way and we are getting quite frustrated and really desperate trying to make our way through these endless plants all of one kind."

"Oh, the maize," sighed Dainty.

"Maize? What is that?" asked Lafina.

"It's food for people and their animals," Dainty replied. "It is challenging for us all, but you'll get used to it. If you can survive it."

"What do you mean, if we can survive it?" asked Lafina, worried at the implications of the little duiker's words.

"Well, these soils here are turned over by huge snarling machines at the beginning of every season," Dainty explained. "These same machines come again and plant the new seeds and the maize grows up. Eventually, the plants mature and the crop is harvested by more big, hungry, noisy machines. The remaining plant material is then either removed by machinery, or burned off!"

"Burned off?" gasped Baylin and Lafina in unison.

"Yes, it is hard to believe, isn't it?" Dainty replied sadly. "The animals that would eat and bring the plant leftovers to the ground are not here. So people either take it away or burn it to make room for the following season's growth. Sometimes animals are brought in to do the work, and then life improves a lot. It is vital for the soil to have all the plants go back in to provide food for the small insects and organisms that the rest of life so depends upon. It's probably not too damaging if the fires only occur every now and again, but burning off everything that grows every year will starve the soil."

"This cannot go on forever, can it? Is no one asking Thutha's question? '*Will what we are doing lead to the future we desire?*' What should be done about this, Dainty?" Lafina implored. "Surely something can be done!"

"This is what your trek is all about!" replied Dainty, with renewed energy as she considered the purpose of the Oglins' journey. "As for getting on with your task, I would suggest to you that you stop heading north. I'd say you should turn towards the yesterdays and you will be out of this maze of maize quite soon. Then you will be able to once again turn north and skirt around through the area where the rainfall is too low and erratic for the growing of maize."

"Why don't you move there yourself, oh Dainty?" Baylin asked, with real concern for the tiny creature that was so willing to help them.

"Well, we duikers are territorial animals, you see," she explained in her delicate voice. "The territories to the yesterdays are pretty well competed for and fully occupied. So, with that society all set up, it would not be easy for a duiker like me to find myself a home out there. None of those duikers are even breeding anymore. In contrast to so many other animals like springbok, wildebeest and such who cannot, we are able to control our numbers, you know. If there is no place for us, we simply do not breed and have young. We wait until there is space. So young duikers like me are bred only to move into these areas or replace our parents. I moved here where I can at least make a meagre living and where I have some special friends."

"So, dear Dainty," Lafina asked, doggedly taking the duiker back to the issue at hand, "what should be happening here? Great Thutha the Tortoise taught us that every time we do something we must ask ourselves if it will lead to the future we must create as described in our creed. If we wanted to grow something for food, would we plant so many plants all of one kind? Would it be the best thing to do?"

"Certainly not," replied Dainty. "Nature just doesn't like a single type of plant living all on its own, in row upon row for as far as one can see. For land to be healthy and more stable, there must be a wide variety of bugs, birds, plants and animals. That way, all of them keep each other in check and balance. If there are fewer types of living things, then the balance goes wrong and one or more will always get the chance to explode into plague proportions. In other words, diversity leads to greater health and stability in nature!"

"So what would you do, if you were the people?" asked Baylin. "What would you suggest for them?"

"Well, it's pretty obvious that people must look around amongst themselves for the answers. First of all, they need to learn to grow these crops in harmony with all of us animals, plants, bugs and such," Dainty responded. "There are plants that can grow here that actually like these so-called "problem" beetles, for example! The beetles in turn are quite happy to live on these plants. If more of these plants were here, the beetles would mostly leave the maize alone! This would rule out the need for fighting with the beetles. Instead of being a nuisance, the insects would then actually be part of the overall balance!"

The Dung Beetle

Just then, out of nowhere, a big rhino beetle flew in and landed in the typical gate-crashing style of a dung beetle. He hurtled into the ground, bounced up into the air and eventually came to rest on his back. Indignantly he then pushed with his wing covers and got the right way up. He slowly folded his wings away, somehow managing to still look dignified after such a ridiculous landing.

Beetle on back

"Ah! Young Oglins! At last! I've been looking all over for you!" announced the dung beetle loudly, slowly wagging his rhino-like horn in an effort to look very important. In ungainly six-leg-drive, the beetle turned to face each one in turn, as his neck was too short for him to simply turn his head and look at them.

Baylin and Lafina looked at one another in amazement and amusement. They knew better than to laugh at the beetle, however, as they had been taught great respect for the dung beetle all their lives. Baylin managed to suppress a giggle as he remembered Lafina imitating that very landing at Vadiera that night in the battends competition. He looked at her with renewed respect and thought about her great fondness for the wonderful creatures.

"I am Digger the Dung Beetle," he announced in a robust fashion before they had even greeted him. "I've been looking all over for you! Knew you were going to get lost in this amazing maze of maize, of course. Ha-ha-ha, excuse the pun!" he chuckled to himself. "We had hoped we'd find you before you lost yourselves in it; save you all the trouble. But now we have found ourselves, you may as well learn all about it here."

"Yes, oh Digger," Lafina replied respectfully, still struggling to suppress a smile. "We are very pleased to meet you and learn more. Dainty has been telling us about this strange place."

"Has she now?" Digger asked, without waiting for or expecting an answer. "Jolly good, you know all about it then. She will have filled you in."

"We were just discussing the situation of what people could do differently," explained Baylin, "to make these areas more healthy."

"Yes, I suppose that Dainty has told you that diversity is the key," said Digger, nodding at Dainty in acknowledgment. "If people must grow crops such as these, and I am sure they must, well, they must try to produce food by growing various crops together rather than all of one sort.

"Look at the sand dunes on the edge of the land," Digger said, pointing towards the edge of the maze of maize where sand piles could be seen in the fence line. "You see that? All that sand has blown off of these lands and settled along the fences! The health of the land definitely depends on never leaving it bare and always maintaining diversity," he emphasised.

"With diversity, there would be food and cover available for all the various bugs and organisms and such so that none would need to be pests. All would happily get on with their own lives, doing what they are meant to do," Baylin added, having thoughtfully processed Dainty's words.

"Of course, with more diversity there'd be more balance," Digger stuck his wings out and hunkered down as if to demonstrate balance. "There would be more stability within the community of organisms here. There'd be fewer cheeky young delinquents, mutating and going rampant in vast numbers over the community, creating havoc as they go.

"If all these plants and organisms were allowed to live in balance, then the organisms would control each other's numbers," exclaimed Digger. Sitting down on his tail and waving his big strong, spiked digging arms around, he warmed to his subject. "The predator bugs would increase in numbers and reduce the bugs that are a problem. Bugs would be bugs again! Keeping each other balanced with the supply and demand principle of predator-prey relations."

Digger paused for just a moment to organise his thoughts before going on a little more slowly than before. "Now, if people ever really have to kill some problem organism, obviously the way to do that is not to go out there and willy-nilly destroy

thousands of beetles and bugs with their technological power. They could possibly do it in a way that is mindful of useful organisms like *us*. The mere and humble dung beetle, who, although we have one of the messiest jobs around, are probably the most important in the cycle of life!"

At this, Lafina and Baylin could not help but laugh out loud in appreciation of the dung beetle's self-important but none-the-less accurate statement.

Taking that as a compliment, of course, Digger went on warmly. "We dung beetles are the crucial link in the cycle of minerals and nutrients in the soil. As you know, in these grasslands, the grazing animal is the only thing on Earth that can take each season's growth of plant material and reduce it in volume into you know what!

"Think of an animal. Any animal!" Digger carried on, looking intently at them past the rhino-like horn that protruded from his face. "It can be an eland or even

one of the people's animals. Think of a cow! Whether an eland cow or a people's cow! Grazing the veld, she takes it into her mouth at one end, feeding the bugs in her rumen that reduce it in volume, and delivers ten or twelve delicious dung pats out the other end. So, many plants become a lot less dung! There is simply nothing else that can do that! There's not even a people machine that can do that!" exclaimed Digger, winking a feeler at them in his irrepressible mirth.

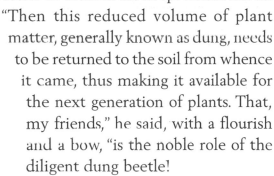

"Then this reduced volume of plant matter, generally known as dung, needs to be returned to the soil from whence it came, thus making it available for the next generation of plants. That, my friends," he said, with a flourish and a bow, "is the noble role of the diligent dung beetle!

"Each season's growth of plant matter must be reduced somehow for recycling into the soil. But since the vast herds of animals that did this have been decimated over these past years, things have changed," said Digger pensively, his feelers sinking into a frown.

"Like what, dear Digger?" Lafina asked him, concerned at his sudden swing of mood.

"They've been burning it!" cried Baylin. "And when they burn it off, all the smoke collects up in the sky! No dung for Digger!"

"It comes down again in the form of sour rain and holds in the sun's heat and warms up the whole Earth. Who knows what changes that will wreak for us all!" the beetle forged on.

"So people are left with only one tool on Earth that they can use to naturally and healthily deal with the seasonal build-up of

 plant material, and that's the animal! That's what animals are for! And that's where we dung beetles fit in. We take the dung and dig it back into the Earth."

Recovering his earlier excitement, the dung beetle took off on his discourse once more. "You see, we take all the structure-of-life and put it back in the Earth where it can decompose. Thus we make it available for plants to use in the future. This plays a very, very key role in the health of the soils. Our burrows and the plant matter that we so faithfully dig into the soil make it possible for all the other bugs and fungi to do their job. Together we bugs make the soil's ability to hold water and nutrients and minerals so much better. So, all in all, as you can see, in the end, we dung beetles are of utmost importance!" Chest puffed out, he dared anyone to challenge him.

Slumping slightly, dejection creeping into his voice, he continued, "But look at us now, wandering like lost souls, waiting pitifully for some animals to provide us with the staff of life. After all, with hardly any animals, there is hardly any dung."

"How dreadful!" lamented Lafina.

She and Baylin were totally enthralled with Digger's story and little Dainty nodded in agreement.

"That's why we rarely see dung beetles except in or near the Oglin homelands," Baylin recognised.

"In fact, just over the other side of the hill is what's nowadays known as a highway. A hot line of black rocks melted together and full of huge machines which make noises just like an animal about to pass dung for us. Before we knew better, many a dung beetle scurried around there looking for dung, confusing the sounds of the traveling machines with the winds-of-promise being passed," he said, chuckling quietly at his own jest.

"Whereas, in the old days, when the highways were still trek routes, people used to actually use animals, like oxen, to pull their wagons and carry freight from one area to another. The oxen would quietly just get on with their work, hooves clicking as they walked along, pulling huge creaking, groaning wagons. Then the sounds of the winds-of-promise were few, but it was the place of plenty as far as dung was concerned. That was, in truth, the new lifeline for dung beetles, whose work was fast disappearing with the demise of the great herds that used to move across these plains and supply us with dung galore!

"In the golden days, literally thirty million springbok in a herd would move across these plains, grazing and tramping the diversity of plants that grow in healthy veld, like grasses, forbs, flowers, sedges and bushes, just to name a few. What was not grazed would be trampled onto the soil, covering and preparing the surface to receive the next rainfall.

"Best of all, though," Digger went on gleefully, "was the massive amount of dung that was produced! Besides the springbok, millions of zebra, eland and other wonderful, graceful animals of the veld were each and every one a source of food for us dung beetles. We would move in just behind the herds, in huge work gangs, almost shading out the sun in virtual clouds of beetles. We would fly in en masse and quickly work the dung right back into the ground. Afterwards the surface looked just like it had been lightly disturbed by a people machine. If people only knew that there is no need for them to have these machines, they could simply bring in huge animal herds to work over the plant material left by the crops. Then we, the dutiful dung beetles, would do the rest for them! We are eager for the work! Nay, desperate for the work!" Once again, Digger the Dung Beetle was bristling with importance, emphasised by the deep silence that followed.

Baylin quietly broke the spell. "My Grand Modra saw one of those herds on a trek to a clan gathering when they crossed the Great Plains. He told about it in battends, but nothing like that has existed for a long time now. No wonder the land is in such poor condition," he mused.

"Talking about Grand Modras," piped up Dainty, getting the attention of the beetle. "Go on, get to the point, tell them about how your life works."

"Yes, indeed," agreed Digger, "that's a jolly good idea. Our young Oglin friends are supposed to hear about that today. Well, you see then, every living thing has a life cycle," he explained. "Life begins with conception, being born, growing up, reproducing and eventually dying. All organisms have something along those lines. Even you Oglins are the same, as you know. Plants, animals, insects, everything has its variation of this. All living things gather nutrients to build their bodies as they grow, and when they die, this nutrient is released to be used by others."

"Yes, we understand that," Baylin agreed, "We certainly do."

"Well, if you've got a living thing, take a bug, a plant, an animal, or anything really, which is busy dying out at a faster rate than it is replacing itself, and you want to save it, then you must strengthen or protect it at the point where it is the most vulnerable in its life cycle." Digger told them. "Now quite often, that most vulnerable time will be just after it's been born or just after it's hatched or sprouted, when it will be very short of food perhaps, or maybe unable to escape from a predator. Normally, addressing the weakest point in something's life cycle would best be done by improving its habitat, that is, the place where it most likes to live and has the best conditions for its growth. Take the tortoises, for example. I know you've spoken to Great Thutha, but he wouldn't have told you about the tragedy of his species."

"Yes, we spoke with him," Lafina affirmed with concern, "but no, he didn't tell us about a tragedy exactly." She was staggered that Digger knew so much about where they had been and with whom they had spoken. "Thutha did tell us about the wires that shock them and keep them in one area for their whole lives. Is that what you mean?"

"Yes, in part, but what he didn't tell you was that tortoises all over the Earth are dying out," said Digger sadly. "They are disappearing, slowly of course, like everything that tortoises do. And the people seem to think that it has something to do with animals stepping on them and killing them. Sure you'll find a few tortoises with wounds on their backs or old scars, but that's not the issue! Really, there were very many more wild animals that used to step on tortoises before the big herds disappeared. Now there are relatively very few animals, and they are much more spread out. Still, people think they must remove even more animals to stop the tortoises from being stepped on.

"What in fact is happening, if they would just take a look at the life cycle of the tortoise, is this. Just after hatching out, the tortoises are very small and there is a dearth of short green grass feed for them. This shortage is linked to the fact that there are too few animals to graze lots of plants, drop the material as dung, prepare the soil by trampling plant material into the soils, planting seeds and making feed available for the young tortoises when they hatch. So in fact, the young tortoises are dying of starvation, nothing else!"

"Oh my," Lafina sighed as one more piece of the puzzle fell into place.

"Now if people understood that they should strengthen the weakest link in the life cycle, they could in fact help by making food available for the young tortoises at the crucial point. They could do this by bringing in herds of animals to trample and invigorate soils, making it possible for grasses to grow again. This would also improve water capture and availability and thus increase the abundance of greenery."

"Yes, we witnessed a huge storm where almost all the water ran off on the Great Plains of the Karoo," interjected Baylin. "It was obvious that even with all that rain, very little growth would have occurred."

"Well, that is what is happening," said Digger. "More water is running off than going into the ground, thus reducing the habitat for tortoises at the weakest point in their life cycle."

"But what about these huge explosions of populations of mutant insects?" asked Baylin. "In this case, it seems that the problem is the opposite: too many of a species rather than too few."

"Precisely, my young Oglin! Well done!" Digger replied. "It works the other way, too, if you address the weakest point in their life cycle. By making it more difficult for them at that point, you will minimise their numbers."

"So," said Baylin, as the concept took shape in his mind, "in other words, if you could find where the most vulnerable point in their whole life cycle is, then change the habitat to make things harder for them at that point, you could reduce their numbers."

"Yes, that's quite right," said Digger. "You've got it!"

"These Oglins are mighty clever things, aren't they?" said Dainty, as they all grinned at one another.

"Well, yes indeed," Digger guffawed. "But they've still got to learn from the likes of us!"

Baylin and Lafina were fascinated. It was easy to get enthusiastic about something so interesting, especially when it was animatedly related by an articulate, dashing dung beetle with a long, sabre-like rhino-horn nose!

"This is so important!" Baylin exploded. "All the Oglins must be told about this!"

"Quite! And quite again!" said the dear old dung beetle, wondering when the Oglins would link the learning back to their greater quest. "That's exactly why you are being told this. You've been sent by the Great Spirit, remember, to take this home to the others."

Then almost embarrassed that he had stated the obvious, making Baylin out to be a bit dense, he blustered on. "You'd better be especially aware of dung beetles from now on! You hear? Don't go tramping on any old dung, you might just squash a few relatives of mine! Wherever you go, in fact, try to arrange for higher concentrations of dung to attract more dung beetles."

Observing the humour he was generating, Digger lifted his entertainment skills to an even higher level and sallied forth. "In fact, if there is lots of dung, we'll come showering down like hail. Enough to frighten any animal off! The odd beetle that gets banged up, well, that's life! If one slightly misjudges a landing and gets concussed, he simply becomes food for a bat-eared fox, an aardwolf, guinea fowl or a francolin.

This is a noble way to go, while getting on with your job. That's what we're supposed to do, either bury dung or get eaten! One of the two."

Baylin and Lafina were amazed once more at this last comment. There seemed to be no end to a dung beetle's dedication to his task!

"So, let me finish now," Digger said slowing down again and suddenly changing the subject. He was clearly not too keen on the getting eaten bit and his discomfort at the thought of it was obvious. "Besides the general knowledge that you should have gleaned today, you need to remember this question that you must always ask yourself when dealing with a living thing: '*Are we attending to the most vulnerable link in the life cycle?*'"

The two Oglins had been so absorbed in the story that they were taken by surprise at the simplicity of the lesson! They looked at each and then in unison repeated the question to Digger, "*Are we attending to the most vulnerable link in the life cycle?*"

"Good, very good then," said Digger approvingly. Then seeming to have had enough, he suddenly said, "Well anyway, young Oglins, it's time that you wandered on."

Baylin suppressed a laugh as he was reminded of dear old Spola who also used to suddenly get grumpy and want to end things.

"We thank you both, dear Dainty and Digger," said Baylin. "It was so very kind of you to speak with us and help us understand so much about the life around us. We will do our very best to pass along this important information to other Oglins."

"Please give my regards to all the dung beetles along the way," said Digger. "There are still very many of them further north."

"And regards to my duiker relatives as well," said Dainty, not going to be outdone by a strong-charactered old dung beetle.

"Thank you for listening so carefully, young Oglins." said Digger. "You now have more keys to the future, and the rest of your journey awaits you. Go well. May the spirits walk with you and guide you on your return. I can assure you that our dung beetle spirits will be looking after you! Head towards the yesterdays and then turn north when you get out of the amazing maze of maize. You will find your route again without too much trouble."

As they were just about to leave, Lafina couldn't help but ask, "Do you know, oh Great Digger, that the dung beetle is the totem of my clan?"

"Oh, yes sirree, the Clan of the Pinnacles!" Digger replied. "We know you very well. We were chuffed to hear about your wonderful battends that won you the competition at the Oglin gathering. That was special indeed! Because you Oglins know about us dung beetles, you are the closest friends we have. When you are homeward bound again, the dung beetle spirits will bear tidings to the Pinnacles Clan of the imminent return of their daughter. Go well, dear ones!"

In honour of their two new friends and all that they had learned, Baylin and Lafina added to their verse.

Dainty the Duiker lives alone
in the amazing maze of maize
where life is oh so arduous
throughout her solitary days.
Yet somehow with the help of friends
she can endure in her own ways.

Dear Dainty made the vital point
that nature likes variety.
With plants and bugs and animals
in plenteous diversity,
this is the most essential key
for true health and stability.

The Dung Beetle crash-lands in time
to make the case for his own kind,
With cleverness and stylish flair,
he tells of nature's current bind.
Who would think a humble beetle
would have so rare and keen a mind?

Behind vast herds across the plains
dung beetles flew in all their glory.
Following the winds of promise,
they swooped down to do their duty.
With never-failing zeal and fervor,
burying the dung galoree.

Distinguished Digger knows quite well
the cycles that all life forms make.
From birth to growth, death and decay,
these are the journeys all lives take.
When we affect a phase of life,
Most careful choices must we make.

THE HIGH VELD

He thoroughly revealed for us
the cycle's strong points and its weak.
For every life goes through each stage
however strong or meek.
This is most vital to be known
to keep life at its utmost peak.

CHAPTER 7

THE CROSSING

"Astonishing!
Everything is intelligent!"

—Pythagoras

The Highway

Following the directions of the duiker and dung beetle, Baylin and Lafina could hear the dull humming roar of the machines in the distance. From experience, they knew it was yet another "highway," as the dung beetle had called them, "an example of the empty 'winds of promise' that had deceived the dung beetles," Lafina remembered with a smile. They had encountered many types of highway thus far. Some were hard stony soil, scraped clear and packed hard by all the traffic. Others appeared to be made of chipped stone glued together with black pitch, where the people's roaring machines would scream up and down releasing their terrible smells.

This highway was different from any the Oglins had encountered before, because there did not seem to be any breaks at all in the steady stream of belching machines. Thus far, highways had meant occasional noise from passing machines, but this one seemed to roar incessantly in the distance. Long before they could see it, the stench reached them. The smell of hot machines and melting black surface brought new tension to the group of travellers. The pala were now getting fidgety, and the Oglins rode with tight jaws.

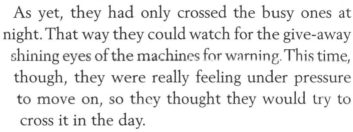

As yet, they had only crossed the busy ones at night. That way they could watch for the give-away shining eyes of the machines for warning. This time, though, they were really feeling under pressure to move on, so they thought they would try to cross it in the day.

They headed into the safety of a grove of the gnarled old wild olive trees at the base of a small ridge. Lafina stayed with the now very nervous pala to quieten them down and to pick some of the olives. The fruits were blue-black, soft, and slightly bitter, but still a welcome treat and a momentary distraction from the danger ahead.

Baylin climbed to the ridge top on foot to check out the situation. He couldn't believe what he saw. There were two black-surfaced strips, each one carrying machines hurtling along in the opposite directions. It was not full all the time, but there were few real breaks at all. Baylin watched for some time before he opted to return to Lafina with the news that they wouldn't cross until dark, hoping that things would slow down.

By the time Baylin returned, the pala had calmed down quite a bit. They had obviously gotten used to the ceaseless noise and were grazing quietly under the olives, close to where Lafina lay fast asleep in the dappled shade. It was hot but comfortable under the trees, and as Baylin dozed off as well, the sound of the highway seemed to become a dull roar in the background and the noises of the veld were once again audible. Birds beetled around overhead and insects buzzed busily. After the previous long hard night when they were harassed by mosquitoes, sleep came easily.

The loud taunting calls of the guinea fowl wanting to roost nearby finally awoke the travellers. It was dusk. Clucking and cackling, the blue-and-white speckled birds scurried backwards and forwards while one by one, they flew with sudden force up into the tree. Landing, they teetered backwards and forwards, red and blue wattles swaying. In the background, the two-note whistle of their mates finished off the evening concerto. The Oglins rolled over onto their sides, facing one another, and sleepily looked into each other's shaded golden eyes. Feeling lazy, warm and comfortable, they held hands and relaxed. The dangerous crossing awaiting them was forgotten for the moment.

They decided to wait until even later when they hoped the highway might have quietened down. In the meantime, they did what they did every night. They recited their creed and discussed their plans in terms of it. Since meeting Great Thutha and Digger the Dung Beetle, they also now checked their decisions using the questions that they had learned from them and from Wallo the Whale when necessary.

After losing themselves for awhile in conversation, Lafina asked if Baylin had also noticed that it was a lot quieter. They listened for a bit, then decided he should go and look again. It was very dark by the time Baylin got to the top of the ridge where he sat and watched. The machines, although a lot fewer now, each had bright white lights shining from their eyes. They looked far more formidable than in the day when one could see the whole machine. Now all you could see was the light shining from the eyes, and the rest of the machine was largely invisible. This made Baylin nervous all over again.

It was at trying times like this that the importance of their mission, the call of achieving their creed and the memory of the last look and words of the Great Wedrela were the only drive to take them forward. Baylin instinctively reached for the amulets in his pacha.

Sitting on the ridge alone, with his back against a boulder still hot from the sun, Baylin's mind naturally slipped back to Vadiera. A moment like this made him long for the companionship of Luka. Just to hug and hold him would be a pleasure. With his thoughts turning to home, they suddenly, with a pang of guilt, sprang to Aga. Other than when going through his amulets in the evenings, it was ages since he had last thought of her. His mind drifted to dreaming of Aga and Luka keeping each other company, and he felt hollow without them. He seemed to be so comfortably growing into a very strong relationship with Lafina, yet he still longed for his family, Aga's sweet company and Luka's companionship. His reverie was disturbed as he noticed a pair of shining eyes with a flashing red light on top, seemingly being escorted by two others with blue flashing lights.

He watched as they sped past and disappeared with their red eyes that shine behind them following them into the night. He suddenly thought that this might be a sign from the spirits to tell him to get on with the crossing. With a deep breath and a knot in his stomach, he rose and returned to Lafina.

They mounted up and bravely headed off around the low

ridge towards the highway. The hum of the machines was much less now, as fewer and fewer passed by. They had no trouble with the fence that bordered the highway; they were used to them by now. Then they stood and waited. For some reason or other the flashing lights that he had seen could still just be made out far off in the same direction they had been going, and strangely, no more machines were coming from that direction at all. For the time being, they only had to watch the nearer strip, which still carried machines whipping past.

Baylin and Lafina had learned that all the lights seemed to first appear in the distance as a single shining eye that split into two as it approached. So when the next eyes seemed to still be only one, they made their move. They rode up the embankment, hearts pounding, and out onto the hard black surface. Only halfway across, Argyl froze. Throwing his head up, he reared and backed off. Baylin had especially put a halter on him and was leading him behind Arto, instead of allowing him to follow freely because he had been worried that he might refuse. Being pulled backwards, Baylin had to spin Arto around to keep up with the now turning Argyl. Hooves rasped harshly on the chipped stone. Baylin managed to regain control of both palas, with Argyl just off the hard surface.

Lafina, on Lara, came back around behind Argyl, talking soothingly to him all the time. While Baylin changed hands with the lead and whispered reassuringly, he began to move the pala forward along the strip. Any movement was better than none at all. The frustration was that Argyl was happy only on the gravely verge and would not step out onto the echoing hard surface. With Lafina on the outside, putting pressure on Argyl, they moved along the strip. As Argyl stepped onto the blackness, Lafina released pressure to reward him.

The star-filled sky seemed to be throwing a lot more light than before; in fact, there were shadows on the strip in front of them. They had not noticed it getting brighter, nor the high-pitched whine of a machine approaching. Their own noise and activity had masked it.

Baylin turned to look, and one single bright machine eye caught him full in its glare. They both shouted at once, the pala spun from the hard strip and onto the loose gravel verge and the one-eyed monster screamed past. They had not seen one of these before! This one was narrow with a single person sitting on top. The single red tail eye followed without seeming to notice them. Suddenly, the Oglins, now riding panicked pala, were instantly enveloped by inky darkness. Grating gravel, a cold chill and a stomach-wrenching drop, and they were all back down the embankment. Poor Argyl was knocked clean over by the other two pala leaping down the bank. He rolled once, then front legs first, scrambled back to his feet. With starlight glinting in the whites of his eyes, he bolted.

Both Oglins were fighting for control of their spinning pala, so they never saw him disappear. They only heard the retreating drumbeat of his hooves. Baylin's heart sank. As Arto got control of his own sliding movement and stopped shaking, Baylin saw in the dim light of the stars Argyl still fleeing; parallel to the highway fence. Baylin called to Lafina to follow and headed off towards where he last saw Argyl. Arto nickered softly to his companion and hearing his reply, went directly to find him. Baylin let the pala lead the way.

Just a little further along, they caught up to Argyl. He was standing in a small stream, quietly drinking and nibbling on the lush water grasses. He lifted his head and nickered softly, warmly greeting his friends as if to say, "What took you so long?" Water dripped, like pearls in the starlight, from his soft muzzle.

Lafina, standing right there with them, while Lara drank long draughts of the crisp, cool water, suddenly said, "Hey, look what the not-so-silly Argyl has found! Let's cross under the highway!"

Reflecting the sky above, the stream that they were standing in flowed away like a starry highway into the mouth of a tunnel and through to the other side.

It was so obvious when she said it. "She is an absolute wonder! How sharp she is! And bless Argyl! He has very obviously brought us guidance from the spirits," thought Baylin. He fleetingly brushed the back of his furry hand gently against the side of Lafina's face and thanked her warmly.

"That is what we need to do, simply cross underneath," he agreed. So, after rubbing Argyl's ears lovingly, Baylin led off down the stream.

"Accidents happen in an instant," Baylin mused. Yet, it seemed that it had all happened in slow motion, giving him much time to think during the action. He realised how lucky they had been. Just a little further and Argyl could have been wrapped up injured in the fence instead of being the hero. An uneasy feeling of guilt pervaded his thoughts. If he hadn't been daydreaming, perhaps he would have been able to avert this near disaster.

The stream was shallow and flowed over a bed of thick water plants with a spongy root base. Every splashing step the pala took was followed by a vibrant effervescence of air escaping from the mud below. The pala seemed pleased to be in the water and happy to be moving under the bridge, even when the echo of the plop and splash of their footsteps reverberated around them. Argyl, who normally would have been overwrought by this alien experience, was acting spirit-sent and led very easily.

They finally came out the other side of the tunnel. Once again, the starlight made jewels of the swishing spray as it splattered out from each hoof fall. Ripples reflected the lights of a thousand stars and the sound was that of a gentle sea. All three pala were enjoying the wading and were now nodding their heads up and down and splashing a little more than they needed.

They were only just clear of the tunnel when a new sound split the night. Approaching from the direction Baylin had last seen it go was the machine with the flashing red lights. Its terrifying siren could have screeched the hair off a gayla! This was another test of their riding skills as the pala shot forward and away from the road. They were soon prancing under control again. Crickets and frogs chirped and croaked again as if nothing had ever happened.

They made an exhausted and quiet camp in some willows on a bend in the channel. The long cold drink from the stream was refreshingly welcome. The two Oglins snuggled up close and slept fitfully.

Baylin's night was fraught with remorse as he replayed the terrifying event over and over in his mind. He was sure that the close call with Argyl was a direct result of his own inattentiveness on the afternoon of the crossing. He had let his mind wander when he should have been more vigilant and thorough in his assessment of the situation. All the angles had not been fully considered and he had gone it alone. Two minds are always better than one. Baylin awoke with the

Great Wedrela's warning ringing in his ears. He knew now that the incident was a warning from the Great Spirits. He must not let his vigilance falter again!

The next morning, with new resolve, they continued their journey north again now that they were clear of the maze of maize.

They added a verse to remind themselves of the lessons of the highway crossing.

A simple crossing caused such a fright!
And a road so narrow seemed so wide!
We did then come to realize,
once safely on the other side,
that the Great Spirit's kindly hand
was ever guiding this great ride.

CHAPTER 8

THE VOLCANO HILLS

"Whoever could make two ears of corn or two blades of grass
to grow upon a spot of ground where only one grew before
would deserve better of mankind and do more essential service
to his country than the whole race of politicians put together."

—Jonathan Swift

The Elephants

Travelling one morning through a heavily people populated area, Baylin and Lafina saw what looked like some rather large kopjies off in the distance. They ran the gauntlet of people activity for most of the day as they made their way towards the kopjies and reached them in the early afternoon. The kopjies were a welcome sight, bushy and quiet, they seemed to stand patiently and watch the activity around them.

The Oglins had to work to get through a huge fence at the base of the kopjies. With great relief, they eventually entered the bushy veld on the other side. They could sense they were in some form of sanctuary. It was quiet and seemed deserted. They moved on, relaxing now, and pretty soon they were gaining height between rock-strewn kopjies. At last, they saw some game! They hadn't seen game in ages. There were kudu, zebra, wildebeest, hartebeest and various other species quietly grazing and browsing in peace. Baylin and Lafina rounded a shoulder and the view of a wide-bushed valley opened up before them with a small group of young elephants, and only young elephants, making their way slowly along the valley floor just below them.

"Ah, this is unusual," observed Baylin quietly. "I've never seen this sort of thing in Vadiera or in the great forest surrounding it. The elephants don't go about in groups of young only; they always live in families with a matriarch cow running the herd. The older elephants train the young ones how to behave. Elephants can behave extremely badly if they are not looked after by their elders! There is certainly something strange going on here!"

Feeling safe from their vantage point on the rocky slope and with growing confidence in talking to animals, Baylin, with only a tiny flutter of fear, called out. "Oh there, young elephants! What are you lot doing all on your own?"

"What do you mean, what are we doing all on our own?" retorted the biggest female of the group, aggressively cocking her head, ears widespread, and slowly raising her trunk towards them.

Even though he had initiated the exchange himself, Baylin was still startled by the elephant's voice!

"Well, where we come from," answered Lafina, picking up where Baylin had left off, "lots and lots of elephants live in the savanna, but they never leave young elephants walking about on their own. They are always in their families! There is always an older female who runs the herd and keeps the young ones in line."

"Yes, that's very true," said the young elephant sadly now, her ears going back to flapping and her head dropping slightly into a more passive stance. "That's a fact. That is how our society works, but we are orphans."

"How can so many elephants become orphans?" cried Baylin, as such a thing seemed inconceivable. "One, yes, but not five of you at once! Where are the other adults that are part of the herd? They should be taking care of you."

"Well, you see, we don't actually come from here, the Volcano Hills." she replied. "We are part of a reintroduction programme of elephants into this area. My name is Khumbula, the One-Who-Remembers, because I can at least remember a bit of where we came from.

"You see," she continued on in a more subdued voice, "this shallow depression and mountain range are part of an extinct volcano and this is a recently developed game reserve. Here people have built a trap for other people that they call 'tourists.' They bring them here to see animals and they have now included us as added attractions.

"There are rumours that this is about to change but we will have to wait and see. So for now it seems people think they can't bring adult elephants here, because they would know our ancient routes and off they would go on our ancestral trails. So they only bring us young ones who have not as yet had the ancient trails taught to us. They shoot all our parents in order to capture us and then move us to these areas."

"Shoot your parents?" Lafina asked. "What do you mean they 'shoot' your parents?"

"Shoot is the word people use for killing with a banging stick. And our parents were shot from flying machines that buzzed above us like mosquitoes. Elephants simply collapsed and died around us one by one. Of course, we couldn't run away from our families. So when the people came, they were able to capture us," explained Khumbula. "They poked us with sharp prickly things that made us slow down and become clumsy so that we couldn't really fight back and knock them down. Even a little baby elephant, like my brother was, could certainly have knocked down a couple of people! Then they loaded us in dark cages on top of big noisy machines and moved us here, where we are still held captive by the high fences.

"Now, if we give them any trouble at all, we will get shot! In fact, we young hooligans quite recently rolled over two of their machines that were making funny noises near us! We squashed them! But the retribution is swift and brutal. Two of us were killed immediately for that."

"Oh my," cried Lafina, full of astonishment and horror, tears welling up in her eyes.

Khumbula had begun to fiddle in the soil with her trunk. Her shoulders hunched much higher than her head that now hung in submission, and only two legs carried her weight.

"We continuously have tourists driving in and around us in their smelly vehicles. They point, click and whir little black boxes at us while they squabble off in some sort of gibberish that our normal people around here don't talk. Sometimes a deep drawl and some times a guttural scrape but very loud in any case. We find it all quite irritating, and I admit we have overreacted at times!"

"But why would they shoot your parents and take you away?" Lafina pleaded, not wanting to accept the very idea of it all.

"We don't understand what they are doing, but..." the elephant's head sunk even lower and her eyes seemed to sadden as she continued, "...how we understand it is that the people where we come from say that we are unable to maintain our habitat. They say that we naturally destroy our environment, as shown by the riverine tree damage, and therefore we must be destroyed before we completely annihilate it. They don't seem to ask why we destroy the riverine trees, when they know full well that our normal food supply is eight-tenths grass, one-and-a-half-tenths small shrubs and bushes and only half a tenth is made up of big trees. They haven't even asked why we are using big trees so much more now than we used to!"

Khumbula's head had come up again, showing off her size. Her passion brought on a new cheeky air. She raised her trunk to form a question mark and went on, "Isn't it obvious that there is something missing in our diet? It's not that there is no grass. There is grass. But look at the stuff. It is mostly old and grey and dead or dying. To prevent it from dying, people burn it, making even tougher and spikier plants come in. Eventually it even hurts to try to eat it!

"What must we do?" she grumbled. "It's not that there is a shortage of food for us. No, it's just that there is a nutritional shortage. People look at the way we behave at the moment, studying our every habit, and they take that as our usual and normal behaviour. For example, we can't live in family groups of more than about twelve because above that, the elephantine nutrition that we need is so difficult to find that we are forced to split up again to look for food. Now people think that this is normal. But our ancestors lived in herds of a thousand or more. And yet still the people don't understand what's going on. We do not have communication with them. Our civilisation is breaking up. The grasslands are dying and so don't provide the nutrition and health that would sustain us. We are turning to the big trees, not to make a statement, but in desperation!"

"So what is making the grasslands die, Khumbula?" asked Baylin, riveted and knowing that these young elephants offered yet another piece of the puzzle for their journey.

"Well, there are no animals to eat it."

"What do you mean there are no animals to eat it?"

"Well, just as people shoot us every year for destroying the riverine trees, so too do they shoot many other animals like the buffalo, wildebeest, impala and zebra. Many of them are shot every year because the people believe there are too many of them. But they, too, are suffering from great hunger because their food source has inadequate nutrition. The grass is not able to sustain them because there are not enough of them to sustain the grasslands. Lots of animals are needed to trample and eat the grass and spread it out as dung again onto the soil. Through the dung beetles, this would go back into the soil, bringing new life and developing the health it needs."

The elephant took a deep breath before she went back to talking again. "The veld is still healthy in Vadiera and the Pinnacles, where you come from, young Oglins. Surely, you've noticed the difference! The big herds, how they trample the soil, how they graze? Have you not noticed how dark green and healthy the perennial plants are? Or how broad and full the leaves are? Have you not noticed how the soils are covered with old trampled-down grasses? How the dung disappears within minutes? Things are different here," she said as she pointed around with a cautious trunk. "Have you not noticed how much of the ground stands baking in the sun, with no cover at all? How much of the far reaches of land are lying barren with nothing but weeds and thickets of bush on it? Or how low-quality, low-nutrition plants and then the spiky, awned self-seeding grasses live alongside too many annual forbs?

"In good rainfall years, those annuals supply a lot of food, but what happens to us when it doesn't rain well? Then the annuals don't make it and we have nothing to eat! Then when it really does rain, it all runs off in floods and takes the exposed soil with it. You've seen the rivers. You've seen the silt in the rivers, haven't you, Oglins?"

The elephant was rocking forward as she continued her interrogation. One forefoot stretched well forward and her trunk snaked up, sniffing the breeze.

Baylin and Lafina were sitting on the rock watching the troop of young elephants, who by now were really relaxed, standing and snoozing as elephants are wont to do for short periods. Their tails were swishing and their big ears slowly fanning backwards and forwards, cooling them down. Their trunks rested on the ground or were draped casually over a tusk. One hung his trunk over the branch of a tree to give the muscles a break. The elephants were standing with at least two feet cocked, while the other two feet carried all the weight.

The whole while they had been talking, the elephants had never really stood still. They were always moving something; ears slowly fanning away, mouths chewing, their trunks shifting around a little bit and their tails swishing.

All the time a gentle, calming noise sounded deep in the elephants' cavernous bodies, grumbling, creaking and knocking as their stomachs worked away at the copious amounts of food they had consumed. Every now and again, one would pass an impressive "wind-of-promise" without even moving a muscle! At the back of the group, one or two were nodding off in boredom, but someone was always keeping watch. None of them really slept, though, just sort of dozed off.

With a heavy heart from the stories they were hearing, Baylin asked, "What can people do differently that would allow you elephants to continue living where you wish and not destroy all the big trees? And I must say that I think that devastation of the riverine woodland is most unfortunate!"

"Yes, the damage we are doing is terrible," agreed Khumbula, leaning back and changing feet to rest the other two, in a slow and gentle move like a dancer stretching the tendons in the back of the leg. "Of that there is no doubt, but we don't have any choice! We are very short of certain minerals and foods that we need. We are such big animals as you see, we've got to get a helluva-lot of highly nutritious food every day for us to survive."

"But where would you get the nourishment you need if you weren't getting it from the trees?" Lafina asked.

"With healthy grasslands and the diet I described, we would be fine. That's not to say that we would never kill another tree. Occasionally we would! After all, there is nothing quite as good as a bit of bark and the fresh leaves from the very tops of the trees to please an elephant!" Khumbula replied, obviously savouring the very idea of such a tasty treat. "But we needn't be wiping them all out. In fact, we quite well understand how to maintain them. You must have heard of our desert relatives in the far northwest. They survive quite happily and they will never break down a tree."

"In the last months of our travel, oh Khumbula, we've been learning a lot about animals keeping grasslands healthy," said Lafina.

"Yes, as you've probably seen, in these drier areas, if the perennial grasses aren't grazed by an animal, they choke themselves out with old dead leaves. After all, old plant material above ground gets in the way of new growth and is therefore only a burden to a grass plant. Did you know that grasses are actually underground plants? In fact, you can ask that grass right there, before I eat it! It's one of a dying breed around here!" Khumbula pointed out.

"We can talk to a plant?" asked Baylin incredulously, looking around himself and almost lifting his feet up in case they were resting on something that wished to talk to him.

"Well, give it a try!" Khumbula encouraged him laughingly.

Baylin looked at the plant Khumbula's trunk had indicated and tentatively asked, "Oh grass plant, are you with us?"

"Yes, of course I'm with you!" came a deep, earthy voice from the ground. Baylin and Lafina looked at one another in utter amazement at this new development. "It's not all grasses that you'll be able to talk to, or you wouldn't be able to hear yourself think with everyone shouting, 'Step on me! Step on me!'" the plant cajoled. "I am Tufty the Grass Plant, and I'm honoured to have been asked by the Great Spirits to speak to you."

"So what have you got to tell us, oh Tufty?" Baylin asked, still bemused and not quite comfortable with the very idea of a talking grass plant with a sense of humour.

"Well, the key is I'm actually the larder of life! I live underground and store the structure of life. Admittedly, I'm not the largest larder as an individual, especially when measured against my mountainous grey friend there. But collectively grasses are the biggest living larders in the drier areas of the world." So the grass tuft began, with a graceful, sweeping bow in the breeze.

"When the weather is good, I chance it and take some of the energy out of my stores to grow some new leaves. These new, soft tender shoots use up some of my larder's reserve to get going. As my new above-ground body grows and adorns the veld with greenery, so this newly visible life begins to sunbathe and gather the sun's energy and turn it into the structure of life. Once they get a good start, this newly captured energy is used for growing the leaves and I can stop raiding my larder to help. Then as these leaves get even bigger, they in turn start to feed me with their excess. First, I refill the larder underground. Then I start to spend the rest on good old self-preservation! I can grow more roots and increase the storage area in my larder, and then I fill it with any extra I can get.

"Just two little things can go wrong and weaken me," the grass plant carried on, happy to share its piece of the puzzle. "The first risk is if these new juicy little leaves get grazed off before they have returned to me the start-up energy I gave them. And you know what that means! Yes, the larder of the world gets reduced and weaker! If this happens again and again, then the larder gets so small that I have to use my living roots to make anything grow. If this goes on too long, eventually I sacrifice myself in a last attempt and pass on to the spirit world of the grasses, a dry and whispery place with nothing but vague memories of life."

"Oh no," Lafina sobbed, moved close to tears by the grass plant's eerie and vivid description, "that's terrible!"

"Easy now, dear Oglin, let me finish my story," Tufty cut her short, though in a sympathetic and friendly way, characteristics the Oglins never thought to attribute to a grass plant!

"The second little thing that can go wrong is if no one comes to graze me! You've heard of this, and need to understand it so just bear with me. You see, at the end of every growing season I have to let all my above-ground leaves dry off and die. This costs me some energy, but it can't be avoided. This little reduction in the size of my larder is normally not a problem if the season that leads up to it and the grazing was such that my energy store is sufficient. Anyway, at the start of the new…"

"Just…sorry to interrupt…I just want to ask something, Tufty. Why don't you just keep your old leaves on?" Baylin inquired haltingly.

"Well, we can't very well do that here," Tufty answered. "You see, our dry seasons are normally so long that we cannot keep our leaves green. Once they have dried off, we cannot reuse them. Winter and frost also kill off the old leaves, especially of a 'summer grower' like me, who prefers the warm season. And because we evolved with animals to trim our leaves for us, we never learned to drop them off as the leafy deciduous trees do every year.

"So in either case, we've got to have that old leaf material removed somehow in order for the sun to reach our growth points down here at ground level. I was about to explain what happens if we have not lost the old leaves by the beginning of the next growing season."

"Oh, I see…I think I'm beginning to understand," Baylin mused. "But what makes the animals move on so you can grow again in peace? What keeps them from grazing you every time you stick your head out? As you said, that is when you are the juiciest!"

"Oh, that's quite easy!" replied the grass plant more excitedly as it stretched in the wind. "As you know, in the old days there were huge herds of animals, and wherever they were, you could be sure there were hungry predators as well, lions, hyenas, cheetah and the like. To avoid predators, the herds bunched up tightly to protect themselves. These herds would stomp all over us. Literally hammering and trampling every bit of plant material down onto the ground, they would break up the soil and push our seeds into the now wonderfully prepared seedbed.

"Now, when you have that many animals in a bunch, you can be sure that their dung, urine and saliva so effectively fouled the soil and plants that the huge herd would move off to avoid their own mess. Then we would be left alone to get on with our growth, and few animals would ever come back until all was cleaned up and quite restored.

"This fouling effect is especially important during the growing season when we grasses will be using up our larders to grow new leaves. This is when we are most vulnerable to being grazed again too soon. The process of cleaning up takes a while, even though the dutiful dung beetles stow the dung away very, very quickly in a healthy situation. The dung beetles are our dearest friends, because they complete the recycling of all our old leaves, the ones that the animals have reduced to dung that is. When they bury it, it feeds the microbugs that then make it available for us to grow again. Isn't this a marvelous cycle of life?" asked Tufty fervently.

Lafina laughed to herself, thinking that if Tufty had a neck and a head the dear plant would have been looking around at them now to see if they were catching on.

"Remember, it's not the number of animals but their timing that could mean the death of me. Now can I go on?" Tufty asked, making sure that the Oglins understood.

"Yes, indeed, Tufty! Thank you very much for your patience while we try to take this all in!" Lafina answered.

"As I was saying, my demise can occur one of two ways," Tufty explained, pausing for emphasis while all the listeners waited with bated breath, "either from being grazed too soon too often, or from not being grazed at all! In the latter case, the new leaves cannot reach the sun's light because of my own choking thatch of leaves left from other seasons. Thus, they are unable to sunbathe and gather the energy to replace what I chanced to take from my larder. This, of course, means that my larder gets smaller, and if this goes on long enough I eventually will start to use up my body stores and get smaller and weaker still. So either way, the pattern remains the same. My larder gets weaker and weaker and in a stress situation I can end up dying."

"This explains why the plants are all dying where Khumbula comes from!" cried Baylin, excited now that it was becoming so clear. "It explains why the grasses are so weak in those gaps in the amazing maze of maize! Dainty mentioned it to us but she didn't quite explain why it happens."

Nodding approval with leafy stalks, Tufty continued "We are glad to be eaten off, time and time again, as much as they like. All that matters is that they mustn't eat us too frequently—or too seldom! With an occasional grazing and trampling, I'll be as happy and fit as ever," Tufty expounded.

"The only way I can stay healthy and keep my larder full is for animals to come by and graze me occasionally and leave lots of wonderful dung for the beetles to work back into the soil," the grass plant emphasised on a jovial note, waving its leaves in the breeze. "Thus, in the gathering and giving of energy, I have helped fill the world's larder and strengthened my friends the animals and the bugs in the soil while they've strengthened me! That's the gift we grasses give."

"It's so simple and splendid, isn't it?" exclaimed Lafina, her mind racing with the new understandings. "The cycle of life is what it is all about! Oh thank you, Tufty. That was really what we needed. This answers so many questions all at once."

Just then rousing from his catnap, the smallest elephant, right at the back, could no longer hold his inquisitiveness at bay. He strolled forward with a typical cheeky elephant gait. Raising his shoulders very high and exaggerating the lifting of his front feet, he bobbed and swayed his head from side to side as he walked. His trunk did a swan-like dance as he came through the others, who barely took notice of him. He sauntered right up to the Oglins and stretched forward as far as he could with his hairy trunk. The trunk's two fingers and double nostril, as if with a life of its own, felt its way all over the Oglins' faces, around their hairy feet and gently pulled at the ends of their toes. The elephant seemed to be having a good feel and smell in order to try to fathom out an Oglin.

The three pala lifted their heads from their quiet head-hanging slumber and, with ears pricked, watched the spectacle. The Oglins sat there smiling and looking at each other while the young elephant's trunk reached further forward and felt at their fingers. The elephant slowly got bolder and his trunk began to dig at their pachas. In fact, he looked all set to start undoing them when Khumbula finally came to the rescue.

She straightened up a little bit, cocked her ears flat and then reached across and blew gently in the smaller elephant's face. Khumbula held her head high in warning as if to say, "Don't be naughty, cheeky thing. I'll sort you out if you're naughty!"

The smaller elephant dropped his head a little lower and then reluctantly moved slightly off to one side. As he walked away, chin up, trunk hanging straight down, he shook his head vigorously making a huge cloud of dust rise up, as he seemed to say, "Well, all right then! I'll bow down to you at this stage. But one day I'll be bigger than you! Then we'll see!"

"Thank you so much, dear Tufty," Lafina said, getting things going again, while still feeling the warmth and sweet smell of the elephant's breath. "There is so much that we have learned from you and Khumbula. It has been very interesting indeed. But I'm wondering, how do we make sure that we do not make similar mistakes and blame the wrong thing for damage that is done?"

"Well, you are supposed to learn, all living things must learn, that it is no good to continually treat the symptom of something!" said Khumbula, still watching out with one eye as the smaller elephant settled to dozing a little way off. "One has to find the root cause of any problem one is dealing with. Roots seem to be at the root of our discussion today!" Khumbula gurgled a deep resonant laugh at her own joke. "Especially if you are dealing with any sort of problem, like we elephants are a problem. There is no doubt that we are a problem. But instead of just focusing on us, and wiping us out, or breaking up our families, people should actually be asking themselves more questions so the deepest, root cause can be found.

"This sounds like something very, very important!" said Lafina enthusiastically. "But how can we discover the root cause of things? How would you suggest that animals, people and Oglins find out what the root cause of something is?"

"I'm surprised you don't know already!" answered Khumbula. "It's not at all difficult. One has just got to ask the question 'Why?' five times. We call it 'the baby elephant test.' Every time an elephant raises its trunk, it is asking 'why?' By the time you've asked it five times, you'll be pretty close to getting down to the root cause.

"For example, 'why' are the big trees dying out? Because the elephants are killing them! So what do we do, kill more of the elephants now?

"Or do we ask 'why' the elephants are killing the big trees? Well, they are short of certain minerals and nutrients that they need to survive.

"Alright then, 'why' are the elephants short of minerals and nutrients? Obviously, those minerals and nutrients are not in the major part of their diet anymore. What is the major part of their diet? Grass. Right, Tufty?

"'Why' are the nutrients not in the grass anymore? It's because the grass isn't being treated well enough, as we've just learned.

"Well 'why' aren't the grasses being treated right? Because people have reduced the numbers of animals and put fences all around them!"

"So," Khumbula waded in for her final point, "the people seem to believe in some of the wrong things. It appears that the root cause is in the people's minds because they are the ones that control this scenario! They kicked out Mother Nature and brought in their own management, believing they could improve on her.

"There," said Khumbula, winding down again, a little self-conscious about her show. "That was exactly five 'whys' and we found it. It's not so difficult, is it?"

"It's peculiar that people don't know this already," observed Lafina. "After all, the ones I've seen do have five fingers on each hand just like Oglins. They could easily use them to count their five 'whys'!"

"Yes, indeed!" Khumbula agreed. "And do you know that when they are little, they ask 'Why?' all the time! What happens is that when the older people get sick of the little ones asking 'why?' they actually stop them from asking 'why?' entirely! Believe it or not, they start banning the word 'why'! And so what happens is that by the time they are grown up, they seldom ask 'why?' anymore. We've seen this strange phenomenon all too often in the tourists that come to see us."

By this time, the other elephants were obviously getting hungry again and they started moving on. Swaying her weight back onto all four feet again, Khumbula apologised. "An elephant's got to eat for most of the day. We can't just stand around much or we will go hungry. Anyway, I think you Oglins understand now, especially with the helpful input from you, Tufty, my providing friend, thank you. The key question you must always ask is; '*Have we found and fixed the root cause of the problem?*'"

"Sorry to cut in here with another question," Baylin interrupted, "but why do the grass plants become so spiky and tough? I know you said it was because there were too few animals, but how does this work? How do more animals make better grassland? I'm not sure that Tufty covered that."

"I'll answer that, if you don't mind, Khumbula," Tufty responded, deftly taking the lead, which was especially impressive for a stationary plant! "Remember what I said earlier about the huge herd trampling the soil to prepare a seedbed and plant our seeds? Well, we broader, softer-leafed grasses, the kind animals like best I might add, have round little seeds that must be trampled into the ground to be planted. Without the herd's hoof activity, we simply do not get very many seedlings started to replace us.

"On the other hand—if you have a hand that is—there are some types of grasses that can plant themselves. They have sharp awns and their leaves are normally tougher, thinner and less tasty to the animals. Fire and little animal disturbance make for the best opportunities and conditions for these types of plants to grow, but this does not suit the animals well at all!"

"Oh, that explains all those kinds of plants we've seen so many of and all the sharp awns stuck in the fur on our feet, doesn't it, Baylin?" Lafina exclaimed. Not really expecting an answer at all she went straight on, "Thank you again, Tufty."

The young Oglins found it absolutely mesmerising to watch the elephants feed from so close up. They sat on the rock and watched the others eat while saying farewell to Khumbula. The elephants would reach out with their trunk, the two fingers at the end shut as the trunk rolled up around some grass. They would tug the leaves off and turn the trunk over onto its back, forming a gentle curve. Carefully the end of the trunk, seemingly with a life of its own, stacked the grass in the curve, fetched more "handfuls" and added them to the rest. Then, arranging the little stack neatly, it rolled it into the end of the trunk and cleverly lifted the stack up to gently and neatly place it in the mouth. Huge lip hanging down, the mouth never stopped chewing. It was amazing that the elephant didn't bite its own trunk off, the way it kept piling the food in!

When they pulled out too much of a grass plant and got a bit of root and soil with it, they just beat it gently against their foreleg, to knock some of the dirt and dust off. Sometimes if the grass was stubborn, the elephant gently kicked its trunk with its front foot to help tear the grass off with a jerk instead of pulling the roots out. For such a huge animal, the movements were so fine and delicate. They packed the grass

so neatly on the trunk, making sure that the little loose roots that sometimes came with it, ended up outside the chewing mouth and fell back onto the ground.

One of the elephants went up to a young tree, reached up, and making a hook with the end of his trunk, grabbed hold of a branch and peeled it downwards until it broke off over a well-placed tusk. The aroma of freshly skinned acacia joined the smell of dust, elephant and fresh dung. The trunk and tusk worked together to hold the branch, turn and twist it, hold it, turn and twist it, so that in a very clever peeling action all the bark was peeled off in the mouth. Slowly, out the other side of the mouth, the turning branch emerged with no bark whatsoever left on it. Meanwhile, another branch balanced nonchalantly on a tusk, awaited its turn. When finished, the last of the branch fell discarded from the mouth, and right away the trunk was already reaching for more.

Baylin and Lafina studied Khumbula's face as she spoke again. Her eyes were deep-set with long eyelashes and were actually quite small for such a large animal. They seemed to have an expression of genuine long-suffering sadness. Amazingly, her ears just never stopped fanning away. Her huge footpads, with deep cracks in them, left massive wrinkled spoors, but were incredibly silent when the giant animal moved. Elephants' feet sag down when the foot is lifted, hanging down in the middle. As they put it down it spreads out flat, actually not even breaking any of the twigs or branches or leaves that it steps on. If anything does break, it is muffled and silent under the massive foot. The only noise the foot makes is a quiet scratching, scraping sort of sound as the rough skin of the pad spreads and lifts again.

"Well it's time for us to wander on now, Oglins," Khumbula said gently around a mouthful of leaves. "It's been wonderful talking to you. You've got an important task ahead of you and I'm glad we could share this time. The Great Spirits had spoken to us about you. In spite of our unfortunate circumstances, they do try and bring some sort of decent behaviour and understanding to us young elephants, even though we are orphans living such a long way from our elders. We're trying to make the best of it and we're glad to have the chance to meet you. Still, if it wasn't for these kind people who have given us a second chance at life here, we may well never have met. Your quest and the opportunity afforded us by these people gives us some hope for a better future."

"Thank you, dear Khumbula!" Lafina replied. "We will always remember you and the orphan elephants of the Volcano Hills and all that you taught us. We wish you well! Oh Tufty, our vegetative friend, thank you and farewell."

"Farewell? Where do you think I'm going? I'm a grass for heaven's sake! Management willing, I'll still be here for ages! You travel well and I shall stay well," rejoined Tufty as an elephant's trunk wrapped around its leaves.

Just then one of the young elephants suddenly raised his trunk and stiffened, causing all the elephants to freeze dead still, in that instant. They stood absolutely still, exactly as they were. The Oglins looked up and listened. Surreptitiously, the elephants slowly raised their trunks, with no movement of their bodies whatsoever, and sniffed the wind.

Baylin and Lafina could hear it now. It was the sound of a flying machine, just like the sound of those that wiped out the elephants' families. With explosive movement, the elephants were silently slipping away, with a high gait and heads up. Their shoulders raised, they moved with phenomenal speed, and yet were almost completely silent. The dust streamed off from behind their ears and backs as they rushed into the cover of the bush. The only sound was the branches scratching along the toughness of their hides.

They heard the sound of the flying machines change. Maybe a change in direction or in the wind and the whole herd stopped again, dead still. As one stopped, they all stopped. There was not a movement. Even the bush was absolutely silent from the violent movement. The only sound was the percussive whopping of the flying machine's straining blades. Then the elephants erupted into dusty action again. The sound of the machine finally faded behind the kopjie. The elephants realised that they were safe for now and seemed to take stock of the situation before returning to the business of feeding their immense frames.

The Oglins were astounded by the whole scene; so sudden and violent yet so majestic. They mounted their now-tense pala, who had also witnessed the whole encounter with interest, and rode off up the valley.

They composed verses for their newest friends and teachers:

> *Khumbula, wise young elephant,*
> *reminded us to always find*
> *the root cause of any problem*
> *and seek to bring that to our mind.*
> *She used five "whys?" quite cleverly*
> *to find answers of a useful kind.*

> *Tufty the talkative grass tuft*
> *explained just how the grasses grow.*
> *Their green leaves soak up sunlight,*
> *and when the rainfall comes they know*
> *to grow their roots beneath the ground*
> *and food in earthly larder stow.*

THE OGLIN

From elephant and earthbound friend
we learned of people's errors past.
The veld needs herds to trample it
and mouths that feed and on do pass.
Yes, grasses need their grazing friends
as much as grazers need the grass!

CHAPTER 9

THE GREAT GREEN RIVER

Real strength never impairs beauty or harmony,
but it often bestows it;
and in everything imposingly beautiful,
strength has much to do with the magic.

—Herman Melville, *Moby Dick*

The Oasis

From the Volcano Hills, where they had met the orphaned elephants, the young Oglins headed north and a little towards the tomorrows. The next major landmark they were looking for was another large river that Old Spola had spoken of a great deal. They made their way through some very rugged country, where rocky slopes and thick thorny bush hampered their every move. Worst of all were the tall, many-strand wire fences that stressed them and their pala to the limit. At least there had been fewer people and more wandering game, which eased their tension slightly.

On a still, stiflingly hot afternoon Lafina and Baylin rode over a rise and before them lay a deep valley scattered with massive "upside down trees," seemingly standing and staring across at the vista. They had never seen such bizarre trees in their lives, but Spola had been right, they did look upside down! Huge and silent witnesses to thousands of passing seasons, these ancient trees pointed their massive blunt limbs into the sky. Each was unique in its shape and the scars on their broad trunks told stories of their long years as living monuments to time. The "upside down" Baobab trees and the dark band of trees along the edge of the river down below, combined with the dryness and bare ground upon which they walked, let them know that they had truly reached a new zone, the low veld. It was low in altitude and even the air they breathed felt hot and heavy.

They wandered on down towards the river course. But where they should have found the Great Green River of Spola's battends, there was only a wide, sandy, and utterly dry riverbed. The fine orangy-cream-coloured sands were like sculptured dunes, high in places, low in others. Along the northern bank of the river course, Baylin and Lafina could see watering holes dug by elephants to reach the underground flow. The Oglins climbed into one of these big elephant holes and dug away a little bit more, and slowly, seeping out of the sand came beautifully clear water. They were able to quench their mighty thirst and wash out the dust caking in their throats. The pala needed no encouragement to kneel and drink; their thirst made learning a new trick simple!

All along the banks were towering trees. Some had been able to stay green and healthy, while others were merely skeletons of what they had been, fallen over and adorned with the debris of past floods. Baylin and Lafina did not hear the call of a single hippo or see sign of a crocodile or anything of the sort, though Spola had warned them of the abundance of such dangers. It was an eerie place, a mere remnant of its past glory.

As they meandered along the river bottom, Baylin and Lafina reassured themselves that this was definitely the river Spola had so clearly described. But in his time, it had been full and running with greasy, grey-green water that flowed in an oily mass down this same riverbed. The battends told of how the river moved, thick and slow, green with the colours of the algae in it and heavy with the scent of hippo dung. The battends also made the Green River out to be as treacherous as ever with huge scaly crocodiles, with tawny unwinking translucent eyes. They watched everything that moved, but did not move a twitch themselves. The crocodiles would lie there, seeming to smile with their huge toothy grins, while they waited for dinner to appear in the form of some poor hapless animal that was not as wary as it should have been.

The size, direction and everything about the river course matched the descriptions from Spola's battends. Sadly, though, where the deep water once flowed continuously, the Oglins were now walking in a dry, sandy bottom. The water they dug up was sweet, so perhaps the river was still flowing a little under the surface, as rivers sometimes do. But it was by no means the beautiful, teeming river of days gone by.

The banks of the river were cut and steep but what remained of the riverine forest was still lovely. Alongside the river were winter thorn trees, bereft of their leaves as usual in the summer season. Broad umbrella thorn trees spread their branches like parasols, wide enough to shade a flock of a hundred bundles. Flittering flocks of birds filled the upper branches with life. They could hear the call of the puff-backed shrike—click-whistle, click-whistle, click-whistle—so indicative of this type of country.

Probably the most stunning sight of all was the spectacular flame rugs, the vines spreading bright crimson, over the top of the tall trees and weeping over the river itself. Some of the dead tree giants were completely draped with brilliant red hanging splendour. The air was heavy with the smell of pollen and alive with the buzzing of bees, as busy as ever.

The two Oglins decided to wander further downstream a bit to see what they could see, as they were in no hurry to leave this oasis of life for the dry country all around them. Soon they found a remnant of the river, a huge pool of water, lying up against the southern side of the watercourse where the current had dug out the sand and created a wide depression. It was full of heavy green water, just as Spola described. Then they heard the familiar call of the hippo, a grunt, grunt, grunt, followed by a wheezing bray almost like that of a donkey as the sea cow drew breath, only to be followed by the grunts again. Spouts of water vapour, like those of a whale, burst hissing with the release of pressure as a hippo surfaced.

The presence of the travellers was agitating the hippos. They could see the nearest one, flicking its stubby, bristly tail from side to side, spreading green dung over the water. The hippo sank beneath the surface and then rose again with its huge mouth gaping wide open, exposing the beast's frightening, creamy-white tusks. Snapping its mouth shut, the hippo let out another of its grunt and bray and grunt and bray calls, snorting white spumes once again. Keeping a safe and respectful distance, the two young

Oglins found a spot in the impenetrable shade of a dark green mahogany tree well up on the bank to watch the pod of hippos for a while. Their pala, grateful for a break from the travel, rested with their heads hanging down and a back leg cocked.

After a little while, Lafina pointed towards a long object below and proclaimed, "There's a crocodile!" Indeed one of the big logs that they had first thought of going to sit on, turned out to be a large crocodile. She noticed it now that it was basking with its mouth wide open and the light orange colour of the inside of its mouth was visible. There were rows of vicious-looking white teeth, sharp as ever, outlining the orange of the flesh. As they watched, a little oxpecker strode right into the croc's mouth! Climbing in and out, the little bird was cleaning away between the rows of dagger-like teeth, working its way around, up over the back, back down the other side, into the teeth, digging away, pulling out food caught in there and having a wonderful time. The crocodile lay patiently, letting the bird do its job and earn a meal in the process.

Finished with the croc's teeth, the oxpecker climbed back out and walked down his scaly, curved legs. By then the hippos had settled down and were wallowing at the far end of the deep pool. Their nostrils were visible just above the water's surface, while their wide-spaced eyes watched, blinking, and their little, round bristly ears flicked from side to side, backwards and forwards. They were listening for anything out of the ordinary, just waiting for the next thing to be bothered about.

Not a problem for the little oxpecker, though. It simply flitted across the pool and landed on the back of the largest of the huge sea cows. The little bird wandered fearlessly around on its back, picking away at scars and scabs that the hippo got from fighting to maintain rule of his domain. Sadly, this big green puddle was all that was left of this part of the old Great Green River.

This oasis in the low veld was a pleasant place, with its welcome green shade and pocket of life, though it was extremely hot during the day. Baylin and Lafina wished they could just cool off a little bit by paddling around in the green water. But it was definitely not recommended, given who lived there!

After a relaxing break from the heat in the relative coolness of the thick shade, the two Oglins reluctantly decided to strike off again. They started out across the rough stony ground that was essentially denuded of vegetation except for stunted broken trees. They were heading north, across the peninsula that separated the Green River from their next destination, the Sand River. When Old Spola's party came through, they had crossed the Green River at the confluence and had continued up the riverbed of the Sand. However, Baylin and Lafina were well towards the yesterdays of the confluence because of their change of direction in the amazing maze of maize. They now faced a long, dry stretch of barren land between them and their next hope of waterholes in the Sand River.

The Eland

Occasionally glimpsing the taller trees along the river itself, the young Oglins made their way to the north. They were on the Kalahari's very edge, a rocky moonscape that was a complete contrast to the soft grass-covered sands of the true Kalahari. Here thick ridges of rugged, glaring bare rock lay baking, hot across their path. They had to climb up and over them, struggling with loose rocks that went clattering away underfoot. The pala had to be led. The footing was far too loose for them to be safely ridden. The little group would get to the crest of one ridge, only to face more of the same ahead, stretching off as far as the eye could see.

Each valley was filled with mopane trees or rustling lala palms with dry, blue-grey fronds rasping and rattling in the wind. They saw much less life than they had expected to see, much less than they should have seen! Such utter desolation was disturbing to the young Oglins. They hadn't even heard a lion's call or any other signs of life in the barren area.

After hours of exertion, they had finally come down into one of the dry riverbeds with steep cut banks and decided to change their route again and follow it downstream. Eventually after trudging through soul-sapping sand and scrambling over scattered fallen trees, they finally came out into the Sand River.

Sadly, it too was just a wide flat expanse of sand from one side to the other. They managed to slake their raging thirst where the elephants had dug for water along the north bank, in the shade under the steep overhangs. Here and there, along the sandy stretch, were occasional pools of standing, stagnant water. Most of them were shrunk down to dry hollows of desiccated algae and cracking mud patterns. Baylin and Lafina found it much better to walk where they could stay on the hard sand and avoid falling into the odd patch of quicksand where it was a little bit wetter.

Travelling along the riverbed, they were delighted to come across a herd of eland that had come down to drink of whatever water they could find. When the eland saw the Oglins, they scattered cautiously back up the bank, their hooves clattering on the stones. They were not quite sure what the Oglins and pala were, as the shimmering heat waves distorted their vision and made the small group of travellers appear to float eerily like ghosts.

"Wouldn't it be interesting to speak with an eland!" exclaimed Baylin, who had long admired the magnificent creatures. "I think we ought to talk with these eland," he went on. "We have to get much closer to them, though. Maybe they don't know what we are!"

So the two Oglins walked to the pool where the eland had been drinking. Through the thicket of tall lala palm trees and umbrella thorns on the riverside, they could see the movement of the nervous animals. The dust rose from where they milled about and hung in the air over them like a shining halo. Baylin and Lafina could hear the distinctive clicking of the hooves and dew claws of the elands as they moved. They could tell that the large animals were agitated by their presence and were ready to break into a long-distance run, as only an eland can.

Hoping to calm them, Baylin and Lafina hailed softly to call them back in. Soon the eland began to drift tentatively back down, closer to the river's edge. The two Oglins moved into the dappled shade of the rustling lala palms. Rattling palms aren't all that good for the nerves of wild game. The sound makes them uneasy and unsure if something mightn't be sneaking up on them. It set their senses a-jangle, making them edgy. The elands' ears flickered, then suddenly stopped, still, to listen. Not a muscle twitched between them. For a moment, even the incessant twitching of the elands' tufted tails stopped.

As Baylin and Lafina watched the small herd with pleasure, a huge "blue bull" began to come towards them. The eland was a tremendous old bull, grey-blue in colour with ribs showing and flanks a bit hollow because the years had taken their toll on his teeth. He carried a massive set of horns that were immense around the base; it would take two large hands to encircle one of them. His old horns, flaking with age, spiralled straight up to a magnificent height.

The elegant eland's proud forehead, covered with thick, coarse brown hair made a dark patch in the middle of his face, against the tan of his long nose. His short, nearly nonexistent coat was a blue-grey colour, almost as if he were hairless. His beautiful, soft dewlap hung penduously down from his throat and swayed gently as he walked. It looked so inviting and smooth, Baylin wanted to stroke and feel it. The towering eland looked down at him kindly in friendship.

The grand old eland lowered his proud neck towards the Oglins in greeting. "I see you," he declared in a deep and gentle voice. "My name is Elanga, which means 'Of the Sun.' You must be the Oglins that are on a journey to see the Great Spirit. He has told us of your coming, as we are kindred to the Great Spirits. After all, we are the spiritual ancestors of the Bushman people."

"Yes, oh Great Elanga, one of our elder clan members, Old Spola, told us about the Bushman people and their Great Spirit Ancestors, the eland," replied Baylin respectfully. "He told us much about you and the Bushmen. We dearly hoped that our paths would cross."

"Would Old Spola be one of the three Oglins who made the Great Journey many, many seasons ago?" asked Elanga.

"Yes, he is from my clan, Vadiera," answered Baylin eagerly. "He was the only Oglin to return to us from that pilgrimage."

"Our Spirit Ancestors speak of such a journey made by the Oglins," Elanga mused. "But, of course, we don't call you Oglins, to us you are called the Tokolosh. In fact, you are feared by most of the people."

"Why would people fear us?" asked Lafina in surprise.

"Only because nobody knows what you really are," Elanga explained in his gentle manner. "Like spirits, you are seen only occasionally, but your work is known. As the Bushmen have such a close link with the spirit world, they don't fear you as others do."

"Great Elanga, you met those Oglins on that Great Journey, did you?" Baylin inquired.

"Oh no, I wouldn't have met them personally, no, I'm not old enough. But being mediums for the spirits, we eland have that knowledge available to us. We have the knowledge of a great many years, of great stretches of history," Elanga explained.

"May I ask you a question then, oh Great Elanga?" Baylin asked. With the eland's nod of assurance, Baylin dared to query him. "As far as I understand, from the Bushman paintings on the rocks that we have seen, you eland are something that is eaten by the Bushman. How can that be? How does that work? Is the Bushman eating his own link to the Spirit Ancestor? We wouldn't dream of eating a Wedrela!"

"Yes, that is so," replied Elanga with a glint of amusement in his noble eyes. "We have a very special relationship with the Bushman people. Bushmen do eat us; they do eat the messenger of the Great Spirits. But it's only right, because the Bushmen can eat the great eland to get strength from their spirit ancestors. It's not like you Oglins, who have the ability to speak with the spirits through your Wedrelas and draw strength anytime.

"We eland appear to the Bushmen in times of great need. We come to them when they do not have any other food, are in desperate need of fat or are terribly thirsty, as can happen out in the remote areas where they live. It can be extremely hot and sometimes their water, cached in ostrich eggs out in the Kalahari, may have been plundered by porcupine or hyena. These robbers find the water by smell and dig it up. It is a thirsty land, after all, and water is the most precious and rare substance in this environment. So when the Bushmen find themselves in dire straits, then like an apparition, the Great Spiritual Ancestor of the Bushman will arrive in the form of an eland and give himself to them. He allows them to hunt him down and use the gifts of his body for nourishment and the liquid in his stomach for water.

"It's not as if we make the hunt easy!" exclaimed the great eland. "It's just that the greatest gift that a Bushman can receive from the spirits is the arrival of an eland to be hunted. At these times, there is always rejoicing and great communication with their ancestors and the Great Spirits."

"But don't the Bushmen that actually kill and eat the Great Spirit Ancestor of theirs feel bad about doing that?" wondered Lafina, trying to understand this unique relationship between a people and the animal they revered.

"No, they understand and rejoice at the gifts of life and the ability to be in touch with the Spirit Ancestors," Elanga reassured her. "That's what it is really all about. It teaches them great things that make their lives richer."

"What sort of things do they learn?" Lafina followed on.

"Most importantly, it teaches them to look inwards at their lives," Elanga explained. "It helps them truly appreciate the positive things. They have their families and such wonderful close relationships. They have the freedom of the world to wander through, the Great Spirits to communicate with and draw guidance from. They have the Great Spirits to look after them and see to their needs if they are in times of desperation. It reminds them of the abundance of the environment that they live in and that the Great Spirit is everywhere. It is also an opportunity for the passing on of knowledge and memories over generations and generations of Bushmen.

"Even so, it is always with great sadness that a Bushman takes the life of an eland," resumed Elanga. "It's not the kind of sorrow of losing a loved one, but a kind of melancholy at the passing of time. It is a moment of deep reflection when the Bushman must assess his life in comparison to the deeper factors that make their lives worth living. They must consider if they are achieving the feelings that give Bushmen their quality of life, if they are attaining the deepest values like love, appreciation, recognition, a strong kinship with one another and relationships with nature, their ancestors and the Great Spirit.

"While they feast upon the eland's meat, drink water from the bowel and use the hide, wasting nothing, they are directly in touch with their essential needs to ensure day-to-day survival: water, food and shelter. This moment of plenty makes them reflect upon what they do, asking themselves if they are doing right, in terms of the deeper requirements beyond their basic needs."

The two Oglins just looked at each other and nodded their heads in recognition. Smiling, Lafina said, "Isn't that interesting. Because that is almost exactly like the creed that we have been given by the Wedrelas! Our creed describes the feelings we most deeply value and how our lives need to be to achieve them. I see that the Great Spirit wants us to learn from what you are saying, oh Great Elanga. We need to look at our creed often, to reassess it constantly and make sure that our lives are indeed moving towards the kind of life that we most want to live!"

"Yes, that is true, but you need to look ahead, at what you are about to do to see if it is likely to create the feelings you value most. So you need to ask the question the other way 'round," the Eland led them on.

"So when we do something," Baylin added excitedly, "we must also check beforehand, *if we feel that it is likely to lead towards the life that will give us what we truly want in our creed*. Just as we have learned from the other animals, so we are learning from you, oh Great Spirit Ancestor of the Bushman."

"My, my!" exclaimed the great eland. "You learn quickly! I know you will add this to the other lessons of your journey so far. Well done!"

Baylin and Lafina beamed with pleasure at the praise and bowed their heads in humility, feeling lucky to meet such a great being.

Elanga then told the Oglins, "There is more. Your Great Spirit has arranged that you talk with some Bushmen. These wise people have information that is vital to your task and indeed for your safety as you travel onwards. So I will guide you to them."

Baylin and Lafina's eyes widened at this news. They doubted that any Oglins they knew had ever met the elusive Bushmen, and they drew in their breaths in anticipation.

Climbing astride their faithful pala, they set off at a trot clattering over the stony ground. They followed the graceful eland with his long loping gait, tail out behind him, bouncing off his back legs. Nothing can cover ground like an eland. His back hardly moving, hanging dewlap swaying under his chin, he ran with an effortless distance-eating gait. The young Oglins on their pala were hard-pressed to keep up, but an Oglin on a pala can fly over ground, too, if needed! Baylin and Lafina were thrilled to be travelling in the company of the magnificent eland, so they kept pace with their companion across the dusty land.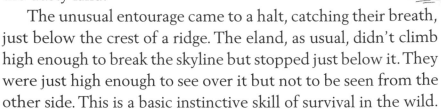

The unusual entourage came to a halt, catching their breath, just below the crest of a ridge. The eland, as usual, didn't climb high enough to break the skyline but stopped just below it. They were just high enough to see over it but not to be seen from the other side. This is a basic instinctive skill of survival in the wild.

As the group surveyed the land before them, the great old eland launched into his final instructions. "It is important for you to know that there are certain Bushmen that can change into a lion. So, what you must actually look for today is a lion," he told them. "You must find the spoor and track that lion down. If you follow the right one you will discover that it is not actually a lion, but a Bushman. I am going to leave you to do it alone, because it would be just too intimidating for the Bushmen if I were there as well. It is you two that need to speak with them, after all. So just climb down off this ridge and find the lion's spoor."

Still in awe, the Oglins thanked the Great Eland profusely, knowing they would always treasure the brief time with the magnificent Elanga. They took their leave of him and with trepidation, headed bravely off to purposely find a lion. Normally, they would go way out of their way to avoid a lion, yet here they were setting off to track one!

CHAPTER 10

THE GREAT THIRST LAND

The legend of the earthbound spirit,
forever roaming the highways and waste places of the world,
bears the stamp of truth, for its poetic value is eternal.
The wandering god, the disguised king,
the mysterious stranger at the wayside hearth,
itinerant poet, tinker and peddler, all those romantic figures
whose appeal to our aesthetic sense is direct and universal,
represent a true archetype, the spirit of the Earth.
—John Michell, *New View Over Atlantis*

On the Spoor

Baylin and Lafina went bravely down the slope, leading their pala through the loose rocks that were blazing hot in the heat of the day. Even through the thick hide of their furry little feet, the Oglins could feel the searing temperature of the stone.

As they reached the bottom of the ridge, the buzzing of flies and the thick smell of the shepherd's tree in flower attracted their attention. The shepherd's tree, white-bark trunk gnarled and bent in many directions, stretching up and disappearing into the flat bottom of dark green foliage. The eland, kudu and impala had browsed it off to a height that no other animal could reach beyond.

Above that, the shepherd's tree spread its branches once more, covered in a profusion of yellow flowers, sprayed through the darkness of the leaves. The air was thick with the heavy stench of the blossoms, smelling bad enough to confuse a dung beetle. The tree teemed with the full activity of life; insects buzzed and ants streamed up and down the trunk.

Right beneath the big shepherd's tree, the Oglins came upon clear signs of where a lion had recently slept. They easily picked up the spoor of the massive cat and cautiously followed it on down the slope. In places the track became very difficult to see. Over stretches of hard, bare ground and exposed rock, they could only occasionally find where a stone had been turned over by the passing beast. The turned-over stones exposed the splashed underside where the soil had been spattered up against it in the last rainstorm.

'The last rainstorm,' Baylin thought wryly, 'whenever that was…weeks, months or perhaps even years ago.' The young Oglins were able to follow over the rocks with a mixture of luck, guesswork and sharp-trained eyes. Fortunately, the lion

seemed to be heading to water and the spoor soon led them straight into the soft sand of a dry riverbed and on down the watercourse.

The Bushmen

It wasn't long before the Oglins stopped cold in their tracks with a shiver, reminded of the fact that they were on the track of the king of the Kalahari! They heard a deep roar of a lion that seemed to start far, far away, deep inside the lion's belly and slowly got louder and louder and louder, building up to the final thundering roar that can rightfully put fear into the hearts of almost every living being. They quietly waited and each time that the lion roared, it was louder than before, sounding ever closer. It sounded as if it was right on top of them.

Finally, when the rolling thunder of the lion ceased, they followed tentatively on, tracing the tracks. Taking great care, they rounded a bend in the river and there, right under a bank, was a little family of Bushmen. Most amazing of all was that the lion's spoor led right into their midst! And there was no lion spoor leaving it! There were just the prints of the little Bushmen's small feet.

Baylin and Lafina could hardly believe their eyes. The Great Eland had told them that Bushmen could do this yet it still astounded them.

In front of them was a little old couple with a cluster of children sitting around them. They wore only the skins of various animals tied together around their waists. The littlest ones had only a thin string of rawhide, with bits of hair, eggshells and beads hanging off them. Some had similar sorts of things hanging around their necks and around their heads. Nearby, a younger man and woman were busy digging in the soft sand under the overhanging bank of the dry river, looking for water. Leaving the pala hidden behind them, the two Oglins stalked quietly closer and nestled down on their haunches to watch.

Upon finding what they were seeking, the Bushman digger picked up a long thin reed and pushed it gently down into the sand, twisting and bending it slightly, all the time gradually inserting it deeper. Every now and again he would put his mouth over the end of it and blow ever so gently. Then he would chat to the others with a very animated clicking and clattering of the tongue and natter, natter, nattering, accompanied by very quick little movements of his lively eyes and lips. All the while, he kept pushing the reed in deeper and deeper until eventually, with a satisfied grin on his face, he heard little bubbles under ground. Then with extensive effort he was able to draw up a little mouthful of water.

In typical Bushman fashion, he did not swallow the first sip. Neither did the young woman. They called the children to drink first. The children did not yet have the strength in their mouths and lungs to draw the water up from the depths of the sand through the length of reed that the Bushman was using. So the young Bushman drew up the water and spilled it into his hand where it then ran down his thumb and trickled gently into the open mouth of the waiting child. The child, having had enough, started making little mewling noises and the Bushman stopped for a moment. Another child then nestled onto the hand for his turn at it. Baylin and Lafina could see the little Adam's apple, under the man's light yellowy brown skin, wrinkled already even at his young age, bouncing up and down with his sucking and siphoning of the water. The tendons on the lower neck and shoulders of the Bushman, who was drawing the water up the reed, stood out straight and his eyes were tightly shut in a scrunch of wrinkles.

When the children had finished, the old couple then moved forward and took their places. After all the others had drunk, the two young people finally quenched their own thirst with the sweet water. Then the others brought precious ostrich eggshells and held them under the trickling thumb to be filled.

These large eggs had been stolen from an ostrich, their tops chipped open and the contents blown out for a meal. Then the beautiful, ivory-coloured eggshells served as water containers for storage or travel, carefully carried in hide pouches that hung over the Bushman's back.

Water was such a precious thing for these Bushmen. Baylin and Lafina took note of how frugally the desert dwellers used it, like running it down a thumb, so that not even one vital drop should be lost. These people came from the Great Thirst Land, the Kalahari, last refuge of the Bushmen.

The old battends told of many more Bushmen than were seen of late. Because Bushmen have no sense of ownership of material things, when hungry they would help themselves to a meal of other people's cattle. Of course, this displeased the cattle owners greatly and the unknowing Bushmen were ruthlessly hunted and killed. This drove the Bushmen further and further into the depths of the Kalahari where they could continue their ancient hunting way of life in relative peace.

The battends also told of the many amazing characteristics of the Bushman people. For example, when Bushmen have plentiful food, they will eat and eat until they are nearly too fat to move! Their behinds fill up with fat and stand straight out almost horizontally, and their whole bodies become round and gleaming, storing the fat almost immediately. Then for the following weeks, with less food available, that body fat is slowly used up. Their skin begins to sag again, like an empty water bag hanging off their bones, like a plant wilting to preserve its last store of water.

The Bushmen that Baylin and Lafina met were wrinkly and dry looking. They obviously hadn't eaten hugely for some time. Every movement of the little people represented great care; they conserved their energy, their water, and every resource they had around them.

After watching them in fascination for a little while, the young Oglins finally called out to the Bushmen, greeting them in traditional Bushman fashion, "Good day, I saw you from afar!" This greeting made sure that one did not prickle the Bushman's complex about his small size. The Bushmen all turned in unison, each with a quizzical little look, from their eyes right down to their mouths. Their smiles filled their faces, causing a multitude of wrinkles to steal across into the loose skin hanging down on either side. There was an inquisitive look of curiosity in their eyes, very much like a naughty little child might look!

The old Bushman answered excitedly, "Oh yes! The Oglins! I see you! At last, you are here! We've been expecting you! In fact, we've gathered together enough water here in the eggshells for you two. Come and have a drink! You must be very thirsty."

The young woman brought forward an ostrich egg full of precious water for the two grateful Oglins to quench their thirst.

Then the whole little clan climbed up the bank of the river to rest up in the shade beneath a huge sycamore fig. The tree, an oasis of life, was filled with colourful birds, all busy about their business. Parrots zipped in and out, with their green heads and little yellow shoulder patches showing against their brown bodies. Rosy-faced lovebirds with bright cheeks and pink heads flew and turned in their flocks with piercing whistles. Above, the cooing green pigeons simply tucked into a meal of figs.

The group sat down in among the massive roots that encircled them like huge arms, welcoming them home and holding them there. There they could sit and talk in comfort and relative coolness of the shade. The little Bushmen children gradually grew braver and snuck forward to light on either side of the Oglins. Tentatively they reached out to feel their furry feet and stare in wonder at the gleaming golden eyes of their visitors. The Bushmen had never seen eyes as bright as burnished gold in anything except a lion and a leopard!

Chatting away, the Oglins complimented the young man on the way that he had drawn the water out from so deep under the ground. They appreciated that not one single drop had been spilt in the process.

The little old Bushman smiled warmly at them and replied, "If you lived in the thirsty land that we live in, you too would learn to treat everything that you use with great respect and as sparingly as possible. We do everything we can to use our resources, water, plants and animals in ways that will ensure their availability for generations to come."

As the Oglins nodded in appreciation, the youngest child crawled up onto Lafina's lap and promptly fell asleep.

"We have very few belongings. We have nothing harder than the wood or rock we find as we travel across the desert. We have the hides of the animals, which we wear; we have our quivers, a few arrows and arrowheads, the calabashes that we find, and our ostrich shells. We waste nothing!

"If we should find a bunch of roots that are edible, we take only some, we don't take them all. The wise old women have taught us that we must leave some behind for others one day," he explained, smiling over at his mate. "If we find some mushrooms, we never take them all. We only take half. The other ones must stay there to grow new ones afresh. If we hunt an animal, we hunt only one. We always try to hunt an animal from a group of animals, rarely one on its own unless it is an eland giving itself to us, because maybe it's the only one here and we certainly want to have them available to hunt in the future."

The Oglins looked at one another and raised their eyebrows again. Lafina said to Baylin, "This is another one of the questions we must learn to ask ourselves. Whenever we do something we must ask: *'Does this activity use resources sparingly and respectfully? And does the way we use it guarantee its availability for generations to come?'*"

Smiling in approval, the old woman removed the leather pouch that hung off her back and put it on the ground between them. She opened it and offered them a feast of small berries and dried worms that she had collected over the last days of wandering. They ate them together. The Oglins were grateful for the nourishment and took careful note of the kinds of things they too could watch for to sustain them as they crossed the Great Thirst Land.

Feeling that their time together was coming to a close, the Oglins thanked the Bushman family warmly and whistled for their pala. The three pala leaped up the bank nearby and picked their way across to Baylin and Lafina. The Bushmen's faces lit up in utter surprise. The children scrambled, wide-eyed, to dive in behind the relative safety of their parents' thin brown legs.

Before mounting, the Oglins introduced the Bushmen to the pala. It was a totally new experience for the hunters to feel and touch a tame, living animal. Being with the animals obviously reminded the old Bushman of food and spiritual power. It prompted him to ask the young Oglins if they had seen any eland along their journey.

They told him of their encounter with the great bull Elanga and explained that they had travelled with him to find the Bushmen.

The younger Bushman's eyes and whole face lit up as he asked. "You saw the eland? Where was the Great Spirit Ancestor going? Did he tell you?"

"No, he didn't tell us where he was going," Baylin replied. "But I feel he just may be waiting for you up there on the ridge, where the lion tracks come from. I think if you follow the lion spoor back, you may find the eland's tracks on the ridge just above the shepherd's tree."

The young Bushman thanked the Oglins. Knowing that his family was well settled under the massive fig tree, he headed out along the lion spoor to see if there was a gift to hunt from the ancestors. The two Oglins took their leave and turned to the north, once more to continue their journey.

In honour of Elanga and the kind Bushmen, they composed more verses:

Elanga the grand Eland bull,
revealed just how the spirits share
their ancient lives through time and space
and taught us how we each must care
for the vast and splendid treasure
of our world so fine and fair.

Eland gives itself to Bushman
in desperate times of dire need
and thus the spirits do provide
and more than hunger do they feed.
For this great gift to be received,

THE OGLIN

We too must live by our heart's creed.

With trepidation we did trace
the lion's spoor across the land.
As great Elanga had assured,
the threat'ning beast was not at hand.
Instead we found a gentle Bushman
sipping water from the very sand.

The Bushmen live in harmony
using just the bare necessity.
They glean a simple life from nature
and consume so very sparingly.
They know that for their children's lives,
they must leave plenty for posterity!

CHAPTER 11

THE GREAT RUINS

There are those who want to set fire to our world;
we are in danger;
There is only time to work slowly;
There is no time not to love.

—Denna Metzger

The Ruins

Following the directions of Old Spola, Baylin and Lafina had followed the Sand River all the way back until it became a tiny hollow in an endless woodland and finally disappeared altogether. They continued north, and as expected, soon found another watercourse heading away to the north and the tomorrows. It became obvious that they were entering an area where the rainfall was higher and thus the grass grew taller. Pools in the stream were more common and bird life was more abundant. When more and more kopjies dotted the landscape, Baylin's heart began to turn towards home.

They were able to recognise some of the specific views and kopjies from Old Spola's battends, which led them to the incredible ruins of an ancient city. Its name, according to Spola, was "Khami." It was obvious that the city had been built with exceptional love, care and attention to detail. They could see that once upon a time many hundreds of people of a long-lost civilisation had lived there. Yet now, these once-wondrous buildings stood empty and in ruins.

In fact, the only living thing the Oglins saw there was a snake that slithered into a hollow in the wall. Exploring the buildings further, they found the vestiges of the wooden posts that once held the roofs over the top. They speculated that wood must have been extremely hard because it had been there for ages.

"What could have happened to these people?" Baylin mused as they wandered in the forsaken city. "Where did they go? Why did they go?"

Built by hundreds of highly skilled masons, the chipped, cut and packed stone walls were utterly perfect in their curvature and angles. The curving walls, almost hypnotising with incredible accuracy and flow, like a honeycomb, had no mud and no gaps between the stones. At a certain height, the stone blocks were not stacked horizontally, but placed diagonally for artistic effect.

They wandered about through the abandoned buildings and eventually came to rest under a big camel thorn tree standing proudly to the side of the ruins. Baylin noticed perched above them a Giant Eagle Owl, sitting motionless with his eyes half closed. The magnificent bird had very lightly striated white feathers over his puffed-out chest and two pointed ears on top of his head. His eyelids covering his half-open eyes were a beautiful pink, with lovely long eyelashes. Baylin pointed up without saying a word and Lafina spotted him too.

The Owl

"Young Oglins," said the owl, in a deep, gentle voice, startling the two Oglins who had the thought the owl was asleep. "I am Uyazi, 'the one who knows.' I've been expecting you!"

Once again, Baylin and Lafina realised that this was another opportunity arranged for them by the Great Spirit.

"How has your journey been up to now?" asked Uyazi.

"Oh, it has been very interesting and amazing, Great Uyazi," Baylin replied. "It has certainly been challenging and difficult at times, but we have learned very much! We have met so many wonderful creatures and seen beautiful things. It's been extremely exciting for us!"

"I'm very glad to hear that! And I'm happy that you have made it this far safely. Now, what do you think of the ruins of Khami?" asked Uyazi.

"We've found them quite fascinating," Lafina answered. "But they are such a mystery. How did they come to be here? Who built them?"

"I'm glad you asked," replied the owl, who seemed more than willing to tell the story. "You see, many, many years ago, my ancestors lived here in amongst these buildings. They saw the people who built them and watched over the people who lived here. The original builders were a brown-skinned people, with long, straight, dark hair. These people came from across the Ocean of the Tomorrows. They came here in search of the metal that is the colour of your eyes, the metal that drives people crazy. They dug it out of these hills around here and carted it off back to where they came from.

"When they first came and found the local people leading simple, comfortable and quiet lives, they whipped things up into a frenzied pace for many years. They got everyone busy digging, building, hunting, growing crops and all sorts of other activities. But when the yellow metal was depleted, they soon departed, leaving the now-exhausted local people to return to their lives," Uyazi explained.

It was obvious that the owl was relishing his role as teacher as he paused and puffed out his chest and tucked in his chin. Baylin and Lafina listened attentively, their curiosity piqued about this mysterious place.

"Nothing much changed here for the local people, though," Uyazi continued wistfully. "The strangers captured them and made them work as slaves. However, they did learn some important things from these long-haired, brown-skinned people from the tomorrows. They learned how to mine and melt down rocks and turn them into metals to work the land with and to make their spear points. That, of course, changed their lives dramatically and added to their technological knowledge quite a lot."

"Why doesn't anyone live in these buildings anymore?" asked Baylin. "Why have they fallen to ruins? Is it because the yellow metal ran out? Is the yellow metal finished?"

"My, aren't you the curious one! And jolly good questions, too," noted Uyazi. "No, the yellow metal isn't really finished, but they had taken out all they could with the methods they had at the time."

"So why, Great Uyazi, did the people move away?" asked Lafina.

"Well the real reason that they left was because they could no longer feed themselves from the lands around the city," the owl replied in his soft and breathy voice.

"But couldn't they easily grow crops around here, the way that people do today?" Baylin wondered.

"Well, with the technology they have today, they can make more food grow here now, out of land that is already tired. They can mine minerals elsewhere and bring them here in order to make this land produce food. But in those days they didn't have the technology to do that. Once they used up the land, it could no longer support them. They planted and planted and planted, crop after crop after crop on the same spot until the soil was tired.

"In many ways, they were very good farmers, those people. They used animals to work their fields and made compost from the dung to help regenerate and fertilise the soil. They planted a variety of crops together, instead of all of one kind like they mostly do now. They brought in water, carrying it from the little stream down below. Of course, they had thousands of slaves who did all that work for them," Uyazi answered and paused, looking at them each in turn before fluttering his pink eyelids with long dark lashes.

"They certainly produced a lot of food here, but slowly, slowly the water for irrigation became less and the river silted from more-frequent flooding," the owl went on methodically.

"Why did that happen?" asked Lafina, the "why?" question slipping easily on to her tongue since their meeting with Khumbula.

"They hunted out all the game on the land around them," Uyazi replied. Looking down at them, he now puffed out his cheeks and flattened his ears. "As they reduced the numbers of animals on the land around them, the grass no longer had a job to do and so it slowly went grey and died. As the grass grew less, the shrubs and bush grew more, but they don't cover the soil like grass and still more ground became bare. More bare, uncovered soil meant quicker runoff of rainfall and more evaporation of water from the naked ground. As a result, there was less water in the stream on a permanent basis and the springs' flow diminished too. The water table underground dropped.

"At the same time, although they were doing their best to maintain the health of their croplands, the erosion of the catchment raised the level of salts in the irrigation water and this built up in the croplands. Over time, their food production slowly declined until the people could no longer grow enough to feed the population of the city."

Uyazi paused, and for the first time slipped his pretty pink eyelids back, revealing frighteningly penetrating, fierce yellow eyes. The intensity of his gaze lent importance to the owl's words, and both Oglins sat up straighter and tried to look like they were really concentrating.

"Eventually, they could not produce enough food to feed the people that lived here. And, as you can imagine, hungry people are a nuisance! They begin to riot and revolt and cause all sorts of problems for their captors. All that those brown-skinned people really wanted here was the yellow metal, not warfare and people problems. So when the social situation became too complicated for them, they simply left!"

"Where did they go?" Lafina asked, her curiosity consuming her.

"Over time many cities were built, some before this and some after; each one even bigger and better with larger towers and temples to their gods. But as they never knew how to prevent the decline of the land, each city eventually fell into ruin as the land around it was exhausted and the people had no choice but to leave. Later on, having given up hope of finding more yellow metal and having lost all prospects of creating something that would last a long time, the long-haired brown people took what yellow metal they could, and returned across the sea from whence they came.

"When the foreigners left, the local people had to scatter back into the bush to live as best they could. With no workable model of how to feed the populations of the cities, the buildings were totally abandoned and fell into ruin. This phenomenon has repeated itself all around the world, until recently when modern technology allowed today's extensive cities to develop. However, the same fate may be awaiting these cities over time," the owl concluded.

Stunned by such an amazing tale, Lafina looked up at the old owl and asked him, "Oh Great Uyazi, could you tell us why it is that people cannot sustain themselves? All our battends of the old times tell of the great diversity and health of the land. Our experience so far is hugely different! What is happening? Are the people doing the same again now? Will they destroy this whole land we live on? How do they do it? Why do they do it?"

Uyazi looked wisely down at the two young Oglins. He pulled in his chin, fluttered his beautiful big pink eyelids and hid his vicious beak in his white-feathered, heart-shaped face. "It's not my place to answer all of your questions, my dear young friends. The Great Spirit has sent you on this journey first of all to learn to ask those questions and then to begin to find those answers for yourselves. But I do have a bit that I can share with you. It will just be a small piece of what you have got to learn in total.

"You see," he came to his point, "people and Oglins alike change the world they live in to suit themselves. In other words, they affect their environment to improve their habitat, to increase their comforts, to provide food, water, shelter and so on. And, when you really think about it, you'll find there are just a very few things they can use to manipulate that world. These, let's call them tools, actually fall into just a few categories.

"Now I could lecture you all about these tools but it will be just so much better if we could discover them together. So firstly, let me see…" The old owl's bright yellow eyes bored intently at each Oglin in turn, then disappeared slowly behind rosy pink eyelids while he considered his next words. "All right then, you Oglins don't like to get wet, do you? So you build warrens for shelter, don't you?"

"Yes…" Baylin's tentative effort sounded more like a question than an answer.

"Well, you see, that is manipulation of the environment to suit you." The owl seemed very pleased with himself as he went on, "What do you build them with?"

"Digging tools…" Baylin answered quizzically.

"Yes!" Uyazi exclaimed. "You see, that is the use of 'technology' as a tool to change the environment, isn't it? 'Technology' means any sort of equipment or things you have built or made to use as tools. People have taken this to a great extreme with all of their machines and such. So this is the first type of tool, or group of tools, that is available to affect the world. Have you got it?"

"Yes, I've got that. There are lots of examples of technology that we have seen on our journey so far," Baylin replied, now seeing the owl's direction, and remembering their close encounter with the speeding machines on the highway.

"Well done! Let's go on to another one, then. Let's say you want to hold a hunting skills competition tomorrow, here on this veld where there is all this uneven, longish grass. What would you do to prepare?" the Giant Eagle Owl continued his line of questioning.

"We would get the gayla to collect the clanta of bundles and pala and…" Lafina was cut off by the owl.

"Sorry I must cut you short there. You, 'would use the gayla

202

to collect the clanta of bundles and pala…' Now that would be the use of the tool of living things! You see, you are using another living thing to affect your environment!" The owl was so pleased with himself that that flattened his ears and lifted them up twice.

"This is a tool that tends to be ignored a great deal these days. Yet every living thing is a worker in nature! Many of them could be employed to do work for you. Take your gayla, for example. They are a living organism working to manage your environment for you and you didn't even know it! They manage your veld with your clanta of bundles and pala every day!"

"I see!" Lafina followed and remembering, exclaimed, "It's just like the man we saw near the Pinnacles who used a dog to work with his sheep, too!"

"Indeed, quite right!" the owl affirmed, and then cocked his head slightly as if to think again. "Now, one of the best examples of this occurs after a big herd of animals has passed over an area. Often huge flocks of quelea birds will fly in right behind them, in their thousands, to pick up the seeds that have been knocked off the grass. They waft through the air en masse like a living cloud and settle like heavy dust. Thousands of tiny feet actually move the loose plant material around on the soil surface and chop it all up as the quelea search for seeds. This prepares the ground for all sorts of other things to happen, like new plants to grow, the sun's warmth to come to the soil and so on. Are you getting the idea?"

"Yes! Yes!" Lafina chimed in again, really enjoying the exchange. "Something very familiar to me is the fantastic work done by dung beetles, of course! Imagine the effect of adding dung beetles back in somewhere where there were none. Their work would improve the soil so conditions would become right for a host of other bugs to get to work too. So add one and you get the benefit of a multiple work force!"

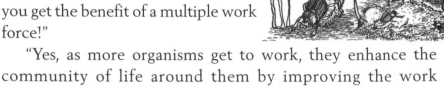

"Yes, as more organisms get to work, they enhance the community of life around them by improving the work conditions for others," Baylin said, adding his thoughts.

"In that situation," the wise old owl followed on, "you would suddenly find that millions and millions of different kinds of organisms would start living in the soil and working there, too. They would build soil structure and break down old plant material so the growing plants can access the minerals in it. So, you now see that in order to use the tool of living organisms, we must help create the conditions in which more of them wish to live. This means covering the soil surface and then life will surely spring forth. Soils are fed from the top down!"

"What we are describing is quite different to conditions in the amazing maze of maize we passed through on our way here," Baylin noted in a very concerned voice.

"Mmmm, that is true," the owl acknowledged, pleased with his students' understanding. "Now let's move on to tool number three," he urged eagerly. "You, young mer, were saying, 'I would use my gayla to collect the clanta…' And what would you do to this veld to prepare for the hunting skills competition?"

"Oh, I would get them to graze the grass in the area very short so that…" Lafina was cut short yet again.

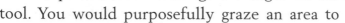

"Yes, indeed!" Uyazi interrupted, wanting to bring his next point home. "Grazing! Grazing is the third tool. You would purposefully graze an area to achieve the change you planned. Now this is a tool that you Oglins have applied unwittingly  for years through your clanta, with the help of your gayla herding them about! And just like you Oglins, most people are also unaware of this tool although they also use it rather unwittingly.

"This tool's main role, as you now well know, is to remove old plant material and to reduce the great volume of old stems and leaves," Uyazi explained. "Sadly, people often use fire now instead of grazing to achieve this purpose, due to misconceptions about the effects of grazing on the environment, but more on that later! The tool of grazing can also be misused and have a negative effect on diversity and ecological health, especially if the time between grazings is not long enough or positively…"

"Yes!" cried Baylin, getting excited now. "It's all a matter of time! If grasses don't get enough time to regrow before they get grazed again, the plants weaken! Their larders get depleted! If the people don't understand this and control their animals, the damage that will be done could easily be misunderstood! And it could possibly even be blamed on the animals, as Khumbula taught us! We Oglins didn't need to know this because our gayla knew and did it for us! We also learned about…" Catching himself, Baylin stopped short and humbly said, "Anyway, go on Uyazi, please," he appealed, as he was suddenly self-conscious after blurting out in the great owl's presence.

His eyes smiling at the young Oglin's enthusiasm, Uyazi continued, "The next tool available for dealing with old plant material, which most people are unaware of, is the tool of animal impact. This occurs when animals are pushed together into a tight bunch so that they trample down the plants and disturb the soil. This automatically helps to address the issue of the barren and bare ground too.

As in the old battends, the vast herds of game and their predators were just doing a-what comes naturally! They were achieving animal impact, just like your gayla do with your herds of bundles and pala."

"Ah!" piped up Lafina. "The people don't make or allow for animal impact to happen, do they? No, they keep their animals spread out, and they keep the numbers too low."

"We saw it once!" Baylin almost shouted. "That man and his sheep dog near the Pinnacles that morning was doing it! He achieved animal impact when the dog drove the sheep past him. Remember? Maybe he knew what he was doing. Maybe we should have talked to him."

"Well done! That's excellent," approved Uyazi. "You are beginning to tie these pieces together and learn your vital lessons! Now…"

Baylin jumped up, unable to contain himself. "This animal impact is the key we have really missed so far! Disturbing soil, and knocking down plants. We have heard it and discovered it so many times, but still haven't really grasped its particular importance!" Baylin stood with hands spread wide in search of words. "The hooves chip the soil surface, which allows the water to enter the soil quicker; it causes the plant seeds to be planted, and tramples the grasses so they are opened to sunlight. We have heard and seen it all. Animal impact has been the key all along!"

Uyazi, looking a lot taller and slimmer as he stretched in surprise at the outburst, now chuckled as he remarked. "My… my…We do have ourselves a bright one, don't we?"

Lafina and Baylin beamed with pride and settled down to listen carefully to the wise old Owl's next lesson. "Now, animal impact that goes on too long in the very same place does not improve the soil surface, though, does it? What happens for example, if a group of animals go every day over the same track?"

"Well, that would create a big path. And if that path was up a hill, it would probably even erode into a donga, as the ground never gets time to heal or grow a cover of grass," Baylin said, airing his thoughts on the question.

"Yes, that is right, of course. So animal impact, if short and intense, is good for the soil and the plants. But if it is repeated too often, without enough recovery time, it can be destructive. Well done indeed!" the owl proclaimed.

"Once again," Lafina interjected, "just like with grazing, it is all about timing! Just think, our gayla do such a wonderful job and manage it all so naturally!"

"Quite right!" continued the owl, regaining his teacherly composure and wanting to go on. "The next tool to change the environment is one that people apply in excess most of the time. It turns out to be a very destructive one when used to excess in certain environments, especially in the drier areas such as you have been travelling through. Could you work out what that is?"

"Well," mused Baylin, "the greatest damage we have seen so far has been caused by not having enough animals to keep the grasslands and the soils healthy. But what kind of tool would that be?" he asked

"Yes, that *is* the tool!" The owl was very pleased with himself and fluffed out his feathers importantly. "It is to let the land rest, in an attempt to heal it. People do this by removing all the disturbance they can. And this can be done to various degrees. They can actually take away all the animals and achieve total rest. Or as they typically do these days, they can partly rest land by just allowing very few animals to spread out over the land. When the soil is rested—either totally or even partly—in environments where it can be very dry for part of the year, it turns out that the plants gradually die and the bare ground spreads over time! I believe you have seen the effects of this on your journey so far?"

"Ah, yes!" exclaimed Baylin. "This was explained to us by Dainty the Duiker and Digger the Dung Beetle. And we had a wonderful time learning how rest affects the plants from Tufty the Talkative Grass Plant!"

"Quite right," Uyazi fixed them each in turn with his penetrating glare to check that they were both concentrating. "So then, what is the last tool for us to look at? What is the tool that the people use excessively these days to try to revitalise the plants that are dying from the effects of the inadvertent overuse of the previous tool of rest?"

"That would be fire, of course!" Lafina exclaimed and smiled broadly as another piece of the puzzle fell into place.

"My, my, my! Well done!" Uyazi praised her. "And the biggest trouble with this tool is that it takes away all the plant cover on the soil surface. The soil is a living thing full of life and activity, a world in itself, and its cover of old plant matter is its skin. Now, what would happen if one of you Oglins or one of your pala was skinned and then left out in the sun and rain?"

The owl waited briefly while he watched the Oglins recoil at the latest graphic description. Not giving them time to answer, he went on as soon as he could see that they were desperate for more. "Yes, a horrible image, isn't it? They would die, of course! Well, that is exactly what happens to the soil, too. Much of the soil's life dies when it dries up. And it's made even worse when the ground is bare and the soil's life has no plants insulating and protecting it from the heat of the sun or the freezing temperatures on cold nights! Of course, the intensity and frequency of the fire makes a difference. The hotter and more frequent the fire is, the less soil life can survive and the worse the situation. Anyway, you know all about that from Dainty and Digger and Tufty."

"Yes, and the veld becomes all tough, and spiky too, as the plant mix changes to one that is adapted to fire. Tufty explained that to us. And Khumbula complained about it as well, as it is so difficult for the elephants to find tasty grass to eat anymore," Lafina added, remembering the orphan elephant's dilemma.

"Indeed!" agreed Uyazi. "People are changing their environment all around them nowadays. They are applying these tools all the time in various ways and much of the time without even realising it! But one day people will obviously learn," the owl said hopefully. "They've learned before about things. They have learned a lot of things! Maybe one day they will come to understand all of these tools that they have at their disposal. And maybe they will learn how to use them to live in harmony with all of nature and to create the kind of future that they want."

"Yes," said Baylin, nodding, "We've learned along this journey that whenever we plan to do something, we must always check whether it is likely to create the future we must have as described in our creed. Now that we understand what the tools are, we will be much more likely to answer this question sensibly!"

Suddenly the stillness of the afternoon was shattered by a raucous noise of a go-away bird, loudly warning all to "gowaaay, gowaaay" in his nasal voice.

The owl immediately shut his eyes and hissed a hushed warning for silence. The go-away bird was seldom wrong. In fact, it always alerted the animals to the presence of a hunter.

The Oglins instinctively crouched down to hide themselves and wondered where their grazing pala had got to. They were nowhere to be seen, but as creatures of the bush, they too would know the meaning of the go-away bird's alarm and hide themselves well.

Soon the sound of loud chattering voices filled the air as a group of people dressed in bright, garish colours made their way past, following a khaki-clad guide. The Oglins watched and listened with interest.

As soon as they had passed, the old owl remarked irritably, "Tourists! They come from all over the place to see these ruins. They haven't noticed us, however, so we can carry on. Where were we, now?"

"Oh, Great Uyazi, it seems that knowing the tools will only take us half the way home. We also need to have a better understanding of the effects they have. We have passed through a number of environments on our way here and I wonder if the tools don't behave differently, depending on where you are?" Lafina asked, voicing her new concern as if there had been no interruption at all.

"Yes, indeed," the handsome old owl agreed with a blink of his pink eyelids. "It would be very wise for you to learn about that. So let's explore the question of different environments. Have you not travelled from Vadiera through a dense, moist forest? And then over the mountains and on to the Great Plains of the Karoo where it was dry and there were vast stretches of bare ground?"

"Yes, we did. That was our route," answered Lafina.

"Well, then, think back to the deep forest. What was the vegetation like? Did you see any old plant material that wasn't rotting?" asked the owl.

"Everything was rotting!" Lafina said. "There was a lovely, heavy smell of wet, damp rotting leaves and plants, everywhere, all the time."

"That's right!" affirmed Uyazi. "That is how it works in the wet forests. When plants die, they fall down because they simply rot off at the base in those wet spongy soils. The bugs, beetles, fungi and every little living thing will break down the remains of all the dead stuff throughout the year. It's warm, humid and very moist in there and it's teeming with life! Did you feel it?"

"Oh yes, we felt that!" Baylin agreed, remembering his comfortable nap one afternoon on the soft, spongy bed of moss under the big tree. Laughing, he said, "I was worried that if I laid still and slept too long, I would be eaten alive!"

Just then the go-away bird flew in and landed in the tree not far from the owl. The new arrival looked down at them out of one dark eye then the other and stretched his grey crest forward like a cockatoo. He then strutted along the branch a little way and wiped his beak with a raised foot, while still eyeing the group.

"So the Oglins are here already! And nobody even let me know. Well, at least I kept the tourists amused so they didn't see you. Gowaay! Gowaay!" the bird cried again with another long look down his beak and a stretch of his crest.

"Do sit still now, you clown," admonished the owl. Then remembering his manners, he introduced the intruder, "By the way, this is Gwaii, the go-away bird. He could possibly be of use to us, although I have no idea how!" the owl added haughtily.

"Let me see now," Uyazi carried right on. "Ah yes, well then, when you Oglins went into drier regions, it was very different, wasn't it? Could you find any old plant material there? Was any of it rotting?"

"Since we left the forest, we have seen lots of old plant material," replied Lafina obligingly, too absorbed to remember to greet the go-away bird. "But most of it was dry and turning grey. It looked like it had probably been there for a long time. It certainly wasn't rotting!"

"Quite right! Let me explain why," the old owl prepared them. "When you are out in these drier areas, you will see that there is either very little humidity, or at least any humidity is occasional, or it may just be seasonal. During those few and far between humid times, there is a great rush for all the plants to grow new growth while they have the moisture to do so. Likewise, there are lots and lots of bugs and organisms that burst into action too, working to break down the plant material into the soil.

"Then in every dry season, those massive amounts of plants die off, above ground at least. And at the same time, when it is dry, there is very little insect or other life available to rot or break down plant materials. Everything goes dormant because of either the cold or the dry or both. As you know, old plant material that is not removed at some stage, just stands around and smothers out any new growth from underneath. When there are enough grazing animals however, they will eat the dry grass and it then 'rots' in the moist environments of their stomachs! This helps recycle all the dormant plants back into the soil and the grazing opens the plants to the sunlight."

"The animal's stomach is like the forest on four legs, it seems," mused Baylin. "Both places are humid and warm all year, so that bugs can get on with their work!"

"Gowaaay, gowaay! That's very good!" applauded Gwaii.

"So Lafina's question now has the beginnings of an answer," declared Uyazi, looking a little annoyed at the bird's unruly outburst. "Tools will cause very different results in varying environments. For example, the tool of rest, in particular, causes opposite effects. In places where humidity and moisture are only seasonal with totally dry times in between, the tool of rest can actually cause plants to die eventually, if used to excess. The opposite occurs in places that are wet and humid all the time; rest allows for all kinds of abundant growth there. We need to then have a simple term to describe these environmental extremes. Thus, the desert between the Green and the Sand Rivers can be described as 'brittle.' At the other extreme, is the forest outside Vadiera, which is always humid; it can be called 'non-brittle.'"

"Let me round this off in a different waaay," interrupted the go-away bird, contributing his first valuable input. "As the owl noted, the tool of rest has a completely different effect depending upon the environment. It can help encourage great diversity and health in the humid, non-brittle environments, but in drier, more brittle tending environments it will tend to result in ever more bare ground.

"Coming through the forest outside of Vadiera, you wouldn't have seen any bare ground, and all the stream banks were healthy and stable. The tool of rest is in application on a broad scale there, with very few animals around. Yet just across the mountains, where the same tool is basically applied, there are likewise very few animals around and the result is nothing but wide spread bare ground!

"To move and change and shift a brittle type of environment to a healthy and a balanced community of many different species of plants, insects and animals can be difficult to achieve and can take a lot of time. Rest is not going to achieve this on any daaay!" The go-away bird slowed down again, realising that the audience was hanging on his every word.

"However, the tools of animal impact and grazing can be used to encourage and maintain health and promote greater diversity of species. This occurs through covering soils and creating the conditions that are right for additional life to get going." The grey go-away bird now proudly strutted up and down the branch a few times. Then, using his beak, he pulled himself over onto a higher branch, obviously feeling very pleased with himself.

"This may seem a little too much to take in all at once. But don't let that worry you," Uyazi inserted, reassuring the Oglins and taking control of the conversation once more. "You are being exposed to this in many ways as you travel along. You will gain deeper understanding over time. The critical things to remember for now are what the tools are and that they will have different effects depending upon how humid the environment is."

"We've already learned where to use this information!" Lafina interjected. "We learned from Thutha the Tortoise that whenever we do something, we must check that it leads towards how the future must be, as described in our creed. Now that we understand the tools, we must always bear in mind how brittle the environment is and what effect the tool will have on it!"

"That's quite right, my dear," Uyazi agreed, smiling warmly at Lafina. "That's very clever indeed. And did the tortoise not take that a step further for you?"

"Yes, he did," replied Baylin. "As soon as we have done anything, we must of course keep an eye on whether it is actually having the effect we think it will. We must assume that we may well be wrong, and keep a close eye out for the earliest signs of that, so we can make adjustments right away!"

"Yes, right again," Uyazi praised. "This may be one of the most important things you learn! I see that the Great Spirit has chosen very well. I have no doubt that the knowledge you are gaining is key to the whole process. There is no one else on Earth that has yet gained all the understanding that you two are acquiring!"

Baylin and Lafina shyly smiled and shuffled their feet a bit awkwardly, humbled by the importance of their task, yet pleased by the great owl's compliment.

"My dear Oglins, it has been lovely chatting with you both," concluded the grand old owl. "Now as the sun lowers in the sky and darkness comes, it's my time to get on the wing and go off to hunt for my dinner! A large owl like me needs a lot of food each night, you know."

"Oops, late for family, late for family, I must Gowaay! Gowaay!" squawked Gwaii as he glided off the perch and flapped and swooped his way home without any formal farewell whatsoever.

"Look at that! Shouldn't even be allowed to fly!" muttered the old Owl disdainfully, not very impressed with the noisy bird's disorganised flying style.

"Farewell, then," said the great owl, regaining his composure as he fluttered his wings and prepared to fly away. "For the future of us all, I hope that you young Oglins are successful in your quest. Please take my greetings to the Great Spirit!"

"Oh, thank you, Great Uyazi!" Baylin and Lafina cried in unison.

"We will always remember the things you have taught us today," declared Lafina, the appreciation very apparent in her voice.

The great owl then gracefully dived forward off the branch, spread his mighty wings and swooped up and away in typical owl fashion, hardly even having to flap his wings at all. He was master of the night sky and needed only occasional little movements from his wings as he soared effortlessly into the deepening twilight. His eyes were wide open now in the dusky light as he set about patrolling his domain, with his treacherous talons pulled up into his underbelly until needed. In the distance, Baylin and Lafina could hear his mate calling to him with a deep, grunting groan, "Whoo, Whooo, Whoooo."

The Oglins, suddenly aware of how late it had gotten, set off to find themselves a safe resting spot for the night. They called up their pala, who had relished the chance to graze while the Oglins conversed with the owl. Together they all walked out among the beautiful kopjies to find something resembling a warren to sleep in, being very wary of course, to not choose a leopard's warren.

They clambered up over some rocks to get a better view. In the half-light of the evening, standing high and proud on one of the great lichen-covered rocks was a klipspringer! He stood motionless, like a statue or sentinel, above them. He perched on his tiptoes as they always do, with his legs stiff and straight. The buck stood utterly still, as if he thought he was a rock, as klipspringers are sometimes wont to do. Only his black nose twitched occasionally, to gather the unseen messages on the scent in the air. He was obviously keeping a careful eye out for a leopard on the prowl!

The Oglins knew that the klipspringer would let them know if a predator was about. They felt that it was watching over them, even though it did not acknowledge them in the slightest.

Finding a cosy little warren just nearby under an overhanging cliff to build a nest for the night, Baylin and Lafina snuggled down together and called the pala in close to share their warmth.

Holding their pachas and precious amulets in their hands, Baylin and Lafina smiled at one another. Touching each amulet in the pacha was a special way of staying in contact with loved ones at home. They all fell into a deep sleep, knowing that however difficult or dangerous their journey was, the Great Spirit was keeping watch over them.

They had added the following to their poem:

Uyazi told the tragic tale
of an ancient city whose land gave way.
Abandoned still, it sadly warns
of people's lives gone far astray.
It's also clear that such demise
is just as great a risk today!

So many people suffer still
from the lack of simple keys.
With these we come to know
that land can change more as we please.
We learned of all the many tools
to make the changes that we need!

217

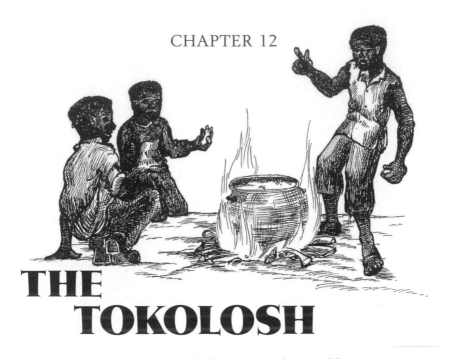

CHAPTER 12

THE TOKOLOSH

It is your mind that creates this world.

—The Buddha

By the Light of the Moon

The two young Oglins were riding at night, taking advantage of the bright moon. They had decided to start riding in the coolness of the evening while the moon was coming up to full and very early in the mornings for the first few days of the moon's waning. This way they could avoid travelling in the intense heat of the day. In any case, it was almost impossible to sleep at night because of the incessant mosquitoes worrying away at them. Sleeping just meant that their eyelids got stung so badly by the mosquitoes that the next morning they would hardly be able to open them up.

It was so much easier to just keep riding into the night and switching away at themselves with a small branch of a tree or a pala tail whisk. At least they could rest up during the day in the shade of a tree and not be worried by the mosi's. So the two Oglins wandered on by the light of the moon.

While making their way through the bush, they both began to notice a distinct smell in the air. It was the smell of a fire with something being cooked on it! It was accompanied by the slow, slightly musical sound of people talking around a campfire. The two Oglins whispered to one another, wondering whether they shouldn't go and have a peek to see what was going on.

As is often the case with Oglins, their curiosity prevailed. They dismounted some distance off and left the pala to rest and graze while they snuck slowly towards the sounds and the smell of the fire. They stalked silently in on their bare but furry little feet, over twigs, branches and dried leaves, and not a sound could be heard. Their little hairy feet were as quiet as an elephant's.

Baylin and Lafina carefully made their way closer, right close up on each other's shoulders so that the sound of their breath was the loudest thing they could hear. They moved in under the hanging branches of a tree, just behind the fire and the people. Ever so carefully with one hand, Baylin gently parted the thorny branches and there in front of them, on a sand bar on the edge of the river was a small band of black-skinned men, huddled around a fire.

Their black faces shone in the firelight as they listened, enraptured, to one man who was telling a lively story with great animation. His one arm was going in every direction, pointing and waving to make a point, then gracefully, seemingly without interruption, swishing and swatting at the mosi's buzzing around his ears in a thick swarm. His other arm, behaving much like an elephant's trunk, would occasionally reach forward smoothly and dip into the cooking pot and come up with a handful of white, sticky food. Squeezing it into a ball and with very graceful movements of the hand turning in different directions, he would stuff it into his mouth mid-sentence and keep talking over and around it without even batting an eye. The story continued, unabated.

All the rapt listeners also leaned forward occasionally, stuck a hand into the pot and dug some food out. They too would squeeze it into a ball, toss it into their mouths and loudly, open-mouthed, chew it with smacking of lips and an occasional wipe across their mouths with the back of the hand.

Every now and again one of them would add emphasis to the story or express their amazement with a "GEE!" or a "HOWU!" And every now and again one of the listeners would slap his thigh and then all together they would roar with laughter, giggling, loving it. Then one or two of them would add a few words in delight. Sometimes this would cause more laughter or someone would roll his eyes back in his head, until just the whites were showing.

Baylin and Lafina looked at one another in wide-eyed realisation. Lafina leaned over and whispered in Baylin's ear, "They're telling battends! People tell battends just the same as we do!"

Just as she finished speaking, one of the shiny black faces suddenly went still, his hand stopped in mid-reach, halfway to the pot, and he cocked his head to listen. The feeling spread to those on either side of him. Total and sudden silence descended upon the whole group. They were all listening intently. Nothing happened. Just silence. Even the crickets had stopped chirping.

After a few moments, the man that originally heard something murmured a few words quietly to the man next to him. His whispers were eaten up by the night and were followed by utter silence.

The teller of the battends was gradually getting impatient. He was all filled up with the courage and conviction of his story. His battends was obviously at a high point, and he really wanted to continue. Finally, he waved his hands all around and with much clucking and telling everybody that there certainly was no problem, he launched back into his story where he had left off.

One by one, the listeners began to unstiffen, listening to the story, except for the one who had originally heard something. He didn't seem to want to relax at all. He was listening with only half an ear, and his eyes were darting around furtively like rolling marbles, whitely reflecting the moon, in a glistening black background. Every now and again his face would light up at the words of the battends teller, but quickly the smile would disappear again and he would cock his ear a little bit more towards the bush.

Baylin and Lafina, sitting in the bush, nudged one another once again, and just by the merest of eye contact and movement of the eyebrows, asked each other, "Should we talk to them?" A shrug of a shoulder, a question, a look at one another and then a naughty little grin came across both their faces, and a little nod. Sure enough, they decided that it was time for the Oglins to talk to the people!

A Voice from the Bush

With great care, Baylin threw his voice so that it seemed to come from the opposite side of the fire. All Oglins learn how to do this when they are little. It is part of their early ability to tell battends. This is especially useful when narrating a conversation.

"Hello! Hello you people!" Baylin greeted them, "I've come to speak with you!" His voice came in out of the darkness, seemingly from behind the trees on the other side of the riverbed.

An instant hush fell over the group of men. Two of them looked about to bolt. The others were hunkered down on a ready-to-take-off basis, but were unsure of which direction to escape.

In the silence, the one who was obviously the leader of the group reached out, grabbed another's shoulder, and tried to hold the men in place. There was deathly silence within the group. The crickets had even stopped chirping again! There was no sound in the bush, something rare in the African night!

After a moment, a little animated whispering began. The men tentatively asked each other: "What? Why? Who?" Should they actually answer this eerie voice? Who was it? What was it? The leader reached down and lifted up a knobkerrie, a short stick with a heavy knob on the end used for fighting. He lifted it up close to his body and then replied with at least the appearance of bravery, "Who-is-it? What-do-you-want?"

Even though they were talking different languages, they were now actually able to understand each other! Perhaps it was part of the gift of the Great Spirit, just as they could talk with the animals, now they were able to understand the language of people.

Baylin took up the cue. "There is no need to worry! No need for you to be afraid," he spoke gently, trying to reassure them. "We're just a pair of small Oglins that wish to sit and talk with you around the fire for a while. Would you be so kind as to pass the evening with us? We are weary of travelling."

While Baylin was offering friendship, he still cautiously threw his voice to come from the opposite side of the fire. In response, the leader of the small band of men stood up to his full height. He was an impressive man, tall and muscular. His dirty white shirt was torn, hanging in shreds and cut off raggedly at the shoulders. His dark trousers stopped below his knees, showing lighter brown skin on the way down to his big, flat feet in simple car-tire sandals. Yet his shabby attire in no way diminished his stature and leadership. His skin was dark and gleaming with sweat. The whites of his eyes and his teeth were shining white in the firelight. His stance surreptitiously widened slightly in readiness for a fight, while his band of followers all secretively pulled weapons closer. Facing the source of the voice in the bush, they waited tensely for the Oglins to appear.

Of course, the Oglins didn't emerge from where the voice had come from. They silently entered the circle of men from the opposite side. Bravely they stepped forward into the light of the fire. One of the hunkered-down men, not expecting it at all, saw them step in from the other side and shouted a warning. The big fellow, surprisingly agile, leaped into the air, doing a twisting turn to face the Oglins, and landed with a "shheeuu" sound as the air was expelled from his lungs. Both his feet planted firmly down on the ground with a thud, his knobkerrie out and ready to fight.

The rest of the gang rolled and shuffled to the other side of the fire. The full flickering orange glow of the fire joined the light of the moon to illuminate the two little Oglins, standing side by side with their backs up against the bush. Upon seeing the source of the voice, the mood of the men immediately shifted. Baylin could detect a very faint quivering on the lips of the leader and one or two of the others looking at one another.

"Tokolosh!" cried the leader, his eyes wide with fear and questioning.

Then there were whispers among the men again while their nervousness grew. The sweat ran down the face of the leader, even as he stood boldly confronting the intruding Oglins.

Baylin, using his own voice this time said, "Please, do not fear us. There is nothing to be afraid of! We are no threat to you! Please, relax and sit down. We are simply passing by and want to share your fire and speak with you."

The two little Oglins then stepped forward and quietly squatted down on the ground in front of the fire. The tall man was now towering way above them. He could easily have delivered fatal blows to both of their heads, with his knobkerrie, before either of them could move. Yet the traditional African way paid off. Show no fear and, much the same as animals will do, take up a vulnerable position. This gesture of submission broke the tension to some extent. Slowly the man's big muscles relaxed a bit. Then as one, the gibbering began. All ten people were asking questions at once.

Baylin raised one furry little hand and silence descended once again. "I can only understand if one of you speaks at a time!"

Immediately another burst of voices erupted from all ten people.

Baylin's hand opened again. With an embarrassed shuffling of feet under the men's haunches, they gradually settled down a bit and spread themselves out around the fire. Even so, they kept well away from their guests! Finally, the leader spoke to the oldest of the men, suggesting that he be the one to speak. Slowly, mouthing the words very clearly, the fellow tentatively asked the two Oglins, "Are you the Tokolosh?"

"I believe that's what you people call us," replied Baylin carefully. "We call ourselves Oglins, not Tokolosh. But yes, I believe that's what you know us as."

"So you are the Tokolosh," the man said in amazement. "Why do you come to speak to us? Have we done something to anger you? Have we done something to disturb you?"

"Oh no," replied Baylin. "We are making a Great Journey from way in the south to see our Great Spirits in the Great Forest. We saw you here and thought it would be nice to sit and talk to you for a little while."

"I see! Well, it's not common for the Tokolosh to speak to our people," the man said.

"No, I suppose it's not," agreed Baylin, "But it is not common for us to be travelling, either. Perhaps it is because people are afraid of us we don't get to speak to one another! Normally we wouldn't have even got near you. If it wasn't for the fact that it is night and you are in a strange place, you would have all just run away."

"Yes, we are terrified of the Tokolosh!"

"But why do you fear the Tokolosh?" Lafina asked.

"It's because the Tokolosh live in the world of the spirits," the spokesman explained. "And it is not good for a person to see into that world. If a person does, it means that he will be leaving to go and join the spirits soon."

With that reminder, there was an indrawn breath around the whole group of men, as they realised that this may well be the last thing that they would do in this life before they themselves were called into the spirit world! In fact, they wondered if perhaps they had already moved into the spirit world, for how else could they be talking to the beings they called the Tokolosh? Their eyes began to shift around, as the men tried to reassure themselves that they were still at their own fire and that the cooking pot in front of them was definitely the cooking pot that they had eaten out of earlier. Gradually assured of this, they relaxed slightly again. The men glanced cautiously around at one another. The tension had eased for the moment and they realised that these little beings seemed to not pose much of a threat.

After a moment's pause, Lafina piped up with a question. "What are those? Are they totems?" she asked them, pointing at piles of beautifully carved animals that the men had obviously been carrying. There were bundles of wooden giraffe, hippos, rhino and other animals piled around the men.

"No, we make them from the trees around here and take them into the centres or to the roadsides for sale," the man answered.

"Who buys them?" Lafina continued her line of questioning.

"Tourists," he endeavoured to explain. "You see, people come here from all over the world to visit our land and to see our animals and rivers. They like to take something back to remind them of this place and so they buy these statues."

"Is that why so many of these big and beautiful trees have been chopped down?" Lafina asked in dismay. "I see them with the smaller branches scattered around them, so I was sure they were not taken for firewood."

"Yes, that's where they come from," the man answered. "We use the trees to make these so we can get money to feed ourselves and our families."

"But doesn't it worry you that there will one day be no trees like these left around you?" Lafina asked with concern.

Baylin then realised what she was really asking: "Did they have a creed or any thoughts or hopes that they were striving for in the long term?"

The leader of the group of men, a bit embarrassed, looked down. He was sitting on his haunches, his feet flat on the ground. He shuffled his feet a little from side to side and moved his weight from one side to the other. He was obviously thinking, and finally replied, "You don't understand, for you clearly live in a land of plenty. We live in a land of great scarcity. I have a family that I must feed. I have a small following, as a chief's son, that have to get food and be looked after. I have a very small patch of land off which to live. My land is weak. It no longer produces the crops it used to. The rain doesn't rain like it used to. I cannot be thinking about tomorrow. Today I am hungry! Today my family, my people are hungry!"

Comprehending at last, the Oglins snuck a look at one another. Without a word, they both realised that in fact the rainfall was unlikely to be what had changed, but more likely, the effectiveness of the rainfall would well be reduced as the land had declined. Many other things were changing as well, and that was the purpose of their journey, after all.

"You mean," said Baylin warming to the man, "that your rain doesn't work as well as it used to, rather than that there is less rain?"

The man simply shrugged his shoulders and muttered, "Maybe..." as an answer. "Either way, we can't grow the crops we used to. We are hungry!" he said, rubbing his stomach. "Today we must survive!"

"Once upon a time there was plenty," he continued. "The crops grew tall and the rains fell widely. The animals and the cattle were fat and we lived here in great health. The children grew fat and tall and strong. Now our children don't get enough food. They have big bellies and runny noses and the flies worry them all the time. In the old days, many of our children died of sickness and diseases, or wild animals and snakes killed them. Today many more of these children survive because of the medicine. So I have to feed them! I must feed them!" He made his point and gained emphasis with a *"gee"* from his nodding mates.

Leaning forward, the two little Oglins peered into the pot of food. They saw how much was wasted and burnt, stuck to the sides of the pot. Their eyes were also drawn to the little wasted piles of it on the ground, dropped when the hurried hands had been grabbing at it and stuffing it into busy mouths earlier on, with not a care in the world. Yet these people were saying they were hungry and didn't have enough food to feed themselves and their families.

Another knowing look passed between them, as they both remembered the gentle Bushmen and the learning they gained from those wizened-up old survivors of the desert. They did not waste even one drop of water! It was no wonder that the Bushmen had survived from long ago times, right through to now. Sadly, the Oglins suspected that these people didn't seem to be set for lasting very long at the rate they were going.

"So," continued the chief's son, "that's the reason why we chop down the trees and carve them into ornaments and totems that we then sell to the foreign people. They take them away also knowing that there probably won't be any more big trees in the future. We all know that the trees won't last long. For us, life is now. We must live for *now!*"

Once again, the two Oglins looked at one another and raised their eyebrows, ever so slightly. They were coming to know one another quite well now, and Lafina's slightest movements, barely discernible to someone else, were as words to Baylin.

"There is a time and a place for everything." Baylin began, trying to convey deeper meanings to Lafina at the same time. "Your current situation will dictate what you are currently capable of doing. You cannot leave a bird's egg, even if it is the last of its kind in the world, if it means you must die of hunger, for example. What you think, what you are willing to consider and, more importantly, are able to hear or understand really depends on where you are, what your past experience is, what your situation is and what you perceive the future to be. This conditioning through life makes you blind to other possibilities or points of view. You may even think you do understand and agree when actually you don't.

"I think this is quite normal," Baylin continued, while turning towards Lafina to let her know the rest was really meant for her. "I also think that this means you have to be ready to truly hear something different to your current mindset or pattern. So it does little good to even be exposed to something truly different until you are ready for it, as you will not recognise it for what it is. Also, the revelation of the new must be done practically and thoroughly the first time or it loses its strength to truly show the difference and be really recognised as such."

Lafina caught on and realised that Baylin was really saying: "We are not really ready to teach someone about any of this. At least not until we have the full picture ourselves, anyway. Besides, they are so caught up with their thought pattern of cause and effect in their situation that they probably would not hear the meanings in our words."

She took up her cue and said. "Well, our new friends, you have so much to do and we have a long way to go. So I think we should be moving on. Thank you for your time and hospitality."

The farewells did take a bit longer but the Oglins were soon able to disappear into the darkness again. It took a little while for their eyes to adjust after being around the fire and to rediscover the brightness of the moonlight. Silent and slightly despondent, they moved on in an introspective mood.

They had just learned that anything judges everything by its own reality. In other words, experiences condition one's individual beliefs and all judgements are made on these beliefs. Further, these judgements are made from one's own point of view and in one's own self-interest. This was a sudden, harsh insight, that perhaps after gaining all the knowledge laid out for them on their travels they would only then come up against their greatest obstacle: the mindsets and patterns of thinking and therefore the beliefs that Oglins themselves, people, and others live by. The seriousness of this realisation weighed heavily upon their minds as they mounted their pala and set out once more on their quest.

THE TOKOLOSH

That evening they tried to capture what they had learned in verse:

Gathered around a fire circle
we did spy of a moonlit night
a group of men telling their battends
and sharing the fire's warmth and light.
So mustering our courage then,
from the darkness we spoke outright!

As people, they thought us Tok'losh
and frightening spirits for to fear.
Yet as we saw and learned that night,
we are not the danger here.
Rather, it is their own reality
and beliefs that they must clear!

CHAPTER 13

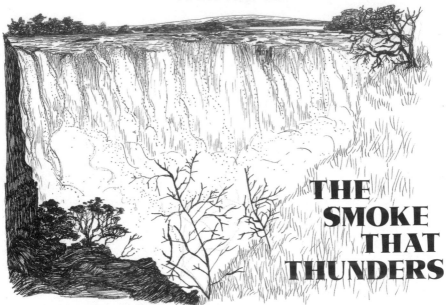

THE SMOKE THAT THUNDERS

From Beautiful images we shall go to Beautiful thoughts,
from Beautiful thoughts to a Beautiful life,
and from a Beautiful life to absolute Beauty.

—Plato

The Approach

Continuing north, the Oglins found themselves travelling through a dry forest. They had reached the huge teak forests that stood on the soft northern Kalahari sand. Here they had to carefully remember the guiding words of the Wedrelas and Old Spola. They knew they had to keep to the yesterdays side of the teak forests. If they let themselves get too far off towards the tomorrows they would come upon the Great Thundering River where it ran through a deep and twisted gorge. This was downstream from where the great river dropped into the massive chasm, forming the cloud of rising mist that gave it the name: the "Smoke that Thunders," the greatest waterfall on the entire continent.

The Oglins knew they had to find a crossing upriver of the thundering falls. They had been warned that to try to cross through the deep valley downstream of the steep gorge would be a horrible trek. The air there was very, very heavy and hot, there were lots of tsetse fly and it was generally very uncomfortable. Besides, it would be a very long way to the first place where they could even think about crossing. So it would be much, much better for them to stay up above the thundering smoke and find a way to cross over among the rocky areas above the falls, where it would be at least relatively easier for them. Little did they yet know how wide the great river was and how immense the challenge that awaited them in trying to get to the other side!

The teak forest seemed to stretch on infinitely for them. Each step, each view seemed to be the same as the previous one. The teak trees were tall with splotchy grey bark and soft hanging green leaves in these summer months and their greyish-brown seedpods hung down and rattled incessantly in the breeze. The lovely dappled shade the trees created on the ground below was the easiest way to keep track of the sun's journey overhead. By this they navigated. In the endlessness of the forest itself, direction could become a mystery. One could so easily end up simply walking in circles, as so many battends tell of unwary travellers.

Reaching the top of a ridge, Baylin and Lafina decided to climb up one of the lovely big trees to get a better view of the surrounding countryside. From the treetop, looking in every direction, they saw a vast sea of green-blue teak, as far as they could see. Yet there, just to the north, rising up into the pale blue sky was a plume of smoke coming out of the valley below.

"That must be the Smoke that Thunders!" exclaimed Lafina with the most excitement she had felt in many a day.

They knew that the plume of "smoke" had to be the spray rising from the great and legendary falls on the Thundering River. They eagerly recalled the battends told by Old Spola about the huge chasm that swallowed the great river in a roaring spray. He had said that one could crawl up to the edge of the falls and look down into the very belly of the Earth.

With renewed energy they rode down towards the river and tried to recall all of the minute details of Spola's battends about the falls.

Old Spola had said, "When you get in close, in the thick mist, you must walk very carefully because the next thing you know, there will just be a huge chasm that opens up underneath you! You must be very careful, because the rocks will be very slippery."

Even so many years after his journey there, Old Spola waxed eloquent about the awe-inspiring beauty, so powerful and intense and yet so serene and soothing. He was so moved by his long

ago visit that Spola had called it "a place where the soul can roar and rise on the wing in freedom, just like the water rising out of the cauldron after tumbling down the falls, set free momentarily from the gripping bonds of gravity."

234

With an enthusiasm that he rarely expressed, Old Spola had gone on to say, "You could spend hours there, just watching the water, the mists, the beauty…" He had drifted off into a smiling reverie as he was transported in memory back to that place and time.

Understandably, the young Oglins were very excited to see this great wonder for themselves. As they moved in toward the smoke sentinel, they noticed the incessant din of a flying machine clattering around up above it, circling and circling and circling. Every time one machine went away, it seemed to be quickly replaced by yet another one. The buzzing machines came back again and again, turning a few times this way and then a few times that way and then going away, only to return again just a short while later. This worried the young Oglins, especially after the experience with the elephants. There were the occasional elephants around them now, too, in the bush they were walking through. Instead of a group of young orphans though, these were dear, lonely old bull elephants, all on their own, grazing peacefully or sleeping, with two feet resting, under a tree.

As they moved in closer to the river, Baylin and Lafina came upon more and more signs of civilisation, dwellings, highways and noisy flying machines. It was all just too much for them, so they decided to retreat to a safe place to rest up a little while, wait for darkness and see what happened, rather than take any risks.

Mist in the Moonlight

As evening came, the settlement's noises began to quieten down. Finally late in the night, it became quite still. The moon was about three days before full, still high in the sky, and the Oglins realised that it was bright enough to light up the falls. They decided to take a chance and go to see the Smoke that Thunders in the quiet of the night, with the shining moon. They were disappointed that they wouldn't get to see it in the day, with all the rainbows in the mist as Old Spola described it, but clearly things had changed dramatically in the area since then! Not willing to risk taking their pala through the settlement, they left them safely hidden in the teak forest.

Baylin and Lafina approached the falls from up river. Just like the water flowing down the river, they still had no idea of the magnitude of depth and power they were yet to experience. As they drew nearer, the spray steaming high into the air above them and the intensifying roar that filled their ears was a contrast to the water that seemed calm and serene as it slipped to its awaiting fate. Still deep green, the water formed into an inverted V, sliding away between moonlit silver and white, as the river was forced together before it fell out into nothing. Encircled by an eerie lunar rainbow, the moon shone through the spray above and draped the whole scene in a surreal white light. The wind, whipped up by the falling water, lashed the palms and trees into a shaking rustle. The Oglins stood and watched in silent awe as the water rushed to its inevitable rendezvous with air, gravity and rock.

"As irrevocable as the endless, unstoppable march of time," murmured Baylin, waxing poetic.

No amount of vivid imagining or eloquent battends could have prepared them for the moving experience of the falls. They stood close together, smitten, quietly soaking up the splendour of the scene. Their emotions stirred and roamed from introspective to free and expansive, as they were filled with reverence for this great wonder of the Earth.

In places there was simply no view at all, just clouds of impenetrable mist and pouring rain. Then magically, occasionally the rain would drift away on the wind, opening up the spectacle momentarily. Baylin and Lafina would catch a glimpse of a curtain of water, gracefully, ever so slowly it seemed, streaking towards the churning white turmoil below. The moon behind the Oglins lit up the falling water fraying into mist on the edges and roaring in anger as it tumbled into the furious confusion at the bottom. As if seeking escape from the canyon in a vain attempt to get back up to its higher level, the river seemed to leap back into the air, creating the plume of white that rose high over the falls. Eventually losing the age-old battle with gravity, the water droplets fell back to Earth as rain.

Gradually Baylin and Lafina had crept around the cliff opposite the falls, from viewpoint to viewpoint, following all the paths to each little overlook and each new vista. Knowing this was likely to be the only time they would ever visit this enchanting place, the two young Oglins drank in every moment. They spent all the night's hours wandering and wondering and getting thoroughly soaked in the process. In fact, it was a delightful contrast to the dry land they had been crossing for so long.

Later still, when the moon was eventually straight overhead, it allowed them to peer right down into the boiling cauldron and behold the wildness of the gorge and its towering cliffs.

As they wandered out to the end of the paths on the edge of the gorge, they came upon yet another wonder, a fantastic bridge spanning the chasm! The Oglins could not help but to marvel at the bridge. A monument to people's technology and power, the bridge stretched calmly over the troubled water far below in the steep-sided gorge. It looked utterly perfect in shape and style and was certainly positioned in the most amazing of places.

"People have so much ability!" Baylin exclaimed. "That is obvious. If only they would use it for good means!" Both Oglins realised that they had better be careful not to judge people too quickly. Perhaps there was just as much to admire about them as there was to be concerned about! This realisation was yet another gift of the magical falls.

The Oglins were reluctant to leave the wondrous realm, even as the first light of dawn appeared towards the tomorrows. If they knew what lay in store for them in their attempt to cross the massive river on the morrow, they would have looked upon that bridge with longing. If it were possible to simply lead their pala across, it would have saved them troubles they could not yet imagine! They remembered their visit with a verse:

> *We found the peak of beauty true,*
> *were smitten to the heart of all,*
> *by the mighty Smoke that Thunders*
> *where the mists cloud up so tall.*
> *Silent river roars to grav'ty*
> *to make Earth's finest waterfall.*

Baobabs and Baboons

After their enchanting exploration of the falls, the Oglins made their way back to the forest and their pala before the people were stirring. They managed to get a short, albeit damp, sleep and then headed out to skirt around the heavily inhabited areas. Drawing upon Old Spola's remembered guidance, Baylin and Lafina found their way to the riverbank quite a good distance upstream of the falls. They literally gasped when at last they saw the enormousness and breadth of the Great Thundering River. They had only been able to see it in sections the night before, between islands and clearings in the mists and rain. In the clear light of the day and with a full view, the river looked truly immense! They both swallowed hard at the mere prospect of trying to cross it themselves, let alone with their pala! Determinedly, they continued to make their way up river as Old Spola had advised them.

"When you get to the river," Spola had directed, "head towards the yesterdays, make your way up the river. As you go along, you'll find that there is very smooth water at first, very broad and very deep, and very difficult to cross, unless you make yourselves a raft. There are two dangers with that option, you can drift too far and go over the falls, and there are some pretty angry hippos in that water, some very angry hippos!" he chuckled. "So you'll be better off to keep on towards the yesterdays to where you reach the rapids. At least there you can go across some rocks for part of the way. And the hippos are less likely to

tarry around the faster rapids. Crocodiles, now, they can be found just about anywhere in that river. So beware! And whatever you do, my dear, dear ones, never, oh never, trust a crocodile!"

239

Spola had cautioned them quite severely, and with good cause. Just the memory of Spola's forewarning sent a shiver up Lafina's spine. She knew she could not let that stop her!

"We scouted the area quite a bit to find any sort of way across the river," Spola had told them. "You must keep going until you get to two massive baobab trees growing right next to one another. In fact, their topmost branches almost touch.

"When you get past those two baobabs, you follow along the closest little stream towards the river. This will lead you to a place where you at least have a chance to get across. You'll have to walk, clamber, and hop from rock to rock most of the way. But beware! Don't think you are across the river when you move from one bank to another, you may well find yourself on an island! At one stage, you may even need to dive into the river itself. If you do, be sure to start high up in the rapids," Old Spola had told them. "The rest of it you should be able to hop from rock to rock and get across the river without too much trouble. It's just that one patch where it is really deep that you have to swim. You have to go way upstream, further than you think, dive in and swim hard and you'll get across that little section. When you think you've gone far enough upstream, go the same distance again. That is much safer than misjudging the speed of the water."

With these ominous warnings in mind, the Oglins rode upriver through the bush. They could not help but notice that once again most of the ground they trod upon was absolutely bare of any plant life. Only occasionally were there spots where the soils were soft and covered with organic matter and grasses.

"This landscape feels so harsh," Lafina remarked. "It's such a contrast to the softness and rotten smells in the small rainforest at the falls where we were last night!"

The Oglins came upon the skeletons of many big baobab trees lying on their sides, their trunks shredded and destroyed by elephants. Once again, Baylin and Lafina recalled their meeting with the young orphans back in the Volcano Hills where the elephants had explained why and how this destruction of trees happened.

The Oglins were now coming to realise that areas where people's fences were few and far between were mostly roamed by wild animals. While it was evident that people had set aside these areas especially for the benefit of the animals, sadly, the Oglins were now coming to expect great deterioration there. They also knew that the damage to the trees was not entirely the elephants' fault. The underlying cause, they now understood, was the way people managed these areas. The Oglins appreciated that the people were trying to do something good for the animals, but worried that if the land continued to decline, the wild creatures would have nothing left to survive on.

Baylin began to wonder if they would actually be able to identify the two specific baobab trees that they were supposed to find. Maybe those baobabs, like so many they saw along the way, had also been hollowed out by the elephants at the base and eventually collapsed and died. Then in the drought, they had been nearly devoured by hungry elephants who gathered around them like mourners. Becoming slightly more apprehensive, but with no choice but to continue, Baylin and Lafina carried on, parallel to the river and upstream.

At least within these wildlife areas, the Oglins did get to see some of the last remaining animals from the formerly vast herds that had inhabited the land. They saw majestic kudu with their twirling horns, grey-and-white striped, and their big ears softly pink inside. Occasionally through the bush they would glimpse a giraffe reaching to browse the leaves of a tall tree. They saw troops of baboons, sitting and grooming each other in the shade. Carefully and with deep concentration, the baboons picked off one another's fleas, ticks and mites.

"They are always so comical to watch," Baylin commented, hoping to ease the underlying tension they were both feeling. "And they look so much like us! The resemblance is quite striking."

Lafina giggled in response, and they both relaxed a bit.

At last they came across a huge baobab tree, standing next to the stump of what had once been another massive baobab. The ruins of it lay off in the underbrush nearby. Perhaps this was the pair of trees they were seeking.

Just a short distance further on, they found a streambed, which seemed to confirm their hopes. Following their instincts, they turned to follow the watercourse, downstream, leading their pala through the thick bush. Eventually they came out onto a big white sandbar on the edge of the river. In front of them, the river flowed past sleepily, cool and inviting in the heat of the day.

However, with great care, the two Oglins stood up on the bank to have a good look around. They both remembered that Old Spola had warned them of the especially large crocodiles on the river, probably the biggest the earlier travellers had come across on their entire journey. Bearing this in mind, the two Oglins scouted around carefully before even going to the river's edge for a drink. The water tasted good, like no water they had ever drunk before. It had a deep earthy taste to it; one could taste the roots and reeds that lined the riverbanks. It left a slightly dry taste in the mouth afterwards, almost as if one could taste the very soil in the water itself. It was very refreshing, and Oglins and pala alike drank deeply of it.

Looking downstream, the Oglins could see a wide expanse of seemingly still water of a lovely deep green colour. Yet, in fact, the water was flowing very, very quickly, although it appeared to be almost still. It was certainly by far the biggest river that either of them had ever seen. It was perhaps as big as all the rivers they had already seen put together!

Downstream, far away, they could still see the huge plume of smoke rising up into the sky, with its people machines buzzing in attendance, like bees around a hive.

Eventually, the two Oglins settled down enough to bring themselves to begin to look at things in terms of having to cross the broad river. They cautiously wandered out onto the rocks between the rapids, hopping from rock to rock. From one little island to the next, on they went. Arto, Argyl and Lara were loose and made their way across behind their companions. Sometimes they slipped and stumbled, and once, Arto slipped in headfirst only to emerge bucking, bobbing, scrambling and dripping up onto the next rock downstream just a moment later. He shook his head and sputtered as he caught his breath and looked balefully at Baylin as if to question what this whole endeavour was about!

All the time they were being extremely careful about watching for crocodiles and being sure that the next rock they were to land on was not a croc's back! And as they discovered on the first little island they were on, they had also to be very watchful for snakes. There were huge snakes on these islands. They had possibly been carried downriver in floodwaters and got stuck on the islands. Once caught on a spot of land, the snakes had nowhere else to go but to live there until the next flood or to swim. At one point, Baylin stepped through a clump of reeds to go down the other side of a small sand dune perched on an island, and suddenly the ground in front him erupted into lightning-quick movement as a massive black mamba slithered off into the reeds! Heart racing, Baylin fell backwards onto the sand. Slowly he released the air trapped in his lungs, then demanded a break for all.

They didn't rest for long, though. The black rocks surrounding them reflected the midday sun harshly and the heat quickly became oppressive. Moving out on the river, close to the cool water and hopping from spot to spot, seemed to take the heat out of the day. However, their pace became even slower and more deliberate, given all the hidden hazards!

They moved to the next island and then the next island and finally to a spot that they thought must be where Old Spola had told them they would have to swim. There was simply no way to hop across any more rocks. The Oglins sat down to rest and try to slow down their galloping hearts as they contemplated the inordinate challenge ahead of them.

Standing on their little island, Baylin and Lafina pondered the vast river. Trying not to let discouragement overtake them, they looked behind them at the wide expanse they had already crossed at such great risk. Then they looked ahead and across to the next bank, knowing it may not even be the other side of the river, but yet another island. As far as they knew, there might be many more rapids and islands beyond that. The first piece of river they had looked at was only one of the channels. The stretch of river they were now facing and contemplating swimming across was really quite wide. The water was moving very quickly, and the river seemed even bigger than Old Spola had described!

Certainly it seemed to the Oglins that the river was a lot fuller, a lot earlier in the season than it was supposed to be. Spola had warned them that they must try to get here before the winter came so they could get across before the river rose to its maximum flow. Although the river arises in a summer rainfall area, the level here would usually peak only in the winter. The large catchment area of this enormous river would normally suck up the summer rainfall and hold it until the soils were full. With subsequent rains, however, the water would slowly rise to its peak. So far down the river, the high water would typically arrive in the middle of winter. By now it was pretty obvious to the Oglins that the water had gotten here much sooner than in the time of Spola's journey. They thought it through and concluded that it was most likely due to the decline of the land upstream and the soil's diminished ability to capture and hold water for a long period. Then they further supposed that by winter the water level would be much lower than in the past.

The little Oglins had a more immediate problem on their hands, however. In dismay, they watched the water as it swept past them through the wide gap, white on either side with the green tongue down the middle, muscling itself on down into the big pool below them, eddies swirling against the banks, seeming to boil up from deep under the surface. All in all, it looked quite wild and woolly! To dive in and try to swim across the seething current just did not seem to necessarily be the right thing for a little Oglin to do.

Feeling a bit forlorn and intimidated, they decided that the old saying, "discretion is the better part of valour" held true here. So they gingerly made their way back across the expanse of river, scrambling from rock to rock and island to island, all the way back to the original white sandbar on the shore. Grateful to be on solid ground, they sat together to rest and try to think over their options.

"What about crocodiles in fast-moving water like this?" Lafina asked with concern. "What do you suppose are the chances of meeting a crocodile in those big rapids?"

"I just don't know," replied Baylin discouragingly, "but crocodiles seem to be able to go just about anywhere! And Old Spola did especially warn us to never, ever, *never* trust a crocodile. Crocodiles seem to be able to do anything!"

A small troop of baboons were sitting nearby under a tree, casually grooming each other quietly and watching the two young strangers consider their dilemma.

"Why don't we ask the baboons," whispered Lafina, hoping for some diversion from their overwhelming situation.

Bravely Baylin called out, "What do you think, oh great baboon?"

The oldest baboon of the troop rolled his eyes back while he lazily lifted one foot and scratched under his bottom. Settling back down, he shook his head. "No, no, no, don't you ever, never, forever trust a crocodile," he agreed. "That would be, extremely, especially, exceedingly silly!"

At this, the young baboons jumped off their mother's laps and ran right past the Oglins, bouncing up and down as they normally do, playing and swatting each other over the ears and screaming in pretended fright. The old baboon reached out and took hold of one. He shook the rascal by the ear, bit him hard on the back of the neck and chased the lot of them away. The naughty ones screamed in true fright this time, loud as ever, and took off out of harm's way.

"Can't carry on a decent conversation with these little beggars running around here," grumbled the old baboon. "No, no, no, you never can trust a crocodile!" he repeated. "Even in the fast, frothing, furious water, a crocodile can take you. They are exceptionally, exceedingly, extremely good swimmers! A croc will climb up on a bank over the top of a rapid and wait there and then float out into the mainstream when they see you in that fast water. They'll be swept down by the current, and when you are least expecting it, they'll catch you! That's exactly what a crocodile will do!" he warned them. "You have to be extremely, especially, exceedingly careful when it comes to crocodiles!"

Sighing, as he knew the baboon spoke the truth, however long it took him to cross the river, Baylin decided they would have to change tactics.

"Then I suppose we'll have to look into using Old Spola's other idea for crossing this river. We'll just have to build ourselves a raft. Now, how are we going to do that?" he asked himself out loud.

"There must be any number of ways to do that," Lafina said, trying to sound hopeful.

They chatted a bit more to the baboon, who belatedly introduced himself as "Boetie." Eventually, the Oglins came up with the idea of tying a couple of old dead pieces of wood together, just holding onto them and quietly paddling across the deep water. But once again, the concern of the crocodiles was raised.

"We certainly mustn't trust a crocodile," Baylin repeated to himself, feeling the responsibility for the safety of his little group. "He'll be watching and lying in wait for us when we try to get across."

"If we tie enough pieces of wood together with
strips of bark off these knob thorn trees, we can sit
on it completely and row ourselves across," offered
Lafina, a bit more hopefully. "Or else we've got to find
someone else to help. There must always be various
options available to us," she said, trying to sound both
optimistic and practical. "If we put together enough
wood and we tie it all together really well with bark
and sedge rope, we can sit on it where a crocodile can't
reach us and paddle our way across. We'll need paddles,
too! How big will it have to be to carry the pala as well? Or
can they swim beside us? A crocodile would probably be happier
to have one of them rather than one of us anyway. So the raft
will have to be big enough for them, too!"

This idea seemed to have some real possibility. So they
discussed it a little while longer and then started gathering
branches and pieces of wood and figuring out how to tie it all
together.

Once they had a sturdy little raft constructed, they took it
into the shallow water in a pool surrounded on three sides by
rocks and with one side against fast-flowing water. They carefully
checked the pool for lurking crocs first until they felt sure it was
quite safe. Then they all climbed onto the raft, one by one, to
test if it could handle their weight. They decided that they had
to add yet another piece of wood to really have enough floatation
for the five of them.

It took the rest of the afternoon to drag a large log down to
the water and lash it to the raft. By now they were pretty sure
that the raft had enough buoyancy to carry both of them and
their three pala. The day was getting on, and all of them were
exhausted from their tremendous exertions and the tension of
the whole situation. So they decided it was better to wait until
the next morning to give it a try. The raft was secure where it

was and as it was so late in the afternoon, they were not going to attempt the crossing until morning in any case.

So the decision was made to spend the night there on the bank. Besides, they still had to find something to paddle with. There were many, many ideas for that, too, but Baylin's idea of lala palm fronds seemed to be the best. Grateful to have an easy task to distract them, they dug around among the fronds until they found a couple that had especially wide, hard bases where they had once been attached to the palm tree. These looked very good for the purpose, as they had a big enough flat and rigid surface to serve as a paddle.

With all their equipment together at last, the young Oglins still had time before dark to sit and think some more as they watched the immense river roll by. This gave Lafina the chance to speculate about yet another concern.

"Maybe we should check with Boetie about hippos in this stretch of river, too," Lafina said, frowning at the long flat stretch of river as it curved out of sight downstream of them. "Hippos can be quite nasty if they are bothered by something floating down past them."

Baylin couldn't argue with that, so off they went to look for the baboon again. By now he had wandered away. They found him without too much searching, standing on two legs picking away at some low-hanging berries on a bush. As the two young Oglins approached, the old fellow looked over his shoulder at them with a typical baboon stare, very shifty-eyed and with eyebrows hopping up and down. He peered down his long nose over his twitchy nostrils at them and said condescendingly, "Yes, can I help you?"

"We had one more question for you, oh Boetie," Baylin said appeasingly. "What do you know about hippos in these pools?"

Boetie raised his head and replied eagerly, "Yes, indeed! There are huge, heavy, healthy hippo pods here! Huge pods!" He turned his head towards the river, baring a set of frightening teeth and barked a screeching "Whaahu!"

The Oglins nearly leaped out of their furry little hides at the noise, so sudden, loud and close. Blinking violently and still reeling from the shock, they heard the river suddenly erupt into grunting, groaning and donkey-like braying of the hippos. Answering the baboon's call, the hippos announced that they were indeed present and in goodly numbers!

The baboon looked at the still-quaking Oglins with a hint of a smile in his eye. He had obviously enjoyed giving them the fright of their lives. "Yes, indeed, there are many, multifarious, multitudinous hippo in this river!" Boetie said. "But you actually don't need to worry about them too much, certainly not as much as the crocodiles," he went on, laughing a bit to himself in a rather sinister way, "because twice a day there are canoes that come down this river."

Noticing the blank look on the Oglin's faces, he added. "Oh, I forgot that you are not from around here. Canoes are long floating things, like hollowed-out logs full of people that paddle their way down past here. All they do is keep their canoes to the shallow water and the hippos go towards the deeper water, and then they don't seem to worry them much. You hear occasionally about a hippo that gets a hold of one of them. But after all, right here you have the second-highest concentration of hippos anywhere in the world. So you still ought to be very careful!"

With frowns furrowing their brows and not feeling very reassured whatsoever, Baylin and Lafina made their way back to the river to discuss their plans. In the end, their strategy for the crossing itself was to launch the raft in just below the rapids and stay as close to the rocks as possible. Here the river eddied up opposite the main current and would help to hold them upstream and give them the most movement across. At first Baylin would stay on the bank and hold a bark rope from very nearby to help guide them across as best they could. As soon as they had a problem or got to the faster water, he would leap aboard and away they would go. They would let their little craft float downstream as much as it wanted to, but all the time they would try to get as much movement across the river as possible by paddling and steering with their fronds.

As darkness finally fell, the young Oglins crept into the skeleton of a huge dead fig tree for shelter. They nestled into a safe place where the main trunk split to spend the night. The troop of baboons climbed up to roost in the higher branches very nearby and the Oglins took comfort from that. They knew that the peacefulness and the soothing sound of the river sweeping by were misleading. The night was still to come. At least they would have the warnings of the baboons if something threatening were to approach.

Baylin and Lafina were utterly exhausted from their day's effort and a very short previous night's sleep. However, both of them slept fitfully and dreamed of wild water, the gaping jaws of crocodiles and the dizzying spin of rafts in the rapids.

During the night, all five companions huddled tighter together whenever they heard the mournful slow whoop of a hyena in the distance. Every now and again, the quiet was shattered by an ear-piercing scream as a young baboon fell off his perch or had a bad dream. Anytime a leopard, genet or any other real or perceived threat approached, the baboons would go absolutely mad, barking very, very loudly followed by an equally loud and sharp drawn-in breath immediately afterwards. "Whaahu, Whaahu." The sounds echoed away across the river into the night, unbelievably loud, and often followed by screaming from some young baboons. At least the Oglins knew that no predator could sneak up on them unawares with the baboons keeping guard.

CHAPTER 14

THE GREAT THUNDERING RIVER

A chain stretched to breaking point will, by definition,
fail at the weakest link.
At any moment in time every chain has one,
and only one,
weakest link that alone accounts for the strength of the entire chain,
regardless how strong other links might be.
To strengthen a chain when resources are limited,
one must always attend first to the weakest link.
—Allan Savory and Jody Butterfield, *Holistic Management*

Crocodiles and Questions

The next morning, with the oncoming light of dawn, Baylin, Lafina and the pala scrambled back out of their nest and thanked the baboons for keeping them awake most of the night. The little group crossed the white sandbank again to the river. The scene, while looking just as beautiful as the day before, was still filled with all the same treachery! The morning sun was shining up the river corridor, with rich orange reflections off the water.

They approached their little craft, which looked rather flimsy in the morning light, and to their shock, just there beside it lay a huge crocodile with his mouth wide open in a yawn! The yellow skin of his inner mouth had just a tinge of orange, like a dry sunrise, and was ringed with a row of harsh and crooked yellow teeth. The crocodile was trying to catch a bit of the early morning sun, and he fixed them with a baleful stare!

The two Oglins and the three pala stopped dead in their tracks at the sight of the massive reptile. It certainly was disturbing to find, right up close, the very thing they had so feared. And he was an exceptionally large crocodile at that! It didn't help that  his great length and massive jaws made their little craft seem ever so very much smaller. One good chomp down the middle, and that crocodile could easily split their little raft in two!

Seeing that they had stopped a good distance off, the old crocodile blinked his eyes slowly. He turned his head and fastened his big yellow eyes upon them. His mouth turned slightly up at the corners, resembling a ghastly smile.

"Sssssssooooo…," the crocodile sighed, "You two Oglinsss trying to go ssssssomewhere? Are you headed to the north, perhapssssss?"

Both of the little Oglins nearly leapt out of their skins at the sound of his voice! They grabbed hold of each other in frightful surprise. The pala, backing off nervously, obviously wanted none of this! While Baylin and Lafina knew that they could talk to animals by now, and in fact were getting pretty used to it, it was nonetheless a shock to be spoken to by a crocodile, let alone one so large, and one who seemed to know where they were going!

Summoning his courage, Baylin replied shakily, "Yes, why yes, we are, oh Great Crocodile," In spite of his quivering inside, he found the wherewithal to add, as if for protection, "We are on our way to see the Great Spirit!"

"Ah yesssss…," said the crocodile, the words seeming to slither surreptitiously from him. "I've been told about your journey to sssssee the Great Sssssspirit," he continued, speaking very slowly in a hissing voice that was especially frightening.

In a burst of bravado, not to be outdone by Baylin, Lafina blurted out, "So can you help us get across the river, oh Great Crocodile?"

Baylin looked at her in shock! He couldn't even conceive of asking a crocodile for help. But he took a deep breath and waited to see how the creature would answer.

Seeming to be smiling once more, the crocodile replied in his languid and dangerous-sounding voice that contradicted his conciliatory words, "I'm ssssure that I could help you get acrossss the river! I don't know whether you would get over there, but I would ccccertainly help you!"

Surprised with such a response, Lafina said cautiously, "Well, we've been warned never to trust a crocodile."

"Ah yessssss……That iss very good adviccce! A lot of animals will tell you not to trusst a crocodile," he hissingly agreed. "But really, we are the mosssst friendly of creaturesss under the right ccircumsstancccesss! You can rely on and truly trussst usss. We will cccertainly help you acrosss the river anytime, maybe even help you to find the sssspiritssss too. No problem what-sssso-ever!"

Rather than reassuring them, the croc's words sent a cold shiver down their spines. As far as the Oglins knew, there were just three ways to find the spirits: communicate to them as

Wedrelas do, go to consult with them as they were enroute to do…or…die! The croc's insinuation could mean anything, but they feared the worst. Old Spola's warning to "Never, never, never trust a crocodile!" rang in their ears. Besides, the crocodile looked pretty lean and hungry to Baylin and Lafina; much too much like he might just enjoy a tasty little Oglin or two or even a juicy pala for breakfast. They weren't at all sure that the crocodile would actually help them get across the river at all, or whether they should even risk it. They knew that they had to be quite desperate to even consider the offer!

Meanwhile, the crocodile seemed intent on other things, on a mission of his own. In spite of their obvious discomfort, he proceeded to ask Baylin and Lafina some very direct and unusual questions.

"Ah yessss, little Oglinssss, I ssssee that you have your doubtssss. But for ssssstartersssss you can call me Ssssssmiler, for that iss my name. Now, regarding thisss river crosssing, firssstly, do you have enough of your equipment together? Have you thought everything through for thisss crosssssing you ssssay you want to do? Have you come up with enough ideasss? Have you been creative enough to get acrossss thissss river? That'ssss the firsst of it!"

Baylin and Lafina looked at one another in utter amazement. This was hardly the conversation they would expect from a crocodile that was planning to eat them for breakfast! But then again, if he was not to be trusted, who knew what trap he was trying to set for them. Still, they needed to cross the river, after all, and his questions made them think hard about their situation.

"Ssssssecondly, do you have to have the ability to produccccce the desssired ressssult of getting acrossss thiss river?" Smiler continued in this surprising line of questioning before they had a chance to get over their shock and think of a reply, in this the most unusual conversation with an animal.

"Thirdly, you have to be ssssssure for yourssssselvessss about how you are going to get acrossss thisss river. Because although you've got yoursssselvessss a little craft and you reckon it can float, you still aren't ssssure if it can get you acrosssss thisss river. Are you? You've got to convincccce yourssselvessss that you can manage to do it, one way or another!"

Grinning at their obvious dismay, Smiler seemed to be quite enjoying putting the poor little Oglins into a state of confusion.

"Ah yessss, my dear little Oglinssss!" the croc continued, "with three ssssssimple quessstionssss you can find the weakessst link in your plan! You sssee, either you haven't got a good enough craft, raft or idea! Thisss would mean your resssourcccesss aren't right.

"Or perhapsss you have not actually got enough character or ssstrength to handle the paddling acrosss the river? Thisss would mean that your ability to convert your ressourccccess into ressultss iss limited.

"Or thirdly, you sssimply haven't adequately convinccced yourssselvessss or thossse three pala you're planning to ssshare the journey with about how you plan to crosss thissss river! Thisss would mean that you haven't adequately 'sssold' yourssselves or otherssss on your plan!"

The two Oglins sat down then, a decent distance from the crocodile to be sure, and proceeded to think over the things Smiler had pointed out to them. They had to admit that the crocodile was making sense and seemed to be playing a role in their overall learning. It did in fact seem to be quite accurate that they had those very three aspects to consider, if they were

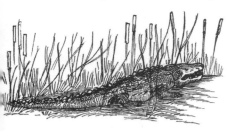 going to cross the river safely and successfully. After all, they had had enough encounters with animals now to begin to trust that the Great Spirit had his hand in these things!

So first they considered the croc's points about the raft, paddle and any other resources they were to use. "Were they set up adequately to attempt the crossing?" Secondly, "Were they capable, did they have the ability? And were they in the right place and the right position to do it? Was the approach route the right one?" And thirdly, "Had they truly convinced themselves and their faithful pala that they could do it?"

All this thinking was a bit much right then. They were both keyed up and keen to make this crossing and the sooner the better! So sitting and thinking things out first was not easy for two tightly wound-up little Oglins, especially in the presence of, not to mention at the very suggestion of, the biggest crocodile they had ever seen!

To break the tension, and truthfully to avoid for a bit the difficult questions posed by the formidable crocodile, they rushed off and got a few more pieces of dried wood. They urgently tied them on the raft on each side with extra strips of bark to reinforce the raft and to build up a bit of a railing on the sides. This, they thought, would make their craft as strong as possible. Just in case the croc tried to come over the top, he would have to contend with some height and maybe, just maybe, an Oglin could stay out of his reach. They also thought that this would make staying on the raft in turbulence or in the case of a violent attack easier for the pala, whose hard hooves couldn't be used to hold on.

Feeling a bit better about their raft then, Baylin and Lafina were about to consider Smiler's second point, when he addressed them once more in his slow and slithery voice.

"Ah yesssss. I ssssee that you Oglinsss have your craft. But…I don't know if you have really lisssstened to the questionssssss I raisssssed. You have already built your raft. Before you added thosssse exsssstra piecccesssss of wood, it wasssss already big enough and ssstrong enough to carry the five of you acrosss thisss river.

You tesssssted it. I ssssaw you and watched you clossssely lassst night. Sssssoooo…ssssurely now, you are putting exsssstra effort into sssssomething that wassss already good enough. Sssssurely your effortsss for getting acrosssss thisss river, for in the end I know that youmussssst crosssssss thisss river, sssssurely thossssse effortssss ssshould be put where you could gain more ressssultsssss for lesssss effort."

The Oglins sighed and thought about it a little bit more, feeling even more uncomfortable at the thought that the croc had been watching them the day before without their knowledge! This line of thinking led them to quickly make another good scan of the immediate area in case there were any more of the stealthy sneakers about.

Finally Lafina said, "Well, yes, Oh Great Smiler, I must admit that you are right. We do have a good enough raft. We have the resources to get across this river. The craft is strong enough, and if anything, now it is stronger than it needs to be. We are in the best possible place to cross, however difficult it might be. We certainly have also got the ability to do it."

Smiler began to smile even wider. The two Oglins looked at one another and, now that their fears had subsided a bit and they were thinking more about the crocodile's questions rather than his teeth, they both realised that it was actually Smiler's third question that most needed their attention.

Finally Baylin stated their conclusion, "The only question is whether we are truly convinced that we can do it. Whether Arto, Argyl and Lara are convinced enough that we can do it, so that none of them refuses to get on or tries to bail out halfway across! Now maybe we ought to talk to others and see what they think. Maybe we ought to ask old Boetie and see what he thinks of our plan."

"No, oh no!" Lafina laughed out loud. "He's got a funny sense of humor, the old baboon. But Boetie won't help us with this one. He'll just give us stern warnings all the time. If we listened to him, we never would have left Vadiera in the first place, for he would have us believe we were doomed, done, dusted before we even began, begun, be-offed!" Smiling broadly at her imitation of the baboon's peculiar style, she went on, "So why bother! I don't think Boetie's the one we need to speak to. Smiler's question makes me realize that we just have to convince the right ones!"

"Well, why don't we ask the crocodile?" asked Baylin, with the excitement of newly surfacing understanding. Suddenly, like a fog had lifted, Baylin realised the crux of the issue and leapt up in excitement. "Maybe we should ask him! The crocodile is our weakest link! We feel that we understand the river enough. We are satisfied enough with our little raft and our plan! We, Arto, Argyl and Lara have been totally unperturbed by it. They'll get on with no trouble and we are ready. The one thing we are totally unsure of and have got no guarantee on is the crocodile!

"Or crocodiles…" he added, his voice faltering ever so slightly at the thought that there were probably many more such creatures lurking in the vast river.

As Lafina nodded her agreement enthusiastically, Baylin spoke up with new confidence, "Oh Great Smiler the Crocodile, we really, desperately need to cross this river. We are on an incredibly important mission. We are on a Great Journey that the Great Spirits have asked us to complete for them. Would you allow us nice young Oglins to cross this river? On this craft, without giving us any trouble?"

Baylin reminded himself of the real and deeper purpose and magnitude of their journey, and felt his fear fade away. Boldly now, he went on, "In fact, wouldn't you like to help us across this river? I am sure that if we had your go ahead, your assurance," he added, almost losing momentum and starting to falter a bit, thinking "never, never trust a…," but still daring to speak the unspeakable, "and if…if we had your help, we would be able to cross this river and continue on our quest in a most timely fashion!"

"Ah, yessssss! I think you two are beginning to learn now!" soothed Smiler, with a smile on his wide mouth that could possibly be called sincere, an amazing and rather unlikely thing for a crocodile, but nonetheless seemingly real in this instance.

"You are beginning to sssee what I mean by the three different linkssss in thisss chain of endeavour. You are identifying which iss the weakessst one! And you are learning that to put more effort into the sssstronger onessss isss alwayssss going to be a wasssste of time and effort. It iss the weakesssst link that dictatesss the ssstrength of the entire chain and that'sss what needsss your attention. If you put your effort firssst into the weakesssst one, you will ssstrengthen the whole chain. But if you keep making the sssstrong onesss sssstronger, the weakesssst link sstill determinesss the maxxximum ssstrength of the chain, and therefore your chain getsss no ssstronger!

"Now you are learning about thisss, and you ssseem to be going in the right direction," the croc continued, "but sssstill, why sssshould I, an untrusssstworthy crocodile, help you tasssty little Oglinssss acrosss the river? I could jussst asss easssily eat you and your juiccccy pala friendsss and ssssatisssfy my hunger thisss fine morning."

Baylin and Lafina looked at one another with a bit of fright and confusion for a moment.

Taking a deep breath and mustering her courage once more, Lafina replied, "We have all the resources we need now. We have the ability to get across that river." Then she pondered, "What haven't we got? Obviously, we haven't convinced Great Smiler the Crocodile to help us! Why would he want to help us? I think the question we must answer now is: 'What's in it for him?'"

With dawning realisation, Lafina then spoke up with confidence and even the hint of a smile on her own face, "Oh Great Smiler the Crocodile, you don't seem to realise the incredible importance of our Great Journey, nor the magnitude of the mission we are on! We have come all the way from the Great Ocean to the south and we must cross this river and go all the way to the Great Forest to the north to see the Great Spirit. We carry with us some of the keys to the future of the world and we have more to learn along the way. We must get there! We must talk with the Great Spirit to discover the rest of the keys! Once we have the keys, the rest of the world will benefit! All of us will be able to live in greater harmony with one another. Including the crocodiles! If we can fulfill our mission, we will help make it possible for there to be more animals, more fish, more birds and more life. Thereby making it easier for the crocodiles to thrive.

"If we can fulfill our mission, in the future the rivers will stay more full of water throughout the year. You don't know much about that, oh Great Smiler, because you live here in a land of great abundance with a huge river to supply you. There are quite a lot of animals still around here for you to survive upon, providing you plenty of food. But so much of the land we have travelled through on our journey is a disaster. Where the Great Greasy Green River flowed, much like this one, across the plains of the low veld, there now stands nothing but white sands and the occasional stagnant pool of water. The crocodiles that live there are forced to live cheek by cheek, in dirty, slimy water. They are so close to one another that they are unable to stretch their legs and get out onto a patch of sandbar without being bullied by a bigger one. And there is a great shortage of food as well as space," Lafina said, really warming to her subject, and the tears rising to the corners of her eyes, as she felt the tragedy of which she spoke and remembered the shrunken rivers they had crossed.

"If you wish this to happen with your river, then stay as you are!" she went on boldly. "Stay just like you are. Don't do any more. Eat us! Destroy our craft as we attempt to cross this river! But, sir, do you wish to see a future that has a river that comes down at the right time of year, with clear, clean water? Do you want to see healthy river banks for breeding sites and surrounding land teeming with all kinds of animals? Imagine all that life throughout the bush, all coming down to drink at your river, all available to you and your youngsters to eat. What do you feel about that, oh Great Smiler? If that's what you wish for the future for yourself and your offspring, out of the goodness of your heart and for you and your future, you had better help us to cross this river safely today!" She finished with a flourish, now quite inspired herself by the purpose and quest that she and Baylin and their faithful pala were on.

Smiler's smile, if possible, widened even further and he winked a slow and friendly wink. "Ah yessss…Now you have it! You have learned that there are the three linkssss in the chain that can be usssed to analyzzze any ssssituation or idea being made a reality. The firsssst one, assss you have sssseen, isss the resssourccccessss you have. The ssssecond is making thossss resssourcccessss into a product you or othersss can usssse for achieving an objective. And the third one is convincccing othersss to believe in you, to buy into your idea! You have done thisss at lassst! I buy it! You are quite convincccing little Oglinss when you want to be! Indeed, I want food today, but I also want food tomorrow and long into the future. I am from a long line of one of the oldessst creaturesss on Earth and I know that your quessst isss urgent and you mussst ssucccceed if life along my river isss to be continued!

263

"Sssoooo. Yesssss, I will help you! Now, my dear Oglins get aboard your raft and let me pusssssh you acrosssss thissss river," he exclaimed, with the widest smile of all.

The two Oglins took one more look at each other for reassurance. They instinctively clasped their hands tightly around their pachas and felt their amulets within. Baylin's shining stone and Lafina's gleaming white seashell seemed extra heavy in their hairy little hands. They thanked the Great Spirit and begged him to let them know they were doing the right thing by trusting a crocodile, the thing they were most warned against!

A Leap of Faith

Together the Oglins arose, taking strength from what they both saw deep in each other's eyes, and they hugged one another briefly. Then, using well-placed poles, they levered the raft into the water. Bravely, Lafina climbed onto the little craft and reached back to lead the nervous but trusting pala aboard.

Arto was first. He dropped his hocks and reared onto his hind legs before placing his front feet on the raft. His weight, always more on the front feet anyway, tipped the craft sharply and pushed it away from the shore violently. Baylin was very nearly dragged into the water as the widening gap split Arto's front and back legs further apart, making it impossible for him to move. Lafina turned to face him, talking soothingly to keep him calm. Baylin fell backwards hard, digging in his heels to try to save his friend from falling in. Lara took fright, reared and scrambled backwards. Her sudden movement actually saved them. She was tied by a lead to Arto's own bundle-rug saddle, and her desperate fight backwards yanked the little craft back to the shore once more.

They had not noticed the old crocodile disappear in the moment of excitement, but Lafina saw him coming at them now. He pushed a "v" wake ahead of his nose in the water. Gleaming eyes nestled on top of his head, like stubby periscopes behind raised snorkel nostrils. Her heart dropped. She didn't even have time to shout a warning as his huge gaping mouth opened while he rushed towards her. Before she could move, the huge jaws thumped shut hollowly on the railing edge of the craft and the croc's gentle but firm shove steadied the raft against the sand bar. By this time, Arto had recovered his balance and was no longer doing the splits. He reared and thrashed the air with his front feet in an attempt to escape the terrifying sight of the advancing croc!

The crocodile's hollow voice, muffled by a mouthful of wooden raft, gently rose from his cavernous depths. "Ffforry, my loveliefff," he mumbled, "I didn't mean to alarm you, only to fffave you from a fffertain accffident. I'm fffforry! Now! All climb on quickly while I hold thifff raft!"

By then, Arto had two feet on the raft and two feet dug into the sand behind. Baylin sensed the moment needed seizing and he did so. He took command as though this was an everyday occurrence.

"On, Arto!" he ordered, encouraging his pala with a little slap on the rump. Arto promptly hopped onboard and turned to look back at Baylin as the rope jerked against Lara, who was still planning her escape.

"Come, Lara," Baylin said encouragingly. He led her gently, looking away to help her relax. Lafina

265

immediately looked away, too, and noticed the crocodile catch on and shut his scary eyes. With no predator-like stares from either Oglin or crocodile, Lara willingly moved forward and leapt onboard to join Arto. She landed hard and squarely in the middle, her nostrils flared and wide.

Argyl needed little coaxing; he was not going to be left alone here! Losing no time, Baylin leapt on to the raft right behind Argyl, shoving the craft off from the shore in a final leap of faith. The crocodile's long body rose slightly out of the water as he held the craft from bucking violently. Then he let go and dropped from sight entirely as he submerged and let the little vessel drift freely over him, out into deeper water.

Just in case, Baylin quickly pulled his toes further onboard as the great scales of the crocodile passed below him. Smiler flashed his yellow belly as he spun from one thrash of his powerful tail and then his nose nudged up against the branches that formed their craft and began to push. With his strong and stubby legs working and long green tail, slightly speckled with gold, sweeping from side to side, Smiler slowly moved the tiny craft and its uneasy passengers out into the river's main current. The Oglins began to paddle towards the far side and built up a bit of a wake streaming out behind them as they floated downstream and across the river.

The crocodile appeared even bigger to them out in the water now that they were sitting practically right on top of him. He was massive! They looked at one another for strength, while a nasty little feeling tickled the back of their jaws: the very taste of fear! Was this crocodile going to just get them out into the deepest part of the river and then flip their little craft up into the air, turn them out of it and gobble them up? He could do it so easily!

Nevertheless, the crocodile steadily followed the route that they would have taken, sticking close against the rapids. Every time the flow of the water got stronger, they drifted downstream a ways. They would cross the fast water going with the flow and then slowly Smiler would take them upstream again in the eddies under the lee of the next set of rocks. Then once again, he would surge them forward into the fast-moving water, causing them to float quite a long way downstream but still make progress across the river as best they could.

The ride was quite challenging to say the least! Smiler steered them as deftly as he could through the mighty forces of the moving water. Eventually, the tiny craft came to a rest in the still water below an island, with the current raging on either side. Smiler backed off a bit and raised his snout just above the water line and took stock of the passengers through his large, languid yellow eyes.

"Ah yesssss…You two ought to really hold on now!" he warned. "It'sss going to be very fassssst through thisss nexsssst current! Isss it possssssible for the juicy onesss to ssssit or lie down to give a bit more ssstability?"

The Oglins had quite a bit more confidence in the unusual crocodile by this point, and they were so wrapped up in the situation that they did not even worry about his name for their beloved pala or the hungry way he looked at them. The pala had learned to sit or lie down in the months of travel through and around people settlements. They instantly obeyed Baylin's hand signal to drop down and lie on their sides. The movement was both quick and, of course, thoughtless to safety. They only knew the command as: "Danger! Now! Lie down!"

As the pala all dropped to their sides, the little craft leaped sideways and launched itself directly into the current, spinning and rolling as it went! Baylin and Lafina tightened their grip on the raft and dropped flat to the bottom themselves to try and make her steady. The flow quickly picked them up, spinning the craft around a few times. The crocodile submerged for a moment, leaving them to drift aimlessly on their own, while he caught his own direction and balance.

At last they felt a bump as the crocodile brought his body up against the side of the raft and it took direction again. Slowly, but ever so slowly, they began moving across the current while still flying downstream at speed. The green water surged and rose up from below, actually lifting the craft from underneath and spinning it wildly.

Finally, with great relief, they reached the eddies on the far side of the river. Smiler carefully pushed them along the bank to a place where they could easily climb out and up the bank. It was a huge elephant and hippo beach, a gently sloping bank where the hippos would climb out of the river every night to go on their grazing forays. It was obviously a favourite place for the elephants to come down to the river to bathe and frolic in the cool water.

As the little raft bumped up against the far shore, Baylin and Lafina scrambled off and onto the sand. With little encouragement, the pala made comically high leaps to get off while the crocodile held the craft firmly with his curved teeth until they were all safely on land.

Looking up at them from in the water, Smiler spoke to them a final time, "Ah yessss…You two Oglinssss are very brave. The Great Sssspirit hasss chossssen very well to sssselect the two of you. Now, you need to continue on your journey, and I wishshsh you the very bessst of luck! Trusssst me, I will hide your raft, watch for your return and help you make it back acrossss thisss Great Thundering River on your way home.

"But, my dear little friendssss, onccce again," he warned them with a smile and a wink, "if you are not an Oglin that hassss been given the blessssing by the Great Sssspirit, never, oh *never* trusssst a crocodile!"

Flashing a last stealthy smile at the grateful Oglins, the crocodile pushed their craft back out into the river, and they watched it twirl away as it went downstream. With nothing more than the tiniest ripple, the great crocodile's head disappeared beneath the water. He spun over onto his back showing his big creamy white belly just beneath the surface. It was a frightening sight! Then with a final swish of his tail, the water splashed up white and he was gone, utterly gone.

Both Baylin and Lafina, wide-eyed and amazed, let out the breath they didn't even know they were holding. Relieved beyond belief to be across the river, they quickly turned and scurried up the tall bank to get up away from the water and its hidden dangers. Looking at one another, they were shaken but felt both extremely lucky and exceptionally pleased to be back on dry land. The pala, meanwhile, had set to grazing voraciously as if that was what they had missed most about not being on land!

Deciding to take a well-earned and much-needed rest, the Oglins found a shady spot under a giant jackal berry tree and went over what they had just learned from the crocodile. Now that the fear and anxiety of the crossing was behind them, they wanted to really take in the essence of the lesson. They knew it was yet another gift from the Great Spirit and another vital piece of the larger picture that their journey was giving them. With no threat in sight, Arto, Argyl and Lara calmly carried on grazing and dozing as if nothing had happened at all.

"There is something important to remember here," mused Baylin. "It's not just about persuasion or begging to get your way. The lesson here is actually about finding the weakest link and working on that first."

"Yes, that's the key," agreed Lafina. "If Smiler was clearly with us from the beginning, if trusting a crocodile was a common thing, if we had easily been able to sell our plan to him, then the convincing part wouldn't have been our weakest link. We wouldn't have had to put so much effort there. If our raft hadn't been strong enough, that would have been a resource weak link. Or if we didn't have the right kind of relationship, if we were not able to work together as a team to use that resource well to produce the result, then that would have been a weak link in the conversion of resources into results."

In a moment of inspiration, Lafina jumped up and grabbed a wild dagga plant and stripped off a few of the flowers. They were lovely, orange-coloured velvet tubes that were narrow at one end and curved, widening all the way to a pretty, fringed trumpet at the other end. She took them, laid them in her lap, and one at a time fed them onto one another. The narrow end of one fitted into the wide end of another, and in so doing, twelve of them formed a circle when the last one fitted into the first. Oglins had used this plant for years as a ceremonial necklace. She made three circles and linked them together, forming a pretty, soft chain with three links.

Holding the chain up with a finger through the end links she named them and pointed to each with her chin and eyes. "When I take an action there are three distinct links in the chain of producing results. Firstly, there are the basic resources," she said, her chin pointed at the first ring. "Secondly, I must convert the resources into a product or result." She pointed at the middle link. "And then," indicating the final link, "there is the sharing of the idea or convincing others, the marketing of the action or product to create the desired result or benefit! Do you see that?"

Not waiting for Baylin to answer, Lafina plunged on excitedly with her perception of Smiler's teaching. "The key is that only one link in this chain can be the weakest at any one point. Watch!"

She gently pulled her fingers apart. Slowly the rings changed shape and certain flowers began to take strain and slip. First one, then another. Then suddenly a flower in the middle ring nearly slid out of its mate next door and Lafina stopped.

"That is the weakest point! See? It is a weak link in the conversion of resources to products, and it is at a specific point!

"Fix it, please," she asked turning to him. "Only the weakest one."

Impressed with her creativity, Baylin smiled and pushed the two flowers gently into one another again. He watched without a word as she started pulling again. The flower right alongside began to pull out of its companion.

"It is still a weak link in the conversion of resources to products or results. Do you see that? It is just at a different point now. It is no good us fixing any of the others. Only the weakest one is worth fixing. That way we continually strengthen the chain with the least effort for greatest results, and we are always better off than before," she concluded with satisfaction. "We can and must use this thinking in anything we do!" Lafina finished her inspired speech with a laugh, amused at her own enthusiasm.

Baylin, haltingly at first, then gaining momentum with the idea, took over. Thinking back on their journey, he reflected, "Another example would be those long lost people of Khami, before it fell into ruin. Their food and thus people problems were worsening all the time and they spent a lot of effort trying to increase their resources to combat it. They began to fetch, produce and raid for food further and further away. This cost lots of effort and must have stretched other resources to the limit. Yet, all the time they were sitting right on enough resources. The rain was the same. The sun shone just the same and their land was still there to produce from. All the ingredients were there. All they did not have was the ability to continually turn all of this into results! Food! If they had thought like this, they would have realised that they simply needed to find other ways to grow food. Ones that built and did not destroy the environment."

"Oh, yes!" Lafina exclaimed, applauding him. "And, if they had found other ways that worked, then their weakest link would have shifted straight away. Just as it did with the flowers the moment you pushed the first two together. Only, in Khami's case the weakest link would immediately have become one of convincing. The new methods would have to be spread to others to make the whole region successful, or the nearby people would have simply come to raid their food!"

Their enthusiasm built as they carried on and realised the wonderful teaching from Great Smiler. With the big crossing behind them, the little Oglins let themselves settle down to rest and discussion well into the afternoon. They could relax and enjoy the cool shade and the calming effects of the water sliding past, green and strong, yet, no longer threatening in any way.

While the pala contentedly ate their fill of the lush grasses along the river, they added the following verses to their journey's tale.

Nothing did prepare us for
the Thund'ring River in its spate.
Our explorations did reveal
that daring action it would take.
So bravely we did build a raft
the fearful crossing for to make.

Our plans did seem in jeopardy
when the crocodile appeared.
Yet much to our bewilderment
his menace was not clear.
And soon we found that he was not
the real danger to be feared.

Sssmiler the crafty Crocodile,
trusstworthy asss a croc can be,
assked quesstionss of the sstrangesst kind
and taught uss linkss in the chain to ssee.
We learned how thiss determiness well
what our ssole focuss then musst be.

The croc taught indelibly that
the weakesst link musst effort gain.
To attend to any other one,
he made quite clear and plain,
that the whole would be in peril
and our endeavourss be in vain.

273

CHAPTER 15

THE SAVANNA

To obtain magical power, learn to control thought.
Admit only true ideas which are in harmony with the end desired.

—Israel Regardie

The Marshes

Relieved to have accomplished the river crossing, Baylin and Lafina made their way across the savanna grasslands, towards the north once more. They were working up into higher country, to the divide between the Great Thundering River behind them and the Great River itself.

The countryside was different here. Instead of there being just the large individual trees dotted randomly around the savanna, here the trees grew in clusters. They formed pretty little thickets of trees with lush, dark green grass beneath them. Upon closer inspection, the Oglins found that each little copse of trees grew on top of a slightly rocky outcrop and around them there was also a little ridge of soil. This was very confusing, of course, until they came to another such clearing in amongst the bush, which actually contained a growing crop. From this, they were able to figure out what was happening there: People had been working the land all around these rocky outcroppings, clearing them of trees and planting crops. So those were the only places left where the thickets of trees had been able to survive. In between them was sparse grassland, not fully recovered from past cultivation.

They also discovered clear evidence of animals, seeing both dung and hoof prints in the rich soil under the trees where the grass grew healthily. While out in the open, where the grass was weak and sparse, they found the soils to be hard-packed, with hardly a mark on them.

"Where the food is better there are more animals, and where there are more animals there is more food. Exactly as we have learned from Khumbula and Tufty!" Lafina exclaimed. "If you think of Uyazi, this is obviously a brittle environment. Without animals, it will gradually turn into a simple plant community. Here it is scraggly grasses. On the other side of the Greasy Green River, it was a thicket of a single kind of large tree with nothing underneath but bare ground covered in lichen," Lafina pointed out, as clear evidence that their powers of observation and interpretation were improving along with their understanding.

Beyond the cropping areas, the Oglins came again to a place that seemed to belong more to the game animals. Here they saw herds of elephant and buffalo out on marshy

275

plains. Baylin and Lafina realised that they were at the headwaters of a major tributary of the Thundering River. Among these marshes, they also saw herds of lechwe travelling through the water, instead of around it. When something disturbed them, the whole herd would move, thrashing through the water in leaps and bounds. The lechwe sprayed the water in sheets so it acted as a curtain, screening them from view as they moved en masse through the marshy grassland.

Moving soundlessly as only an Oglin can, they snuck closer to the lechwe for a look, they recognised it from Old Spola's battends; neither had seen one before. The lechwe's hide is a reddish-fawn colour right across the whole upper part of the animal. There is a distinct line where the reddish colour turns to the creamy white long hair underneath the body. Their faces are a deep red-yellow colour, the same colour as the rocks on the cliffs at Vadiera where they drop down into the sea. The lovely lechwe has a dark muzzle and dark eyes with a little bit of white just visible below the eye.

The males have lyre-shaped horns that sweep forward at the top in a great spread. The magnificent horns are rippled at the bottom, then become smoother and smoother towards the tips. The females have no horns, but their large ears complete a pretty picture.

The lechwe graze in and out and around the great reed beds, shallow flood plains and pans around the catchment areas of the river. There was a stark contrast between the yellow- and khaki-coloured veld and the deep green of the wet pans and waterways where the herds lingered.

Rather than try to cross through the treacherous marshes and shallows filled with huge crocodiles, the Oglins decided to skirt around towards the yesterdays. They left the waterways and rode up through the savanna with sparsely spread trees and shrubs. Rocky boulder outcrops, like pebbles loosely dumped in piles by a giant, were littered across the wide expanses of waving grasslands.

The Cheetah

At the base of a kopjie ahead of them, Baylin pointed out the sentinel statue form of a cheetah sitting on its hindquarters in the shade of an umbrella thorn tree. Seated on its hindquarters with its front legs straight, it struck a most regal pose, fitting the cheetah's royal place among animals. The sleek cat was gazing out across the plains, watching silently and patiently for prey.

The distinctive spots, spread loosely over its lean body, accented its lovely tawny yellow colour. The long thin tail wavered and twitched occasionally out behind the haunches, as if it had a life of its own. With a noble glance and a raised chin, the cheetah stared out of its yellow eyes. A distinct black tear line from the point of the eye, around to the corner of the mouth, gave the sleek feline the appearance of a saddened expression.

The Oglins looked at one another, knowing full well that if a cheetah were so inclined, an Oglin could easily become its prey. Even a pala could be enjoyed for a meal by a cheetah. Nonetheless, being brave Oglins and knowing they were on a great mission, they decided to move forward and see whether they could strike up a conversation with the noble cheetah! As they made their way across the plain towards the kopjie, they stuck tight together with their pala. As a group, they tried to look bigger and stronger than a little Oglin alone normally might. With chests puffed out and strutting their arms out wider than normal, they attempted to make themselves appear to be more imposing targets than a cheetah should really be taking on.

As they approached, the cheetah regally turned her head and fixed them with her boring-straight-through-you stare that nothing but a cat can do. Her eyes were set in the front of her head, as they are with all predators, not on the sides of the head as the eyes of prey animals are. At that moment, the Oglins both became exceedingly aware that eyes on the front of the head are far more intimidating! The cheetah, having waited patiently, broke the standoff and greeted them.

"Good day to you, brave Oglins! I am Checha! 'The one who hurries'!" the cheetah called cheerfully to them.

Breathing out at last in relief, guessing that she was less likely to try and eat them if she were talking to them, Baylin answered. "Good day to you, oh Great Checha! May we join you in your shade and share your view?"

"Why, surely!" Checha replied. "I've especially chosen this spot and have been expecting your arrival! The Great Spirit has asked me to meet you here today. The Great Spirits know where you are all the time. They have been keeping an eye on you two! They tell me that while they are not easily pleased, they are greatly pleased with the two of you."

"We are grateful to hear that, oh Checha," answered Lafina, blushing with joy and pride. "We feel that the Great Spirit is pleased with us whenever we work our way through our amulets and connect with nature, memories and the spirits each night."

Feeling a bit more at ease now about the cat's predatory instincts, the Oglins left the pala to graze just a little way off and joined the cheetah in her shady spot. They sat down on the soft grass and inhaled the sweet scent of the summer and the slightly sour smell of the drying seed heads. The air was thick with heavy pollen.

"Great Checha, what are you doing today?" Baylin asked politely.

"Well, I'm sitting here in my usual fashion," Checha began, "watching and waiting to see which of the animals will give itself up to me today to feed me and my two cubs. They are still too small to come on a hunt with me."

For the first time, the two Oglins noticed that the cheetah's nipples were heavy with milk.

"They are hiding in the rocks behind us in that thicket over there. They'll be sitting there watching me today," Checha told them.

"They watch you?" Lafina wondered.

"Yes, from when they are very young they must watch and learn what they can," the cheetah explained. "I take them with me and place them in a good vantage point to watch me make my kill within their view if possible. It becomes even more important later on, when they are bigger, as they must learn how to hunt from watching me in action, as I learned from my mother. They must observe how I do it and how I go about it so they can become successful hunters, too.

"We cheetahs are not heavy like lions or leopards. We are lightweights. We hunt with speed, and it is extremely dangerous. We must strike our prey at just the right spot and get the timing absolutely right; otherwise, we won't be able to bring it down.

That's what my young cheetahs have got to learn from me, timing and placement. They have to see me ankle-tap the prey and then watch my eyeline go in and take a hold of the soft spot at the throat. There is a right spot, a different spot for each different type of animal. I hunt the animals that I know, and pass on the generations of knowledge."

"What is your favoured prey, oh Checha?" Baylin queried, his interest piqued.

"Well, if a lechwe happens to wander out onto the drier plain, as they do occasionally, I'd be very interested," Checha answered. "But I'm not that keen to go after one in the water. I prefer to be on the dry land, thank you! My main forte, of course, is a nice tasty impala! That's what I'm really good at! And that's what I'm hoping to get hold of today. I'm watching that little group of impala down there. Can you see them?"

Looking off in the direction of Checha's gaze, Baylin nodded. "Oh yes, I see them. But how will you choose the one that you want?"

"Well, you see, we cheetahs have to judge things very, very carefully. We only have a certain amount of energy to expend in a run. I've got to get myself into exactly the right position, to force one impala out into a different direction, so that I will be able to take a shortcut and take it from the best angle. It's an art, really. It's an art that a cheetah must master if one is to survive! But you see, you can only learn how to do it by always asking yourself a specific question: Which move will give me the most advantage for the least effort? This releases the mind for deeper concentration. Otherwise, our heads would be filled with questions like: 'Which action must I take now? Which impala must I choose? Which angle of attack must I choose? Where do I go to next?' You see? Lots of questions, too many questions to make the kind of decision we must make! So, the simple question: 'Which move will give me the most advantage for the least effort?' is the answer for uncluttering the mind," Checha explained.

"This I must ask myself continually, so that when I go in for the attack, I do it with the least amount of effort and gain the greatest amount of return from my actions. I simply can't afford to expend excess energy and miss the kill—at least not very often! Of course, I miss occasionally! But I must minimise any wasted effort and maximise the prospects of success.

"It's the same issue once I make my kill, too! I need to eat as much as possible and as quickly as possible. If I get too exhausted by the run itself, I can't start eating soon enough and other predators will chase me off before I get a full meal. With two young ones to feed, it is critical that I eat enough for myself and for them!"

The eyes of the cheetah fixed on the Oglins, as she finished her explanation. Baylin shivered inside with instinctive fear, wondering how any animal could face those fierce eyes and drive them off a kill.

"That question is the key that helps me achieve the greatest success!" Checha concluded "And you, my dear young Oglins, can do the same thing. In every action you make, strive to ensure that everything you do gives you the greatest possible return towards where you want to be and what you want to achieve.

"You need to ask yourselves this question once you've been through all your other thinking. Evaluate all the options you have. Then you must actually learn to weigh your options one against another by asking yourselves: '*Which one of these options will give me more movement towards my creed for the same amount of time or effort?*' If you start asking yourselves that question every time you must choose between different options or actions, it will help you greatly!" Checha assured them.

Even while talking with the two young Oglins, Checha never wavered from her constant surveillance of the plains out in front of them. She cocked her head as the impala finally moved towards them and softly whispered, "I want you two to stay right where you are, stay perfectly still and watch me. My time has come."

The cheetah crept forward, crouching close to the ground to stay beneath the tops of the grasses swaying in the breeze. Her head was held low beneath her shoulder blades, showing gaunt through the spotted blanket of her skin. As the tension in her neck relaxed, her back hung even lower, slung between shoulder and hip. Her tail curved up, twitching still, dark at the tip.

She stalked slowly forward, moving with utter grace and stealth. She stopped occasionally, watching and sniffing at the wind. The impala hadn't picked up her scent as yet.

It was a fantastic view for the Oglins, from the high point looking out over the plain. Checha moved relentlessly towards the impala, adjusting her course to move directly into the wind. Just as she moved slightly into the wind, the impala suddenly picked her up. Their heads jerked up in unison, the wide horns of the male gleaming in the light. They grunted and snorted loudly as they all turned in her direction. Ears up, all of them pointed at the cheetah and alertly watched her.

The two Oglins looked at one another in surprise and Lafina whispered, "Why did she do that? Why did she let them know that she is there?"

With nothing to do but watch and learn, they were riveted by the scene, as the cheetah then turned and walked away. The impala, wanting to keep the cheetah in sight, immediately stepped out and moved forward, noses high and their tails flickering nervously. Snorting loudly through widened nostrils, they kept coming towards her.

Checha deliberately moved out of the impalas' line of sight, down into a low hollow. The impala watched, stamped their feet and watched and watched where she disappeared. After a while, they slowly began to relax again and returned to their grazing. Meanwhile, Checha had headed through the lower ground of the hollow, beyond and downwind of the group of shiny red and khaki antelope. Then the cheetah stepped out onto the open plain again, quietly watching and sitting down on her haunches. The impala were grazing their way up wind again, slowly, spreading out.

The closest, bravest male had moved quite a distance ahead towards the spot where the cheetah had disappeared from sight. He moved forward still a little further, grazing, lifting his head and watching warily, mouth still working fast. The handsome buck stamped his feet and shook his head vigorously occasionally to rid himself of flies.

The cheetah then began to move forward, stalking in towards the side of the impala. The buck had his head down grazing when Checha let out a low growl. The impala started with fright. He snorted and spun around as he realised that the cheetah was right there. The buck bolted in the direction of the rest of his herd, where there was greater safety in numbers.

It was too late. The lightning-fast cheetah leaped into motion, cut across the corner with a phenomenal burst of speed and caught up quickly with the young male. Dust spurted out from under her claws as she dug divots of soil with every movement and flung them far and wide behind her.

Checha flew over the ground and caught the impala across the hindquarter, ankle-tapping him. Almost as if in slow motion, the impala's back legs slid out from under him. His tail hit the ground and dust burst in a cloud around him. Fear took over the features of the impala's face and his mouth opened in a silent scream. Drawing on all of his strength, he rose again in one fluid motion and stretched forward in his first great leap. Meanwhile, the cheetah had checked her forward motion with a low turning action, heavy on her front feet, and positioned herself for just that very move by the impala.

Spinning, the impala tried to bolt in a new direction. The Oglins could see the indecision in his eyes, as he tried to choose which way to go. He exploded into a full gallop with a turn to the right. The cheetah was right there, on his heels again. Reaching out a slender foot, she ankle-tapped him again. He came down once more, tumbling, dust exploding in sprays around him.

Instinctively escaping, but beyond judgement now, the impala leaped straight into the cheetah's clasp. The cheetah's movement flowed through the drifting dust like liquid gold. The impala's scream choked short in the deathly grip of her jaws. Like the dust settling to ground, so the fight subsided in him. Going limp, he gave himself to her. The cheetah held on for a moment longer and then slowly released her prey and sat back on her haunches. Her whole body gasped for breath from the incredible exertion of the chase. It was over.

She had got her prey just in time, before she herself was exhausted. Checha sat alongside the kill for a few more minutes, panting hard, catching her breath.

As a hunter, Baylin was struck by her skill and phenomenal speed. Every action had been brilliantly planned, perfectly set up, and efficiently executed.

As soon as she was able, Checha went back to work, tucking her head down into the soft underbelly of the impala, ripping and taking her share of the meat. As she had told them, a cheetah must feed very quickly before some other predator or scavenger comes along to compete with her. She engrossed herself in the business of eating, though every now and again she looked up, her muzzle bright red, covered with fresh blood, to check her surroundings.

Only a few moments passed before there was a whistle of wings in the air above. A huge tawny eagle swooped in and landed on the tree above the Oglins' heads. From way up out of sight, a watcher in the sky, the great bird had seen the kill take place and swooped down. He was hoping to get his share as soon as the cheetah would leave.

Nervously, Checha raised her head to watch the massive bird land in the tree. Her eyes fixed on the bird briefly. She knew she would have to feed quickly now and leave before the thieves got too thick. Lion, hyena, even a large pack of vultures would be impossible for a single cheetah to fend off by herself. For now, she had to swallow only chunks of meat to regurgitate for her two cubs later. Her muzzle dropped back into the body of the impala as she continued eating voraciously.

As she fed on, Checha occasionally raised her head alertly at the sounds of the incoming birds. The vultures began to arrive. From far above the tawny's aerial station, they had seen the eagle go down and had begun to follow. One by one, the movement passed itself on like an invisible telegraph through the sky.

285

A lappet-faced vulture arrived, huge, with pink head and bare blue around his cheeks. Over a vicious, hooked bill, his beady eyes looked mean and intent. Swooping in with feet outstretched, to land with a hop, a skip, hop and a run, wings out, the vulture terrorised the other birds, to prove that he was the biggest and strongest there and to lay his claim to the kill. Finally, he dared to move towards the still-feeding cat, head down, running, and beak open, ready to attack the cheetah. Checha crouched down and rushed aggressively forward to swat at the bird as he lifted up off the ground. His great wings flapped vigorously, white feathers coming loose, as the cheetah's claws grazed his body. The vulture swished up above the cheetah and landed over to the other side of the impala's remains with a hop, skip and a run. Again, with feet stepping out and wings trailing, he managed to stay just out of Checha's reach, taunting her.

One has to defend one's kill in Africa. Hang on to what one has got! Otherwise it will surely be claimed by others and nothing will be left. That is the nature of life in Africa!.

The number of vultures was quickly increasing, and their pressure on the cheetah was building. Across the plain, Baylin and Lafina spotted the first pair of jackals approaching, tails up, running along, sniffing the air for the scent of the kill. They stopped occasionally to quarter the ground for other smells or to make their territorial markings on the bushes, then trotted along towards the kill.

By now, a hoard of vultures were hopping around in a group, impatient for their turn at the kill, all the while cackling, fighting with each other and pecking and beating one another violently with their wings and beaks. The squabbling was their way of sorting out their own pecking order before the kill was available. Then, almost as if it had been planned, three huge lappet-faced vultures, their wings outstretched and overlapping, bounded in towards the feeding cheetah. It reminded Baylin of three Oglins riding in on a hunt! Heads held low, like crooked lances, the vultures rushed in towards the cheetah. Checha crouched and sprang forward in defence, but the vicious birds bearing down on her were just too much. Knowing it was time to abandon her prize, she spun on her back legs and ran off a short distance before turning and growling angrily at them.

Finally, she turned away for good and walked stiffly back towards the Oglins under the big tree, licking the blood from her muzzle as she approached. Her tail still twitched with a life all of its own. As always, she had eventually lost her kill, but this time she had eaten quite well, as could be seen by the full stomach that hung much lower to the ground than when she left them.

Looking back at the site of the kill, Baylin and Lafina could see that the vultures were now all over the carcass, their long featherless necks stretching deep into what was left of the body of the impala. The remains were being tugged every which way. Birds were squabbling and fighting one another, while still trying to tear away a bite for themselves. Even more vultures came roaring in from behind. There was no room for them to get in on the kill, but they dove in anyway, pecking at the others' backs and forcing them up over the top of the body. The bubbling frenzy of noise swelled as they dug into the kill. The largest of the lappet-faced vultures got hold of a piece in his mouth and went hopping and skipping off, trying to keep it for himself while other vultures chased after him. This opened the way for a couple of the hangers-on birds to get in and try to steal a morsel of food.

The cheetah came up to Baylin and Lafina, still breathing rather heavily and licking her muzzle clean. She spoke to them once more in her regal fashion, "Remember, young Oglins, always ask yourselves, *'Which of these actions that I could take now will give me the most return for the same amount of effort?'*

"Now I must go and thank the impala spirits for feeding my cubs and me once again. I wish you the best of luck on the rest of your journey," she said most graciously. "Take my best regards to the Great Spirit."

With a twitch of her tail, Checha sauntered off to feed her cubs, leaving the Oglins speechless in awe of her beauty and amazing skill.

Baylin and Lafina sat still for a few more moments, absorbing the impact of what they had just seen, savouring the brutal, bittersweet splendour of life in balance with death. Later they relived what they had just experienced and thought through the important lesson they had received from Checha the noble Cheetah. They added the following verse to their growing poem of the journey.

Sleek Checha the Cheetah gave us
a fine spectacle for to learn
that ev'ry labour, ev'ry action
must the sharpest focus earn.
It must exceed all other options
to make the most of every turn.

CHAPTER 16

THE GREAT DIVIDE

Man feels himself an infinity above
those creatures who stand,
zoologically, only one step below him,
but every human looks up to the birds.
They suit the fancy of us all.
What they feel, they can voice, as we try to;
they court and nest,
they battle with the elements,
they are torn by two opposing influences,
a love of home
and a passion for far places.
Only with the birds do we share
so much emotion.
—Donald Culross Peattie, *Singing in the Wilderness*

The Hangman

Mounting their pala once more, the Oglins continued on up to the saddle that marked the Great Divide and then down into the catchment of the Great River at last. They were in high rolling country with no spectacular mountains or peaks. It was simply more endless African savanna.

In the heat of the day, the Oglins would stop and relax in the shade of a tree. They would lie on their backs, gazing up at the blue sky, as it seemed to move between the fluttering leaves and listening to the buzzing of the bugs and beetles. In this way, they would rest for a little while and the pala had a chance to graze nearby.

The veld was beginning to ripen and dry off as the summer season wore on. Winter would be coming around in a few months. Although in this part of the world winter was not really as cold a season as it was further south nearer the Pinnacles. In this region of the continent, winter was just a dry season, a bit cooler and typically very dry. Slowly the tall grass veld would turn to golden yellow, khaki and red. The winter colours would range from pale cream through golden to brown to dark red and eventually pink, and every colour in between. Against the backdrop of the veld, the grey or dark brown trunks of the trees would stand in stark contrast as their leaves began to turn colours as well. Some trees would lose their leaves while the leaves of others would just wilt and turn a grey-green colour and remain like that throughout the dry season.

One particular afternoon the Oglins were lying under a large tree looking up through the branches, when a small bird flitted across from another tree. It came and perched on a low branch near the bottom of the tree, still hunting, holding dead still except for the occasional twitch as its head moved to look around.

"After all," observed Baylin to himself, "it is all very well being a predator, but you are always still someone else's prey and you must therefore keep a watchful eye!"

It seemed that the little bird could sit there watching like that for hours, waiting for a bug, beetle or butterfly to fly past. Timing it just right, it would dart down off the perch, catching its prey in mid-air. Fluttering and turning, the bird would fly back to rest and look around. Then briskly hovering, the bird impaled the bug on a thorn to kill it and keep it for later. Job done, the bird returned to its perch to watch and wait again for the next unsuspecting prey. That is why this bird and its family are known in Africa as "the hangman," as it "hangs" its prey out for later.

Baylin lazily raised an arm and pointed. "Look at what that bird is doing!" he indicated to Lafina.

The bird cocked his head at them and spoke in a tiny but nonetheless commanding voice, "And so you should be watching the birds! Welcome, young Oglins. I am Jackie Hangman. I am a red-backed shrike!"

Both the Oglins bolted upright, startled but interested! A little way off the pala raised their heads in unison, mouths still full of grass, no longer chewing, ears forward, like zebras alert at the first sign of danger.

Another bird! It hadn't crossed their minds to talk to a small bird, of which there were so many along their daily treks. This red-backed shrike's body was only a little bigger than an Oglin's foot. Its red back contrasted nicely with the white underbelly, and the white inverted "V" at the base of its tail. The redness of the cape accentuated the bird's grey hood over its sinister black eye mask and vicious bill. The red-backed shrike is a true image of a hooded and masked hangman. And the shrike is a skilled hunter, sitting on low branches to watch and then hunting down insects that fly past.

"We are pleased to meet you!" Lafina replied, recovering herself enough to answer. "Where is your nest, oh Jackie Hangman? Is it in this tree? Are we disturbing you?" she asked.

"No, no," replied the little shrike. "I don't even make a nest in Africa! I'm only a seasonal visitor, not a resident."

"That's very interesting!" Lafina said sincerely. "I know you only visit us at the Pinnacles in the summer months and then go away again at the first signs of winter. Do you migrate far?" she asked, wondering how far such a small bird could travel.

"Why yes, indeed, young Oglin!" Jackie answered proudly. "I am a world traveller, in fact. My true home, where I am a resident and raise my family, is very, very far from here. It is across another continent, across a few oceans, far to the north in a land that, at this time of year, is in the grips of icy cold and all covered with snow. It is summer there when I go back home to avoid your winter. The meadows are green and surrounded by trees in full leaf. The streams that are now frozen stiff run with lovely clear water. There are rocky hillsides and steep mountains solid with ice now that will be covered in green grass and flowering shrubs when I am there," the Hangman explained, while his eye still roved restlessly, ever in search of more prey, as all predators are.

"That is my home, where I build a nest and raise young. It is far, far away from here," Jackie continued, not sounding anywhere near as mean as he looked. "But I fly south with my mate, each year for these summer months. As it is now soon to become autumn here, we are storing up for our big journey. We must eat lots of fat, juicy bugs and wait for the weather to turn in our home in the north. As soon as it is warm enough there, we will leave and head home. There we will build a nest and have our young in a tall tree or in the shrubs along a river valley. There we will raise our family before we return here again next year, and bring them south with us, to show them the route as our parents did for us, and our ancestors have done for many, many generations."

"That's a mighty long way for a small bird like you!" Lafina exclaimed in wonder.

"Indeed, it's a very long way," the shrike replied. "It does take us a while, but we do it in stages. It's too much flying to do it in one go."

"What is it like to fly such long distances over land and sea?" Baylin asked the bird, in awe of his great accomplishment.

"Well, young Oglin, it takes a lot of thought. We have a specific route and we use it each year. It is the same passage we shrikes have used for generations. We, too, have battends that we tell to our young ones each night, as they are growing up in the nest, about how our great ancestors discovered these routes and found their way on the winds of the seasons. The intrepid explorers that they were! They pioneered the way from place to place for us and now it is easy. It is imprinted in our minds. The challenge now is to watch one's course along the way."

He checked to see if the Oglins were listening and found them rapt, chins on their knees with their arms hugging their legs to their chests. Assured that he had their attention, Jackie continued his tale.

"As with all animals, all birds, and all organisms, one must have a plan! Every time you are doing something, you have to have some sort of plan in mind. 'Where do you want to be? When do you want to be there? What are you trying to do? Why are you going? Who are you going to go with? How are you going to go about achieving that end destination? And what are you going to do when you get there?'

"Continuously along the way we must carefully observe and monitor our progress. This is to ensure that we stay on course, achieving each step as we planned it to be. The moment we go off plan, adjustments or controlling actions must be made, to bring us back on course. So every step of the way along our plan, in our case, along the journey to and fro, we carefully monitor our positions according to our memories. We then immediately make any adjustments or do any re-planning necessary to bring us back into line with our plan."

Once again, the Oglins realised that they were being given yet another important piece of the picture, from the seemingly unlikely source of the little Hangman!

"We constantly realign ourselves with our plan," he carried on, not missing a beat. "We redirect, flying slightly further into the wind, or a little bit more downwind, constantly changing our course a little bit or changing the order of the flight patterns for better direction than before. We try to make many small corrections and stay as close to our ancestral route as possible, but sometimes a big storm will blow us far off course, or perhaps the timing of our trip has to change slightly. Therefore, we must make adjustments all the time. The whole way through life, we've learned to do that with every decision we make. We plan, then monitor our progress along the way, and quickly correct the deviations or even re-plan entirely when we must. We do not want to just monitor our results and congratulate ourselves for doing well. We want to create a specific result and we are constantly monitoring to make this happen!"

Jackie paused, searching for the best finishing line.

"You young Oglins could learn greatly from this. You and all animals and organisms could benefit hugely from what we, the red-backed shrikes, do in our day-to-day life: *Plan, monitor, control and re-plan to create the desired result!*" he finished with a flourish.

The two Oglins looked at one another in realisation, and Lafina exclaimed, "I think we have found the final step in checking our actions towards our creed! We now have a series of questions to ask ourselves about each action, in terms of achieving our creed. This comes right on top of Checha's fine words of testing one action against others to see which will give us more progress towards our creed for the same effort. We must assume that we could be wrong when dealing with our environment and the Hangman has now taught us that we must monitor what we are doing to create the desired results. Jackie Hangman the Red-Backed Shrike has shown us how to do that! Check your movement towards what you want, with every action you are doing, to make sure that you end up where you want to end up!"

Baylin stepped in to help saying, "Don't forget the importance of making adjustments before you get too far off course, as Jackie explained."

Listening to the two Oglins discuss what they had just learned, the Hangman realised they had grasped it all. Now, feeling he had completed the role assigned to him by the Great Spirit, he needed to go back to his hunting. So, they said their farewells and thanks and the little bird flitted off to the next tree in search of prey.

Baylin and Lafina excitedly talked over the learning they had made so far. It was becoming more and more clear now as they began to see the role of the questions, their creed and the everyday usefulness of all that they were experiencing. Again, they added a new verse to their poem:

THE OGLIN

Jackie Hangman, world travell'r,
does check and change his route with care.
To go the farthest distances,
we too must plan and compare,
and ever mindful and attentive be
To stay true to our course so fair.

CHAPTER 17

THE LAND OF CLOUDS

Do all the good you can
By all the means you can,
In all the places you can,
At all the times you can,
As long as ever you can.

—John Wesley

Bananas

The Oglins' general direction was north, following the flow of the Great River basin. Their plan was to follow the higher ground between the catchments of the two main tributaries: the Merma River to the yesterdays and the larger Modra River to the tomorrows. This route would take them through woodlands and savannas rather than following the rivers through thick forests. Eventually they would have to go down into the forests to reach the Great River at the confluence of the Merma and Modra rivers. There, they were hoping to find the ruins where the Great Spirit would be.

Their route took them into higher and higher concentrations of people. The more dense the populations became, the more evidence there was of bush clearing and soil erosion. Away from the river, only islands of the forests still existed on tall hills and mountains.

The days were hot and humid. The discomfort made Baylin and Lafina's thoughts turn longingly to their home in the south, where the season would have been cooling down by now. Here, as they were getting closer to the equator with the sun more overhead, the weather was decidedly different. At home the rains were over by now, but here the main rainy season had begun in earnest. It was raining heavily every afternoon and on some days, it poured all day.

They were crossing through a banana plantation in the afternoon, sinking deeply into wet, almost waterlogged soil. The banana trees whispering overhead were lush and very green. Ahead, they could hear an extended line of people singing as they worked. The Oglins changed course across the plantation rows and up the slope towards the forest to avoid the people.

They stopped as they entered the forest and watched the people wandering forward, singing as they swayed upright, then swinging down, moving ahead all the time. They had sharp objects on the end of sticks that they were thumping into the ground. They were digging to loosen up the soil to plant another crop. It was quite a gentle sound and the smell of the freshly turned earth was heavy on the air. It was a lovely sunny afternoon and steamy as ever in the heat. The workers' bodies shone in the sun, with the sweat glistening off them. The skin of the people here was exceptionally black, much blacker than any the Oglins had seen in the south. There were no men working, just the women moving calmly forward, many with babies strapped to their backs.

The Oglins moved deeper into the thickening forest. The air became even heavier and their movement more difficult. They decided they would climb up onto the forested slopes of the hill to wait for evening and travel then. They continued to battle their way upwards through the dense undergrowth. The air itself seemed liquid and heavy; it was so laden with moisture.

Suddenly, they came upon an open path. Something or someone had been clearing it. This made the going so much easier that it was even possible to ride again. So the travellers moved more quickly now, up towards the top of the slope in the midday heat. The buzzing of flies and the incessant noise of bugs and beetles filled the air, and the decaying plant material, wet under their feet, cushioned their footfalls. Lafina could not remember when the hair on her feet and hands had last felt dry!

Gorillas

As they moved on a little bit further, Baylin and Arto, in front, suddenly stiffened and stopped. This happened so quickly that Argyl, Lafina and Lara all bumped into Arto from behind. Baylin pointed ahead noiselessly. Lafina saw it, too, though neither was sure what it was. Whatever it was, it consisted of a huge amount of black fur and bare patches of black skin. Scared to move, the Oglins stayed frozen where they were and watched. The pala, dead still now, ears pricked forward, stared nervously ahead.

Suddenly, a huge black leg, furry and with a bare-skinned foot and black toenails, rose up and rolled over to the other side. A massive head with an egg-like point at the top rose up out of the greenery. The beast had almost no nose, but his cavernous black nostrils slanted slightly off to each side. The animal's thick white canine teeth went to nibbling along the edge of its foot, trying to catch a flea or something. It finally dawned on Baylin and Lafina what it was: a gorilla! Though they had never seen such a magnificent creature themselves, they recognised it from the battends of Old Spola.

By then their eyes had adjusted to the gloom and the closeness. They began to see even more gorillas in the grove, lying up in and around the bases of the surrounding trees, resting and gently having an afternoon nap. The Oglins had ridden right into a family of gorillas! They then realised what had created the convenient path they had been following through the bush.

The pala were watching, ears forward, the whites of their eyes showing and bodies leaning backwards as if trying to widen the gap. Arto, deciding that this was a little too close for him, snorted and shuffled backwards into the others.

Surprised by sound and movement so close, the first gorilla sprang to his feet. Upright, he was colossal! The silver hair on his back, massive shoulders and long, muscular arms dangling down in front of him made him all the more impressive at this close proximity! He raised up his chin, put back his head, and screamed at them, baring his fierce teeth, stark white against his orange tongue. He beat his chest with his powerful fists, resounding like someone beating on a drum.

Wide-eyed and down on their haunches, the pala backed as fast as they could. They couldn't take their eyes off the towering gorilla but were fleeing in reverse, panic rising in an instant sweat. Instinctively, the Oglins rode the storm and concentrated on their pala. They did not want to turn and run, but to face the mighty gorilla and show submission to settle him down. Argyl, only on a lead, reared and, muscles bunched, spun on his hindquarters, very nearly knocking Lafina off Lara. Lara, having little room to manoeuvre, overbalanced and toppled gently into the mass of undergrowth. Head up, she struggled to rise.

Baylin quickly realising the total disarray of his entourage, spoke out, "We mean no harm! We are only travellers!"

"Ah, it's you! Oglins!" laughed the gorilla, recognising them and dropping onto all fours then sitting roughly down like a baby who has only just learned to walk.

"Please forgive my display! You took me quite by surprise!" the gorilla added with a quizzical look on his face as he watched the Oglins battling to regain their composure. "I am Gumbo the Gorilla, 'Grandfather' to this family you see before you."

"We are very pleased to meet you, oh Great Gumbo," said Lafina humbly as she fought her way up from under the vegetation and a departing Lara, leaves stuck in her hair and a small branch still hanging around her neck. "We are sorry we gave you such a start."

Baylin had yet to say another word as he managed the shying Arto and set about calming him and gathering the other two escapees who had run off down the path a little way.

"No worry whatsoever! I'm happy to see you both. In fact, I've been expecting you to arrive anytime," Gumbo replied gently. Waving Lafina to join him, they sat and chatted generally about her trip and awaited the return of Baylin.

It wasn't long before Baylin arrived on foot followed by three wary pala, stepping very gingerly and dubiously. Not trying to get too close, Baylin dropped the reins and leads so the pala could stay off a bit. With kind words to reassure them, he walked on to join Lafina with the gorilla.

"Sorry about that," Baylin sighed, as he settled down. "None of us ever expected or knew what we were seeing!" He laughed lightly.

"No, I am so sorry." The huge gorilla apologetically laid a massive hand on Baylin's arm. "You see, we must constantly be on the alert. We live in grave danger here. Our way of life, our home forests, all are being destroyed! More and more and more we are being reduced to smaller and smaller communities on little hills in the mist and in the moisture, with the people filling in the gaps. Recently there have been many new people encroaching more and more on our country. So we are pretty nervous and we find it very difficult to live our lives out, quietly on our own. Therefore when anything sneaks up on us, we elders defend our families with great aggression to try to give the others time to get away."

Nobody had even noticed how all the other gorillas had disappeared during the uproar, but looking around now they saw them returning out of the bush. Just as Lafina had done, they were brushing off the various decorations of plant material hanging all over them.

"In fact, they hunt us!" Gumbo continued, in too much of a hurry to let everyone become acquainted. "They hunt us down and shrink our skulls and cut off our hands and feet for mementoes! Many of these people actually don't think twice about eating a gorilla or just selling parts of us for medicinal or even decorative purposes."

Baylin and Lafina gasped in horror at this news.

"We do have some people, warriors who fight for us, I know, but their numbers are few. There are so many people here now; they are putting a lot of pressure on the land. It's not easy for them to find the amount of food that they need. They war and fight with each other often. Chopping each other up, not giving anyone time to plant and grow crops. Which means there is never enough to go around! In fact, most of the wars are caused by a lack of available resources."

"Goodness me!" Lafina exclaimed, feeling sorry for the people who had grown so desperate.

"We hear that you have been sent for by the Great Spirit," Gumbo continued. "And you are wandering the world to find the keys to the future and that it will be your duty to carry this across to the people later on."

The two young Oglins looked at each other in alarm.

"The people? We are going to have to teach the people?" Baylin asked tentatively, this being the first they had heard of such a thing!

Old Gumbo smiled gently, with a knowing look, his eyebrows pulled down over his eyes, set deep back into his head. "Yes, I'm sure that's going to be your task," he replied.

"But what about the fighting and the wars?" asked Lafina, her voice trembling at the very thought of it.

"I'm not sure what the Great Spirit has in store for you," Gumbo assured her. "But I'm sure you'll work it out when the time comes, one way or another. And I'm sure the Spirits will ask you to do only things that you are truly capable of. Look how far you have come on this Great Journey!"

The rest of the gorillas, now all seemingly back from their disappearing act, gathered around their grandfather Gumbo and the young Oglins to see what was going on. A particularly bold young gorilla had snuck forward and actually climbed onto Lafina's lap. He was pulling at her hair and climbing all over her, playing with her feet and twiddling her toes. The little gorilla then took a dive down at Baylin's toes, grabbed them, stuck them in his mouth and bit them. With a sharp, indrawn breath, Baylin had to yank his foot away from the rascal. Old Gumbo looked on with a very sad smile on his face, watching the Oglins play with the cheeky young gorilla.

"We would love to pass away the afternoon with you," Gumbo finally said. "But I'm afraid it's time for us to wander on into the forest to gather our food for the day. You see, we must eat while we can; we never know when some hunters will disturb us."

The Oglins asked Gumbo for directions and the best route for them to take on their journey.

"We don't really know that much about the outside world anymore," Gumbo answered. "But as far as I am concerned, the best way for you to go from here is to head straight towards the yesterdays. Follow the gorilla track down off this ridge. Then if you stick to the thickets along the ridge edge, in and out of the banana plantations, you will follow a long line of these ridges down to where you want to go. Travel well! I wish you success on your Great Journey. We are all counting on you!"

"Thank you, oh Great Gumbo. We will always remember you and your family," Lafina said sadly in parting. Baylin ruffled the head of the young gorilla who had been playing with them.

The great silver-backed gorilla raised himself up on all four legs and began to rouse his family to move through the forest. They quietly wandered off, each picking away at shoots and shrubs as they moved through the dense thicket.

Hunters

As the gorillas moved off, disappearing once more into the jungle, Baylin and Lafina began their descent back down the slope. They hadn't gone far, making their way down through the thicket of ferns, thick bush and heavy moisture, along the track made by the gorillas when suddenly, there was the smell of people! It was the smell of people who lived in small huts and carried the smell of their fires with them. It was the thick heavy smell of wood smoke, mixed with a bit of tobacco and strong stale sweat; a queer mix of smells, very particular to these sort of people. One didn't come across these smells just anywhere. The Oglins had smelled it when they had bumped into people before.

Having been warned about hunters, the Oglins were nervous. Acting on an impulse, Baylin and Lafina quickly crawled off the track into the thickness of the undergrowth and forced their pala into the bush ahead of them. They didn't get far. The growth was extremely thick, with tall, heavy stems, reaching up and closing over the top of them and the track like a canopy. In the otherwise complete silence, they heard quiet footfalls and whispers and the occasional slash of machetes if there was something in the way.

The sweat was dripping off the faces of the people as they struggled up the hill. They were carrying banging sticks over their shoulders. The leader's banging stick was at the ready. As they came to the spot where the two little Oglins lay hiding and quivering in the bush, so close to the track, the leader stopped. He knelt down. Two more men caught up from behind.

The leader was pointing at the tracks of the Oglins and pala! They exchanged hand signals. In silence, the rest of them squatted down on their haunches, leaning on their banging sticks or machetes. Baylin and Lafina could actually see the sweat on the hunters' bodies. They could see it moving, slowly trickling in rivulets down the dark black skin, shining in the soft green light of the forest. The continual buzzing of the flies was the only noise. They buzzed their way around from person to person.

The two little Oglins had never been so dead still. Their golden eyes, gleaming bright, were fixed on one another. They were listening desperately, deeply and ready for communication by eye contact if necessary. There was just a question in both eyes. They each had a hand on a pala, standing tense and still, like a drawn bow.

The Oglins' track obviously led back into the gang of people. The three men with the leader were looking back at those behind, pointing at the ground and signing for them to look for the tracks. It was in a particularly thick bunch of fern and bracken and they were not sure if they could see the spoor. They were gently parting the leaves and looking. Then the Oglins saw the left and right sweep of the hand and shake of the head, signaling, "No track." The leader made his way backwards, searching the whole way. He followed the path, just a little way short of the Oglins. He, too, finally indicated that the track was gone. The leader raised his hands, pointing left, and pointing right again, palm up in question. The tracker, with a scrubbing motion of his hands, pointed to his chest and then at each person in front of him to say, "No spoor, the tracks have been destroyed by us. This is where they ended."

Unsure of what to do, confusion reigned among the hunters. Should they backtrack to where they might be able to find the unusual tracks again? Or should they forget the distraction and carry on in search of the gorillas? The leader stood up and signaled for them to retrace their steps. He obviously wanted to know who or even what had made these tracks. Slowly, the worm of people turned and headed back down the hill to see if they could find where those tracks might lead. They made their way back down past the Oglins once more.

Once the people were completely out of sight, the little Oglins squirmed back out of their hiding places, mounted the pala, and made their way back up the hill to the thicket where the gorillas had been. This was something they had never experienced before. Their hearts beat wildly in their chests. The two Oglins huddled together.

"We can head out here, down this other track, and we can probably get away from them," Baylin whispered. "The tracking is very slow in this thick bush, and we'd be gone before they get back to this junction. Or should we get across to Gumbo and warn him and his family? I'm pretty sure they are after the gorillas, not us."

Indecision once again. It was a very difficult choice for the little Oglins, and they knew they had very little time!

Lafina looked longingly down the track that would lead them to safety but away from the gorillas. The other way, the gorillas' spoor was very obvious and clear.

Baylin, with a hand on her shoulder, whispered in her ear "Would it lead to our creed to leave without warning them?"

"No, it wouldn't," Lafina replied, immediately sure of what they must do. "Not even the very first thing! We would like to live in harmony with all those around us. We must warn Gumbo!"

The Oglins both instinctively reached for their pachas, fingering their amulets and especially their most recent acquisitions, the dazzling white seashell in Lafina's pacha and the stone with the fire in its heart that Baylin carried. They swung their palas as one and quickly took off in pursuit of Gumbo and his family.

They hadn't trotted for long along the gorillas' pathway, ducking and dodging the overhanging vegetation, when they caught their first glimpse of the gorillas through the trees. Unwittingly they fell into exactly the same trap as before. They spotted a gorilla and headed for it. They hadn't kept an eye out for the Great Gumbo. Suddenly rearing up out of the forest was the massive form of the silver-backed grandfather, beating his chest and baring his ferocious teeth under snarling nostrils. With dark fiery eyes, he came roaring and crashing towards them.

As before, recognition dawned across his face and the great roar turned into a laugh, as a joke, so typical of Gumbo. The two cowering, terrified little Oglins, barely keeping their seats on the spinning, frightened pala, started to giggle lightly in stark relief, before they remembered the seriousness of the situation. Hurriedly they  told Gumbo that they had come across the gang of people tracking through the forest.

Gumbo reached up to put a mighty hand on the high back of his head, and quietly muttered under his breath, "They are coming more frequently these days to hunt my family. We are prizes for them, not only for food and skins, but also for ornaments in their homes. We must go!"

Baylin felt much braver and much better now that he had faced up to his mission and the odds drawn up against him. "We could split directions," he suggested to Gumbo. "That way the tracks will confuse them, and they may just decide to follow us instead of you. They seemed very interested in our spoor. Maybe it's unusual for them."

Gumbo, with one gentle hand on a shoulder of each of the little Oglins, thanked them dearly, and said, "We will disappear, as only we can."

He signaled his family and they all climbed up quietly into the canopy. Slowly, from tree to tree they made their escape. The great weight of the silver-backed gorilla made it more difficult for him than any of the others. Where he could go, the rest could travel easily. Later they would drop back to the ground into the undergrowth and make off again in total silence, their track effectively broken. It was their only way of breaking the spoor. It was their only hope of getting away from the experienced trackers and hunters.

The two Oglins were now faced with their own difficulties. Once again they could hear and smell the people coming up the track. They were probably coming quickly now too, having heard Gumbo's roar of attack. The route that the Oglins must choose would be difficult. To get to the other path off the hill they had to initially go back to where they had met the gorillas the first time. This would take them directly towards the people. It was just a matter of who would get to the junction first! It was dangerous, but it was the only option.

Baylin picked up a strong sapling stick from where it had been discarded by the gorillas moments earlier and mounting up, he called out to Lafina. "We cannot sneak off into this undergrowth without leaving a track. We must return to the other path. The people may well get there before us, but we will have the element of surprise on our side. We must ride. Ride like the wind!"

Without hesitating, they spun their pala around and charged off down the path. Baylin was in front on Arto, dodging from one side to the other to avoid standing trees and branches. Leaping high over one log, he lay flat down on Arto's neck to avoid the next low branch. With the trees whipping past, there was no way he could look back to see how and where Lafina was. Arto needed no urging to extend into a flat gallop, and Baylin could only hope that Argyl and Lara were doing the same. The dappled shade made judgement and visibility very difficult. Arto, surefooted, seemed to understand this and took over the navigation. Baylin only had to watch and avoid the overhead obstacles, as he flew along on the most dangerous ride of his life!

He rounded a curve and everything seemed to slow down for him; it was just like the hunting competition again. There were two hunters crouching at the junction of the two paths, studying the tracks. The others had not yet come into view around the last corner. Both of them looked up, startled. Eyes wide and white, one behind the other they tried to turn and point their banging sticks ominously at the flying pala and Oglin. Baylin knew, in that split second, that he would be through them and turned off down the path before they would be able to fire at him; but he also knew that Lafina would not make it. They would be prepared by then and would probably gun her and Lara down as they approached.

He didn't have to think about it. His only course of action was clear, and years of pig hunting practice made it possible. Baylin took full control of Arto again, slowing his headlong rush slightly and collecting his body ready to spring. He turned him straight at the closest man. He brought the sapling to bear, like a familiar pigging lance, as the hunter attempted to rise. Baylin swung his lance and went for the gap between the man's chest and his banging stick. The sapling's point sailed neatly through the narrowing gap and Baylin let Arto's forward speed force the banging stick up and out of the man's arms, hitting him in the face as it went and sending him sprawling backwards, narrowly escaping the flying hooves.

Now was the most dangerous moment. The second man had more time than the first. Baylin had to almost stop as he collected himself and his lance and slowed the pala's forward speed. He steered Arto slightly further to the right in a dummy run, and the man responded by slowing the arc of his banging stick, anticipating a need to fire to his left. That was all the chance Baylin needed. He spurred Arto forward and left again straight at the man, who, surprised again, couldn't change the weapon's direction in time. Baylin pushed Arto into a powerful jump, hitting the hunter full in the chest, crushing his weapon against him. The man fell, rolling backwards on the mat of soft plants, but didn't let go of the weapon held tightly in his now-outstretched arms. Baylin brought Arto to a bounding sideways halt. Holding the sapling lance down he charged in again, stopping with the roughly chewed, sharp end resting hard against the man's throat as he struggled to regain himself.

The hunter seemed to suddenly stiffen and lose his urge to fight when he looked up into eyes of burning gold, holding him cold in their stare. At that moment Lafina and Lara with Argyl right beside them burst around the bend. She was low over the neck, stretching forward and driving the pala on. Her eyes widened as she took in the scene in front of her and she slowed in hesitation.

"Ride!" Baylin cried. "Go for the left-hand path and don't stop till you hit the bottom. Go! Go! Go!" he yelled, as he noticed her distraction with the first hunter who was now crawling after his weapon lying half in the undergrowth.

Lafina needed no more encouragement. Lara bravely changed stride twice, jumped clear of the fallen men and turned down the path towards safety. With only a slight hesitation, Argyl dived down the steep turn after her. At that moment, a shout rang out and around the bend more hunters streamed into view, diving for cover. Baylin lifted the point of the sapling slightly, as he pushed Arto back into action, and drove the lance into the soft ground alongside the man's ear. It was now pegged between his body and his weapon, effectively preventing him from being able to pull his weapon back towards his body without letting it go first.

Spinning, Arto leaped forward and in two strides dived into the open mouth of the waiting path. The world behind them erupted into roaring flames and earth-shattering noise. Trees cracked, splinters flew and leaves were shredded as the air filled with the whiplash cracks of near misses. In a flash, pala and Oglin were gone, straight down the path at breakneck speed. The crack of bullets flying past and the snap of them striking wood around them drove them at an insane pace down the almost vertical path, strewn with logs and branches. Only Arto's miraculous control of his flying hooves could save them. Baylin gave Arto his head entirely and let him fly. "Find Lafina!" he instructed and leaned way back to help bring Arto's hocks under him and increase his control of his death-defying flight down the tunnel of forest.

Finally, they burst headlong into a thicket at the bottom, unable to make the last turn, and ran straight into Lafina, Lara and Argyl, who had also missed the final bend! Above them they could hear the heated shouting among the people. However, they had some distance between them now, thanks to the pala's phenomenal speed. Together, more quietly, the little group scrambled their way through the thicket and back onto the track down the hill. This led them down onto the flats, where they could finally get a glimpse of the sky, pregnant with rain and grumbling with thunder.

"Let's go!" Lafina shouted. "Along the edge of the ridge and away from here! The rain will be upon us soon and will wipe out our tracks!"

Their instincts had been right. Their creed had guided them well! The gorillas were safe, at least for one more night. Their bravery and skills had been tested to the full and all they wanted at the moment was some distance to separate them from the scene of the action and the hunters.

That night they added a verse for the gorillas:

Gentle Gumbo of the mountain mists,
taught us that every life is dear,
that even when the paths diverge
and when there is so much to fear,
if we live by our creed each day,
the hardest choices will be clear.

CHAPTER 18

THE GREAT FOREST

A holistic perspective is essential in management.
If we base management decisions on any other perspective,
we are likely to experience results different from those intended,
because only the whole is reality.
—Allan Savory with Jody Butterfield, *Holistic Management*

The Forest

The Oglins made their way through the Great Forest where the moisture dripped incessantly. They were constantly wet. They just did not find it easy to be in that sort of climate. It was not really ideal for an Oglin who prefers wide-open spaces and sunny weather. Finding clear pathways to use was extremely difficult, too. Once they did find one, they had to be exceptionally careful because, much like in the forests surrounding Vadiera, one could not hear the footfall of another animal or a person. One could practically walk into a band of people waltzing along, without any advance warning that they were there. The Oglins' keen sense of smell was of little use in the heavy, humid environment; the smells just did not travel far. Any smell was rather quickly wrestled down and overpowered by the heavy damp and rank smell of the rotting vegetation.

Getting around the huge trees became very arduous, too, as their roots grew high above the ground, standing out almost like the upright wings of an eagle, snaking their way along before they finally disappeared underground. This was the anchoring system for these huge trees. It was the only way that they managed to stay standing for so many years with their great girth and towering height on the loose, wet soils.

Many days it was very misty, a heavy, cloying mist with big droplets. This was something they just could not get used to. Even Old Spola's battends about the mists could not prepare them for the disorientating and debilitating effects of the sodden, swirling veil that shrouded them. It closed in around them, shifting this way and that way, making it very troublesome to tell what direction they were heading.

Becoming despondent and losing heart, the two Oglins sat down to rest a lot. They were wet through and the pala were soaked to the skin. There was an eerie, creamy, half-light throughout the forest and the leaves were a luminous green. Huge fronds offered a little shelter as they hid underneath them, trying to rest up for what could well have been night or day. It became difficult to even tell.

Where possible, they would make use of one of the numerous paths. This way they covered much more ground, but then the paths always led to people and habitation. So with the continual worry of running into people, they moved through the rough thickets whenever they smelled or heard any villages.

On these occasions, the thick jungle undergrowth really slowed them down.

The Bat

For two or three days, Baylin and Lafina had to continually struggle and fight their way along around the far of smells of a settlement. Their progress was painfully slow, as they had to chop and hack their way through. Taking it in turns they slashed everything in front of them, cutting a swath just wide enough to allow them to pass. One after the other they worked away in the heat and humidity. The pala nibbled at shoots and walked along behind them looking wet and crestfallen. The two sopping wet and miserable little Oglins did not look any better. They were feeling quite desperate and getting utterly sick of it.

They stopped in a small clearing, opened up by the fall of a massive tree, and sat back-to-back on the girth of its trunk, swatting away at the mosquitoes buzzing around them continually. It must have been midday, although it was still very, very gloomy in the Great Forest even here, where the race for the new light now streaming in through the new opening in the canopy had only just begun. Thousands of young plants were growing at high speed to capture the light and thus to close the gap again.

In despair, Baylin asked the question that was on both of their minds, "Aghh, Lafina, how much further of this, do you think?"

"Well, I don't know, but I'm so tired of it. I don't think I can go much further," she sighed. "And even if we were to turn back, we'd have to struggle our way through this stuff again! It grows up so quickly behind us, I'm sure that within four days or so our path would be completely covered again! What are we going to do? Have we not got another plan?"

"Well, there is obviously one way to get down the Great River," said Baylin, with the beginnings of a smile on his face. Somehow, he was always able to be cheery in the most difficult of times. "What if we built another raft and floated down the river?"

"Oh, I don't know," said Lafina. "There are a lot of crocodiles to trust! Remember what Smiler told us! And the Merma is such a big river, we could wander off on all sorts of channels that we don't even know are there and pass the confluence entirely. We could end up missing the ruins and the Great Spirit altogether!"

"You're right," laughed Baylin, "I was just pulling your leg. We haven't got much choice but to keep going. Sooner or later we must get onto a rather large path that will take us down to the Great River."

"If only we could see where we're going," moaned Lafina. "It is so gloomy and dark. There are just too many plants stealing the light that filters through the canopy. What I would give to see the sun for a change! We could actually know what direction we were travelling in and how we are going. How do we know that we're even going the right way?"

"We're continuing downhill," soothed Baylin, trying to reassure her. "That's all we can do, is carry on downhill. It will take us north and north and north and eventually turn us around towards the yesterdays as we get close to the Modra River. That's the direction that we've just got to keep following. As long as we're going downhill, we're fine."

"Well, how do we know that we aren't going down the same hill and back up and round and down it again…I mean we could just be going around and around in circles here!" Lafina complained, obviously nearing the end of her patience.

"I suppose we could, but it's not really likely," Baylin answered gently, becoming a bit amused. "We do have the downhill continuing pretty steadily. Sure, occasionally, we've gone uphill a bit, but we seem to only do that for short spaces of time. And each time we've continued down, we've come back into sight of the Merma River. As long as we are going parallel to this river, we'll be all right."

"Wouldn't it be nice to get above and have a view of the whole forest and know roughly where we are?" Lafina sighed longingly, calming down and feeling more relaxed now that her breath was returning after her last arduous spell of slashing undergrowth.

"Yes," agreed Baylin, "that certainly would make a difference." Then with a flash of brilliance he exclaimed, "What we must do now, I think, is just climb up a tree! We'll find a tree and climb it as high as we possibly can. Let's do it, come, right now! Shall we?" Baylin challenged. Doing anything was better than wallowing in frustration.

"Yes!" Lafina cried, instantly getting excited about the idea. "There's a likely looking tree right there! Let's go!"

She jumped up and headed toward the base of the big tree.

"Mind what you put your hands on when you're climbing, though," Baylin cautioned, half-teasing and half-serious. "There are snakes and lizards and geckos and chameleons and all sorts of things that live on these trees. I'd hate to get a fright like that!"

Heeding Baylin's wise warning, the two little Oglins began scaling the tremendous tree. Up the vines and trunk they clambered, slowly but surely, occasionally resting and enjoying the views from the increasingly lofty heights. By late afternoon they were high up in the branches of the towering tree, but still seemingly a long

318

way from getting to the top of the elevated canopy.

They took a long rest on a lovely broad branch as the evening pressed the gloom to darkness on the forest floor below. They had left all their belongings with the palas so that they had something familiar to be with. Now, as the dusk deepened, they lost sight of their companions far below. The Oglins gladly resigned themselves to spending the night right there, welcoming the change from the dank forest floor. Just to one side was a huge orchid, hanging down over the sides of the branch. The orchid's wreath of leaves were a pale greenish blue colour with pretty delicate little white flowers. To their surprise, from underneath the orchid a squeaking and shuffling began, then became louder and more agitated. The Oglins looked at each other in amazement, wondering what in the world could be going on.

Lafina nudged Baylin and whispered, "Well, talk to it! Maybe it will talk back to us!"

Taking her suggestion, Baylin said, "Oh, you who squeaks in the flowers, can you hear me?"

The squeaking and shuffling stopped abruptly. From within the leaves, a voice inquired, "Whom is that?"

With a sly grin, Baylin replied, "Whom is that asking 'Whom is that'?"

Much to their amusement, the indignant voice responded once again, "Whom is that asking 'Whom is that' when I'm asking 'Whom is that'?"

Not to be outdone, and almost giggling now, Baylin rejoined, "Whom is that asking, 'Whom is that, asking "Whom is that," while I am asking "Whom is that"'?"

"Whooo…"

Suddenly, from between the orchid leaves, poked a furry little upside down head, with pointy ears and a perky little nose. Baring terrible canine looking teeth grimacing around a pink tongue, the creature demanded sharply, "Whom is that talking to me?"

It was a bat! Both Oglins started back in alarm. Baylin almost fell off the tree, remembering to hold on only at the very last instant.

"Dear, you did give us a fright, didn't you?" Lafina scolded the bat.

"Well, you certainly surprised me!" replied the squeaky-voiced little creature. "It's not often that a bat hears a voice speaking to it where it lives, hanging upside down here in this orchid high up in the treetops!" Pausing only to lick his muzzle with a little dog-like tongue, he went on righteously, "In fact I would say that this is probably the first time ever that anyone has climbed up here to talk to me! My family and I live quite nicely here on our own without anybody coming to bother us, thank you very much! And by the way, for your information, my name is Birdoke, which means Bird Person!"

"Oh Great Birdoke the Bat, please excuse us for disturbing your peaceful evening," Baylin said appeasingly, trying to hide his further amusement at the little bat's haughty attitude.

"Oh well then, never mind, the daytime slumbers were over, after all," Birdoke answered in a more conciliatory tone. "We are just now preparing for our nighttime sortie over the Great Forest in search of food."

"Are you an insect-eating bat or a fruit-eating bat?" Lafina asked him, her curiosity overcoming any fright that may have remained.

"We happen to be insect-eating bats," he replied, "one of the many kinds in this Great Forest of ours."

"What sort of insects do you eat then?" she asked.

"Well, there must be thousands of kinds of insects here," Birdoke informed her. "There are probably millions of insects.

But our favourite food is those big juicy mosquitoes that seem to be sitting on you and drawing lots of blood out of you. You're looking a bit pale there aren't you, Oglin? A little bit pale, yes?" teased Birdoke, peering forward with his dark eyes but still looking ever so warm, dry and furry.

The Oglins looked at him with naked jealousy in their eyes. "How do you stay so dry, oh Great Birdoke?" Baylin questioned.

"Well, I live high up here in the forest and I hang upside down under these orchid leaves all day long. The orchid leaves turn away most of the moisture and protect me from rainfall. It's only the humidity that remains underneath. We get a little bit musty, but we can survive it," Birdoke said proudly.

"Well," said Baylin, "we are just dripping wet all the time down there on the forest floor. And the mosquitoes just love us to bits. It's not very pleasant at all!" Baylin complained.

"Well, it's a pity that the two of you can't fly," jested Birdoke. "Why don't Oglins learn to fly? That would be such a clever thing to do!"

"Oh, that is a grand idea," laughed Baylin. "But we don't have wings! So it's not too likely for us! People have learned to fly, though! But sadly their marvelous flying machines seem to also make a frightening noise and they often use them to poison things or to carry banging sticks to shoot elephants with. We're not too keen on that!"

"Ah, yes…people," agreed the bat. "People are wreaking all sorts of havoc here too, you know. They are chopping down great sections of this forest. Magnificent old monarch trees are being cut down and floated away down the river. They are disappearing from the forest forever instead of gradually returning their life to everything else when they die, as it should be. It is a serious loss, and one we simply cannot sustain. I rue the day they come to cut down this tree that has been my family's home for generations," Birdoke said sadly. "So I take it you are the two young Oglins on the way to see the Great Spirit."

"Yes, we are the very ones, oh Great Birdoke," Lafina replied.

"But what are you doing so high up in a tree then if you have no wings? Oglins normally live on the ground. Walking things, aren't they?" Birdoke seemed determined to poke fun at them.

"Yes, that's true. But we happened to be feeling a bit lost down there," Lafina replied.

"Oglins don't get lost, do they?" Birdoke quipped.

"No, we're not lost exactly, oh Great Birdoke," Baylin explained a bit defensively. "We're finding our way down the river as we are supposed to. But we wished to get up high and get a view of the Great Forest and see if we could find out where we are and what the best route is from here."

"Oh, I see," said the bat, smiling smugly. Then, in a friendly tone he offered, "I'll tell you what! I'll be taking off soon anyway and can do a little reconnaissance for you. I happen to know this forest very well and will look to see which way would be best for you. Sorry I don't have the answer straight off the bottom of my head, but I am a bit above all that wandering about on the forest floor, you know.

"After all, you Oglins and all life could learn, that to get a decent overview of what's happening is the only way to do it. Stand back and take a greater view. You must learn to look at the whole, rather than the bits and pieces that occupy your vision day-to-day. All of you miss out because of the nature of your lives, being so closely linked to the soil and so closely linked to what's happening just in front of you on the surface. You don't have the opportunity of standing back, or like a bird, getting high above the world and observing it as a whole and working out your best routes forward from that. Plans should be made from the whole point of view, rather than a narrow perspective.

So, young Oglins, if you will excuse me, I'll go out on my recce now."

The bat dropped from his perch and spread his thin-skin wings, his little claws sticking out at the front. He deftly arced and soared up to the top of the canopy, breaking out above it all. Slowly turning on one wing tip, the bat hailed the Oglins, "I will be back with a report for you!" With that, he flew off out of sight.

One-by-one more bats scrambled out from under their orchid shelter, warmly greeted the Oglins and dropped away onto the wing. The Oglins were, to put it mildly, very jealous of the cozy, dry bats, so capable of winging away over the surreal moonscape of the forest, now washed with silver light.

The Oglins had nothing to do but wait patiently while the bat was gone. At least being up in the tree was a pleasant change from the past few days of bushwhacking. They both stretched out on the wide branch and drifted off to sleep. After many hours and a much-needed and much-drier rest, they awoke at the first hint of light. The sound of wings approaching heralded the return of the night fliers. The Oglins both sat up just in time to see Birdoke come swooping back down to the branch to deliver his report.

"Well, I have made quite a survey for you," Birdoke started importantly. "Here's what I have seen. The Merma River continues north from here, but it is beginning to turn towards the yesterdays slightly. If you head in a straight line towards the yesterdays from here, for a day or so, you will then come to a broad track. You will be able to turn and travel north on that track. It should be quite easy to recognise, as it is being used a lot by both the local people around this area and by many elephants. If you are careful to avoid the people, it will certainly speed up your progress very much.

"The track eventually turns towards the yesterdays and comes out into a clearing right on the banks of the Great Merma River. From there, follow the path alongside the river. In the distance, I could already see the Great Modra River. I could not see the ruins where you will meet the Great Spirit, but the trail will be found near the confluence, where the waters change colour."

"We are ever so grateful," said Lafina sincerely.

"Indeed, glad to help," replied Birdoke. "But remember the most important thing of all, dear Oglins: Whenever you are in trouble, stand back and look at the whole picture. Whenever you are busy planning something, stand back and look at the whole. Plan from the whole and look down to the finer detail rather than from the finer detail out towards the whole, for you may never get to the larger picture if you approach it that way!"

"Thank you, oh Great Birdoke. It was very kind of you to help us," said Lafina appreciatively. "It is so nice to know that we are on track and in fact very close to our destination. We have come a long way and we are anxious to complete our quest! And rest assured, we will remember what you have taught us!"

"Well done, then," said Birdoke in parting. "Travel well, dear Oglins. We are counting on you!" With that, he scurried back under the orchid leaves to escape the coming light of day.

Going down the tree was just so much easier than going up. They were able to slide down the great vines with ease. Both the little Oglins felt much more light-hearted about the whole journey after having met up with Birdoke the Bat. The pala were also very pleased to see them back, nickering softly and nuzzling up to them. After a night away, Baylin and Lafina saw their pala friends with new eyes and noticed how lean and hungry they were looking after being in the forest without grass for so many days. Just nibbling on leaves was not doing them that well. It was time to get on with it now! Knowing that they were on track and getting close was very encouraging, and they hacked their way towards the yesterdays in the early morning light with renewed energy.

The bat's directions held true. The Oglins found the big track and followed that readily to the Merma River and then on towards the yesterdays. The broad track was much easier to travel along and it was so wide that it even had short very lush green grass along the sides. The pala really took to that and seemed to become themselves again. Being right along the river also seemed to allow more breezes to blow through and more light to filter down, changing the climate entirely. The edge of the path was also indistinct so that there was not a solid wall of forest. This gave them the space to easily hide off the side of the trail whenever people came down the path. The little group's progress was so much better and quicker than before and their spirits soared again with anticipation.

Singing happily as they rode along the road, they added another verse to their poem for the wonderful bat who had helped them so greatly:

Brave Birdoke the Bat lives on high
and flew still higher in the night
to assure our journey's end was nigh
and helped to end our larger plight.
He taught that we must see the whole
and view the world in a broader light.

The Great Merma River

Coming through a wide clearing, Baylin and Lafina encountered huge thick vines, the size of a mo's thigh, hanging down from the upper branches. The monkeys would use these to swing themselves from tree to tree through the forest canopy. High above, they could hear the cacophony of birds and insects and other small creatures that lived their entire lives above in the denseness of the forest's treetops. There were many more birds in these trees, meaning there was a change in vegetation. In fact, the path had once again come out on the edge of the Merma River.

It was a good time for a break and there was plenty of grazing for the pala. So Baylin and Lafina went to have a closer look at the wide river they had travelled half a continent to reach. They crawled up onto a root of one of the towering trees. The root itself was enormous, as big as Smiler the Crocodile's waistline. They shinnied up the root to the base of the tree, where the next roots led down into the fast-moving, muddy, orangy-brown water of the Great Merma River itself. This was the Great Merma River at last!

The deep mass of water was flowing past, with the sun shimmering off its surface, a gleaming ribbon between the shadows of the Great Forest on both its banks. This was the first sunshine the young Oglins had been fully exposed to in quite some time, and the bright light almost hurt their eyes! Far, far across the vast river they could see the forest on the other side, at least what they thought was the other side.

Baylin and Lafina just sat for a bit watching the mighty river. Their only movement was to swat away at flies and mosquitoes. They especially enjoyed watching the dragonflies, with their pretty oranges, blues and purples, hovering just over the surface with their delicate wings, thin little legs and long tails. It never ceased to amaze them how the dragonflies could be flying and yet so still!

Lafina suddenly tapped Baylin's arm lightly and pointed upstream. There, half entwined in the branches of a young tree on the river's edge and half-stretched out across the mud of the riverbank was a huge python! Stretching for almost as long as a giraffe stands tall, the snake was as big in its girth as a springbok's body. It was just lying there, ceaselessly watching with infinite patience as only a snake can do. Its splendid colours, whites, yellows, creams, dark browns and blacks, formed an exquisite pattern.

"Now that's a snake!" Baylin whispered into Lafina's ear. "It's big enough to swallow a whole Oglin! Spola told us about the exceptionally large snakes here. Do you remember how they came across a python one day that had swallowed a duiker? They could see the shape of the antelope, distending the snake's belly and the poor creature's horns were sticking out through the python's body."

"Let's keep an eye out walking through here!" Lafina cautioned, looking around her with a new regard for the dangers at hand. "We don't want to wind up walking into one of those! You'd better ride in front, Baylin."

Baylin looked at her and a roguish look snuck into his eye, a little glint of naughtiness. Trying to sound guileless, he said, "I seem to remember that the battends told that the snake usually gets the second person in the line!"

Lafina shivered. Knowing he was simply trying to provoke her, she returned, "Never mind! I'd still rather ride second, thank you!"

Grinning at one another, they carefully scrambled down off the root to go back to the pathway. Both of them relished the bit of afternoon sun they got sitting on the river bank. The endless canopy was broken open at last by the wide expanse of the water. It was such a pleasure after days in the dark and dingy light and incessant moisture of the forest, to feel the sun and really dry out. They had so longed to see the sun! But sharing it with the enormous python was persuasion enough for the little Oglins to move on.

CHAPTER 19

THE GREAT SPIRIT

There are two ways to live your life.
One is as though nothing is a miracle.
The other is as though everything is a miracle.

—Albert Einstein

The Road to the Ruins

They had been out on the path for only a little while that afternoon when Lafina called out to Baylin to stop. He crossed to where she was riding down towards the river on an ancient but now ignored path. The shrubbery forced them to dismount and walk, peering ahead. There in front of them was an ancient dock. Built strong, straight and neat, the dock had stood for years alongside the river. Now it was covered with moss and small stunted trees grew on the shallow soil that had formed on top. Hidden as it was, this was the signpost along the river that they were searching for!

Under the dock the river slowed, swirled and eddied, as two colours of water from different streams met and joined their power. Barely noticing how beautifully the sun danced on the rippling water, they turned towards each other. Feeling the intensity of the moment, they shyly smiled and hugged. They held each other for a long time before Baylin leaned back and looked into Lafina's gleaming, golden eyes.

"We are nearly there," he whispered with a sigh. "Let's go so we can get there as soon as we can!"

"Yes! Let's go!" she agreed. Suddenly nervous and a bit unsure of herself, she broke away.

They headed back across the main path into the jungle to find the ancient road. Although it was grown over to a great extent, the deep gully was open enough to ride down. This was a real relief. At least they could move along more quickly and get to the Great Spirit sooner.

The little entourage made good time but the daylight ran out before they reached the ruins, so they decided to stop and go on in the morning. Baylin and Lafina built a small shelter for the night. They chopped down stalks that carried leaves the size of elephants' ears and stacked them in a circle. They added more until a small hut was erected. They had to wriggle their way inside. As always, it was wet to start with, but once their body heat warmed the leaves they almost dried and it became a quite cosy little nest. It was a trick that they had learned after seeing the bats so snug and dry under their orchid leaves.

Sleep did not come easily to the little Oglins. Tomorrow should be their big day, meeting the Great Spirit at last, thought Baylin, nestling alongside Lafina. As they were performing their little nightly ritual of revisiting their creed and feeling their amulets, both noticed and mentioned to one another how heavy their pachas had become. Both the white seashell and the beautiful stone with the fire in its heart felt especially powerful and warm that night. The Great Spirit was near, they could feel that!

They spent the night nervously huddled together under their shelter. The water dripped off the trees and landed on their little tent with a heavy, loud crack, just like the heavy crackling of wood in a fire. It went on all night but was never consistent so that one could predict the next drop. The night was filled with a continuous crescendo of noise from the beetles and bugs. Insects and life of all sorts crawled all around them and rustled in the undergrowth. The thick smell of deep, damp humus rotting away filled the air. It was so potent that it occurred to Baylin that if he were to fall asleep and spend a little too long there, he might actually just rot where he was sitting! This endless dampness, the matted hair, was not good for the complexion of an Oglin.

He whispered quietly to Lafina, "What do you think the Great Spirit will be like? Can't look much like an Oglin, 'cause it's so uncomfortable for an Oglin to live in this kind of humid, dripping, environment. Really, our hair is wet and matted all the time! In fact, if we don't get to see the sun again within a few days, even we will start smelling old and mouldy."

Lafina giggled in agreement, as she wiped the water from her forehead, again.

Baylin's mind slipped back to the final battends told by Old Spola the night before they left Vadiera. He shared his memories with Lafina to help pass that long and dreary night.

They had all gathered for a feast, the Wedrelas and Essedrelas, Baylin's family and Eldrin and Essine who had hosted Lafina during their preparation for this Great Journey. They were all seated around the fire, watching and waiting while the huge orange globe of the full moon emerged from the sea, towards the tomorrows, as the sun disappeared towards the yesterdays. Above, a small line of clouds, shining bright orange underneath, reflected the moon's light, while on top they still shone bright pink from the last rays of the sun. They were trading places, the sun and the moon. The sun was going to bed and the moon was coming out to do its duty.

"Tonight I'm sure we will hear the raised voices of the jackals, the hyenas and rumble of the lion," the Great Wedrela had said. "We'll surely hear them tonight."

The background noises of the evening savanna had distracted Baylin. He could make out the yipping, barking whinny of the zebras, as the stallions called their herds closer together for protection against the predators already out and stalking them.

"The journey that Baylin and Lafina are leaving on is a dangerous one," the Great Wedrela had continued, snapping Baylin's attention back to the gathering. "Spola left with two other Oglins and returned alone. We certainly hope that is not going to happen again with this Great Journey. But still, the dangers are real. It was wonderful that the Spirits brought Spola back to us with the knowledge that we needed. It is wonderful that they have kept Spola alive for so long that he was now able to tell these battends to Baylin and Lafina. These are battends of such importance, with information that is vital for them to find their way and to know where to go. Old Spola is now going to tell us his final battends."

Old Spola had began slowly. He told how the three Oglins who had ventured out on that journey long ago were all still together sitting in the thick heavy darkness of the Great Forest.

"It's totally different to anywhere else in the world, when you are in the deep, Great Forest," Spola described. "The vegetation grows high up above an Oglin's head, and that's just the bottom vegetation. You can climb; you can climb your way up out of that vegetation. But as you climb, you'll find still more. There's layer upon layer of foliage. Each level up, the leaves are just a little bit sparser. In the daytime, there is an opaque, greenish light down on the forest floor. In fact, it's almost dark. You can't see the sun. You can't see the sky. As you climb up, when you are halfway up you'll be able to see the light, the pale green light filtering through, but you won't be able to see the sky. We climbed and we climbed but we never saw the sky.

"At night it's dark black, the darkest black you can imagine. Maybe that is how it might be when one is moving on into the Spirit World. But I don't think that on the journey to the Spirit World you would be able to hear the incredible noise and smell the incredible smells that one smells in the Great Forest. Perhaps I'll find out soon enough! At night in particular, the smell of the dampness and the rotting plant material rises up around you and engulfs you. The air itself seems heavy to breathe. The air itself is full of water. The water drips off everything. It drips all day. It seems to drip endlessly. In fact, you've got to be very careful, we discovered, and sleep under nice big leaves 'cause if you don't, you'll have this water dripping down your ear at night and that will give you a big fright! It makes it very uncomfortable.

"And the insects, the bugs, all the organisms, it's just incredible how much life there is there! While you are trying to sleep, they crawl all over you. They get inside your hair. They tickle along your skin. They climb in under your ears. Sometimes you want to start cursing the Great Spirit for even making you come to this horrendous place! It is so different from a place that is comfortable for Oglins. It is so different from the beautiful, open savanna and tall grasslands of Vadiera. Some days in Vadiera it's humid, but even at its most humid here, it's only a touch of what it is like in the Great Forest.

333

"We had finally come near the Great Temple, which I have already told you about in a different battends. We laid up there for the night. When we woke, we tried to shake as much of the insect life and organic matter out of us as we could. A spray of moisture came off of us, like a gayla shaking itself after a swim," continued Old Spola, smiling slightly at the memory.

"We began to walk along. Walking along is not easy in the Great Forest. There is always thick undergrowth. You've actually got to fight your way through it. We each had a stick that we'd sharpened, interestingly enough," laughed Old Spola, "that didn't look much different to the short stabbing spears that Baylin and his mates used to win the competition the other day. Ours was only slightly shorter. We made them a bit thicker and we scrubbed them down on rocks to sharpen the side of them so that we could slash the undergrowth to make our way through it when it got thick.

"At last we came across the ruins and stopped in front of the temple. We had a feeling that the Great Spirit was near. Our pachas were feeling especially heavy. We took hold of the amulets that were given to us for communication with the Great Spirits. And we stood in awe. The Great Spirit spoke to us. We never saw the Great Spirit, but she spoke to us. She spoke in a wonderful voice, lilting, almost musical, with poetry to it. It was a warm voice, generous and gentle, full of wisdom and kindness. It made us feel utterly at peace and completely safe, as if no harm could come to us in his presence.

"The Great Spirit asked us many questions of our journey. We answered all her questions, but she already knew the answers! You see, the Great Spirit is everywhere, with the rest of our ancestors, watching over us all the time. They know where we've been, what we are doing, and what we've done. She seemed to ask us these questions only to check whether we had understood the meaning of our experiences or not.

"Then the Great Spirit made it very clear that I was to return home, to return home to Vadiera for the Oglins of Africa. But the two that I had travelled there with were to be sent away to far-off shores.

"The Great Spirit then inquired if we had ever seen a whale. We had all seen a whale before and soon came to understand why she asked. Our next instructions were to go back to the Great Merma River, make ourselves a sturdy raft, and float our way down to the sea. Reaching the ocean, we were to go out to where the water changes, from sweet and fresh to salty. There we were to just sit and wait for a pod of Great Whales.

"As certain as I am here, it happened just as the Great Spirit said it would. When the pod of whales came to us, we were to bid our farewells to one another, never to see each other again. It was a sad moment after making such a long journey together; we had grown very close. We were each to step into the mouth of a whale. My whale was instructed by the Great Spirit to bring me home to Vadiera and land me on the beach." Old Spola's eyes began to mist over with tears at the memory of his long-lost companions.

"My coming back to Vadiera would feed the knowledge we had gained to the rest of the Oglins in Africa and north. By returning here to Vadiera, my message would reach all the Oglins through the gathering of the clans, and the knowledge would spread through all of them. Vasca was sent far away where his work will also spread far and wide across another great continent. The third Oglin, Rupa, was sent to yet elsewhere but he had an especially difficult task, because from that continent there are many islands, many small pieces of land. The communication between Oglins on those islands is sometimes very difficult. And I, the lucky one, was returned home to Vadiera. I was brought home by that whale. Maybe the Great Wedrela should tell you about how they found me, because I think he'd do better than me."

Old Spola sat down to appreciative cheering from the small crowd gathered. By then the tears were streaming his cheeks. A happy toothless grin spread across his face. He knew that at last his great duty as an important mo Oglin over the years that he spent on this planet was now done. He had done his bit for the world. He could now sit down and relax once and for all. His eyes blinked and then closed, as he drifted off to sleep, an exhausted, but satisfied, old Oglin. All present looked upon him with warmth, admiration and wonder. So old now, and so frail, yet such a brave and special old soul. Spola's name was known and revered in every Oglin burrow across Africa further north and towards the tomorrows.

The Great Wedrela stood again. With extreme enthusiasm, he told of how one morning, the Whale Crier Oglin blew his horn with exceptional vigor. This particular Oglin lives in a small warren, in the face of the cliffs looking out over the sea. He blows on a great kudu horn to announce the arrival of the whales so that everyone can come down to sit upon the cliffs and watch the whales play and give birth. It is a time of great joy for the Oglins of Vadiera.

"Very, very early on this particular morning, the Whale Crier blew his kudu horn much more, much louder, much longer, and much more frequently than normal," told the Great Wedrela. "In fact, it woke the whole of Vadiera and all the Oglins poured out of their warrens and rushed down to the cliffs to see what it was all about.

"Just offshore from the beautiful white beach was a huge whale swimming back and forth! When the crowd of Oglins gathered on the sand, the whale turned and headed straight onto the shore and beached itself. This happens on rare occasions, we all know. It is a special gift from the Great Spirits for us Oglins because it's a huge source of food and other wonderful gifts. When it does happen, we have a great butchering session, which goes on until there is nothing left of the Great Whale. All of it is used for something, the bones, the fat, the baleen, everything. Nothing whatsoever goes to waste, and we give thanks to the Great Spirit for the whales who give us such bounty.

"On this day, I was a young Essedrela in training with the Great Wedrela whose totem was the whale. He went and stood in front of that whale and thanked the Great Spirits, and thanked the whale for giving itself to the Oglins. And to the amazement of everyone gathered there, the Great Whale spoke so that all the Oglins present could understand.

"The Great Whale proclaimed, 'I have brought more than a gift for the Oglins of Vadiera, to confirm the great bond between whales and Oglins. We the whales of the Great Oceans are your eyes and ears to communicate with all Oglins in all parts of the world. Yearly we return to your coast. Yearly we visit you and speak with your Wedrelas. This is the covenant between the Great Spirits, the Whales and the Oglins.

Now, your gift, of course, is my body for your benefit. But you need to open me quickly for I have returned, inside me, one of your own."

"The Great Wedrela thanked the Great Whale, his own totem, and blessed it. Then with great haste and wonder, the Oglins began to work to open up the whale. From inside the whale came our dear Oglin Spola, having been returned to us from the Great Spirit in the Great

337

Forest, by means of a whale! It was a glorious symbol. With him, however, came the sad news that his fellow travellers, a mo and a mer Oglin, would never return to our shores again. Yet also with him came the confirmation of our connection with the whales!

"With that tale we hope to inspire these two young Oglins as they embark upon the greatest opportunity and challenge of their lives. They go, willingly, to do as they have been called. Whether they will return or not to our shores, whether Baylin will return or not to Vadiera, is something we do not know. Yet it is something we do not have to fear, because wherever they go, even if the Great Spirit calls them or one of them into the world of the Spirits, it is for the good of the Oglins and the world as a whole. Whatever becomes of you is the will of the Spirits and for the good of the Earth.

"Oglins are never tearful when we say goodbye. We are only tearful with joy when you return, for we have suffered the sadness of the time of missing you, the time that goes by without you here. But we will not be sad at your going. It is not the Oglin way. Rather we will rejoice and be thankful for the times we've had together."

Lafina sighed deeply as Baylin finished the tale. Tears welled up in their eyes at the memory of that last evening in Vadiera. How very long ago and far away it seemed now! How lucky they had been to have Old Spola's battends to lead them! Would they ever have made it this far without his guidance? Not very likely! They were so near their destination. All they could do now was to nervously wait for their own encounter with the Great Spirit, which they expected to occur the next morning.

So much was still unknown. What would the key to their future really be? How would they get home again to share it with all their fellow Oglins? And what about Gumbo the Gorilla telling them they would have to teach this to the people as well?

Would they be sent home in a whale, too? They became even more nervous thinking about that prospect! Old Spola never told them what it was like sitting in a whale for however many weeks. Could pala travel in a whale? What if they were sent to different destinations, never to see their families and homes again? And even worse, never to see one another again?

So even while they anxiously awaited morning, there was nothing sure about the future for these two young Oglins. They had already risked their lives many times over to get to this damp, dank place in the Great Forest, half a continent away from everyone they knew and loved. The amulets grew warmer and heavier as the night drew on, providing the only solace they could find in that black, black night.

The Ruins

As soon as there was enough of the dim light that meant morning had come, the young Oglins roused themselves and started to move on. It wasn't worth lying around any longer. There wasn't a place for really resting in the incessant dripping of water, rain and the continual bombardment by insects. Just as Old Spola described, they shook themselves off and leading the soggy palas, moved on. Lafina had taken the broad, flat frond of a banana-like plant and carried it over her head like an umbrella to try to ward off some of the falling water. Leading the way, Baylin had no spare hand for that, as he had to clear the new growth that had sprung up and the huge spider webs that crisscrossed what pathways they could find as they struggled to follow the ancient road.

Finally, upon pushing aside yet another thick-stemmed creeper, the two Oglins stepped into a clearing. Suddenly, there in front of them, were the stone ruins of an old temple that had been built many, many years ago.

"This is amazing," whispered Baylin. "They must have carried these stones from very, very far away. We haven't seen any stones for days! No, not for weeks! Except at the dock. I suppose they brought them in by boat."

One wouldn't even necessarily know that the ruins were built of stones until they went right up to then, for everything was covered in a mass of green moss. The walls were standing like an old ruin would stand, but they were being swallowed up by the forest. There was an old tower in the corner. Baylin and Lafina made their way across to it. They pushed their hands up into the green mass, and it was soft as could be and dripping with moisture. The Oglins were in awe! So in awe of the sight they were seeing—so very different from the ruins at Khami that they had seen all those many memories and days ago, where it was dry and arid and there was no forest seeming to consume the rocks! Although there had been lichen on the rocks at Khami, there certainly was no moss growing on them.

"Not like the brittle environment at Khami," said Lafina, still keeping her voice low, as if she felt they were intruding on some special place.

"No," replied Baylin quietly. "This is definitely non-brittle. This is amazing. Look! Look up there. There is a tree growing out of the joint in those two rocks! Can you see that? There's enough moisture that the tree can grow on its own up there! Anything would grow anywhere here if you left it alone long enough!"

"My! You wouldn't get that at home, would you?" exclaimed Lafina.

"No way! It wouldn't have enough moisture to grow in such a place. It would take forever to create enough soil in a little pocket like that to grow anything," said Baylin.

The two Oglins were so mesmerised by what they were seeing that they completely forgot that this was where they were to meet the Great Spirit! They were totally engrossed in exploring the ruin when they heard a voice, a Great Voice, a soft voice, very gentle and very peaceful. Though startling when first heard, it calmed them down very quickly. It was the voice of the Great Spirit.

The Voice in the Forest

"Welcome, young Oglins! Baylin of Vadiera and Lafina of the Pinnacles, you have made the Great Journey and reached the ruins here in the Great Forest at last! You have seen the Great Merma River! You have seen and observed many a thing on your travels. You have braved many dangers and overcome many obstacles. You are truly Oglins of exceptional value to the world!"

Stopped in their tracks by the voice, the two little Oglins huddled next to one another in wonder. Looking about them, they saw only the ruins they had been exploring and the three pala now standing straight up, ears forward and attentive. They could see no one! But the voice they had heard was unmistakable!

"Thank you, oh Great Spirit," Baylin and Lafina finally managed to whisper back, in awe of speaking directly to the Great Spirit. They looked all around them, in every direction.

"You will not see me, dear Oglins," the voice of the Great Spirit said gently. "I am not visible. But you will hear me, and you will know that you have been with me! Before you two, this Great Journey has only been made once before by your kind, by the brave and true Oglins of Africa. There were three Oglins that made that journey, one of whom you know: the Great Oglin Spola! He made the journey all the way here and travelled back to Vadiera in the belly of a whale. The other two Oglins are also still in the land of the living and are active in their communities of Oglins on the far-flung continents that they were taken to by the whales.

"Now the two of you have succeeded in making this journey once again. This time you are here for the most important of reasons. You have been called on this journey to discover the key to the future, not just the future for the Oglins, but the future for all manner of life on Earth, including people.

"While people have great potential, they have much to learn! They have not yet discovered how to live in harmony with all other beings. Their numbers are currently exploding and they are putting tremendous pressure on the rest of life and all the resources that sustain it. In the name of what they call progress, they are destroying the habitat of many other species and endangering the future of all life. Including their own! Thus it was absolutely vital that you make this journey now! It is not a moment too soon!"

"Oh Great Spirit, Gumbo the Gorilla told us that we would have to speak to the people at some time, to carry this message across to them!" Baylin ventured to say.

"Oh yes, young Oglins," the Great Spirit replied, "you will indeed be charged with that duty. You will meet with some people and find a way to convey the knowledge to them. That is how the ancestral legends say it will come to pass. But you need not worry yourselves about that now; you will know what to do and when to do it, and you will do well when that time comes.

"Now, please sit and make yourselves comfortable. As comfortable as you can be in this environment, anyway! My dear Oglins, tell me what you have learned on this Great Journey," inquired the Great Spirit kindly.

"Great Spirit," Lafina replied bravely, "we have learned from all manner of things, birds, animals and insects. From all manner of life and opportunity we have learned. We have kept our eyes and ears as open as we could. We have felt and smelled our way right across this continent to you. We think we have learned a lot along our journey!"

"What have you learned, young Oglins?" the Great Spirit asked, encouraging them.

"Well first we've learned from our own Great Wedrela, the need to have a creed for our lives and for all life on Earth," Baylin answered humbly. "And that creed must first describe how we want our lives to be now. Secondly it must describe what we need to do to achieve the kind of life we desire. And thirdly we must describe our community and the land as it must be, far into the future! This creed acts as a guiding star so our daily activity will lead to the way of life we desire."

"Birdoke told us to try to take a look at the big picture, see it as a whole rather than in fragments. This is essential to making the rest work," Baylin continued.

"We've learned from all manner of other living things, about how to ensure that we achieve that," Lafina chipped in. "We've learned from wise old Uyazi the Owl, about the tools available to us and people to change the environment in which we live. From Thutha, we've learned to check that every action we take with any of these tools will lead towards the description of our land and communities far into the future.

"We've learned about the workings of life and land from various teachers, like Dainty, Tufty and Uyazi, too," Lafina continued. "About how water and life cycle. And how brittle and non-brittle environments respond to the different tools. Just this morning we have seen a wonderful example of a non-brittle environment, these ruins being swallowed up by the forest,

343

in contrast to the brittleness of our homelands and the stark ruins of Khami."

"That is true," agreed the Great Spirit. "You have learned this well, young Oglins! It is a vital key to understanding and forecasting changes in different situations."

"We've learned to check first that we are dealing with the root cause of a problem," Baylin contributed, "not just treating symptoms. We've learned to ask ourselves, as Great Wallo the Whale taught us, that we must check whether this action might cause a problem with others whose help and support we need."

"We've learned from Great Digger the Dung Beetle that if we ever want to increase or decrease an organism's numbers, we must deal with the weakest link in its life cycle," Lafina went on. "Weakening it at that point if it is a problem organism, or strengthening or protecting it at that point if it is an endangered organism."

"We've learned from Great Smiler the Crocodile to always address the weakest link

in our chain of production, if we are producing anything, or if working our way through something," added Baylin. "The links are the resources available to us, production from those resources, and the need to convince others so that we can achieve the desired results."

"We've learned from the Bushman," Lafina said, fondly remembering the kind family that took care of them in the desert so far away and long ago, "to be wary of the sustainability of the source and the way we use energy and resources. And to be sure that both the source and the use match our creed."

"We've learned from Great Elanga the Eland to check whether what we are about to do will lead towards the way we want our lives to be as described in our creed," explained Baylin.

"We've learned from beautiful Checha the Cheetah that we must use a process of checking any options that we have considered this far. We must check them against one another to pick the one that will give us the most movement towards our creed for the same amount of effort that we might put into it," said Lafina.

"And," added Baylin, "we have learned to be humble now and assume that we are wrong whenever we are dealing with anything in nature. It is too big and too complex for us to understand the whole of it from our little fragmented and limited views of it."

"And most importantly," Lafina emphasised, "Jackie Hangman the Red-Backed Shrike taught us that we must monitor as closely as possible the results of our actions, to see if they are leading us towards or away from where we want to go. We must watch them carefully! And as soon as something shows that we are off course, we must change and adjust as quickly as possible to get back on track towards our creed!

"We also learned around some peoples' fire," Lafina went on, "that no one will grasp anything that they are not ready to grasp. They will judge most everything by what they already know and unless they are ready, they will push anything different away, no matter how obvious it is!"

"My my, young Oglins!" said the Great Spirit. "You have done very well indeed! You have been very observant. You have learned what needed to be learned. You took full advantage of every opportunity. I am not easily pleased, but today I am greatly pleased!"

Baylin and Lafina hugged each other in joy. They had pleased the Great Spirit! All of the difficulties, all of the dangers, all of the troubles they had encountered, they were all worth it!

"There is one last learning that you must make here," the Great Spirit continued. "It is more a reminder than something new. All that you have learned is common sense type of knowledge. Easily learned and made part of daily life. And this is what must happen. Oglins and people need to start thinking like this all the time. Then it will become a day-to-day way of life and decisions will improve all 'round. This will lead to the outcomes that are both desired and necessary."

"Now that we know this, oh Great Spirit, we can never see things the same way again! And like those poor people we met, our beliefs will be reflected in what we do!" said Lafina.

"Now we have one final step to complete your understanding," said the Great Spirit, in the most serious voice yet. "I want you both to reach into your pachas and draw out your new amulets, the ones that I placed there myself. For it was I that chose you two to make this Great Journey."

The two Oglins reached into their pachas. Lafina pulled out the dazzling white seashell. As she held it to her ear, she could hear the roar and memory of the sea that seashells never ever forget. The shell roared louder in her ear than ever before, bringing the strength of the sea to Lafina's heart. From within his pacha, Baylin drew out the radiant stone with the fire inside its heart, and raised it up. The fire shone from within it, brighter than ever before, bringing the fire of conviction to Baylin's heart!

"Now, my dear Oglins," the Great Spirit continued, "what you must learn to make these two link together is a very, very simple extension of what you learned from Birdoke. You see, our whole world, the universe itself, works as one. It is one. We are not separate entities that can live or operate on our own. You, me, the forest, the animal, the bird, the water, the sea, we are one life. With no grass, there is no grazing. With no grazing animal, there is no dung. With no dung, no beetle. No beetle, no soil. And so on and on. We are one living organism. That organism is the Earth, which is a whole. The organism of this world is only one whole within the great whole of the Universe.

"Now, the way for us to move forward is to use the knowledge that you have discovered, step by step. It will make a great difference if we make every decision, consider every action in the way you have learned and in light of the view of all life and the Earth as a whole. As Birdoke said, no sense or success will be made out of anything in a whole like the Earth and nature if it is looked at in pieces, from narrow points of view, or as individual unconnected parts. The path to the future we must create will come from seeing it all as a whole.

"That seashell that you hold in your hand, Lafina, is the result of a small creature that lived in the sea," the Great Spirit explained. "It lived inside that shell, until its life was over and then gave its life back to the cycle of living things. That seashell was raised from the deep blue sea and brought to the hands of the Oglins by the Great Spirits. If left in the sea, that shell would slowly but surely have been covered by sand, deep below the ocean. Over time, over millennia, that seashell would have been heated by the Earth's core and compressed more and more and more by further silt and sand and the great weight of water above it. And over years, that fine seashell would merge with those around it. The pressure would concentrate the shells down into the original matter that they are. Over time, as the pressure got great enough, and that little piece of the Earth was not disturbed for long enough, it would eventually turn into the shining stone with the fire in its heart like the one Baylin holds in his hand right now.

"So even though all things may appear to be different, in the end they are all one. They are all of the same source and they are all of one whole," concluded the Great Spirit.

"Now," the gentle voice instructed them, "join the seashell and the stone together. Put the fire of the stone into the beauty of the dazzling seashell. If they join together, you have the answer to the future of the whole."

Lafina and Baylin's hands drew closer and closer together; their furry little hands shook in excitement. For at this great moment the truth was coming together. Their two hands joined and the seashell slipped perfectly around the stone. The fire of the stone joined the enveloping seashell and they became one.

"This is the key to the future," said the Great Spirit.

Lafina and Baylin glowed in the wonder of it and knew their lives were forever changed.

Eventually, the Great Spirit spoke once more, tenderly. "Dear Oglins, now from here the two of you will wander back south to your home, along the same route. You will journey as directly as you can to Vadiera. The next gathering of the clans will be there to greet you. It will be earlier than usual, and once again, it will be held at Vadiera. The two of you will arrive back as the gathering begins. Do not stop at the Pinnacles, pass by and go straight to Vadiera. There will be a few little surprises saved up for you on your way home! Soon the Great Whales will come, as they will come every year, to take messages to and from the Oglins in other parts of the world."

With rising intensity, the voice now reverberated around them. "You Oglins have been chosen to receive the gift of this knowledge for the future to share with all, including the people of this Earth! That is the task of the Oglin! We will let the people's great fear of the Tokolosh slip away, and the Oglin become a symbol of hope, health and a great future for the whole Earth and those that dwell upon it!"

The Great Spirit's voice quieted. "Now travel swiftly, my dear young Oglins, with your faithful pala and brave souls. Head south with haste and take my word with you."

The Oglins looked up into the forest canopy, where the dappled light of the sun shone through, the patterns dancing on the leaves below. They could feel that the Great Spirit had left. The invisible yet unmistakable presence was gone.

Taking a deep breath, the two Oglins looked at one another and stepped into one another's arms to embrace. They each still had one hand clenched around the seashell and the stone, joined together. Finally, Baylin leaned back and looked into the depths of Lafina's bright golden eyes framed by damp curls.

"Come, let us go!" Baylin's thoughts sprang to his lips. "My heart yearns for the great cliffs and the deep blue sea of home. Your eyes remind me so much of the colours in the Vadiera veld as it receives the first kiss of the sun at dawn and my heart longs for it! I think the seashell is also calling to go home to its own place. It is time that we left. Let's make this journey home and let's make it quickly! The world needs us. We have a mission to accomplish now. It's not over yet; it's only just beginning! It's not over until every living thing on this Earth has heard of this. It's not over until the people have learned about this and learned the means for restoring and taking care of the Earth for sustainability into the future."

Holding hands with the seashell and the stone still one, Baylin and Lafina looked down at the two joined pieces.

"What about this?" Baylin wondered. "Does this go into one of our pachas? They obviously have great power when they are joined together."

The two Oglins slowly separated their hands, Baylin holding the precious amulets. He turned them over and the stone neatly slipped back out of the shell. He handed the shell to Lafina saying, "I think we have the key now. We can place these two together anytime we need to. All we need to do, if we are in difficulty and we are having problems, danger or struggles getting these ideas across to others, we must simply join these two together and take courage from them."

Lafina reached out, knowing it was the right thing to do, and took the dazzling white seashell and pushed the stone with the fire in its heart back into Baylin's hand. Smiling, she gently placed the seashell back into her pacha and Baylin followed suit. The glow next to their chests, radiating from the amulets, still heated from the power and energy of the meeting with the Great Spirit, warmed their hearts.

The young Oglins turned to Arto and Lara, who hadn't moved a muscle through the moments of conversation, and hugged them. Argyl, not wanting to be left out, nuzzled his way into both embraces and they joined, all five together. The urge to travel was upon them, so soon they turned and followed their path back through the forest to make their way back to the light and sunshine of the African savanna.

They remembered their precious time with the Great Spirit through the following verses:

The Great Spirit gave us blessings
far beyond our wildest dreams!
For deep within the jungle ruins,
where life is much more than it seems,
she gave us the gift of knowing
we can trust in our own discoveries!

Through a miracle of joining
the Shining Stone and White Seashell,
we found our own source of courage,
which comes from deep within ourselves.
We knew then that our task ahead
would one day be achieved as well.

CHAPTER 20

HOME COMING

"Roads go ever ever on
Under cloud and under star,
Yet feet that wandering have gone
Turn at last to home afar."

—J.R.R. Tolkien, *The Hobbit*

Homeward Bound

The journey home was long and hard, but the young Oglins kept up a swift pace and made good time. They felt a great sense of urgency, to arrive back in time for the clan gathering and to share all that they had learned with their fellow Oglins.

It was especially hot to start with, but cooled as they moved south. Once they had crossed what was known as the Greasy Green River and began to climb out of the low veld, it began to get colder. It was very cool at night where the tinder-dry grasses stretched away as far as they could see, in pastel shades of yellows, golds, reds and creams. They crossed the Great Red River and within a few days, more shrubby vegetation mixed in with

the grasses lent a little bit more colour to the landscape, adding dark greys to blacks with starkly contrasting greens.

They knew they were drawing nearer when they came across the tracks. It was Lafina who first saw them, recognising straight away what they were. They were riding slightly apart, one towards the tomorrows and one towards the yesterdays, simply because it was much easier that way and they could talk and look around. She called Baylin over and hearing the excitement in her voice, he rode straight across to her. Both the pala they were riding were snorting and prancing. Arto was almost dancing on the spot, his nostrils wide and neck arched proudly. He also knew who it was. Argyl in the meantime had trotted ahead, head swaying from side to side, to the top of the crest ahead of them to look into the distances.

Lafina explained that it was the track of the Oglin's entourage that had headed off from the Pinnacles to go down to Vadiera. She recognised the tracks of certain Oglins. She pointed out among them, the spoor of her Modra and eldest badra. She couldn't make out any other individual's tracks, in amongst that lot. But it was very exciting, for it confirmed that the word of the Great Spirit had reached them. It meant that the next gathering of the clans was being called and that they would all be at Vadiera waiting for them!

Their whole journey home gained new momentum and excitement. They travelled on top of the tracks of the Pinnacles Oglins and their spirits were lifted as they headed for home. It helped to break the monotony of the long reaches yet to be crossed.

In the far distance, they began to see the heads of blue mountains beginning to rise above the horizon, slowly but surely.

"Just beyond them, one set more, and we'll be in Vadiera," Baylin enthused. And they both quickened their pala's pace without thinking.

That evening, they came upon a campsite where the Pinnacles Oglins had spent the night. Baylin immediately set to picking up bits and pieces of bedding material that they had used and making a nest for the two of them.

Lafina went off on a mission of her own, wandering around looking at things. She jumped up at one point and excitedly called Baylin over. He rushed to see what she had found this time. She had discovered the tracks of her favourite gayla! It was a gayla called Doda, who had very distinctive footprints because one of his toes was missing. Sure enough, there next to one of the sleeping places, was the track of her gayla.

Even though the group had clearly been travelling with several pala, there was very little dung to be found, because the dung beetles had buried it all, of course. Baylin and Lafina could see the softly turned up ground where the dung pats had been. She found a pat that looked whole and picked it up. It was just an outside shell, everything from the inside was gone and had been worked into the ground. The

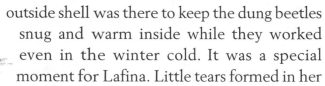

outside shell was there to keep the dung beetles snug and warm inside while they worked even in the winter cold. It was a special moment for Lafina. Little tears formed in her golden eyes, because it was her people, her gayla and her totem following them. To find evidence of all of them together was like the first welcome home.

Finally, Baylin and Lafina were only one day out from the forests of Vadiera. The two of them were greatly excited! The tracks of the Pinnacles Clan they were following were about three days old, so they knew that everyone would have been there for two days ahead of them. The last morning, at the first sign of light, long before the sun was sighted, in the bitter chill of predawn on the Great Plains, the two young Oglins were up and going already. Steam rose from their breath. Their little hands were folded up and tucked into their furriness for warmth. Wrapped in their bundle rugs to ward off the bite of the early morning cold, they were off, heading across the plains.

They kept up an eager pace all day, pulled by the vision of home and all their beloved family members and friends. By late afternoon, they were scrambling down the final slopes of the mountains, towards the beginning of the forest that surrounds Vadiera. They had to choose their way carefully to find the secret Oglin path that led into the forest and through to the hidden valley. They came down towards the little clearing where the head of the trail began. Below them, on the edge of a clear flowing stream that seemed to dance over the rocks, they could see two Oglins with their pala.

It was the Great Wedrela, who had especially come out to meet them! And it was Baylin's littlest sadra, Aga! They each had a pala and there were two gayla with them! One of the gayla was Doda, whose tracks they had been following, and the other was Luka! These were the first gayla and Oglins that they

THE OGLIN

had seen in so long, the very sight brought lumps to their throats, tears to their eyes and joy to their hearts!

A Welcoming Feast

Baylin and Lafina watched them for just a moment from on top of a little rise. The Great Wedrela and Baylin's little sadra sat close together, talking quietly. Aga had one arm draped over Luka's back and Doda lay at her feet. Their pala were standing nearby, heads together, one leg cocked as they were resting.

Baylin and Lafina looked at one another as wide smiles spread across their faces. Then they began the final descent to meet the others. The first one to see them was Luka, who picked them up on the breeze. He leapt up, silent, frozen except for a wildly wagging tail. Then he broke into a yipping call of joy and bounded easily up the slope towards Baylin and his friend Arto. Luka ran straight to Arto and bouncing all about, licked his friend's nose a few times. The gayla spun around twice then leapt up towards Baylin, licking his face as the Oglin leaned over to greet his eager friend. Putting a paw on each shoulder, Luka pulled Baylin in a gentle slide to the ground. There Luka stood over Baylin, licking madly at his beaming face and whining gently while his tail wagged furiously. Wrapping his arms on either side of the gayla, Baylin laughed aloud and roughed the hair on his gayla's head and neck.

"Go on!" he protested and Luka ran off down the hill to catch up with Arto, who having lost his rider, had sped off with Lafina to meet the others. Luka bounded up to Lafina, who with tears of joy streaming down her face had just finished hugging the Great Wedrela. The gayla jumped up, two feet on her shoulders and a cold wet nose in her face, and nuzzled her a

356

few times in greeting as she giggled in delight and hugged him back. Then he turned around and, tail down flat, rushed straight back to Aga, pressed his cold wet nose to hers, and sat down beside her.

"Looks to me that little Aga has got a new pal! So this is the way it has gone," laughed Baylin arriving at the reunion.

Argyl, in the meantime, overtaken with the joy of the occasion, did a galloping circle, head down, bucking and fly jumping as he went. Luckily, the load on his back was secure enough to survive the antics.

The Great Wedrela stood with an irrepressible smile on his face and tears rolling down his cheeks. He was trying, without much success, to regain the composure of an ancient and Great Wedrela, who probably shouldn't be showing his emotions quite so freely! But he couldn't help it; the joy was so great.

"After so many moons on Arto you still can't stay on his back going down a little hill like that? It's a wonder you made it to the Great Forest and back without serious injury!" jested the Wedrela, trying to cover his emotion before greeting the young mo.

Little Aga, on the other hand, had no need to contain herself as she leapt into the waiting arms of her bodra, Baylin, with a cry of delight. When at last he put her down, she very bravely made a great show of handing Luka, whom she had looked after so carefully for so long, back over to Baylin.

By now, Lafina had her arms around the neck of Doda, petting him and cooing sweet greetings in his ear. She was so chuffed to see him!

After talking for just a little while, the four of them mounted up and headed into the forest in the afternoon light. Argyl, leading the way, knew where he was going. Baylin realised how much little Aga had grown and how well she handled her pala, as he saw her ride ahead and deftly duck under the branches of the first great tree. He thought how good it would be to hunt with her. She had the balance and she had the style! And most interestingly, both she and the Great Wedrela's saddles now had the new leather stirrups that he and his mates had revealed at the last gathering of the clans.

They headed through the forest and came out into the open to see the wonderful vista of Vadiera bathed in the glorious slanting light of late afternoon. The kopjies shone in the distance and the savanna grasses still held the last vestiges of green, before fading into the winter golds. There, visible on the far horizon, was the dark blue sea. This was Baylin and Lafina's first glimpse of the sea since they had left. Baylin stopped and took a few deep breaths to take it all in: the thick scent of the waning autumn, the song of the rustling, drying leaves of the veld and the sweet feeling of being home. His eyes turned and picked out the tree that he and Luka had laid under when the elephant had come and visited them. Memories came flooding back, of Vadiera and his youth. How wonderful it was to be at home, but also how extraordinary to have had the opportunity to make the Great Journey and all that he had seen and learned from the adventure!

He looked at Lafina and urged Arto over towards her. He reached out, putting a hand on her shoulder, squeezing gently and said, "Welcome back to Vadiera! It's good to be home."

The two of them burst into speed and caught up once more with the Great Wedrela and Aga, who hadn't stopped. As they came round to the kopjies, the sun was disappearing behind the mountains. The light was dimming. Wispy, high clouds above them towards the tomorrows, shaped much like a pala's tail, were beginning to turn red and purple, fringed with gold. As they came into the burrows of Vadiera, it looked much as it had

at the last gathering of the clans, just before Baylin and Lafina had left. Clusters of tents served as temporary homes to hundreds of assembled Oglins. They were all drawn together around the central fire for the opening feast.

Argyl took the opportunity to have his moment of glory. He galloped, bucking and jumping wildly, through the tents and around the gathered people. All the gayla instinctively leapt to their feet and, yipping excitedly, tore off after the racing pala to try and round him up. Noise and dust rose around the crowd who enjoyed the entertainment. With his exceptional speed, Argyl outstripped the gayla easily, then suddenly checked and spun. Going straight through the following entourage of gayla, he raced back to Arto's side where prancing and proud, he took up his station.

It was an unusual gathering with no competitions or other normal activities planned. It had been less than a year since the last one. A great many Oglins had made this special journey, some taking a full moon to reach Vadiera from their far-off burrows.

The five pala, with their important passengers astride, and Luka following, as he used to, right in the tracks of Arto, rode into the gathering. Little Aga's shoulders were back, accentuating her beautiful seat on her little bundle-rug saddle with the leather stirrups. Arto and Baylin immediately seemed to just click back into the mode of the last gathering. Putting tension in his seat, Baylin shifted Arto into a well-remembered prancing gate, raising front feet high and arching his neck like the proudest of all animals. Baylin pulled back his own shoulders, and memories came flooding back for all the Oglins there of the great moments when this young Oglin and his mates won the hunting competition so splendidly.

A great cheer arose from all the Oglins present. With that, they shouted praise for the two young Oglins that made the Great Journey. Then the festivities began in earnest. It was a time of great excitement with feasting, battends, music, tears, fleeting hugs from Modra and Merma and bodra and sadra all around. There were tears and welcoming words all around, leaving a deep sense of recognition, pride and a feeling of importance.

The evening flew by for the two young Oglins. They were the centre of attraction and their battends went on late into the night; no one wanted to leave and return to their tents and sleeping rugs.

The Bacor

Over the following days, things quieted down. Every afternoon and evening, Baylin and Lafina gradually told the battends of their whole journey and everything they had learned. They told the stories right from the start, beginning with the creed that was given to them by the Wedrelas before they had even left Vadiera. Each evening they told the next segment of their travels, including all their encounters with the various animals and all their learnings along the way. All the Oglins gathered around, a rapt audience.

It took Baylin and Lafina days to get enough time and opportunity to meet up with all the individual Oglins that they knew and loved so well. Lafina's whole family was there, except her Great Modra and Great Merma, who hadn't made the journey but asked for her to promise to come and visit them at some stage.

Then came the sadness of meeting up with the two elders of the Bacor, Essine and Eldrin. They discovered that Eldrin had had a serious hunting accident when a stirrup had broken as he was leaning out wide and driving his short assagai into a wild pig. The pig had tossed him from his bundle-rug saddle and his pala had fallen as well. The short stabbing lance had actually broken underneath him and gone into his leg. He now had great difficulty in walking but, as with everybody around him, he was very thankful to still be alive.

On this particular evening, just before the final battends about Baylin and Lafina's magical meeting with the Great Spirit in the dark, rank depths of the Great Forest, there was a moment given to Eldrin and Essine to make an announcement. The announcement was a grave moment for everybody. Eldrin and Essine wished to retire from being the elders of the Bacor. Eldrin had only recently gotten back onto his feet. He was very crippled and finding it difficult to get around, spending most of his days being moved from the sun to the shade outside his warren. It was time to hand over the leadership of the Bacor. There had been a discussion among the clan and new leaders of the Bacor of Vadiera had been chosen.

Eldrin, standing with the help of Essine and the Great Wedrela, announced emotionally, "It is the choice of the clan and the Bacor that you, Baylin and Lafina, will lead Vadiera over the next years of your lives. Whether they have already chosen to be together or not, Baylin and Lafina are the new leaders of the Bacor, and we are very proud to have them!"

Baylin and Lafina were seated next to one another with the main group of Oglins, Eldrin and Essine, the Wedrelas and Essedrelas, and all the Great Oglins, including the leaders of the Bacor and chief Wedrelas of all the clans. The two of them looked at each other, tears welled up in their eyes, two furry little hands reached out for one another and they held hands. Their hearts were beating wildly, the blood roaring in their ears. They could not have been more excited about it. They had slowly become so close and their lives and thoughts and hearts so intertwined, that it had never occurred to them that they would not be together! And now it was confirmed for all to know.

A great cheer went up from the crowd and celebrations were held for the new leaders of the Bacor. As they sat down to share their final battends, Baylin's eyes met Lafina's. She passed him a knowing look of great love, support and honour. In that moment he knew that she had intuitively known for some time that this was how it would work out. It was only he who had not realised until now. A wave of respect and deep love swept through him and with a lighter heart, he and Lafina hugged. Then they began the battends about their magical meeting with the Great Spirit and the joining of the dazzling white seashell and the beautiful stone with the fire in its heart.

They re-enacted the meeting and the joining of the two amulets. Once again, the glow emanated from within the dazzling seashell. It was actually shining so that it could be seen from some distance. This was the great conclusion to the journey as such. All the information they had discovered was tied together in this last battends. With the same shock that Baylin and Lafina had first felt, the whole crowd gasped in amazement when they learned that they must carry this information to the people of the world.

Taking the cue from the battends that the Great Whale would be the key to the whole experience, the Great Wedrela stood up and said, "Tomorrow the Great Whale is coming and we will have our midday feast on the beach beside the bay. That is where the Great Whale last came in and gave its life to us when it returned Old Spola."

Spola was also receiving endless praises and being really thoroughly spoiled throughout the celebration as well. The dear old thing just had tears running down his face all of the time. His tear ducts seemed to have become incontinent over the last few days. He was getting all sorts of praise and appreciation for how well his battends had worked for Baylin and Lafina. However, everyone was deeply disturbed about the drastic changes in the land since Spola's journey.

Spola especially loved the battends about Smiler the Crocodile. He smiled widely every time he thought of it, chuckling and shaking his head while muttering under his breath, "Never, never, never trusssst a crocodile."

The Great Whale

The next morning, the whole gathering of Oglins made their way joyfully to the beach. All but the Vadiera Oglins were wondering what it would be like to see a Great Whale, and up so close. The excitement was building by the moment! The sand was dazzling white in the clear morning light. The setting was dazzling, with the forest behind them and the mountains in the distance, dark greyish blue against the bright brilliant blue of the sky. White clouds floated overhead, and the sea was a deep turquoise, accented by the white splash of the breakers and plumes of white spray breaking off the cliffs on each side of the narrow entrance to the hidden bay of Vadiera.

The Oglins drew up on the beach, overlooking the calm waters of the bay. The anticipation was building as they got themselves situated, chatting away animatedly. Then the Great Wedrela raised his staff and quieted the crowd. With the hush, he turned and faced the water and seated himself on the sand.

There was a slight ripple on the surface of the water from the wind. Suddenly, from deep beneath the bay, rose a mountain of a whale. Cries of awe and wonder arose from the gathered Oglins.

Water was streaming off the whale's sides, rippling like rapids over the barnacles that had attached themselves to its great body over the years. It raised up and then slowly toppled over to one side and fell with a great crash back into the water. A wall of water jetted away from the body of the whale as it landed. The whale turned and glided forward arching its back as it went down. Following the movement of the body, the tail came into view, water slowly cascading off it. Raising its tail higher, the whale stood on its head and showed its great length and gracefully shaped tail to the delight of all the Oglins on the beach. Then the magnificent creature slowly disappeared under the water once more before coming back up to bask in the sun just off the shore.

The Great Wedrela spoke to all the Oglins. "The Great Whale has arrived! The Great Whale who knows everywhere and every corner of the oceans! He has brought with him today the news that he will take on the great honour and duty to spread the word to all the other Oglins of the world. In this way, the keys that the Great Spirit has given us will be carried to all Oglins. That is the Great Whale's promise to us and her gift to all Oglins.

"The Great Whale also promises to create an opportunity for us to pass these messages across to the people of this world as well. As decreed by the Great Spirit, part of our role is to convey this knowledge to people.

"We wish to thank all you Oglins for making your own difficult journey to come to this gathering, which was out of time and out of place. But, as you surely observed in your travels here, time is of the essence to spread this new knowledge. This is an important moment for all of us. Each Oglin clan is asked to leave one mo and one mer Oglin behind to spend time with us in Vadiera to learn the finer details of the knowledge. They will then carry it home to their own clans. All the young mos and mers in this gathering can now reach into their pachas. Those that find amulets that were not there before have been chosen by the Great Spirit to stay on with us here at Vadiera for a while."

There was much excitement as the ones chosen for this next mission were revealed. Amongst them were one of Lafina's sisters and one of Baylin's cousins from the Great Flat Top Clan. The chosen Oglins raised their new amulets high above their heads and the crowd applauded them.

The applause grew to a crescendo as the whale slapped its tail on the water as if clapping too. "Go well, until we meet again, oh Great Whale," greeted the Wedrela as the whale slipped quietly below the surface.

The festivities went on late into the night, with all the young chosen Oglins introducing themselves one by one to Baylin and Lafina. For the first time in an age, there were no battends, but no one was perturbed, for tonight was a night that battends were made of.

CHAPTER 21

HOME LIFE

A new light is coming into the world.
We are on the border of a new experience.
The veil between spirit and matter is very thin.
The invisible passes into visibility through our faith in it.

—Ernest Homes

Settling In

While Baylin and Lafina had been away, a group of friends, young Oglins that Baylin had grown up with, had set to building a new burrow for him and Lafina, under instruction from the Wedrelas. The Great Spirits had told the Wedrelas of the plan to bring these two together for the long term. The first day after the gathering of the clans was over, there was a great moment of excitement for all his friends when the secret was finally to be revealed. Walking between them, just as he used to before their

Great Journey, the Great Wedrela took Baylin and Lafina by their hands and led them to see the big surprise.

He walked them down to a kopjie, adjacent to the kopjie where Baylin's family lived, but separate, where there were very few 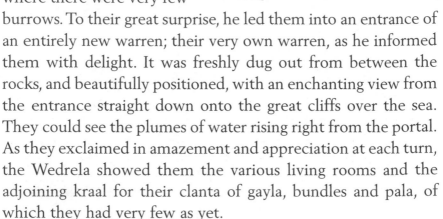 burrows. To their great surprise, he led them into an entrance of an entirely new warren; their very own warren, as he informed them with delight. It was freshly dug out from between the rocks, and beautifully positioned, with an enchanting view from the entrance straight down onto the great cliffs over the sea. They could see the plumes of water rising right from the portal. As they exclaimed in amazement and appreciation at each turn, the Wedrela showed them the various living rooms and the adjoining kraal for their clanta of gayla, bundles and pala, of which they had very few as yet.

Then, as Baylin and Lafina emerged out of the entrance to the burrow once more, another incredible sight awaited them. An entire clanta stood waiting, including Arto, Lara, Doda, Luka and Luka's mate with a litter of six playful pups, a flock of bundles and some female pala with young, some brown and white and others all brown. All of them were calmly bunched around the mouth of the burrow and with them, all the Oglins that had brought them along. Baylin's Modra and Merma, little Aga and the rest of Baylin's family were together, grinning from ear to ear. Lafina's whole family was also present with a shower of gifts besides the clanta that they had brought. A profusion of bundle rugs, cooking and milking utensils, candles and other necessary household belongings were laid out with care. Baylin's hunting mates, and each of the young representative Oglins that had been selected the night before by the Great Spirit, had brought with them another bundle or a pala from their clan. All of these were gifts for Baylin and Lafina for taking the Great Journey and for making this great effort for them.

What was unusual was that some of those bundles were not just white, some were black and white and some were brown and white, special breed types that had been brought by various clans from around the country. So, this would be a continued tradition. Baylin's family was the first one in Vadiera to have and to introduce the brown-and-white pala. Now Baylin and Lafina would be the first to have brown-and-white and black-and-white bundles from the other clans. The art of singing and acrobatic dancing as part of the battends, as practised in the Pinnacles, would also come to Vadiera through Baylin's family now that Lafina was to be a part of it all.

So there was great excitement. Baylin and Lafina now had their own home and to make the family complete, they had their own clanta of pala, bundles and gayla. They belonged to one another; and no Oglin would be complete without a clanta, and no clanta complete without Oglins.

There would be a ceremony and feast that night so the young Oglin couple could become complete as a freestanding family of their own. They would be respected and honoured among Oglins as the makers of the Great Journey. In addition, they were to be the new leaders of the Bacor of Vadiera.

Over the months that followed, the two young Oglins really got to know one another and to develop a great affinity for their clanta. They came to feel completely at home in their new burrow. Although it was so amazing and interesting to learn all they had learned and to travel those great distances, Oglins really feel at their best when they are at home in their own burrows with clanta and family. For an Oglin, home and family is what life is actually all about. Their greatest joys are being able to stroll out in the evenings under a full moon, to climb up the kopjies and sit on top to watch the moonlight playing on the sea, to see the colours in the sky and listen to the nightjars calling in the distance. For an Oglin, this is the way to experience the wonders of the Great Spirits. Besides, these were opportunities to enjoy fond trips down memory lane.

The only sad moment for Baylin and Lafina had been the departure of Lafina's family. They had ridden with them through the forest and onto the Great Plains. There they travelled with the Pinnacles Clan Oglins for two days before turning back. Travelling home again was like reliving times gone by for the two young Oglins. Just the two of them with their pala, riding out on the Great Plains!

One of the first things that the young couple did was to create their own family creed just as the Great Wedrela had taught them. They then encouraged all the families in Vadiera and the visiting mos and mers from all the other clans to do the same. Their creeds were set in the same way as they were taught: how they wanted their lives to be, what they need to do to make that happen and how things must be in the future to keep it happening. Once all the families had set their own creeds, a feast was organised to create a clan creed. Arrangements were made so that this feast would happen again regularly, twice a year for all years to come. This was so that all the Oglins of Vadiera could get together and revisit and change their creed as times and circumstances and clan members changed over time. From then on, all the decisions to be made by the Bacor were checked towards the creed, using the knowledge and questions discovered on the Great Journey. Similarly, each decision made by Baylin and Lafina in their own home was done in the same manner.

The young Oglins from all the other clans took the feast as an opportunity to set their own creed. It served to give them drive and hope for the future and an aim for where they wanted to go. Over time, they learned to use their creed to create the life and future that they truly wanted.

Baylin and Lafina's life settled down, soon enough, into the lovely daily pattern for an Oglin. It was up in the morning, wandering about while the clanta were herded off to do their day's work in the veld, grazing, caring for their young, and at the same time preparing the soils for the seedlings and

371

young plants of tomorrow. Then at home in the evenings, to kraal the clanta and for battends with the family.

Visitors

Some moons later, Baylin and Lafina, with the Great Wedrela, called the second gathering of the Vadiera Clan to revisit their creed and to see how they had been getting along towards it. Their added purpose was to say farewell to all the young Oglins of the other clans who were now to set off on their journeys home. They were to take what they had learned and experienced back to help their own clans develop their own creeds and progress towards the future. The gathering had been set for the afternoon so all the clan would be able to be there and in the light of the day begin the discussions. Later they would have the last of the battends from each of the visiting young Oglins to tell about their clans and their totems, and to describe their home country. This was to give all the other Oglins present a taste of the greater wide world beyond their own clans and beyond that of Oglins.

It was a cloudless evening and the Oglins were gathered for the feast and to listen to the battends. As the last battends was finished, the colour began to drain from the sky and the midday heat was lifted away by the coolness of twilight. The gentle evening breeze shifted uncertainly and turned to come from the sea. It was the night of the full moon. As the sun disappeared from view in a splash of colour behind the mountains, everyone kept watch for the moon towards the tomorrows, over the sea. With the silent slip into view of the magnified orange moon, came a strange and unexpected noise.

It was the sound of the Whale Crier's horn! It was a different call, an emergency call, not the usual call announcing the coming of the whales. What on Earth could it be?

The Oglins all streamed out of the gathering down towards the sea. They followed the urgent call of the great kudu horn of the Whale Crier, the hermit Oglin who lived on the face of the cliffs, was ever vigilant for the coming of the whales and faithfully announced their arrival. The Oglins hastened down to the bay. There was nothing to be seen in the water. Yet from high on the cliffs, the horn continued to sound. All the Oglins drew up on the beach. Silence descended. Floating in across the still air, the Whale Crier announced the arrival of a boat. A people boat!

Fear immediately arose in the Oglins. They were unsure what would happen with people if they should discover where the Oglins were! Vadiera was, of course, not known to any people. The entrances to all the clans' homelands were absolutely secret and impossible to find by people, so none had ever entered on purpose. If by some miracle a person had ever managed to enter an Oglin clan home, they never remembered anything of the access afterwards.

And now they had a boat coming! Bringing people! Through the mouth of the bay, on what seemed to be an unusual current, there drifted a small, bright orange, little tent-like structure, floating along on a mirror surface. As the Oglins watched in apprehension, the call of the horn changed. The call was now announcing the arrival of a whale, one that the Oglins on the beach could not yet see. Floating high and seemingly rudderless, yet staying on course, the buoyant little tent turned and came along the deeper channel of the still bay. Then, just behind the little boat, the Oglins saw for the first time, the spume of a whale.

The small tent-like structure was being pushed along on the nose of a huge whale! The water was boiling around the smooth flanks of the massive whale as she created the thrust to push the little orange boat along. The sight of the whale with the tent calmed the hearts of the Oglins. The Great Whale would never deliver them into danger. This had to be something special! The Oglins gathered along the edge of the beach again, jovial now, as the Great Whale stopped just off the shore and with the aid of a light breeze the small tent-like structure beached gently on the sand.

The Great Whale raised her head up to show her might. Then, backing she slid into the water with a final jet of pressurised steam, from her blowhole. She surfaced again, facing the open sea floating high like an empty ship having unloaded its cargo. Her great tail slapped down on the water three times in greeting and the whale sounded. She headed back out to sea, out of the danger of the shallow inlet, where very few whales had been known to come before.

The bigger Oglin mos waded into the water to grab the sides and ropes that hung off the little boat. They dragged it up onto the beach, grating onto the sand.

All present stepped aside for Baylin and Lafina to reveal what lay inside.

"I do believe this is for you," said the Great Wedrela, adding drama to an already stretched moment.

The tent flaps were half open, shifting listlessly in the breeze, seemingly with memories of violent seas and as if oblivious to the solid earth upon which it now firmly sat. Reaching forward with apprehensive hands, and locking their eyes briefly for fortitude, gold to glittering gold, Baylin and Lafina opened the flaps all the way.

The half twilight, made more surreal by the opaque orange of the tent, revealed two people, a man and a woman. They were lying in the bottom of the little boat, facing each other with an arm draped over one another in embrace. Their skin was blistered and dry from the harshness of the sun. They looked more dead than alive, except for their breathing, which kept lifting some of the wild long silky hair that billowed from the woman's head.

The whales had promised that they would bring a means to help the Oglins to get the new knowledge to the people. Now they were here, two people, albeit almost expired and unconscious in a deep sleep of exhaustion. They wouldn't have seen the Great Whale that raised them from the sea and brought them in. They would not have seen the entrance to Vadiera nor know how they got there.

Willing little hands, knowing now the importance of the job, were helping to lay the people out on the beach. The Wedrelas came forward to practise their magic and call the people back into the world of the living. The Great Wedrela stepped forward with a wicker basket with a hide stretched over it. For some reason, he had brought it with him. The Wedrelas, as usual, seemed to know what the Great Spirit had in store for them. The Great Wedrela dipped the basket down into the warm water of the sea and brought it to the people. Wetting his hand, he gently patted them on the forehead. One of the Essedrelas came running up with a skin full of fresh clear water brought from the stream that flowed past the kopjies and into the sea.

The eyes of the people began to flutter as gradually they regained consciousness. They were given sips of water. Their eyes opened bright at last, blinking as they looked at each other then at their rescuers. The visitors seemed confused, but were not in great fear. They reached for one another, holding hands. Their eyes locked and tears of relief and joy at simply being alive rolled down their faces. Then they seemed to relax, almost as if they knew where they were. They seemed to at least sense that the world of the Oglin was a place of great safety. It was a place of warmth and a feeling of security, offering great hope for all the world.

Baylin and Lafina caught one another's eyes and that familiar, knowing smile passed between them. At the soulful wail of the crier's horn, they looked out to sea once more to catch a final glimpse of the Great Whale as she disappeared into the waves, breaking silver on the moonlit surface off towards the tomorrows.

THE BEGINNING

Upon Vadiera's finest shore
the Spirit's promise was fulfilled.
The Great Whale did deliver there
the people, as the myths foretell.
All the Oglins remember well
the way their very hearts were stilled.

Dear friends, if you a people be,
who yearn for Earthly harmony,
if you perceive the task at hand
and are keen for opportunity,
if you asp're towards the 'morrows
full of grand possibility,

Then we, the Oglins, ask of thee.
Please join us in this Great Journey!
Become a champion for the Earth!
Tell this tale and you will see
that this, dear friends, is the greatest joy
that there can ever, ever be!

The Oglins' Great Journey

Poem by Rio de la Vista
based on the story The Oglin
by Dick Richardson with Rio de la Vista

This life is oh so sweet and fine,
on this we heartily agree.
Smitten by the vast savanna,
sheltered by the towering tree,
smiling under sunlit sky,
and joyful by the wild blue sea!

Yet all of this is now at risk.
There is no destined guarantee.
To make our future more secure
we must seek our capacity
to serve the self and help the whole
and share responsibility.

We look to the past for wisdom,
and live by our hearts for today.
Together, we do dare to dream
and face the challenge of our day.
We reach for a bounteous future,
where life can prosper in every way.

THE OGLIN

In each and every heart there dwells
a creed for life to be drawn out.
With care we craft it part by part,
a common goal found and vowed
to live our joy and to protect
what we most fiercely care about!

With this guiding star to steer by
as we traverse along life's way,
we follow it unfailingly
making choices day by day.
And find that in the run of time,
steady on our course we stay.

Wallo the Whale opened our eyes
to animals as mentors true.
From travels on the sea so wide,
she cautions that the deeds we do
we must with care and wisdom choose,
for we affect all others too.

She taught us thus to always ask
"Will this a new divide give rise?
Or upset those whose help we need?"
For if we use our ears and eyes
our choices then can fortify
the strength of those most vital ties!

Old Thutha lives for centuries,
and with tortoise's common sense,
he looks so very far ahead
to see the future consequence.
He cautions that our deeds may well
have unforeseen significance!

To best proceed we ask ourselves
with each and every step we take,
with plans and dreams and choices made,
with actions and the words we state:
"Will this sustain the life we love,
and a most splendid future make?"

Dainty the Duiker lives alone
in the amazing maze of maize
where life is oh so arduous
throughout her solitary days.
Yet somehow with the help of friends
she can endure in her own ways.

Dear Dainty made the vital point
that nature likes variety.
With plants and bugs and animals
in plenteous diversity,
this is the most essential key
for true health and stability.

THE OGLIN

The Dung Beetle crash-lands in time
to make the case for his own kind,
With cleverness and stylish flair,
he tells of nature's current bind.
Who would think a humble beetle
would have so rare and keen a mind?

Behind vast herds across the plains
dung beetles flew in all their glory.
Following the winds of promise,
they swooped down to do their duty.
With never-failing zeal and fervour,
burying the dung galoree.

Distinguished Digger knows quite well
the cycles that all life forms make.
From birth to growth, death and decay,
these are the journeys all lives take.
When we affect a phase of life,
Most careful choices must we make.

He thoroughly revealed for us
the cycle's strong points and its weak.
For every life goes through each stage
however strong or meek.
This is most vital to be known
to keep life at its utmost peak.

A simple crossing caused such a fright!
And a road so narrow seemed so wide!
We did then come to realize,
once safely on the other side,
that the Great Spirit's kindly hand
was ever guiding this great ride.

Khumbula, wise young elephant,
reminded us to always find
the root cause of any problem
and seek to bring that to our mind.
She used five "whys?" quite cleverly
to find answers of a useful kind.

Tufty the talkative grass tuft
explained just how the grasses grow.
Their green leaves soak up sunlight,
and when the rainfall comes they know
to grow their roots beneath the ground
and food in earthly larder stow.

From elephant and earthbound friend
we learned of people's errors past.
The veld needs herds to trample it
and mouths that feed and on do pass.
Yes, grasses need their grazing friends
as much as grazers need the grass!

Elanga the grand Eland bull,
revealed just how the spirits share
their ancient lives through time and space
and taught us how we each must care
for the vast and splendid treasure
of our world so fine and fair.

Eland gives itself to Bushmen
in desperate times of dire need
and thus the spirits do provide
and more than hunger do they feed.
For this great gift to be received,
We too must live by our heart's creed.

With trepidation we did trace
the lion's spoor across the land.
As great Elanga had assured,
the threat'ning beast was not at hand.
Instead we found a gentle Bushman
sipping water from the very sand.

The Bushmen live in harmony
using just the bare necessity.
They glean a simple life from nature
and consume so very sparingly.
They know that for their children's lives,
they must leave plenty for posterity!

Uyazi told the tragic tale
of an ancient city whose land gave way.
Abandoned still, it sadly warns
of people's lives gone far astray.
It's also clear that such demise
is just as great a risk today!

So many people suffer still
from the lack of simple keys.
With these we come to know
that land can change more as we please.
We learned of all the many tools
to make the changes that we need!

Gathered around a fire circle
we did spy of a moonlit night
a group of men telling their battends
and sharing the fire's warmth and light.
So mustering our courage then,
from the darkness we spoke outright!

As people, they thought us Tok'losh
and frightening spirits for to fear.
Yet as we saw and learned that night,
we are not the danger here.
Rather, it is their own reality
and beliefs that they must clear!

THE OGLIN

We found the peak of beauty true,
were smitten to the heart of all,
by the mighty Smoke that Thunders
where the mists cloud up so tall.
Silent river roars to grav'ty
to make Earth's finest waterfall.

Nothing did prepare us for
the Thund'ring River in its spate.
Our explorations did reveal
that daring action it would take.
So bravely we did build a raft
the fearful crossing for to make.

Our plans did seem in jeopardy
when the crocodile appeared.
Yet much to our bewilderment
his menace was not clear.
And soon we found that he was not
the real danger to be feared.

Sssmiler the crafty Crocodile,
trusstworthy asss a croc can be,
assked quesstionss of the sstrangesst kind
and taught uss linkss in the chain to ssee.
We learned how thiss determiness well
what our ssole focuss then musst be.

THE OGLINS' GREAT JOURNEY

The croc taught indelibly that
the weakesst link musst effort gain.
To attend to any other one,
he made quite clear and plain,
that the whole would be in peril
and our endeavourss be in vain.

Sleek Checha the Cheetah gave us
a fine spectacle for to learn
that ev'ry labour, ev'ry action
must the sharpest focus earn.
It must exceed all other options
to make the most of every turn.

Jackie Hangman, world travell'r,
does check and change his route with care.
To go the farthest distances,
we too must plan and compare,
and ever mindful and attentive be
To stay true to our course so fair.

Gentle Gumbo of the mountain mists,
taught us that every life is dear,
that even when the paths diverge
and when there is so much to fear,
if we live by our creed each day,
the hardest choices will be clear.

THE OGLIN

Brave Birdoke the Bat lives on high
and flew still higher in the night
to assure our journey's end was nigh
and helped to end our larger plight.
He taught that we must see the whole
and view the world in a broader light.

The Great Spirit gave us blessings
far beyond our wildest dreams!
For deep within the jungle ruins,
where life is much more than it seems,
she gave us the gift of knowing
we can trust in our own discoveries!

Through a miracle of joining
the Shining Stone and White Seashell,
we found our own source of courage,
which comes from deep within ourselves.
We knew then that our task ahead
would one day be achieved as well.

Upon Vadiera's finest shore
the Spirit's promise was fulfilled.
The Great Whale did deliver there
the people, as the myths foretell.
All the Oglins remember well
the way their very hearts were stilled.

Dear friends, if you a people be,
who yearn for Earthly harmony,
if you perceive the task at hand
and are keen for opportunity,
if you asp're towards the 'morrows
full of grand possibility,

Then we, the Oglins, ask of thee:
Please join us in this Great Journey!
Become a champion for the Earth!
Tell this tale and you will see
that this, dear friends, is the greatest joy
that there can ever, ever be!

THE OGLIN CREED

The way of life we most value: We want to feel close as families with strong bonds between our clans and friends. We want to feel healthy, loving and at peace with ourselves. We want to feel in close contact with nature and in harmony with the world around us.

What needs to be for this way of life to become a reality: We Oglins need to live with loving, open hearts, sharing our thoughts and feelings honestly while caring for one another. We need to have respect and recognition for one another and all life around us. We must live close to and constantly learn from nature. Everything we do must be good for us, must be good for and enhance nature and must lead to the health of the whole world, for both the near future and the far future. We must create opportunities to grow, to learn, to explore and build upon the beauty and artistry of our way of life.

Far in the future: Others must see us as being kind and fair, as sharers and keepers of great knowledge that serves as guiding principles for Oglins and the world. Our clans must be in harmony with one another and with all the world's living things. We must have the ability to understand one another and to communicate freely

Our warrens must be comfortable, safe and pleasant places where we and all of our animals can enhance one another's lives.

The land where we Oglins live and all the lands around the clans must be healthy and thriving. The soils must be covered and sheltered by plants so that they teem with an abundance of life and activity. When it rains, the water must go into the soil so that the springs will have life and the rivers will have water that is living and clean. All the plants and animal droppings and all manner of nutrients on the land and in the oceans must be absorbed quickly in order to be useful again for other living organisms. A great profusion and mass of plants must capture the sun's life-giving energy, and support abundance and an ample variety of life forms.

GLOSSARY

Aardwolf A small grey, black-striped hyena-looking animal. It was persecuted wrongly for killing livestock for years. They actually eat ants, bugs and beetles. Yes, even dung beetles!

Acacia Acacias are a family of thorn tree that has many different species. They tend to be thorny, have small leaves arranged along opposing sides of twigs and have small, pompom-like flowers.

Amulet An object of special importance, usually conceived to be a charm and vested with magic for protection or spiritual connection.

Apron veld Veld (grassland) along the edge of high ground but not quite flat or "vlei."

Assagai A short spear for stabbing prey or enemy.

Baboon Large dog-like apes that act very human at times and are quite inquisitive. They are very noisy and spend a lot of time grooming each other. Baboons are the favourite prey of the leopard.

393

Bacor The committees of respected Oglins that govern their clan. Members are chosen by their service to the clan.

Badra Oglinese for "Brother."

Banana tree A broad flat-leaved, multi-stemmed plant that produces the bananas eaten for breakfast.

Baobab tree Massive trees that live in the low-lying hot climates of southern Africa. They hardly ever have leaves on, and their big strong branches as well as their twig and branchlet free limbs look like roots pointing at the sky. Thus its common fun name: "the-upside-down-tree."

Bat The furry mammal that flies at night with membrane wings. Some eat fruit and others eat insects, which they catch on the wing. They roost hanging upside down by their back feet.

Bat-eared fox A small grey fox with black facial markings, a little like a racoon. They have disproportionately large ears, a bit like those of a bat.

Battends A central tradition of Oglinicity, battends are the stories typically told each evening in the family burrow. They comprise the oral history of the clans. Over the generations, Oglins have developed battends into an art form; there are battends competitions at all the clan gatherings.

Black Korhaan Large, long-legged terrestrial bird with black head and belly. White patches on the cheek and surrounding the wings form a stark contrast. The bird's back is khaki coloured with small black horizontal striations; the bill is red on the male and pink on the female. The males make a very load crackling noise and when disturbed, fly off, then suddenly drop their feet and come in to land noisily like a helicopter or a wounded bird.

Black mamba The fastest snake around and one of the deadliest, too. They can grow to be very long and are jet black. The inside of their mouths is gunmetal blue.

Buffalo Brown to black, very large cattle-like animals that live in huge herds that can number in the thousands. Both male and female have massive horns in a "w" shape when viewed from the front. Males have much heavier horns that join over the head to form the "boss." Their ears are large, often tatty and hang down below the horns.

Bundle Animal companions to the Oglins. Resembling a cross between sheep and goats, the bundles provide wool, milk and other products necessary to Oglin life.

Burrow The extensive cave-like excavations used as dwelling places by the Oglin families.

Bush Across vast stretches of Africa, bush is a mix of trees, shrubs, grasses and more. It can range from quite dense to more sparse, depending upon the average rainfall and many other environmental factors. May also refer to an individual bush—which is a small shrub to a medium-sized tree.

Bushbuck Secretive antelope that frequents thick bush. Males have shaggy dark coats with white dots on the face and white stripes on the neck and legs that vary a great deal. The males have horns that are short and twist straight upwards. Females are a light fawn, with no horns and have classic "Bambi"-style spots.

Bushmen The Bushmen are small, light-brown skinned people who inhabited southern Africa long before the arrival of either Europeans or Bantu people. They were persecuted by both and were driven into the Kalahari desert where only a few still remain today. They are incredibly hardy and well adapted to the harsh climate, and can go ages without good food or water while using up their bodies' reserves.

Bush pig A wild pig-like animal found in the thicker bush areas. It resembles the wild boar of Europe and is very dangerous when cornered.

Camel thorn tree The camel thorn is another acacia, and a very beautiful one at that. They have gnarled trunks with

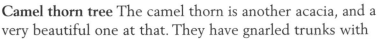

tortured and twisted bark. Their leaves are small, typically acacia, and the flowers are small, sweet-smelling yellow pompoms. The pods are white, flat and broad and when held up they form a camel's hump. The thorns are white, straight, thick at the base and in pairs along the twigs and branchlets. These thorns can get very large and become dark, the colour of dried blood at the point. The camel thorn is very tough and adapted to the dry regions of the continent and found throughout the Kalahari (Great Thirst Land).

Cape Poncho-like garment worn by Oglins. It is made either from woven bundle wool/hair or from very supple leather.

Cattle If you do not know what cattle are yet or spent time around any, you are one of the most deprived people that we haven't met yet. Cattle, or cows, as they are mistakenly called in the USA, are the producers of beef and milk, which are two of the primary reasons people were able to develop so well. Yes, because cattle provided the necessary protein to feed and grow healthy bodies and minds! Cows are actually female cattle and bulls are male ones. Oxen, steers and bullocks are cattle that have been neutered; heifers are young females that have not yet had a calf, which is what we call baby cattle.

Chameleon A chameleon is a very slow-moving (so much so that it seems to be totally indecisive) arch-backed reptile with independent protruding eyes. They tend to curl their tails up and have long sticky fingers that help them stay on branches and twigs. The chameleon is best known for its long sticky tongue that it uses for catching prey and the way that its body changes colour to blend in with its environment.

Cheetah A large spotted cat with a lanky "greyhound" build. It cannot retract its claws and is known to most as the fastest animal on Earth. The cheetah is very shy and typically lives singly, very seldom seen in pairs.

Cicada A beetle with a green head and clear wings that comes out in summer and rubs its wings together to make an endless high-pitched "tsweee" sound.

Clan A community of Oglin families, all related by tradition and dialect or accent. Clans live in close proximity to one another and perceive themselves as being one whole.

Clanta Oglinese for the animal companions of the Oglins, including their pala, bundles and gayla.

Clapper larks A brown lark, nondescript except for its very special display after rains. The bird flies upward clapping its wings loudly before dropping in a glide while whistling an ascending note. This display is repeated ad infinitum all around one as one walks or rides in the veld.

Copse A thicket of trees or bushes forming an island in an otherwise more open grassland.

Covey A family of game birds living as a unit.

Creed A set of guidelines one has agreed to follow. A creed will often be used as the basic point of reference and direction for a group.

Crocodile One of the largest reptiles on Earth. This giant lizard lives in and around water where it preys on various

animals, birds and fish, which it kills by clamping its massive jaws around the unlucky animal and then drowning it as the croc rolls in the water. The crocodile is a shy and secretive killer that watches for mistakes and habit to capture its prey.

Donga A gully formed through erosion of soil by water movement.

Duiker A group of some of the smallest of African antelope. The common duiker is the one that features in this story. It is brown with a black face that is distinctive. The males have small, very straight horns. The duiker's ears are disproportionally large and are a pale cream on the inside.

Dung Animal droppings. Nature's gift to the soil. Dung is the result of nature's efforts at reducing the volume of standing plant material and placing it back on the Earth, i.e. the process of grazing. Dung is very important as soil cover with great potential for feeding soil organisms if there are dung beetles present.

Dung beetle A vital contributor to a healthy mineral cycle, dung beetles work fresh dung back into the soil, to eat and to lay their eggs in. There are over 2000 species in Africa. Some roll balls, some bury the dung directly and others even rob other beetles' balls for a way of life! They also mate for life! They previously existed in huge numbers to match the vast herds of Africa. Now dung beetles are less prevalent and even at great risk in some areas. The reason for this is the shortage of dung in large enough concentrations and the indiscriminate use of pesticide dips and chemical doses for livestock.

Eland The eland, the size of large cattle, is the largest of the African antelopes. The last of the majestic eland live from the mountains to the deserts all across southern Africa. The eland has long been sacred to the Bushmen, who depend upon it for sustenance and who regard it as a spirit ancestor. They are khaki in colour, and both sexes have horns. The males have a knot of dark brown hair on their heads. The older the males become, the more hair they lose; they eventually end up a deep blue colour, known as "blue bulls." Thus the name of South Africa's famous Pretoria rugby team "The Blue Bulls."

Elephant Elephants are the largest living land mammals.
They must eat most of the day to obtain adequate nutrition
through their inefficient stomach system. They then deposit
huge amounts of nutrient-rich dung. This dung is, of course,
the lifeblood of many more "cycles,"
all adding up to the great mineral
cycle and contributing to the water
cycle by covering lots of soil with
organic matter. They are a highly
intelligent, family-oriented animal
whose future is seriously in jeopardy
if current conservation thinking does
not change. The decline of the
grasslands and the savanna
ecosystems causes the elephants to move into the riverine
woodland areas even more, looking for ever more scarce
food sources. This leads to their further demise in the name
of conservation, through "culling," i.e. the killing of entire
elephant families to reduce their numbers, although as this
book explains, the numbers are not the problem! As this
book attempts to reveal, a change in thinking could change
their future along with the future of all of Africa's wildlife.
If you haven't grasped what this means, please re-read this
book and call someone to learn more!

Essedrelas Oglins in training to become Wedrelas, who
provide healing and spiritual services to their clans. Their
training takes the form of an apprenticeship stretching over
many years. They learn the art of herbs and medicines for
healing purposes. And they develop the ability to
communicate with the spirits and to provide guidance to
the Oglins in their life decisions. They also receive the
magical gift of being able to communicate with animals.

GLOSSARY

Fig tree and figs The fig trees of the region are numerous but remain the same in principle. They carry figs and have softish leaves and smooth bark. The particular figs featured in the story are the sycamore figs, which are among the largest of them all and have a powdery yellow look to their branches. They are massive trees that grow nearer moisture, and often their roots travel laterally, spreading around them.

Francolin Grouse-like birds, very much like wild bantams. They live in coveys or families and are generally very noisy and conspicuous in their behaviour. There are numerous Francolin species in Africa, most of them unique to a certain habitat. They are still widespread but are coming under pressure in certain areas. The main reason for this is found by studying the weak link in their life cycle, as this book teaches. You've got it by now, yes, their food source, bugs and beetles, are disappearing due to the amount of chemical insecticides being used. The insecticides in question are in particular for crops and the dipping and dosing of livestock against ticks and other insects. In the game parks, the loss of biodiversity and baring of the soil surface is resulting in a dearth of beetle activity and thus, there too the bird numbers are going west! Yes, towards the yesterdays!

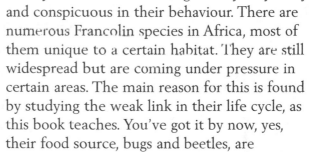

Gayla Animal companions to the Oglins, similar to people's dogs. Gayla perform the important task of daily tending to the bundles and pala, herding them out onto the veld for grazing, moving them constantly to fresh forage, protecting them from predators and then returning them to the safety of the kraals in the evening. The gayla also instinctively keep the animals away from the grazed areas for long enough to allow soils and plants to recover. While people train herding dogs to assist them in this work, the Oglin's gayla perform their vital role entirely on their own.

Gecko There are many types of geckos. The most common are the gecos found in houses, which vary in colour, walk upside down across the ceiling and have poppy eyes. The one lot in the story are outdoor tough, desert animals but do not look very different. These barking gecos sound like they are rubbing two stones together at dusk and on full-moon nights in the drier regions of the subcontinent. The other lot in the story are more like the house geckos, which are paler in colour and hunt insects in the forest.

Gemsbok A gemsbok or oryx is nature's answer to the arid areas of Africa. The buck has straight, long and sharp horns above a striking black-and-white "painted" face. They also have black-and-white markings on their front legs, which accentuate their movement when viewed from the front. These hardy animals can go without water for days in the heat of the Kalahari (The Great Thirst Land).

Giant eagle owl A very large owl, about 70 cm in height. Light grey in colour with an almost white underside with very fine barring. These owls have a black ring around the face surrounding the most penetrating yellow eyes and the most terrifying beak one ever saw. Their favourite food is vervet monkey, which is a medium-sized grey monkey.

Giraffe The tallest animal, another that surely all of you know about. It has a long neck, a very high wither and a sloping rump all the way to the tail setting. Giraffes have lovely long eyelashes, pretty mosaic spots and tufted short horns on their heads for fighting. They have very long legs and yet run very gracefully. When they drink though, grace is over and they have to do an ungainly stretch with their front legs to get their heads down to the water. If something disturbs them while drinking, their grace returns immediately as they elegantly swing back up into the upright position with their feet together again.

Gorilla A very large ape with heavy facial features. They are being hunted out of their natural habitat and fast disappearing. The females are quite a bit smaller than the males, which become hugely impressive, with their almost hairless "silver" backs, when they get older. They are very human in their behaviour and live in tight-knit extended family groups.

Green pigeon A very large pigeon that is a lovely lime green colour and has a very red base to its bill. They love sycamore fig trees.

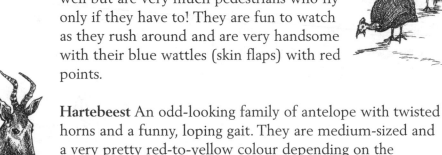

Guinea Fowl The chicken of the bushveld. They are grey-blue with fine white spots and live in large flocks when not breeding. They fly and fly well but are very much pedestrians who fly only if they have to! They are fun to watch as they rush around and are very handsome with their blue wattles (skin flaps) with red points.

Hartebeest An odd-looking family of antelope with twisted horns and a funny, loping gait. They are medium-sized and a very pretty red-to-yellow colour depending on the specific species. Both sexes have horns.

Hippopotamus A huge beast that surely you have all seen pictures of. They tend to spend most of the day lying in the water or mud resting. At night they go onto dry land to graze. Their terrifying and very dangerous tusks are displayed as a sign of aggression and although used effectively in both fighting and attacking people who threaten their territory, they are not used for grazing. The hippo kills more people in Africa than any other animal!

Hyena A heavy dog-like creature. There are two types in the area; one is the shy, shaggy and elusive brown hyena, which although a scavenger also eats a lot of berries and insects. The other, most often referred to in this book, is the spotted hyena. This hyena, although a scavenger, is actually a vicious, opportunistic hunter. In fact, of all the hunters to fear if you are lost in the bush in Africa, this is the boss!

Impala A medium-sized antelope with a thin stripe on the flank separating the darker, tanned upper body from the fawn-coloured under body. The males have handsome, ribbed horns that start out parallel and then turn out and in again in a lyre shape. Impalas live in herds around water points throughout the bushveld. They are largely responsible for the browse lines that one sees on the bush and trees around the waters.

Jackal A a small dog-like creature not unlike a fox. They are a little taller and not as stocky. There are a few types of jackal but the one featured in the story is the black-backed jackal. It has a dark silvery black back and a stripe on each side. Other jackals are a pretty ruddy yellow colour. They run with a bouncing gate, always nose to the ground in search of any opportunity. The jackal has survived very well for years by hunting for sheep and lambs.

Jackal berry tree A very big, dark evergreen tree that offers the most wonderful deep shade. The leaves are small but the stature of the tree gives a lasting impression, as it stands tall and proud over bare earth. These trees invariably stand on bare beaten earth and have a definite browse line at the height that browsing animals can reach.

Karoo and Karoo shrubs An area of low rainfall in the south central west covering a large area of southern Africa. The Karoo veld has a high percentage of shrubs and is often termed a desert. The Karoo lies in a rain shadow behind the coastal escarpment. The greatest difficulty for the weather patterns in the Karoo is that after all these years it is still unsure if it wishes to be a summer or a winter rainfall area, thus every now and again the weather becomes totally confused and gets no rain whatsoever!

Karree tree A medium-to-large tree with long thin leaves reminiscent of willow trees. It remains green through the winter but suddenly drops and replaces its leaves in midsummer. Its bark is rough and dark, almost black, and broken into uneven squares.

Klipspringer A robust little buck that lives on the rocky outcrops called kopjies. They nibble the plants that grow out between the rocks and jump and land with perfect balance from boulder to boulder. When fearing detection, they stand absolutely dead still, in sentinel-like statue form.

Kloof A ravine or gorge.

Knob kerrie A knob kerrie is exactly what its name can be translated to. A knob stick. That is a stick with a heavy knob at one end that is used to hunt or beat an opponent over the head. In other words, a club with a narrow shaft and heavy rounded end. According to Zulu tradition, a warrior's knob kerrie (Saghile) must fit in its wielder's mouth, or the carrier would be put to death.

Kopjies Small hillocks often just a jumble of boulders or rocks standing out in open veld.

Kraal A corral or holding yard for animals, typically where they are kept at night for protection from predators.

Kudu Medium-to-large antelope. They are abundant and becoming more so in southern Africa, as the massive encroachment of bush occurring due to the loss in biodiversity suites, their browsing habits. The males have huge twisted corkscrew horns raised over a very regal nose. They have a very clean white "V" on the nose, big fawn eyes and large rounded ears, pink on the inside. The coats are grey on the males and lighter brown on the females, but both have thin white stripes down their flanks. They are very beautiful and graceful and jump fences with consummate ease, making the colonisation of farmland very easy for them.

Lala palm A Lala palm grows in two distinct forms. Either tall and straight in the style of the classic palm, or as a stunted and untidy bunch of fronds near the ground. This stunting occurs from fire, ingestion by elephants or human activity as people tap them for sap to make a deadly liquor. The fronds are a green-grey colour and rustle endlessly in even the smallest breeze. The palms make a nut-like seed, which the elephants love to eat.

These seeds are passed by the elephants with only the pithy outer husks digested. If you pick up one of these you have a long struggle ahead to break it open and discover the small hollow nut inside, known as vegetable ivory. These nuts can be labouriously carved into trinkets for loved ones.

Lances A lance is a long cane or straight stick with a sharp point. It is wielded with one hand from horseback at a flat gallop. It is only really effective in a full frontal charge. The rider learns to follow the point of the lance with his shoulder and pull it out of the victim for reuse. If it did not come free, the rider would have to change over to a sword.

Lapet-faced vulture The largest and ugliest of all the vultures in the region. They have a little downy white hair on their lower necks and shoulders but otherwise their necks are pink, blue, purple and bare. They have an exceptionally strong beak and wattles (flaps of skin) that hang down on each side of the face. The Lapet-faced vulture flies the highest of all the vultures and descends only once it has seen the lower-level vultures swoop down out of sight. They will drive almost any competitor off of a kill with their ferocious approach to other scavengers.

Lechwe A medium-sized antelope with lyre-shaped horns. The body is two-toned, reddish above the hock and a tawny white below. The females have no horns and look very gentle with their longish ears. The lechwe lives in herds, fewer now than in the old days, in the marshes of the Chobe, Zambezi (Great Thundering River) and the Kafue, which is where the Oglins encounter them running in the shallows.

Leguaans (Pronounced Leg-a-varn) Monitor lizards, as they are known in English, measure up to about a meter or so. They are very aggressive when cornered but tend to keep out of the way. There are two types, one that hangs around water and one that prefers dry country. They are mostly a drab olive, camouflage colour, with flecks of yellow. The water monitor has more yellow striping. They eat birds, snakes and beetles.

Leopard The Leopard is another well-known cat. It is a strong yellow colour with rosettes of black spots all over its body. It hunts alone and readily climbs trees. A leopard often takes its kills up and leaves them hanging in the tree to eat later.

Lion A lion? You all know what a lion is: a large, tawny cat that hunts and lives in "prides." The male is known as the "king of the animals" and has a darker mane around his neck and shoulders. The Kalahari lions are particularly well-known for their very dark-coloured manes. A lion's roar sends a shiver down your spine and is a sound you will never forget!

Lizard A small reptile with a long tail and four legs. There are various sizes and types but the general appearance is agile and slender; most have the ability to drop their tail off if they are under too much stress. A new tail will be grown out again later.

Lynx An agile cat of medium-to-small build, much larger than the domestic cat and a whole lot smaller than the leopard. The lynx is a red colour and has long pointy tufted ears. It is a revered predator and hated by many who perceive the damage it does to livestock as being a direct challenge to their right to survive as stockmen.

Mahogany tree These trees have the lushest dark green leaves you can imagine, usually growing over a very dried-out soil. The shade is thick and as cool as anything can be in the very hot places where they grow. Mahogany trees always have a very distinct browse line that makes it possible to see through underneath. (A browse line is a clear-cut height below which there are no leaves because animals have eaten everything off.)

Maize Maize, or corn as it is known elsewhere, grows up to 2 meters or so tall with broad leaves and a flower on top. Crops of maize tend to be planted in broad-scale monocultures (single species crops). This is now the staple food for people across most of southern Africa.

Matabele ants These ants are black and grow very large and have a vicious bite that stings for a while afterwards. They release an interesting smell when disturbed and in the evenings. They can be used to stitch wounds by forcing them to bite the closed wound then nipping off their heads between thumb and forefinger. The "stitches" last a long time and are very effective.

Mer Female Oglin.

Merma Oglinese for "Mother."

Mo Male Oglin.

Modra Oglinese for "Father."

Mopane tree The mopane tree comes in two distinct forms. One is stunted and becomes only a tatty, medium-sized bush. This stunting can be caused by fire, elephants or pole cutting. The other is a magnificent, tall, strong and hardwood tree. The leaves, in the shape of a cloven hoof joined by a stalk at the one end, taste like quinine. The leaves in various forms have been used for all sorts of medical conditions, most notably to address both malaria and diarrhea.

Oglin A race of beings, known widely across Africa as the mysterious Tokolosh, mystical creatures that are rarely, if ever, seen by people. Evidence of their existence includes the occasions when a cow is dry in the morning, and the Tokolosh are accused of drinking the milk and drying up the cow. They are thought to be the size of children, around 130 cm., when full grown. They are commonly mentioned with a tinge of fear, as unknown spirit beings.
All over southern Africa, people still put their beds up on bricks to avoid the Tokolosh, and mention of the name strikes fear into hearts.

Olives and olive trees The wild olive is a gnarled, very slow-growing tree with silvery green leaves that are a paler colour underneath. They grow well on rocky slopes where there is a little less frost. The olives themselves are very much like domestic olives, just a lot smaller and edible as they are, without any preparation.

Orchid Very pretty flowers that are associated with wetter environments and tend to cling to other plants and therefore live higher up in the forest. This particular one's leaves hang down and create a nice roosting canopy for bats.

Oxen Neutered bulls, also known as bullocks or steers, whose horns are left intact; they are used as draft animals. They pull wagons and do all sorts of other farm work. Due to horse sickness, which seriously reduced horse populations in southern Africa, most draft work was done with oxen rather than horses.

Oxpecker There are two types of oxpeckers in southern Africa. They are medium-sized birds that live in small flocks. Their bills are bright yellow and their food source is mostly ticks, flies and scabs, all gathered from the animals that they hitch a ride on. They are in dire straits as a species due to the use of chemical insecticide dip commonly used on livestock today. They are one of a few bird species that will enter a resting croc's mouth and search for food trapped between the crocodile's teeth.

Pacha A small pouch made from the hide of the first bundle born after an Oglin's birth. The pacha hangs around each Oglin's neck and holds their sacred amulets for spiritual connection.

Pala Another companion animal to the Oglin, the pala are comparable to the horse or zebra, only of much smaller size so as to be rideable by Oglins.

Pan A shallow hollow or depression that collects runoff water, which is far more likely to evaporate than penetrate, due to the pan soils being mostly impervious. Pans are often very white due to the salts and calcium left after the water evaporates from them.

Pinnacles A secret Oglin homeland near the Orange River (Red River). To enter it, a hidden entrance opens up for the Oglins in what seems to be a solid grey wall of rock in the side of a mesa known as Klipkrans (rock cliff). To find the secret entrance, there are two conical hills, the Pinnacles themselves, with rock nipples on top that must be aligned with each other.

Poort A poort is a kloof or gorge, but definitely cuts right through, allowing access through an almost impassable range of ridges or mountains.

Porcupine A small pig-like animal covered in quills. The quills are black and white and get very long and thin along the back. The tail is not long and has very short, sharp and strong quills which are used for defence. These quills will go through skin very easily and many a predator has suffered as a result of tangling with a porcupine.

Puffback shrike The puffback is another bird from the shrike family. It is black, white underneath and has a white stripe down each side. It has a startlingly red eye and during mating time will stand all the feathers on its back up into a white puff ball. The puffback shrike has a distinct call that is synonymous with the bushveld: "Chick weeee, Chick weeee…"

Python A very large constrictor snake. This means it catches and strangles its prey before it swallows them whole! There are a number of species of python in Africa.

Queleas Small finches that live in massive flocks that travel like smoke through the air. They roost in thorn trees en masse and, due to their great numbers, they become so heavy that they can break all the branches off. These birds still long for the large herds that they used to follow for the seeds they knocked off. Today they are a notable pest of crops like wheat, which they devour out of the head in the land, wiping out entire crops at one sitting. They are "controlled" using bombs that explode, burning fuel over the colony while it roosts en masse at night.

Reims Rawhide ropes cut from an animal hide and softened with animal fat and a beating and twisting action.

Sadra Oglinese for "Sister."

Savanna A mixture of grassland, trees and bushes. Grassland savannas are mostly open grasslands with occasional trees and bushes. A woodland savanna has a tree canopy over grass with occasional open areas.

Scherm A kraal fortress against predators, made by cut thorn trees and shrub, pulled into a circle with the stems towards the inside, forming an impenetrable barrier.

Shrike Shrikes are medium-to-small birds with very strong beaks. They prey on bugs as well as fledglings, lizards, frogs, etc. There are a number of different kinds, but the particular type referred to in this story as Jackie Hangman, is the red-back shrike. Unlike its sadistic cousin, the fiscal shrike, the red-back only occasionally impales its prey on a thorn or barb of a fence to save it for later. The red-back shrike's markings are classic for the hangman appearance with his red coat and black eye mask. It is an intercontinental traveller, migrating as far as from Finland to southern Africa!

Spoor The tracks left behind by people and animals. Tracks do not necessarily mean foot or hoof prints but all the signs that can be left behind by the passing of the animal. For example, graze marks, dung and bent grass.

Springbok An antelope the size of a reasonable goat. Springbok are beautiful. They are white underneath and fawn on top, split by a brown stripe. They have small tight lyre-shaped horns. They are highly gregarious but the breeding males hold territories to which the herds of females come during the rutting season. They are called springbok, which translates into 'jump buck' because they love to jump for the joy of it. In fact, when the rains come they go into "pronk" mode. Pronk means to drop their heads down, raise all the hair up from their tails to their withers, and then jump straight up and down with their legs straight and their heads down. They are amazing to watch when there are large groups doing this together, jumping to great heights.

The sad thing about springbok is that historically, they were recorded as travelling in herds so vast that it would take two weeks to go by on a five-mile-wide front. These herds were so tightly packed that they would trample animals to death and break wagons into splinters. The days of the great springbok migrations are now over and only a few remain in some sanctuaries, which are wonderful in that they have saved this animal for now.

Tawny eagle A large eagle, usually a tawny khaki colour. They have a piercing, yellow eye and a terrifying beak. The tawny waits on the wing high above and out of sight, but not as high as the vultures. The tawny eagles are the first to see a fresh kill and dive down towards it. The vultures fly even higher up and descend when they see the tawny go down.

Teak tree Teak is a common name for various trees from different famillies. This particular teak grows on the sand veld south of the Zambezi River (The Great Thundering River). They have small leaves and pretty flowers. The teak has been persecuted, being cut first as sleepers or railroad ties and now for the curio industry. Buying wooden curios must be one of the worst things anyone can do. Every day, thousands more beautiful teak trees are sacrificed for this insatiable and unnecessary industry.

Tortoise A hard-shelled reptile that withdraws into his shell at the first sign of danger. Tortoises can grow to quite a large size.

Totem The specific animal or bird one chooses or is given as a guiding spirit.

Towards the tomorrows Oglinese for "East."

Towards the yesterdays Oglinese for "West."

Trek Move or travel.

Umbrella thorn tree This is one of the acacia family. This particular acacia has a straight thorn and a hooked thorn and therefore hooks and pricks. Its Afrikaans name can be translated directly to mean exactly that! The tree also grows with a very flat, spreading crown, which earns it the other common name, umbrella thorn.

Vadiera Vadiera is a secret Oglin homeland that has still never been purposely entered by humans. It is situated near Knysna somewhere on the east coast of South Africa.

Veld The African name for rangeland, often distinguished as high veld or low veld for the elevation or as sweet veld or sour veld for the flavor of the grasses. The outdoors is also termed the veld.

Vlei Low-lying, flat country that can occasionally be wet in the rain seasons.

Warrens Another name for the cave-like dwelling places, or burrows, of the Oglin families.

Warthog A grey animal that is pig-like in its appearance, habits, skin and features. The warthog is far more robust in the forequarter and light in the hindquarter. They sport really big tusks and are vicious when wounded. They have a hairy mane and when they run they raise their tails straight up like an antenna. When in family groups, they always run in a row from the biggest in front to the smallest at the back.

Wedrela Wedrelas are the spiritual leaders of the Oglin clans. They provide healing services to the Oglins, using the wealth of knowledge handed down over generations regarding plants and their medicinal uses. They are also able to communicate with the Spirits and to provide guidance to the Oglins in their life decisions. In addition, they have the magical ability to communicate with animals. They train their assistants called Essedrelas in the healing arts.

Whale The whale is the largest of all mammals and lives in the sea. The particular whale in our story is the right whale, known as such as it was the right animal to hunt! The right whale returns every year to South Africa's southern coast to calve and breed. The growths on their heads are not barnacles as told in our story but are in fact growths called callosities. The largest one is 'the bonnet' on the front of the nose.

Wild dagga plant The wild dagga plant is a forb that grows very upright with rings of leaves interspersed up the stems. The flowers, also arranged in a circle high up on the stalk, are curved orange trumpets. When you take them off they can be arranged into a circle by pushing them into each other.

Wildebeest A grey-coloured, horse-like animal with horns. We refer to a group of animals of which the most common in southern Africa is the blue wildebeest. Its horns are similar to the buffalo's but much lighter and thinner. The blue wildebeest has some dark hair on his face and looks not too different in the face to the bison of north America.

Willow tree Willow trees grow along water courses. They are not indigenous to this part of Africa but have thrived since their introduction. There are two types, one with upright branches that break off readily in floods and spread downstream to sprout again. The other is the weeping willow, whose soft willowy (excuse the pun) branches droop down around it creating a lovely house effect inside.

Winterthorn tree Winterthorn trees are huge trees that grow in vleis on heavy soils. They are green in winter and in spring drop their leaves and huge pods that look and smell like dried apple rings. These pods are sought-after food for many animals.

Zebra Heck, every one knows what a zebra is, don't they? It is the only animal that starts with the letter "Z" and therefore every kid who ever went to school has seen a picture of one! Oh. OK! It is a horse-like animal that never ever took off its black-and-white striped pajamas!

Give the Gift of
THE OGLIN
to Your Friends and Colleagues

CHECK YOUR LEADING BOOKSTORE OR ORDER HERE

❏ **YES**, I want _____ copies of *The Oglin* at $24.95. each, plus $4.95 shipping per book (Ohio residents please add $1.56 sales tax per book). Canadian orders must be accompanied by a postal money order in U.S. funds. Allow three to four weeks for delivery.

My check or money order for $_____ is enclosed.

Please charge my: ❏ Visa   ❏ MasterCard
                  ❏ Discover   ❏ American Express

Name _____

Organization _____

Address _____

City/State/Zip _____

Phone_____ E-mail _____

Card # _____

Exp. Date_____ Signature _____

Please make your check payable and return to:
BookMasters, Inc.
PO Box 388, Ashland, OH 44805
Call your credit card order to: 800-247-6553
or Fax (419) 281-6883
order@bookmasters.com   **www.atlasbooks.com**
www.Oglin.com